I0669290

By KARA NASH

With Caitlin Ricci
DARE
Dare to Risk
Dare to Hope

Published by DREAMSPINNER PRESS
www.dreamspinnerpress.com

Readers love *Dare to Risk*
by KARA NASH & CAITLIN RICCI

"Thanks, Kara and Caitlin, for a whirlwind story. I'm looking forward to see what happens next."
—Rainbow Book Reviews

"…an exciting, emotional roller coaster with a great set of unique characters."
—Three Books Over the Rainbow

"I had really good fun with this story."
—Prism Book Alliance

"*Dare to Risk* is a really enjoyable start to a new series with a bunch of interesting characters."
—Gay Book Reviews

By CAITLIN RICCI

Blood Slave
Country Strong
Cuddling (Dreamspinner Anthology)
For the Asking
His Lion Tamer
Marked by Grief
Reckless
With Cari Z: Worth the Wait

A FOREVER HOME
Rescuing Jack
Of Monsters and Men

A PLANET CALLED WISH
To the Highest Bidder
Fantasy for a Gentleman

THORNWOOD
One More Time
About Last Night

With Kara Nash
DARE
Dare to Risk
Dare to Hope

Published by Harmony Ink Press
Crush
First Time for Everything (Harmony Ink Anthology)
Weathering the Storm

Published by DREAMSPINNER PRESS
www.dreamspinnerpress.com

KARA NASH & CAITLIN RICCI

DARE TO HOPE

Published by

DREAMSPINNER PRESS

5032 Capital Circle SW, Suite 2, PMB# 279, Tallahassee, FL 32305-7886 USA
www.dreamspinnerpress.com

This is a work of fiction. Names, characters, places, and incidents either are the product of au-
thor imagination or are used fictitiously, and any resemblance to actual persons, living or dead,
business establishments, events, or locales is entirely coincidental.

Dare to Hope
© 2016 Kara Nash & Caitlin Ricci.

Cover Art
© 2016 Anna Sikorska.
Cover content is for illustrative purposes only and any person depicted on the cover is a model.

All rights reserved. This book is licensed to the original purchaser only. Duplication or
distribution via any means is illegal and a violation of international copyright law, subject
to criminal prosecution and upon conviction, fines, and/or imprisonment. Any eBook format
cannot be legally loaned or given to others. No part of this book may be reproduced or
transmitted in any form or by any means, electronic or mechanical, including photocopying,
recording, or by any information storage and retrieval system, without the written permission
of the Publisher, except where permitted by law. To request permission and all other inquiries,
contact Dreamspinner Press, 5032 Capital Circle SW, Suite 2, PMB# 279, Tallahassee, FL
32305-7886, USA, or www.dreamspinnerpress.com.

ISBN: 978-1-63477-412-3
Digital ISBN: 978-1-63477-413-0
Library of Congress Control Number: 2016913066
Published November 2016
v. 1.0

Printed in the United States of America
∞
This paper meets the requirements of
ANSI/NISO Z39.48-1992 (Permanence of Paper).

Chapter One

Samuel shot out his hand to grab his phone off the bedside table before the device even had time to ring properly. Being a light sleeper had its perks at times. In the dark the screen's brightness almost blinded him, but not enough to keep him from seeing that the number was an overseas one—an American one if his memory served him right.

His heart sped up as he put it to his ear. "Hello, Samuel speaking."

"Hey. So…. It's Chris. And I just remembered it's pretty late there. Shit. Sorry."

Samuel sat straight up, leaning his bare back against the headboard of his bed. "Chris? Hey, how are you? Is everything okay?"

Chris laughed, but for some reason Samuel couldn't quite name, it sounded a little off. Maybe eight months of not hearing Chris's laugh, or even his voice for that matter, had begun to mess with his memories of the sounds.

"Of course things are okay. I'm good. Just hating winter here in New York, as usual. There's snow everywhere, and the cabs can't drive even half the speed limit because of it. I've been late to three meetings this week because of the traffic and accidents. We get snow every year, but it's like people suddenly forget how to drive the second those flakes start to come down. It's insanity. Tell me you have gorgeous weather or something. Please?"

"Actually, we do at the moment. It's summer here, so maybe it's time to make use of Bran's kindness and come pay us a visit?" The idea of seeing Chris actually made him look forward to something, because settling into life back in New Zealand hadn't been as easy as Samuel had thought it would be. Too much had happened to them all in Montana. New friendships were formed and lives changed, some dramatically, like Kaden's, since he'd now hooked up permanently with Bran.

"That's kind of what I wanted to talk to you about. I've got some time away from the firm, and I was hoping to come see you. If you'll have me. But the catch is I don't want Bran, or Kaden, or anyone else in New Zealand, except you of course, knowing I'm coming there. If you snitch it'll be a lot longer than eight months before I decide to talk to you again." His laugh was back, but it sounded even worse this time, almost desperate.

For Chris to hide something from his best friend was huge, because the two men were practically joined at the hip. How they had survived the last eight months without their cuddles and twisted passion for the game of truth or dare, Samuel would never know.

"Chris, keeping anything from Bran spells disaster. You know that, right?" Samuel would respect Chris's wishes but had to at least try to get Chris to do right by his friend.

This time there was no laughter in Chris's voice, only a hint at something painful that Samuel couldn't even begin to guess at.

"I do know. He's my best friend. His mate, as he's taken to calling me since moving full-time down there on the other side of the fucking planet. But I need a little time with just you." The brightness was back in his voice a second later, as if Chris had flipped a switch. "Gotta try to get into your pants again, this time without an audience. You know? So what do you say? Can I come visit you, or are you going to make me continue to freeze my ass off in this snow?"

It didn't take a genius to know something was wrong, but Samuel played along. He had to until he had Chris where he could see him in the flesh and determine what the hell was up with the man. When it came to acting, Bran and Chris used to be masters at it, and Samuel knew pushing at anything over the phone would drive Chris away. And he didn't want that, not when Chris had finally reached out to him for help. Yeah, the sexual innuendos were still there, but they were what Chris was hiding behind at the moment.

"Please? I'll be good. I promise."

A fist clenched around Samuel's heart, and he went cold. Chris did not beg for anything, and this was Chris doing almost exactly that. Something was seriously wrong, but Samuel kept his voice calm, despite the sweat breaking out on his forehead.

"You? Be good? Ha-ha, but of course you can come and see me. Getting in my pants on the other hand, let's just say, good luck with that." It pained him to joke with Chris, but he had to keep things light or Chris would never board a plane to New Zealand.

"Yeah, we'll see. So. Tomorrow work for you, then? I'm looking at a flight that gets me into Auckland at six, and I can take a cab to you if you text me your address. They are called cabs there, aren't they?"

Samuel chuckled. "Nope, they're called taxis, and you'll do no such thing. I'll pick you up at the airport. Fortunately I am the boss here, so I can take the milking off."

Chris sighed loudly and sounded very much like he was getting frustrated. "Not gonna work. Please? I'll take a taxi. It's not a big deal. Just don't fight me on this. I can't argue with you right now. Not about a fucking taxi from the airport to wherever you live. Text me your address or just tell it to me now. I'm heading out to JFK. And remember, no telling Bran."

The pleading in Chris's voice stopped Samuel from arguing any further. "Okay, have you got a pen or online maps ready? Have a look at taking a shuttle from the airport to here, because it'll be cheaper than a taxi."

"Shuttle. Right. Pen. Go for it."

Samuel gave the farm address to him, making sure he understood it was the driveway with the purple mailbox with the cow painted on it. "Think you can find it?"

"Purple box with a cow, pretty sure I still have my eyes and can spot it," Chris said sarcastically but still playfully. "Thanks. See you tomorrow. Don't bother putting clothes on before I get there! They aren't part of my plan!" Chris kissed him through the phone, then promptly hung up.

Like an idiot, Samuel lowered the phone and stared at it while still sitting in the dark. It was almost one in the morning, and he had a whole workday to get through before Chris would arrive in Auckland the next day. New Zealand was roughly seventeen to twenty hours ahead of the States, so Chris's tomorrow would be the following day for them. Chris's flight would take a good twenty-three hours or so, excluding any stopovers for the aircraft to refuel.

He placed his phone back down and lowered himself back onto his pillows. With his eyes closed, he tried to go back to sleep, but the effort was futile. His thoughts traveled back to their time spent working on Tobias Wilson's farm in Montana for about two years before Bran and, by default, Chris stormed into their lives and changed almost everything. Kaden fell hard for Bran, a guy who made their blood boil for a long time with his selfishness and greed. In the end, however, and fortunately for Kaden, Bran redeemed himself by revealing he had a heart of flesh and blood after all.

The two lovebirds lived on the larger of Kaden's two farms, about a twenty-minute drive away from where Samuel and Trent co-owned a large two-thousand-cow dairy farm stretching over seven hundred acres of Waikato country. They saw the other two men regularly when having meals together or when they went out for a night of drinks, fun, and dancing. Surprising all of them, Bran had easily adjusted to living in a rural town after the hectic lifestyle of Manhattan. Samuel had at the least expected Bran to have some withdrawal symptoms from the five-star lifestyle he used to have, but apparently Bran's finances were still flourishing, even with him living on the other side of the globe.

On the downside, Samuel found it hard to hang around them for too long at times, to see the love, passion, and affection they shared, because Bran reminded Samuel of Chris so much, and a phantom ache started in his heart for a man he would probably never have.

Even the lighthearted, often absentminded Trent hadn't walked away from Montana unscathed after laying eyes on Chris's crazy, dark, ex-army half brother, Misha Romanoff. Forgetting he was lying down, Samuel tried to shake his head but didn't quite succeed in the gesture. Trent needed all the bloody help he could get with that nutcase if they were ever to pick things up where they left off after saying good-bye in Montana. They were such opposites, and if it wasn't so ludicrous to imagine the two together, Samuel would've found it totally hilarious.

Samuel would never again think of Montana as the green, flat, peaceful, crop-growing, blue-skyed land of promise, as they always described it on television or in movies. No way. To him Montana brought back memories of shitloads of drama, fighting, worrying, and confusion. Not to mention a healthy fear of truth or dare, but whether the fear came from the drama that unfolded during the stupid games or the raging hangovers the next day, he wasn't quite sure.

Hell yes, they had heaps of fun too, but there had been so much heartache and self-destruction in the midst of it all. Mostly centered around Chris, and Samuel hated the moment Chris returned to Manhattan at his homophobic father's command. Samuel hadn't been sure Chris had been healed up physically or emotionally enough to deal with his controlling family, but Misha had left with Chris and promised to keep a close eye on him. Despite the latter, Samuel had been uneasy since then.

His thoughts returned to the unexpected phone call from Chris and the strange request for Samuel not to let anyone know Chris would be in New Zealand. He couldn't help the dark sense of foreboding rising within him. For Chris not to want Bran to know he was in the same country or even the same town, only twenty minutes away from each other, was not only strange but a big deal on so many levels.

Not only would Bran feel betrayed, deceived, and hurt if he ever found out, which was bound to happen with them living in such a small community, but Samuel worried over the impact this would possibly have on their very special friendship. Furthermore, Samuel's concern grew at the possible reasons why Chris would want to seek refuge with him, at his home, when his best friend lived almost down the road. What was so bad for Chris to want to hide away from the person who knew and loved him best?

From all he had heard tonight, spoken and unspoken, during their long distance call, Samuel concluded Chris was in trouble. What kind of trouble and the damage to Chris because of it, he couldn't decide. Some time later, still without any easy answers for his questions, he fell into a restless sleep.

CHAPTER TWO

THE TAXI dropped Chris off at a house that made his jaw drop. Yes, he knew Samuel lived on a farm and had prepared himself for a farmhouse similar to the one Bran's grandfather had lived in back in Montana. Samuel's house was anything but similar to the dwelling Chris had imagined.

The modern and yet rustic wood and glass house took his breath away, and all he could do was stare for a long time. The more he looked, the more he saw Samuel's signature all over the materials and design. Samuel fit the house, or rather, the house fit the man perfectly, considering his native blood and ties to the land the Maori people called *Aotearoa*.

From what the online maps had told him, the closest town, Thames, would be only a fifteen-minute drive away. Looking around him, Chris found it hard to imagine civilization so close, because as far as he could see there were cows, paddocks, more cows, milking sheds, corn, and green. Plenty of green. If he hadn't just been driven by taxi from the Auckland international airport to this breathtaking place, he would've found it hard to believe cities and towns were so close.

Slowly walking closer to the front of the house, he looked through one floor-to-ceiling glass panel facing the deck, through the open blinds he could see a man he was particularly familiar with sitting in the living room, watching TV.

He was only too happy to be out of the taxi. After nearly thirty hours spent between planes and airports, he wouldn't feel anything like himself until he was able to get a shower and spend some one-on-one time with Samuel, but first he had to go up to his front door.

Chris pulled the shoulder strap of his duffle bag, the only luggage he'd brought with him, up a little farther on his shoulder before stepping closer to the front door. A glance at Samuel, sitting there with his back to Chris, told him that Samuel hadn't noticed him there yet or heard the taxi arrive. He took the second he had and breathed deeply in a futile attempt to calm his nerves. He could do this, he knew. He was certain of it.

Looking at Samuel again, he saw that his time was up. The beautiful man, as dark as the creamy coffee he'd sipped to stay awake on the second plane ride over, was now standing up and looking straight at him through the window. Barely more than five feet separated them, after eight months of being apart. And the worst, most surprising part of it all was the way his body still reacted instantly to having Samuel around.

It was as if he couldn't get enough of Samuel, like his body needed him, even if he had only kissed Samuel a few times. Ridiculous as it was to Chris, his palms were suddenly sweaty, and he couldn't do anything about the stupid smile springing across his lips as Samuel opened the front door.

"Hi," Samuel said.

Chris swallowed thickly, his words getting stuck somewhere between his racing heart and his brain, that had suddenly turned to mush. Samuel was still so perfect, and Chris had tried so hard not to think about him over the past eight months. It hadn't worked, but his attempts at keeping his mouth shut and not bothering Samuel every time he happened to think about him had. He'd almost managed to last a year without having to run to Samuel for help. If he didn't feel so absolutely fucking desperate, he might have actually been proud of himself for lasting as long as he had.

"Ready to come in?"

Nodding was the best Chris could come up with as he stepped into Samuel's house. Chris felt like an idiot for thinking Samuel would live in a simple bachelor pad. The interior of the house consisted of more wood, and in the middle of it all sat a gorgeous open fireplace made of what appeared to be flat stones. To his right, an iron and timber staircase curved up to an upper level, but more than that Chris couldn't see right now.

"Thanks for letting me visit," Chris remembered to say as he stopped to remove his shoes beside the front door. Samuel's hardwood floors looked recently mopped, and there was no way in hell he wanted to get them dirty from his shoes. There were far better ways to do that once he had Samuel naked.

"I was surprised to hear from you after so long."

Samuel moved back a little when he came forward and out of the summer heat behind him. The door was closed, but some of the hot air had still followed him in, and it made Chris anxious to get his extra layers off. Winter had been in full force back in New York, and though he'd expected the warmer temperatures in New Zealand, it was still a shock to step off the plane and land right in the middle of summer.

Chris didn't have a good reason for his silence over the months, at least not one he could share with Samuel, or anyone else for that matter. "Yeah, well, I'm here now. I may drop off the face of the planet, but you can't get rid of me. Not really anyway." He forced a smile, but Samuel didn't look convinced. "Mind if I take a shower? I'm disgusting from traveling."

"Sure. It's upstairs. We'll talk about why you're really here when you're done."

Chris was sure Samuel wouldn't be getting the answers he wanted out of him without a heavy negotiation. He wasn't so eager to get thrown out of Samuel's house already that he wouldn't put up at least some fight. But with Samuel looking at him with so much worry in his eyes right then, Chris already felt himself wanting to open up and let him know it was all okay.

"Sounds great. See you soon," he said with false cheerfulness as he pushed Samuel's worry aside.

Being clean after his shower felt amazing, but he knew he couldn't stay under the hot spray forever. Feeling like himself again, and not like some grimy airplane person, came with the usual clusterfuck of emotional baggage he'd become accustomed to. He hadn't done anything to help himself in more than twenty-four hours, because he hadn't had the time or the privacy while traveling, but now that he had a few minutes of quiet, while he could hear the TV going downstairs, he couldn't help the intense need that rushed over him to release it all.

Chris clenched his hands into fists at his sides and shook his head, stepping back from the slim black case in his travel bag that seemed to be screaming at him for attention. He shouldn't have brought it with him, not if he really wanted to get better, but he hadn't been able to just leave it in his apartment back home either. He fixed his hair, brushed his teeth, threw on some shorts and a T-shirt, and smiled as he realized which tee he'd grabbed first. A giant rainbow rooster lay across his chest. It'd been a Christmas gift from Bran, and it made him a little happier just looking at the ridiculousness of it. If nothing else, it proved to be a good distraction from where his thoughts wanted to go.

"Chris?" Samuel called from outside the bathroom door.

His moment of privacy gone, Chris tried for normalcy, or some imitation of it anyway. He really needed that. "You're welcome to come in and join me. Your shower looks like it's plenty big enough for two."

Samuel sounded like he was choking on whatever he'd intended to say after that, but Chris didn't let him linger there for long before he opened the bathroom door. "Hey." He leaned against the sink and saw Samuel give him a thorough once-over. Coming to New Zealand and seeing Samuel hadn't been about sex, but if they chose to go there, Chris certainly wasn't going to be upset about that turn of events. Sex was healthy for most people, and he trusted himself with Samuel where he knew he'd be a mess with anyone else.

"I wanted to make sure you were okay."

Plastering his brightest smile into place, even as it felt as if he was cracking around the edges, Chris picked up his things and left the bathroom with a deliberate sway in his step. "Of course I'm okay. I'm always okay. Now, where am I staying?" he asked, running a finger over Samuel's muscular abs with his free hand, while the other was currently clutching the duffle bag in a white-knuckled grip. Samuel's stomach was hidden from his view by a shirt, but that did little to diminish the hard abs Chris remembered being there the last time he'd had a glimpse of Samuel's stomach and now traced.

"Spare bedroom. I'll show you where."

It wasn't a secret that he wanted Samuel, and the last time they'd seen each other, Chris had been practically begging Samuel to screw him. But he could see that the silence he'd let stretch between them had confused, and might have even bothered, Samuel.

"I'm here now," he said, even though Samuel hadn't spoken a word to make him say this.

"Yes, you are. But we'll both see how long you end up staying this time around."

Chris frowned at his back as Samuel turned away from him and started heading toward a bedroom. "That's unfair," he mumbled, but he knew it was the truth and exactly what he deserved.

After Samuel had him put his things in the extra bedroom, Chris knew his time was up as he turned to see Samuel sadly watching him, a thousand questions swimming in his gaze. He'd lost weight, and a good deal of it too, but he knew he didn't look that bad because of it. Definitely not enough for Samuel to be staring at him the way he was now.

"Question time now?" Chris asked him with some trepidation.

Samuel gave him a slow nod and stepped aside so Chris could leave the bedroom. "Downstairs, on the couch. We'll be comfortable there."

Chris led the way, and once Samuel was sitting next to him, he pulled his feet under himself and turned toward him. "I'll tell you everything you want to know, answer any question you want," Chris promised him with a soft smile as he ran his finger down the side of Samuel's neck, finishing his path along Samuel's collarbone.

Samuel swallowed thickly, and Chris leaned forward to press his lips to the side of his Adam's apple before he leaned back a little.

"It can't be that easy to get answers out of you. What do you want in return?" Samuel asked him.

He had to be normal if he wanted this to work; to flirt like he had nothing to lose, to act like he only lived for sex. Just like every other time he'd been around Samuel. So he gave Samuel his biggest smile and moved his fingertips to Samuel's sternum, then lower to Samuel's stomach, before resting his hand with the gentlest of touches on the front of Samuel's pants, right over his zipper.

"I think you know what I want, Samuel." Chris played with him in the sultriest voice he could possibly manage. When Samuel's eyes went wide, Chris knew he had to tread carefully if he hoped to get anything at all. "Not sex. Not yet." He gently kissed the side of Samuel's throat and felt Samuel's racing heartbeat hammering against his tongue when he flicked it out to taste Samuel's skin. "Something much easier than that. I want to be on my knees for you, my mouth wrapped around your cock, your hands in my hair."

He squeezed Samuel through his pants and kissed his throat again when he felt how hard Samuel was for him already. He was so close to getting exactly what he wanted, if only he could control his excitement long enough to enjoy it.

"You want my secrets. I want to watch you come. I've been thinking about it since Montana. That's my bargain. Do we have a deal?"

When Samuel hesitated and Chris was sure he'd turn him down, he decided to backtrack a little or risk losing out on Samuel altogether. "Or a kiss for each little secret if you'd rather. I know you want answers, and I'm not going to push you into something you don't want. We've kissed before, if you remember. It wasn't a big deal then, and it doesn't have to be one now either." That was a lie, as just being near Samuel was pretty massive for Chris and the first time they'd kissed nearly broke his heart. He pulled his hand away from Samuel, but he wouldn't change where he was sitting. He liked being able to feel Samuel's warmth through his shirt too much to move to the other side of the big couch and give Samuel some space.

He'd tried so hard to be good after Montana but knew he'd failed at it. Needing to leave Manhattan in a hurry was enough evidence of that. Being here with Samuel, Chris knew he should have tried harder. And he should have left New York a lot sooner than he had. Maybe then he would still feel a little like he had some sanity left.

Samuel frowned but nodded slightly. "Kisses I can do, but before anything else happens between us, there needs to be some truth on the table first."

"You were nice enough to let me visit, so I guess I can do that. Ask me anything you want. I won't have secrets from you." Realizing that, even as he was saying it, shocked him more than a little. He'd been keeping something big from Bran for the past four months yet somehow seemed ready to spill everything to Samuel despite hardly knowing him. But it was as if he did know him, like Samuel had been a part of him since the first time he'd laid eyes on him in the farmhouse in Montana nearly a year before.

Chris expected Samuel to fire away, now that he had Chris's permission, but instead the man seemed nervous and almost fearful. Samuel swallowed hard and stared out the window at the beauty outside. And Chris couldn't resist leaning forward and kissing his neck again.

"What is so bad that you're hiding away from Bran?"

Each word resonated against his lips as Samuel spoke them softly. Carefully.

Chris nodded, supposing it was best to get to the most awful truth right away. "I'm cutting myself again," he quietly whispered, leaning his head against Samuel's shoulder for support as he trembled.

"Cutting? You're hurting yourself? Why would you do that?" Samuel's eyes were filled with shock, and he pulled back to stare at Chris.

With the taste of Samuel's skin still on his lips, Chris reached for the button of his own shorts.

"You said no sex," Samuel reminded him.

Chris couldn't look at him, not while he was about to show him what he'd been hiding most of his life, so he simply shook his head and pushed his shorts down a little, making damn sure not to expose himself or the intricate tattoo flowing over his ribs in the process. The scar was small, but against his tanned skin, it was easy to find, even after so many years of trying to forget about it.

"I was ten the first time I opened up my pocket knife and cut myself," he slowly began, his voice a trembling mess as he tried to get the confession out. There were dozens of other scars on that hip alone, and if Samuel had asked him, Chris would have bared each of those small marks to him. But when he didn't say a word, Chris quickly fixed his shorts and pulled his shirt down as far as he could over them, covering himself up again even if he knew it wouldn't make any difference. Samuel knew his terrible secret, and he was afraid to look at Samuel and see what he thought of him now.

"Living with my dad has always meant there was a lot of pressure on me. I excelled in everything, but I did so because I had to, not because I had any real desire to be better than anyone else. Romanoff men aren't failures, he would tell me. And anything less than the absolute best was failing. My college career was planned out before I was eight. If my father could have gotten away with it, I'm sure he would have arranged my marriage to some pretty little girl and had the names of our children picked out for us before we were in high school."

Chris shook his head and groaned as he looked up at Samuel, who watched his every move. "I felt like I was suffocating all the time and had no control over any part of my own life. I didn't pick out my own clothes, my own music, what I ate, where I went, what I did with my time, who my friends were, none of it. Looking back, there isn't a single thing from my childhood I can actually point to as being something I did simply because I wanted to. It was all in an effort to make him happy, to be the best son I could be for him. Misha wasn't a disappointment to him by any means, but now that I'm an adult, I feel like he made different choices with Misha, had lost control of him and his future somewhere, and didn't want to make the same mistakes with me." He took a deep breath and wished Samuel would say something instead of continuing to stare at him like he was a freak.

"So I started cutting to release all that stress. No child should be under that much pressure, that much absolute need to be perfect all the fucking time. I still did everything I was supposed to do and never faltered even once. But every night I was making little marks on my hips. Never my wrists or anywhere else that someone could see, always just where my underwear would cover. It was how I took control of it all. I didn't get a say in anything else, but when I was cutting, everything was mine. I decided how deep I went, how far I cut, and for how long. Sometimes it was enough that I just put the knife against my skin and held it there, not cutting at all. Others it was all I could do not to cut so deeply I hoped that I bled out."

Samuel's dark skin had gone pale while Chris opened his heart and spilled all of himself to a man who might not want anything to do with him after his fucked-up confessions, but Chris forged on. He felt like he had to, now that he'd begun talking.

"When I was eighteen, I went to college, and everything changed. I was no longer under his thumb all the time. He still controlled when I came home, the degree I got, and what my extracurriculars were. But I got to have some actual fun for once. And I met this crazy kid who was just sixteen and wanted to do everything I did and more. I was so scared the first time I had sex, but I was also drunk, and I'd had a fight with my dad about taking more classes and getting an additional degree, even though I promised to be a lawyer and be everything he wanted for me.

"After that first time, I realized sex gave me power and control, even more so than cutting did. I stopped needing to drink to have sex with guys and instead drank because it was fun. I had sex with anyone I wanted to and got as extreme as I possibly could. I would pick a guy at a party or in a bar, no matter who he was or who he was with, and knew I could get him to have sex with me. Even while his girlfriend or wife was waiting for him to come out of the bathroom, I could have him. And I never had to work for more than an hour to get someone to come with me.

"After Montana I tried to be better. I stopped drinking, stopped having sex, and for a while there, I was completely fine. Misha was over all the time, and even though I didn't have Bran right down the street, we still talked daily. Then Misha left for the Middle East, and I started to slip a little. I don't want Bran knowing I went back to cutting. In Montana I bombed into his life, and he doesn't need that again. I know he'd drop everything for me and that he loves me enough to come back to Manhattan with me just to make sure I don't hurt myself anymore, but I don't want that for him. He's happy here with Kaden, and he deserves to have that kind of a life with the person he loves. I won't ruin that for him. You know my big secret now, so whatever you do with it, don't tell Bran. It'll hurt him if you do, but if you need something from me to keep your mouth shut, I'll do it. Whatever you want."

Chris sighed as he realized he'd left out one of the more important things. "When I called you, I'd had a rough night. It was stupid to react badly to something my dad had said, but I did, and I cut myself deeply in my frustration and anger. I called you right after since I knew I needed a break from all of it. I can go to a hotel if you want. I am thankful that you let me run here, and I do understand if you want me gone now too. It's a lot to deal with. Sometimes I feel like I'm even more screwed up than Bran ever was."

Samuel wiped his hand over his face and his short hair before pinning Chris to the spot with icy gray eyes. "I think you may be right about that last bit. But why the hell would I let you out of my sight when I know you are doing this to yourself? I won't be able to sleep without checking on you to make sure you're not cutting yourself and perhaps going too far."

Chris appreciated that; he really did. But he didn't think it was fair of Samuel to take that kind of responsibility on either. "My safety isn't your responsibility, and you can't have that all on your shoulders. Are you going to tell Bran?"

Samuel sat forward and invaded his personal space. "Leave Bran out of this for now. I decide what's my responsibility or not, and the first time you kissed me and I returned that kiss, that's where you became part of my responsibility. You claimed you wanted me, and this, caring whether you live or die, bleed or not, that's part of wanting someone in your life."

"I think all of those confessions deserve at least one kiss," Chris tried with a weak smile to lighten the mood some when Samuel didn't say anything else. There was anger there in his expression, and Chris knew he deserved it. But he hoped at least some of Samuel's rage was directed at his father too. Chris had been mad at him most of his life, but the feeling had been getting steadily harder to ignore. In the past few months, there had been times when he'd been sure he nearly hated the man, which left him feeling sick.

Samuel cleared his throat. "I'm so angry right now—firstly at your waste of space of a father, at your equally useless mother for not ever stepping in to stop the asshole, at Misha for promising to keep an eye on you and then fucking off and leaving you alone without letting us know. And I'm mad at you, so mad I wish I could spank your sassy ass, but all I want to do right now is kiss you."

Samuel grabbed his face between two warm palms and pulled him forward. He leaned back against the side of the couch, almost pulling Chris over his chest to kiss him.

Being in Samuel's arms again felt great, but they'd never been like this before. In Montana, the few kisses they'd shared had been nearly innocent. This was anything but. He felt as if Samuel was being possessive of him, nearly squeezing him too hard as Chris lay over him and crushed his own mouth against Samuel's. Unlike their kiss in Montana, Samuel held nothing back from Chris this time. He parted Chris's lips with his tongue and swept inside to taste all of him. Samuel sucked on his tongue and dragged a stroke over his teeth, as if he couldn't get enough of Chris, and for the second time, Chris lost his heart and mind over the man whose strong tattooed arms protected him from the big scary world he'd always feared.

He felt wanted and needed. But there was guilt there too, because Samuel was too good to him and he'd brought his cutting tools into Samuel's home, all neatly wrapped up in a shiny black case. He should have left them in Manhattan. He felt like he should have somehow known he wouldn't want them there with him.

Reluctantly Chris pulled away. "One second. I need to get something from upstairs."

"It can wait," Samuel said, sounding unwilling to let him go.

But if there was one thing Chris was absolutely certain of, it was that Samuel would never force him to be where he didn't want to be, and when he tried to get up, Samuel released him without a fight.

"I'll only be a minute," Chris promised as he headed back upstairs.

CHAPTER THREE

SAMUEL WATCHED as Chris disappeared up the stairs, wondering what was important enough for Chris to interrupt their kisses. It wasn't long before he heard Chris come down again, and he walked right up to Samuel and held out a small black box to him.

"Here. I'd like you to hang on to this for me. I shouldn't have brought it with me, but now that I have, I think that if you have it, maybe you won't have to worry about me hurting myself so much while I'm here with you. I will need it back, so please don't lose it."

Realization dawned, and Samuel stared at the innocent-looking item in Chris's hand before reaching out and taking possession of it. He hoped he never had to give it back to the man, because he hated Chris hurting himself.

"You can look at it if you want," Chris offered, but Samuel couldn't get himself to open the little case. Not yet. Maybe never.

When Samuel didn't open it, Chris shuffled his feet uncomfortably. "Are you okay? You hardly said anything while I was talking. If you do want me to go, that's fine. You can keep the box with you, and then you won't have to worry. I'll pick it up before I go back to Manhattan."

Samuel shook his head and reached down to the floor beside the couch, where he placed the kit to take care of later. "You're not going anywhere. I just feel a bit old, you know? I sort of didn't know people took to practices like this to deal with emotional challenges. When I went through stuff, it was the usual—alcohol, marijuana, methamphetamine in severe cases. I guess I'm a bit shocked and trying to process what you've told me." He wiped a hand over his face, then tapped the space next to him. "Sit down."

Chris folded himself onto the seat and tucked his legs beside him, facing Samuel. He laid his head on the soft cushion, and Samuel could see the dark smudges under his expressive eyes and the exhaustion lines all over his skin. He resisted the urge to smooth them away with his fingertips. In his heart, he wished it was as simple to stroke away Chris's inner pain.

"Do you still have to milk and do all the stuff you had to in Montana, or do you have people for that now?"

Samuel smiled weakly at his attempt to change the subject. "I do some days. It's nice being the boss, but I like to stay busy too. So if I'm not milking, I'm somewhere else on the farm doing work."

"That explains why you're so buff," Chris teased. "Tell me about your place here. I must say how beautiful it is, the scenery, the mountains in the distance. It's so green wherever you look."

Samuel snorted as he turned sideways and copied Chris's pose. "Wait until late summer comes and it doesn't rain much. Then it all goes yellow and brown. The only green paddocks you'll see then are the ones with maize in them. The Waikato is renowned for having droughts."

Chris's gaze ran over his face, down his chest, and over his outstretched legs. After having his shower earlier, Samuel had put on a T-shirt and a pair of long khaki shorts. "Trent and I own this operation as mutual partners. At peak time we milk approximately two thousand cows through three rotary milking sheds. So in effect the property is divided into three smaller farms, and I manage one, Trent another, and we have Daniel on the third. We each then have three staff—a herd manager, assistant herd manager, and farm assistant—working with us. There are twelve of us in total, and one bloke is a qualified mechanic by trade, but he loves milking cows more. He makes it easy to maintain and service equipment, motors, tractors, and bikes, and if he can't fix it, we send it into the dealerships in town to take care of."

Chris's eyes were wide when he stopped speaking. "Wow, twelve? That's a hell of a lot of employees. Where do they all live? In town?"

Samuel got up from the couch and held out his hand to Chris. "No, there's housing for everyone on the farm. Come to the kitchen so I can make something to fatten you up. Would you like a hot drink?"

Chris's fingers were cold when they landed on his palm, and he pulled him to his feet. He rubbed Chris's fingers between both his hands. "Are you cold?" Looking closer, he almost thought he saw Chris shiver.

Chris chuckled. "No, I actually think my body is in a bit of shock right now. I think I'm crashing from being on a continuous adrenaline high at work and the shit I have to deal with there. Now my body is so relaxed and calm that it doesn't know how to deal with peace. I love being around you. You make me forget about all the crap in my life."

Samuel pulled him closer and felt Chris wrap his arms around his waist to hug him tight. They stood there for a few minutes before Chris slowly withdrew with a deep sigh. He gave Samuel another once-over, his gaze coming to rest on the crotch of Samuel's shorts.

"Sure you don't want that blowjob?"

Samuel laughed before pulling Chris toward the open-plan kitchen. "You don't give up easily, do you?"

"Not when the reward is so huge," Chris teased and waggled his eyebrows.

"Oh, resorting to flattery now?" Samuel pulled out a barstool by the stone and wood bench and indicated Chris should sit there.

"No, even with your clothes on, I can see well enough what's hiding under there."

A red flush touched Chris's neck and cheeks, and to Samuel he looked a bit better, so he walked away and opened the fridge to see what he could make them for dinner before Chris fell asleep at the table.

"Now who's being a tease? Showing off your tight ass now, are you?" Chris taunted him. "If I wasn't at risk of falling flat on my face from exhaustion, I'd come over there and slap it."

"Yeah, stay right there, or you'll sleep on the kitchen tiles tonight," Samuel warned.

"No I won't. My guardian angel would carry me to bed," Chris bragged.

"Ha-ha. Okay, I've got fresh organic farm eggs and sliced champagne ham. How about a fluffy omelet with a side salad?" He turned around and had to clear his throat to get Chris to stop looking below his waistline. "You've got a one-track mind."

"With you I do. I know what I like, and yes, an omelet sounds great. Thank you." Chris slid off his chair and walked closer. "Show me where your cutlery is, and I'll set the table for us and get the kettle boiling for our drinks."

Samuel removed what he needed from the fridge and placed it on the island in the middle of the kitchen. He showed Chris where to find all he needed to make their teas and ready the table for dinner.

They worked in comfortable silence for a bit, and as Samuel poured the egg into the pan for the first omelet, Chris sat back down and watched him.

"What's fun to do around here?"

"First of all, New Zealand is not America, and secondly, we're out in the country here, but we can still have lots of fun. On Friday nights, all the families get together at the local school sports fields, only about six kilometers from here, and we play sports—netball, touch rugby, tennis, or whatever you like. In Thames, about twenty kilometers away, we have a cinema, large supermarkets, public heated swimming pools, indoor go-kart racing. The nightlife is not too shabby either, with three nightclubs, some pubs, or bars as you would call them, but a bit more rustic than your version. Oh yes. One of the nightclubs is a gay one." Samuel turned over the omelet and put the cheese, ham, and herbs in before folding it in half and allowing it to cook another minute or two.

Chris yawned when Samuel slid his food onto his plate and placed the bowl of green garden salad beside him.

"Eat up. You're about to fall asleep in your plate."

"I am so hungry but tired too. Thank you. It smells great." Chris picked up his knife and fork and cut off a piece, which he blew on a bit before eating. "Yum."

Samuel went back to the stove and started his own food.

"So where's the closest city from here?" Chris asked in between bites.

"Hamilton and Auckland are almost equal distances from here. About an hour's drive or so, and there's no limit to the fun you can have in either of them."

While his egg cooked, Samuel poured the boiled water into the cups Chris had placed by the kettle. He stirred and added milk before placing them on the table, noticing Chris's plate was almost empty.

Chris shook his head. "Thanks. I don't think I want to go back to Auckland again so soon after just coming from there, but I would like to see Hamilton sometime maybe, if we have time."

"Sure. Whatever you want."

That made Chris smile, but the expression was gone as quickly as it had come. "Though Hamilton is probably fairly small, and I imagine the chance of running into Bran, Kaden, or Trent is going to be highest there. That trip will probably have to wait until I've told Bran that I'm here. I need this time to get sane again, but I'm not looking forward to what will happen when he finds out I was within driving distance of him." He shook his head before finishing off the last of his dinner. "And, speaking of Bran, I need to call him. We talk daily, and if I miss one I don't want him to think something's up. Can I trust you not to give anything away while I'm on the phone?"

Samuel frowned. "Wouldn't it be easier just to tell him?"

"Probably. But I can't. Not right now. But I'll see him before I go back to Manhattan, which won't be too far out. I don't have that much vacation time saved up. Let me know how long you're okay with me staying after my phone call. Are you going to give me away?"

Chris looked so helpless, nearly desperate, and Samuel simply shook his head. The idea of Chris going back to Manhattan had him feeling angry all over again, but he couldn't very well force Chris to stay in New Zealand either.

Chris pulled out his phone, and Samuel quietly kept eating, his mind circling on thoughts of how he was going to get Chris better and no longer hurting himself before he went back home. There was no easy solution, especially when Samuel felt so out of his depth with what Chris was doing to himself.

"Hey, you," Bran said warmly as soon as he picked up the call. Samuel was surprised Chris had put it on speakerphone.

Chris glanced at Samuel, as if making sure he wouldn't reveal his secrets, before turning back to his phone. "Hey. How's life as a weird little flightless bird?"

Bran laughed, and Samuel was glad to see Chris smiling. "Really nice. Quiet. Kaden does his farming stuff. I get to enjoy what it does to his body. He's so fucking hot. Damn. What's going on with you? Why do you sound so tired?"

Samuel saw Chris stiffen even from a few feet away and reached over to touch him on his lower back, offering some silent comfort. Chris gave him a small nod before answering Bran.

"Because I am tired. Hard day at the office. I'm going to be crashing soon, but I wanted to say hi first."

"It's still early there...."

"It is."

Bran sighed loudly. "Your dad being an asshole again? When are you going to let me pay someone to kill him?"

"He wasn't too bad today. And you can't kill him, or pay someone else to either. He's my dad." Chris leaned forward a little. "I'm gonna let you go. I'm barely awake here, and I don't want to fall asleep on the phone."

"Okay. First, though, quick questions. Misha and therapy?"

Samuel shook his head as he saw Chris round his shoulders forward, looking like he was getting upset.

"Misha's good. He's coming over tomorrow. And I go to therapy in two days. Lots of progress. Still not drinking or having random sex. Saving myself for Samuel and marriage like a good little virgin bride. I'm okay, Bran. You don't have to worry. Go enjoy your hot Kiwi."

"I'd pay good money to see you dressed up like a bride. With a veil and nail polish. Some killer heels. You'd be so pretty!"

Chris snorted and shook his head. "No way in hell. Night."

"Night. Talk to you tomorrow. Wish you'd come down here. You're welcome anytime. I know we'd all love to see you again."

"I know. I will soon. Promise."

"Yeah, yeah. You said that six months ago too. Be good."

Samuel couldn't stop staring at Chris. He lied so easily, even to Bran, not letting even his best friend know the most basic details of what was going on in his life. It was unfair to Bran, and by his expression, it clearly hurt Chris to do it.

"I always am. Good night." Chris hung up the phone and went to put his empty dishes away. "What?" he asked Samuel once he'd turned around.

"You clearly have practice lying to him." Samuel couldn't disguise the anger in his voice. He was so mad at Chris in that moment for not taking care of himself but also refusing to even let anyone know how badly his life had spiraled out of control. If any of them had known, they would have been able to help him. It never had to get this bad, and Samuel was pissed off over Chris letting it. "When was the last time you went to therapy?"

Chris shifted uncomfortably. "A month after Montana."

That was hardly enough time to get anything resolved. "Why did you stop?"

"Romanoffs don't go to therapy." Chris's voice had gone hard, and Samuel had a fairly good idea of where the words were coming from. It seemed Chris's father had not only caused his problems but had stopped him from getting help as well.

"Thanks for dinner," Chris said, coming away from the dishwasher. "I need to get something out of my kit. But I'll bring it in here so you can see what I take and make sure it's not my knife."

"What do you need?" Samuel asked him as he watched Chris go back into the living room and pick up the small black case, which was barely longer than the space between his wrist and the tip of his middle finger, and bring it back into the kitchen.

Chris put it on the island where Samuel could see and opened it up, revealing a simple knife with a smooth edge strapped to one side and a plastic bag full of first aid supplies on the other.

"It's beautiful, isn't it?" Chris asked him instead of answering Samuel's question. "It's lightweight and sharp as fuck. It cuts cleanly and only leaves a minimal scar."

"It's what you use to hurt yourself with," Samuel said plainly, not liking the way Chris seemed almost to fawn over it. To Samuel it was something ugly, something he wished Chris would throw away and never think of again. But from the way Chris stared at it, he knew that wasn't going to happen right away, and it saddened him to realize that.

Chris nodded, then went for the plastic bag. He pulled out a large piece of gauze and some medical tape before sealing it up again. "The deep cut I was telling you about? The one I made right before calling you? I need to change that bandage. It should be fine by tomorrow. I'm good at patching myself up. Scared me more than anything."

He closed the case and passed it over to Samuel, who ignored it in favor of watching Chris.

"You should have told us what you were going through," Samuel said as he tried to touch Chris, but Chris moved out of Samuel's reach before he could touch him, and Samuel let his hand fall limply back to his side.

"I wanted to be better," Chris whispered before taking off up the stairs.

Samuel sadly watched him walk away, feeling helpless as to what to do to help him.

CHAPTER FOUR

MOST OF the time, if it was four in the morning, Chris would be fast asleep. But this was not a normal morning, and he'd barely been able to get any sleep. After so much travel, it also didn't feel like four to him. So when Samuel went into the shower at four, Chris heard him. And he was half tempted to go in there with Samuel to surprise him. But he'd only been joking about having a shower with him the day before, and Chris wasn't quite ready to show Samuel the tattoo he'd designed on his ribs. It meant a lot to him, and he knew someday he would show it to Samuel. But he wasn't up for it this morning. Instead he pulled out a clean shirt and a pair of loose shorts and waited outside the shower for Samuel to emerge.

He got his wish no more than ten minutes later and wondered how anyone showered that quickly and actually managed to enjoy the experience. "Hey," he said, as quietly as he could, when Samuel opened the door. If someone had startled him that early, he would have screamed so loud his neighbors would have called the police. But Samuel only opened the door all the way and gave him a nod.

"Did I wake you?"

Shaking his head, Chris pulled the clothes he'd be changing into closer to his chest, holding them up like a shield even though there was no reason at all for him to feel so defensive around Samuel.

"No. I was up already. It's a little hard to sleep without sirens going by all night and people yelling under my window. It's nice here. Peaceful. I can see why you all like it."

Samuel gave him a soft smile. "It is. I need to go help with the milking for a few hours. Will you be okay here alone?"

Chris tried not to feel like a child as Samuel looked at him as if he expected Chris to get into trouble while he wasn't there, and instead reminded himself that Samuel was likely just worried about him.

"I'll be fine. You have my kit. That's the only real trouble I get into anymore. I know you still have to handle farm work, so go for it. I'll see you in a few hours for breakfast." Chris gave him his best smile, but Samuel still didn't look quite convinced, so Chris stepped up to him and gave Samuel a quick kiss on his cheek. "Go do farmy things. I'll probably just go right back to sleep after I shower. Worst case scenario, I walk around for a little while and keep a low profile. You don't have to worry. I'll be okay."

Samuel gave him a nod, but the concern lingered in his eyes.

"Or… we could go to your room, and someone else could milk those cows this morning," Chris offered him as he shifted his clothes into his left arm and used his now free right hand to trace the top of Samuel's pants, right over his button.

"It's a little early," Samuel said, even as he smiled.

Smirking, Chris moved past him and into the bathroom. "If you say so. You ever get a craving for something American this early in the morning, though, you know where to find me."

Chris shut the bathroom door on Samuel's quiet laughter. It felt good to be able to flirt with him, to touch him and know that Samuel would be good to him when he took him up on his offer. The waiting wasn't fun, but as long as he could make Samuel see reason and that they'd be good together, Chris was willing to work a bit harder for him.

He took his time showering as he let the hot water run over his skin and wake him up. His bandage was off, and he knew from experience he was healing nicely. He'd been stupid to cut so deeply or to leave such a long mark on himself. But he knew cutting himself at all was pretty ridiculous.

When he was in that moment, though, where it felt like he was suffocating from his own life, he couldn't think of anything past that moment and the release he knew he'd feel in it. Sex worked too, but he hadn't been with anyone since Montana. Waiting and being good sucked, but if Samuel ever said yes to him, he was sure all that time would be worth it. He just had to get his head out of his ass long enough to make Samuel see they could have fun together.

Sure, it had only been about twelve hours since he'd arrived in New Zealand, but he'd had this idea, this wonderful, fantastic fantasy, of how Samuel would see him, pick him up, and take him straight to bed, and for once Chris had been sure that he would just stop hurting and be able to deal for a little while. Of course that hadn't happened, but he wasn't ready to give up hope either.

Freshly showered and dressed in clean clothes, Chris tried to fix his hair in the usual way his stylist had showed him made him look the best, but his hair, which had grown a lot longer since she'd fixed it for him, refused to go up where it was supposed to. After fifteen minutes of playing around with it, he called it quits and went downstairs. He'd told Samuel he might go back to sleep, but by the time he was done getting ready, the sun was already up and he felt newly energized as he looked out over the green pastures, lying there as if waiting to be explored by him.

Chris left a quick note to Samuel on the kitchen island, letting him know he would be back soon and had gone for a walk. He doubted Samuel would be back before him, but just in case he was and didn't think to use his phone to call him, Chris didn't want him worrying. He got the feeling Samuel was worrying about him enough already, and he didn't need to be. Sure, Chris had gone to a pretty dark place and done something stupid, but that wasn't normal for him. And he was in New Zealand now, taking a breather and getting his head back on straight before he had to go back home.

He left the house and started wandering aimlessly, though he did keep in mind the stories Bran told him of the bull he'd nearly been killed by in Montana. To avoid that happening to him, Chris only went through smaller gates and walked along fences that would have been much too low to keep a bull in, at least in his mind. He knew exactly nothing about cows, other than how he liked his steak cooked and what toppings he wanted on his cheeseburgers, so everything about their care was simply a guess.

"Hi," he said, seeing a man mending a fence as he walked through what might have been his sixth gate but might have also been his tenth. He'd lost track wandering around the farm, which was far larger than the Wilson Dairy Farm had been back in Montana. This man was nearly as dark as Samuel, and from the look of him, he was Maori too, but he wasn't quite as big. His Samuel could still take him in a fight. Chris was sure of it. Not that he expected them to go at it or anything like that. It was simply a wayward thought that made him smile.

"Good morning. Ummm, are you lost, by any chance?" he asked as he rose up from his crouched position at the base of a post.

"Actually…. Yeah. Kind of. Mind pointing me back in the direction of Samuel's house? Assuming you know who he is. I thought I was going the right way, but all of these pastures look the same to me."

"I'm Daniel. You're a friend of Samuel's?"

"Little more than that, actually," Chris said with a wink. With the sun warm on the back of his neck, he was fairly certain he'd been walking for at least an hour, if not two, and getting back was starting to be important. He'd promised Samuel breakfast, after all. He could have checked his phone, if he'd thought to bring it with him on his walk. Unfortunately it was still plugged in beside his bed, where he'd left it that morning. "So, directions to get back?"

Daniel lifted his hand and pointed Chris south. "Four pastures down. Stay on the cow track or race and out of the pastures, though, or you may get even more lost."

That made sense to Chris, and he remembered what a cow track was from talking to Bran. Apparently it was also called a race, from what the man had just said. Different words, but it was the same thing as a trail, only this one was far more permanent since it was built into the ground almost like a road for the cows to use while going from the pastures to the milking sheds, and it was easy to spot.

"Thanks. See you."

"Wait, what's your name?" Daniel asked, stopping him.

Answering truthfully wasn't going to be an option, since he was pretty sure Daniel would know Kaden and therefore Bran, since he worked on the farm. Chris went with a shortened version of his middle name instead of the truth. He wouldn't answer to the different name, but it was something to give Daniel.

"Eddie." Short for Eadric.

"Nice to meet you, Eddie."

Chris gave him a nod and let himself out of the nearby gate. "You too." He shuffled off in the direction of the closest cow track, made of dirt and stone, that he saw cutting through the middle of the pastures. He hadn't come this way, instead choosing to cut through the pastures in the hopes of not seeing anyone, and he was glad of his choice as soon as he came up to a small group of buildings. They weren't milking sheds, he knew that much from the few days he'd spent with them all in Montana, but he figured buildings might mean people, and he really didn't want to see Bran, or even Kaden. He was nice enough, but Chris knew Kaden wouldn't hide him being there from Bran. And Chris wouldn't have asked him to either. That would have been unfair of him.

He stayed low as he made his way past the buildings. He didn't hear anyone in them, but that didn't mean no one was about. He moved as silently as he could, just as Misha had taught him the time he'd taken him out to a paintball field. He'd been shot within minutes, by the guy he'd been screwing at the time no less, but he'd learned a bit from Misha that day too. He'd also learned that assholes that will shoot a guy with a paintball gun in the gut can get really whiny when sex is withheld from them. But that wasn't a lesson that mattered right then. Staying low and being quiet was.

Unfortunately for Chris, though, the goat that came around the side of the shed had different ideas as it butted its head up against Chris's shoulder, then as he stood up, against his hip.

"Go away," Chris hissed, pushing against its head. "Shoo. Go." The stubborn thing kept beating him with its short, nubby horns, though. "Fucking annoying little goat. Go. I swear to God I will eat a nice goat stew in your honor the minute I'm back in New York if you don't—"

"Chris?"

Busted! He bit back a groan as he turned to see Trent smiling at him as he leaned against the side of the shed Chris had been trying to hide behind. "Hi. So. Your goat I take it?"

Trent smacked his hand against his hip, and the goat, the little shit, trotted right over to him to take a treat out of Trent's hand. "Something like that. More like he's a friend. Surprised to see you here. Bran know you get in yet? I just saw Kaden, and he didn't say anything, so I bet he's planning some kind of a party. I can't wait to see Samuel's face when he sees you, though. He's been missing you."

Chris needed to fix this situation, and fast. "Here's the deal," he began with what he hoped was his sexiest grin. "I'm spending a few days with just Samuel before Bran finds out I'm here. Bran's been wanting us to get together for so long, and I knew if I had just a bit of alone time with him, I'd get Samuel for good. It's going to be a surprise to Bran, since he loves playing matchmaker." Really, Bran just wanted him to be happy, and if Samuel did it for him, then Chris knew Bran would have been fine. But by Trent's smile, Chris was pretty sure he didn't know that about Bran yet. "Which means that you can't say anything about me being here to Bran. At all."

"You do know keeping something from Bran is the worst idea you could possibly have, though. Don't you?" Trent asked him. "It's disastrous."

As far as bad ideas went, it was up there. But it was hardly his worst. That was all stupid crap he'd done in the past, though, and none of it was something Chris felt like sharing with Trent in that moment. "Pretty sure I do know that. But if you tell Bran I'm here before I tell him myself, then I find out your worst secret from Samuel and I tell it to Misha. Got it?"

Trent took a few seconds to respond, because his kind face went pale and his ever-ready smile dropped away.

Chris hated to threaten Trent like that, especially when he gave Chris an outraged look, as if he couldn't believe Chris had just gone there. But keeping Bran happy and not knowing how much of a fucking mess he was right then was worth any kind of issue Trent had with him, as far as Chris was concerned.

"Sure. I won't tell him."

Grinning, Chris put his arm through Trent's. "Great. Now, are you done working for the morning? I promised Samuel I'd make him breakfast, and you're invited too. Not your goat, though. I'm pretty sure he hates me."

Trent chuckled and led the way back to Samuel's house. "He doesn't. He just thinks everyone has treats in their pockets, like I do." Trent fed him another treat, as if proving his point, but Chris wasn't convinced in the least.

The walk back was much more direct, and therefore a lot shorter, than the path Chris had taken, and they stepped into Samuel's house less than half an hour later. "Hey," Chris said as soon as he'd kicked off his shoes. Samuel was watching TV in the living room, and Chris went right over to him and kissed him on his cheek. "Look who I found. And a goat." He glanced back at Trent to see him standing in the doorway. "He won't tell either," Chris whispered to Samuel before giving him another kiss on his cheek.

"How did you manage that?" Samuel asked him.

Chris wasn't about to tell Samuel about his deal with Trent with the other man standing right there, though. "Breakfast time!" he declared, clapping his hands together before he headed into the kitchen to see what was available. Cereal... eggs.... He shook his head. Some smoked salmon that looked promising, but there wasn't enough left in the package for three people. There was, however, some fresh fruit he could cut up, enough cheese for some good scrambled eggs the way he liked them, and of course a stack of eggs, since there was a chicken coop not more than a hundred feet from the house.

Within minutes he had the eggs cooking, bread in the toaster, and some water simmering for tea. He would have preferred coffee but had yet to find any in Samuel's house, which was a bit disappointing. Next time he came to visit Samuel in New Zealand he would have to remember to bring some.

Samuel and Trent came into the kitchen a few minutes later and readied dishes for their breakfast, and Chris saw Trent open a small cupboard to one side to reveal a fancy stainless steel coffee machine. Trent pressed a few buttons, and the aroma of delicious coffee permeated the air.

"So, you do have coffee!" Chris said excitedly.

Samuel laughed. "Of course I do. I can't go without my daily caffeine intake."

Chris finished slicing up the fruit—a mixture of melon, peaches, pear, and some grapes—and placed the serving tray in the middle of the table before sharing the scrambled eggs between them. Samuel added the buttered toast, Trent wandered over with their coffees, and they all sat down and dug in.

The smell, then the taste, of the coffee was exactly what Chris had needed to feel more like himself. "Do me a favor, please," he said, looking up at Samuel with the coffee mug still held between his hands. He hadn't even started eating his breakfast yet.

"What's that?"

"Don't ever give me tea again. Not when you've got the good stuff here." Chris gave him a little smile over the rim of his mug and kept drinking. Breakfast food could wait. His coffee was more important to him.

Chris caught Trent looking between himself and Samuel with a frown on his face. "What's wrong?" Chris asked him, putting the mug down but not letting it go far.

"Aren't you worried about what Bran will say when he finds out? He's been missing you for eight months, talks about you constantly. And now you're a twenty-minute drive away and you won't go tell him? He should be here. They both should. And Misha should be eating breakfast with us too."

Trent finished speaking with a shake of his head, and Chris tightened his mouth into a hard line as he turned to stare down at his food for several seconds while he tried to think of something to say, aside from the truth.

He couldn't come up with anything reasonable, so he just said the first thing that came to him. "I plan on telling Bran as soon as Samuel lets me into his bed. Then Bran and I can go out drinking to celebrate the end of my dry spell." It sounded ridiculous, even to himself, but it seemed like exactly the kind of thing Trent would expect him to say. "If you want Bran knowing sooner, you could always help me convince Samuel how much fun it would be to have me naked under him. Or on top. That's up to him."

Trent coughed, and Chris grinned, glad he was still able to make Trent uncomfortable. It was a talent as much as anything else he was good at.

"Mate, I don't know if you're being so clever this time, because I'm telling you—I've seen Bran pissed as hell, and things don't look good for any of us if he finds out we've all been part of this. And Kaden is my friend too. Keeping stuff from each other is not our way. But I guess you're a grown man who can do what you want. How's Misha, by the way?"

Chris was infinitely glad for the change of subject. "Misha is fine. He's back home. He's probably eating pizza and watching a football game right now. American football. Not soccer or rugby or whatever else you have here. He—" Samuel stopped him by clearing his throat, and Chris frowned as he put down his fork. Fine. If Samuel thought Trent needed the truth and that he could handle it, then Chris would tell him.

With a sigh and a drag of his fingers through his hair, he turned back to Trent, who was now watching him intently. "Actually, the truth is that Misha hasn't been in the States for a little over four months. He got bored with retirement and took up with an ex-military unit that does contract jobs. It's hardcore stuff, and he's not allowed to tell me where he is or what he's doing, but I get a text every Saturday letting me know that he's okay. He's fine. I'm sure he's happy being active and shooting at people again. He's in the Middle East right now. That's all I know. And that's another thing Bran can't be told."

Trent put down his knife and fork and stared out the kitchen window. "Fuck, this is so damn hard," he mumbled almost to himself, already seeming deep in thought.

"Are you okay, buddy?" Samuel asked, a worried frown creasing his forehead.

Trent's green eyes shone brightly as he looked at them. "No, I'm not. I haven't seen or spoken to the asshole for more than eight months, despite him having my number and e-mail address. The few e-mails I shot off came back undelivered and the text messages unanswered. Now I hear he's probably being shot at or sidestepping landmines, for all I know."

Chris nodded. He was worried about that too. "If it helps at all, he's been shot before."

Trent looked even worse, and Chris realized that was definitely the wrong thing to say to him.

"But he is an ass for not answering your text messages. He doesn't answer mine either, but him being my half brother and him being into you are two completely different scenarios."

Trent shook his shaggy head. "I think he's having far too much fun and excitement without me, so it makes sense. Why would he bother with me if he's living life on the edge? I can understand why he would easily forget about my existence. We live continents apart, so it's too much hard work, but that's okay. I can deal with that. Actually, I should be fucking used to shit like this by now."

If Chris hadn't seen it for himself, he wouldn't have believed the jovial, softhearted Trent could get angry. He watched in amazement as Trent pushed his chair back and dumped the rest of his breakfast in the rubbish bin. He downed his coffee in two swallows, rinsed the cup, and put it out to dry on the rack.

"Thanks for breakfast, Chris. I'll see you two later." Trent left via the back door, which softly clicked closed behind his retreating back.

By the looks of things, Samuel had lost his appetite too. He rubbed both his palms over his face and short hair before looking at Chris.

"It wasn't a good idea for me to come here, was it?"

As Chris moved to get up, Samuel clamped a hand over his arm, keeping him seated.

"It's not you...," Samuel began.

"It is me! I stayed away from you all because Bran and I caused so much drama in Montana, and I didn't want to be a burden to anyone anymore. It sucks when people see you in that way. I want to be strong, independent, and healthy. So I come here to try to get better, and look now! I'm lying to my best friend and pulling you and Trent into this. And Trent is right. When Bran finds out, it's going to be like fireworks from hell! He's gonna be so mad, I find it hard to predict what he's gonna do. And he won't just be mad at me—he'll be furious at you and Trent too. Because of me!" Chris ended in an almost shout, his heart pounding a hundred miles a minute in his chest.

Samuel watched his meltdown in silence, and when Chris ran out of steam, Samuel came around the table and picked him up out of his chair. The next moment Chris felt the soft fabric of the couch touch his back as Samuel lay him down before stretching out his big body beside him. Chris hid his face in Samuel's neck and let the tears of frustration and disappointment in himself overflow.

CHAPTER FIVE

IN HIS arms, Chris's frame shook as the sobs ripped through his chest and out his throat. Samuel held him close as the storm broke, the tears of heartbreak wetting his skin as they flowed down his neck.

The pain gripping Chris wasn't only about the lies to Bran. Chris's whole life had been taken away from him by two people who should've been declared unfit to have kids to start with. Like Samuel's own biological parents. Disillusionment and distrust in those whom you were supposed to trust the most were not foreign to him at all. In so many ways, he had so much in common with Chris, but the younger man didn't know that.

Samuel let Chris cry and purge some of his pent-up emotions. Chris's father had probably conditioned his son to never cry or reveal any softer emotions. Asking for help with counseling apparently didn't carry the man's approval and was seen as a weakness. So why would he and his wife care if their son felt unwanted, abnormal, inadequate, and unloved?

Like an echo, Samuel heard the words yelled at him so many years ago. "Why are you crying, boy? Crying is for girls, not men. Toughen up and shut your mouth, or I'll smack it shut, just like your eye!"

When Chris calmed down, Samuel stroked his back, still holding him close as he started to speak. "I've never told you about my childhood, and I know none of my friends will, because it's not their story to tell."

Chris pulled away, his face all puffy and his eyes reddened from his tears. "I thought you all had wonderful, normal, and innocent childhoods," he mumbled and tucked some hair behind his ear before laying his head down to watch Samuel.

"Kaden and Trent pretty much did, but not me. Not until I lived through a few years of hell first," Samuel offered with a weak smile.

"Were you sexually abused? Is that why you don't want me?" Before Samuel could even say a word, though, Chris was already groaning. "That sounded so much less selfish in my head. Please pretend I didn't just ask you that." He took a deep breath and curled his hand in

Samuel's shirt. "Okay. Starting again. And better this time. I promise. Do you want to talk about it at all? I'll listen. I'm fucked up enough that I probably won't be of any help, if you do need any help still, since you seem incredibly put together, but I promise to listen and not ask you any more stupid questions if you do want to talk about it."

Samuel smiled and pushed Chris's head back down into his neck. "Shhhh and listen."

"Okay," Chris sniffed and mumbled against his skin, giving him a soft kiss, making goose bumps break out over his skin.

"My parents drank and did drugs, lots of them. I seldom saw my dad sober, but more than anything I remember the fights. The yelling, the swearing, breaking stuff, and of course the punches and slaps as they beat each other up."

"What about you?" Chris quietly asked him, as if he was afraid of Samuel's answer.

"Let's put it this way—if my dad lost the battle, my mom pretty much saved my ass. If he won, I was usually next." Samuel rubbed a hand across Chris's back when he felt him tense.

"I never thought I'd be the one with the better dad, and I'm sorry that happened to you. What happened to them? Do you still talk to either of them?"

"After one particularly bad night, I managed to escape my dad's grip and ran off into the dark. I wandered as far as I could with only one eye, because the other one was swollen completely shut. Much later I found a small stream with some long grass and thought it safer to sleep there than risking going back home with my dad in such a rage. I never realized I'd actually stumbled onto the neighbor's farm." Many of the memories were foggy for him, but he remembered the comfort of the place where he'd spent the night.

Chris's hand tightened in Samuel's shirt, keeping him close, as if Chris couldn't have even an inch between them. "Random guess, and I'm probably wrong, but was that Kaden's parents' farm?"

"It was. Long story short, Kaden and Trent came to swim in the stream early the next morning and found me there, all beaten up. They took me home, and Kaden's mom took one look at me before grabbing a baseball bat and paying my folks a visit. Half an hour later, she came back with a plastic bag with some of my clothes, wrapped me in her arms, and told me I was never going back to that horrible place again.

And that was that. I was happy to stay there. A few months later, my parents moved away to who knows where."

Chris slowly nodded against his neck. "No wonder you three never went into specifics when I asked how you all met. It was good of his mom to take you in. I'm glad she was there for you."

"I've never heard from my dad since, but my mother got in touch with me via a distant relative about six months ago. Apparently my dad almost killed her for real a few months prior to that, and waking up barely this side of death made her rethink her life at that late stage."

"Was that weird for you? To hear from her again after so long? I don't know if I could have talked to her."

Samuel nodded his understanding. "It did surprise the shit out of me, but you know what? All that stuff happened a very long time ago, and she was as much a victim as I. I know she played a role in the mess by drinking and doing drugs too and not looking after her kid, but she was also very young. I'm not saying I'm ready to live happily ever after and so forth, but I'm saying I was willing to reach out because she was."

"You're a strange man. And a lot more forgiving than I think I would have been, if I was in that situation." Chris nuzzled the side of his neck for a few seconds before giving him a kiss.

"The mending is not over, and I didn't just dive headlong into it like a little lost kid. She told me she had separated from him and went to rehab for the alcohol and drugs. She now lives with her sister, and she has managed to find a decent job in town. So before falling for it all, I verified it was all true, which it proved to be. So we've had a cup of coffee a few times, and so far so good. She's never been here, though, and I think it will be a while before it gets to that point."

"Does she know you're gay?" Chris asked.

"She did the first day she called me. I told her there was no point in catching up if she couldn't handle a gay son. She insisted it didn't matter to her. So we'll see how it goes or how long it takes her to try to introduce me to some woman or something." He chuckled.

"I hope it works out for you, however you want it to."

Chris pulled away from him, and it was good for Samuel to see that Chris's eyes were no longer puffy from tears.

He gave Samuel a weak smile and smoothed his hands down the front of Samuel's shirt. "So…. This is pretty random, but I was just thinking about it. Do you remember after Richard? When I was lying down in bed all fucked up with bruises and stitches and you came up to check on me? That meant a lot to me, not only that you would make sure I was okay but also what you said. About how I'd get better and that I deserved better than I'd gotten from him. How I deserved better than being fucked in random back rooms by nameless guys."

Chris took a deep breath and met Samuel's gaze. "Thank you for that. Richard was just a stupid mistake, but he wasn't the first, and it was good to hear someone actually say that to me. I want you to know that I did listen to you. And I did try. I failed, clearly, but for a while there, I was completely normal, and I actually felt like I was in control of myself for the first time in a lot of years. So thank you. It might not have meant anything to you, and not a big deal if it didn't, but it did mean something to me. A lot to me. Anyway, I just wanted you to know that."

With incredible slowness, Samuel turned them so he was on top of Chris and slid his hand over Chris's stomach, coming to rest at his hip. He'd lost weight, and some of his beauty along with it, but he was still attractive. No, he was more than that. To him, Chris would always be beautiful, but now that he knew the truth, he couldn't help comparing Chris to a violent storm in his mind. He was drawn to Chris, but the man's self-destructiveness needed to stop, and Samuel was afraid of who he'd end up bringing down with him before he finished hurting himself.

"I want you better. I need you to stop cutting yourself," Samuel murmured softly.

Chris easily moved under him without having to be told what to do. "How about worrying about that later, and I'll go upstairs and get a condom out of my bag?" he suggested as he lifted himself up to kiss Samuel's neck.

His offer was tempting, and Samuel did want him, but he wanted to enjoy Chris first. There were things they had to work out before Samuel would be taking him to bed, but denying them both was nearly impossible. Chris had said, multiple times, that he hadn't been with anyone since meeting him, and from the eager kisses Chris gave him as Samuel bent to meet his lips, Samuel believed him.

He pushed Chris's shirt up a little, enough to gain access to the button of his shorts, but Chris was quick to bring his shirt back down.

"What are you hiding now?" Samuel asked. If Chris said he'd cut himself on his chest too, or if it was something worse and even more self-destructive, Samuel had no idea what he would do. He was barely hanging on as it was.

"A tattoo that I don't want you to see right away. Later, but not this second."

That surprised Samuel, as he didn't remember Chris having any tattoos before, but if Chris didn't want him seeing it right then, for whatever reason, Samuel would respect that. He refocused his attentions on Chris's shorts, opening them up and pulling them a little over his hips, enough to give him access to Chris's thick cock. He was waxed, beautifully hairless, and seemingly perfectly ready for whatever Samuel would give him.

He tried to ignore the little scars that ran over Chris's hips and the thicker pink cut that lay over his inner thigh. But it was impossible, and soon he found himself tracing that pink line. It was a dangerous area and sensitive too.

"This is the one you did before you called me," Samuel said, even though the words were needless. Of course it was. It was the newest one, and as he touched it, even gently, he saw how Chris shivered, as if it still hurt him. "You are not to do this ever again, Chris. I mean it." Samuel looked away from the cut to make sure Chris had heard him.

"I won't. No more cutting there. Or that deeply."

That wasn't good enough, though. Samuel took his thick shaft in his right hand and leaned over Chris's body. "No. You can't cut yourself anymore at all."

But Chris only shook his head. "I can't promise you that. I'm sorry. I wish I could."

Samuel didn't understand, and he wasn't happy about it, but he could see plainly enough that Chris believed in what he was saying. To Samuel, he could have stopped at any time. But for some reason, Chris didn't seem to see that, and it broke Samuel's heart. Samuel kissed him, hoping to drive away his own worry, along with Chris's pain, with his rough kiss. He used his left hand and pinned Chris's hands loosely to the arm of the couch as he gripped him with the other.

Soon enough Chris's lips parted and his breath escaped in a rush with each quick stroke over his shaft. Samuel wanted to be inside of him, to have Chris's body flush against his, but this was as much as he was willing to do while Chris was still such a mess. Each of Chris's harsh gasps filled him with need, and he knew, given half a chance, that if Chris was well, he would have already had him in bed.

Surprisingly, Chris didn't try to pull his hands down. He only kept them where Samuel held them, though he could have easily brought them down to touch him. Seeing him stretched out like that, with his face flushed with pleasure, made Samuel so hot.

Chris's orgasm seemed to surprise him too, as Samuel slowly squeezed him, milking him as Chris stared up at him. "Sorry. I told you it's been a long time for me."

Samuel didn't mind how quickly he'd come at all. "It's okay." Samuel leaned down to kiss him before getting up to wash his hand. While he was at the sink with his back turned, he heard Chris go upstairs. When he came back down, Chris had changed his clothes, this time wearing a pair of comfortable-looking shorts and a simple gray T-shirt.

"Thanks for that," Chris said, sitting back down beside Samuel on the couch. "Can I treat you now too?"

He reached for the front of Samuel's shorts, but Samuel took his hand before Chris could touch him. "I do want to, but I would like you to be healthier first. I need you to stop hurting yourself. You can't keep doing that."

Frowning, Chris pulled his hand back. "And if this is the best I'm ever going to be?" Chris asked him, almost bitterly.

Samuel didn't believe that for a second. "Then I would only be comfortable being your friend. But with therapy and work, I'm sure you could move on from this. You don't have to hurt yourself. The stuff that happened to me was long ago, but the scars are still there, and the pain I went through was enough to last me forever. If you hurt yourself while you're with me, it would hurt me too. In a very bad way, because you'll be part of me, and if you're down on yourself enough to cut, then I won't make any difference in your life. I need you well for you and for me. Otherwise I would start doubting what my purpose in your life is, and if I'm not enough, then there's no point for us to go down that path. It will save us both a world of heartache."

Chris shook his head and moved to the other side of the couch, putting a few feet of space between them. "I can't be just friends with you. That would hurt too much." He took out his phone and started tapping away loudly on the screen.

"Who are you calling?" Samuel asked him, wondering what Chris was doing now.

Chris didn't look up from the screen of his phone. "I'm booking a taxi. And a hotel room. I'd like to see you again while I'm here for the next few days, but I need some space to think. I can't do that with you around. You can keep my kit here. I'll pick it up before I go back to Manhattan."

Samuel reached across the couch to him and put his hand over Chris's, making him lower the phone. "Don't do this. You're welcome to stay here for as long as you want to."

Chris looked as if he was near tears as he slid off the couch and got to his feet. "I know I am. And thank you for that. But I can't stay here. If I was capable of being just friends with you, this would be so much easier. That's just not possible, though. I wish it was. The taxi will be here in a little while, so I should go pack."

Samuel got to his feet as well. "I can take you to whatever hotel you want, then."

Chris hesitated on the stairs and looked like he was considering Samuel's offer but slowly shook his head after a few seconds. "I'd rather take the taxi. Thank you, though."

"Why?" Samuel demanded, not understanding in the least.

Chris looked away from him, his hand tightly gripped on the railing of the stairs as he visibly shook. Samuel took a step toward him, but Chris moved back, silently showing Samuel that he had no intention of being touched by him again anytime soon. "My best isn't good enough for you," Chris quietly explained.

He licked his lips and shook his head before bringing his gaze back up to meet Samuel's. "I tried. I didn't fuck anyone, and I stopped drinking. A few cuts a week, or a day even, aren't a big deal to me. The one on my thigh is a problem, but that's the first time in years that I've cut that deeply. You're asking me to drop it all before you'd even give me a chance, and I can't risk that. This is my best. I don't know how to be better than this. Not yet. I don't know if I'm even capable of more than this. I was good for eight months for you, and it wasn't enough. So please, I need some space to think and figure this out. I'm going to go pack, I'll take a taxi to the hotel, and tomorrow I'll call you and see if you want to do something. But right now I just can't be around you without breaking down."

"I don't mind if you do that around me," Samuel said, Chris's words hitting him in his gut and closing around his heart, nearly strangling him at the same time.

"I do." Chris quietly headed upstairs and closed the bedroom door behind him. He came back down half an hour later, right as the taxi was pulling up. Samuel stood in front of the door, and Chris sighed once he saw him waiting there.

"Please let me go?" Chris asked him, sounding weary. "I can't do this."

Samuel had wanted to fight him, to keep Chris there with him for as long as he was able, but seeing him looking practically miserable at the prospect of spending another night under the same roof with him had Samuel reconsidering that prospect.

"Chris, I know you think this is your best, but hear me out. You stopped sleeping around and drinking, and I'm really proud of you for that. You were on the right track with counseling, but thanks to your father, you stopped getting help. What you've achieved is wonderful, and you've been strong. I'm not saying it's not good enough for me. You being well is a necessity for you, not me. I want you healthy for your own sake, and only then do I matter. If we go into this relationship as it is, I don't think we'll survive. Either of us. We both deserve better than that. I want more than just a small chance to make it work."

Chris gave him a slow nod and pulled the duffle farther over his shoulder. "I hope you find someone that can give you that. I'd like to go now. Please."

Samuel knew Chris wouldn't give an inch right now. "You will call me tomorrow."

Chris nodded. "I will."

Believing him, Samuel stepped out of the way and let Chris go, and somehow this time, it was harder than back in Montana. How many more times did he have to let Chris walk away from him, he wondered as he closed the door with a heavy heart.

CHAPTER SIX

WHAT'S A bar Bran wouldn't be at? Chris texted Samuel nearly two hours later, when he'd given up trying to be entertained by the TV in his hotel room. It was a damn nice room, but it would have been a lot better with some company, and he wasn't about to ask Samuel to come out there when he'd only just left him back at his house. It was barely even dinnertime, and he could have been out doing any number of things that the TV commercials had said were available in Hamilton, from hang gliding to rock climbing to the scenic horseback rides. But he hadn't wanted to run into Bran while taking a little outing, so he'd stayed right where he was and quickly grown bored.

Planning to throw your good behaviour away already? Samuel texted him back.

Getting a text from him at all was a surprise, but he'd kind of expected the anger he could practically hear coming out of Samuel's typed words.

He shook his head as he texted back. It shouldn't have hurt that Samuel would think that about him. He should have been able to simply ignore whatever Samuel thought, about him or anything else, but he wasn't that easy to ignore. *Wanting to dance.*

Renegade. It's in Thames. Seven months ago one of the servers acted like a jerk to Kaden and we haven't been back.

That would work for Chris. *Thanks.*

Twenty minutes later, with the pop music blasting so loudly it seemed to shake the building around him, Chris paid the cover and stepped into Renegade, a club the online reviews called the hottest gay club in Thames. It certainly had some of the hottest guys in it. He'd give it that, he decided as he made his way over to the bar so that he could better see everyone. He hadn't come to hook up, certainly not, but the music and dancing would be good distractions for him if he decided to take advantage of them.

He found an empty seat next to a guy that gave him a heated once-over, but when Chris didn't respond, he went back to talking to the guy beside him.

"What'll you have?" the bartender asked him, coming over and putting a napkin down in front of him.

Eight months of not drinking had felt good, but being rejected by Samuel again had left him with a distinct need to figure out a way to deal. And throwing out all the work he'd tried to do seemed like a good plan. That was until he actually went to order the shots he was thinking of starting the night with.

"Soda."

The bartender was cute, especially when he lifted his eyebrows like he was surprised at the order.

"To start with," Chris clarified. Maybe he'd drink. Maybe he'd just order something and look at it for a while. Maybe he'd get completely wasted and end up in the bathroom with some guy he wouldn't even remember the next morning and only really know he hadn't imagined it by the awful taste in his mouth. He didn't want to go there in his mind, especially not with the happy music around him and everyone smiling like it was the best night of their lives. But he wasn't exactly feeling like being good anymore either. Not when being good hadn't gotten him Samuel.

"Where you from? Not anywhere around here, that's for sure," the bartender said, putting the soda down in front of him.

Chris smiled and downed half of it in one drink before he came up for air. "No. I'm from New York. America."

"I know where New York is, mate," the bartender said, smiling. "I'm Jeff."

"Chris." Chris offered him his hand, and Jeff shook it. "Busy night?" There were people everywhere around him, most of them dancing, all of them drinking.

"Usually is. Visiting or planning on moving here?"

He must not have been that busy, Chris decided, if Jeff was available to make small talk with him. Whatever, he didn't mind the conversation or the attention. He wouldn't be taking Jeff home, but it was nice to have someone good-looking actually notice him instead of treating him as a nuisance, like he thought Samuel was doing.

"Vacationing. Thought I'd spend some time with a friend, but that didn't work out. Still have a few days left, so I'm exploring the area a bit. Getting into trouble."

Jeff laughed and handed him another soda. "I remember when I thought like that. I came down for two weeks, then realized I didn't want to live anywhere else."

"Oh yeah? Where are you from, then? Originally?" It was a nice sentiment to fall in love with a country and just decide to stay, but Chris was damn sure that wouldn't be happening to him.

"Portugal. Brought my brother, Aaron, down here with me as well." Jeff nodded to a man that couldn't have been much over twenty-one who was bouncing around in the middle of the dance floor, completely oblivious to the attention he was getting from the guys around him, or just not caring.

"He's cute," Chris said absently. The family resemblance was obvious, even past the darker skin and slick black hair. They had the same eyes and the same curved lips. Either of them could have passed for Latin movie stars, but Aaron was far more in that category, with perfect looks that hadn't yet been chipped away at by life.

Jeff shook his head. "He's twenty-two. Likes to dance, but the guys here…. They're good people, for the most part, but they're not careful, not like he needs someone to be with him."

Chris looked back over his shoulder at Aaron and noticed a few guys getting a bit close. None of them had touched him yet, but Chris knew the look they were giving him. Plenty of guys had given him that look too, especially when he was that age. It was the kind of look that said, in no uncertain terms, that they'd have him up against a wall within the hour, whether he liked it or not.

"Shit," Jeff swore behind him. "I'll send my bouncer over there, let him handle it."

"No need. I've got this," Chris said.

"What are you going to do?" Jeff asked when he was already heading toward Aaron and the three guys beginning to circle around him like sharks.

Chris threw a smile over his shoulder. "Watch."

Getting up to them was easy, and surprisingly, so was coming between them. He touched Aaron first, bringing his body flush against his and dragging his fingers through Aaron's long black hair. He pressed

Aaron's face against his neck as he ground them together, the movement sexual even though his intentions weren't. He met the gazes of the three men who had planned to be with Aaron and grinned at them, letting them know that Aaron was his and they weren't welcome to play with him.

"Who are you?" Aaron asked him as they started moving away.

"Chris." He knew how to dance, how to make men want him with little more than a smile and a shake of his hips. That knowledge had come after years of being around men much older than he'd been when he was even younger than Aaron. While Aaron's dancing was sensual, he wasn't where Chris had been at twenty-two, and that told him quite a bit and made him smile. He danced like he knew what he wanted, like he wanted to play with whoever would let him, but like he hadn't been down that road yet. He was hesitant as he touched Chris's stomach and sides, as if he knew what he should be doing but didn't have the confidence to actually go through with it.

"Let me buy you a drink," Chris said huskily in his ear. "You look like you're burning up." The old line had worked on him dozens if not hundreds of times, and it didn't fail to have Aaron following him off the dance floor and right back to his brother.

"Fuck if you aren't sex incarnate," Jeff said, shaking his head at Chris.

"Got him out of there, didn't I?" Chris shot back with a smile.

Aaron looked confused as his gaze went between the two of them. "What did I miss?"

Chris took a big drink of his soda before ordering one for Aaron as well. "You need to be more careful when you're dancing. Those guys would have eaten you alive and picked their teeth with your leftovers."

But Aaron only rolled his eyes at the warning. "I could have handled them."

Snorting, Chris shook his head. "Bravo for the macho attitude, but take it from someone who has been there—three guys like that, at your age, and you would have been hurting for at least a week." He finished off his soda and looked to Jeff for another, but like any great bartender, he already had one waiting for him.

"What do you know of it?" Aaron said defensively.

His attitude and the fearlessness Chris saw in him made him instantly miss Bran. Talking to him and seeing him out there had been like watching Bran all over again. Only he hadn't screwed up this kid.

He leaned in close so that Aaron would have to listen to every word he said. "I know you're inexperienced, maybe even a virgin. I know that at your age I thought that sex and love were practically the same thing, and that if I wanted something enough, sex would get it for me. And I know that whatever you want from a guy, you're not going to get it here, with these guys around you looking like you're one cute buffet all served up for them and just waiting to be stripped down. You're cute. Work with that, but don't ever be cute and stupid."

"You don't know that a good guy isn't in this crowd. Maybe my Mr. Right is."

Chris thought he was far too young to be thinking about Mr. Right, but at thirty-five he'd never had a relationship that lasted longer than six months, so really what the hell did he know about dating and relationships? The only thing he was absolutely great at when it came to other people was sex, but at least he knew that much. "He could be. But chances are, if he's trying to buy you drinks and wanting to get you alone the first time he's met you, then he's most likely not the guy for you. Unless you want that. But, tip from someone that has been there, the guys that want to fuck you in the bathroom aren't really the kind of guys that call the next day. Or if they do, it's so they can take you out and fuck you in another bathroom."

He shook his head, remembering plenty of exes that fit that bill. "My point is that hooking up, if that's what you want to do, is fine. But you say you're looking for Mr. Right, and he doesn't come from quick sex. At least not in my experience. And I've been with more guys than are in this club. And then some. Decide that you're worth it and make the guy wait for you. Go out on a real date that doesn't involve clothes coming off unless you're going swimming. Have fun and decide if you actually like this guy before you end up wasting yourself with him or anyone else. Sex is by far the most fun thing I can imagine doing. But it's also really empty when everything is said and done."

Aaron gave him a shrewd look, then lowered his lashes as if he was considering something. "What about you?"

"What about me?" Chris repeated him.

"Want to go out sometime?"

Being hit on by someone barely old enough to drink was refreshing, and he wanted to laugh, but he held it back once he saw how serious Aaron actually was. "Thanks, I'm flattered, actually. But I'm far too tainted for someone like you. I will dance with you, though, if you want to. I like dancing."

Thankfully Aaron didn't look all that upset by his refusal. "Yeah? Sure. We can dance."

Aaron got off his stool, and Chris moved to follow him onto the dance floor, but a hand on his shoulder stopped him, and he turned to look at Jeff.

"Thanks for that. I've been trying to tell him that for months, but I think you were actually able to get to him."

Chris gave him a nod. "He reminds me of my best friend when he was Aaron's age. Maybe if he'd had someone with half a brain talking to him, instead of me, neither one of us would be as fucked up as we are right now. Hopefully he won't waste himself on horrible guys before the right one comes along and decides that he's too much trouble to be with."

"That what happened to you?" Jeff asked, pulling his hand back and looking sad.

Chris nodded and forced a smile. "Yeah. We're going to try to be friends, though, so it's all good." The lie was easy, but the truth of it hurt. Jeff gave him a nod, and Chris went back to the floor and danced with Aaron. This time there was nothing sexual between them as they danced together, their movements sensual but friendly. They bounced around and laughed when they ran into each other and some people around them.

Dancing again and meeting new people, having fun was just what he'd needed, Chris thought as he smiled on his way back to the bar and Jeff for another cool drink. His shirt stuck to his back from the heat and exercise, but he felt more alive than ever. Stopping at the bar, he watched Jeff, who obviously watched someone else. Chris leaned forward to see what the other man was staring at and lost any and all rational thought in his brain.

There in the dark corner against the wall at the end of the timber bar top sat Samuel as Chris had never seen him. His eyes were obscured in the low light in the club, but Chris's body went cold then hot when he ran his eyes over Samuel. He'd never seen him in jeans, and he counted his lucky stars he hadn't, because he would've climbed Samuel like a cat in heat. On his upper half, a skintight black muscle shirt showed every ripped bump, dip, and detail. The cuffs appeared stretched to their breaking limit around Samuel's massive biceps, and his tattoos beckoned Chris closer like a drug. And Samuel looked straight at Chris.

"He's something else, isn't he?" Jeff commented from the other side of the bar.

"Fuck, yeah." Chris couldn't take his eyes off him.

"He appears to like you too," Jeff added dryly.

Chris snorted without breaking his stare off with Samuel. "Believe me, he doesn't want me. Not really."

"Oh, the 'just friends' guy?" Jeff managed to piece it all together.

"Sad, isn't it? I'm just too messed up to make it worth his time." He tried to pass it off as lightly as he could. Only it didn't feel like nothing to Chris. It felt like he'd made a thousand little mistakes that had all led up to one very big one. And that one was why Samuel didn't want him, but he couldn't do anything to change any of it now. Part of him didn't even know if he would have gone back and done his life differently if he'd had the choice. Up until Montana, everything had been perfect. Fucking hot Kiwis had completely changed his priorities up on him.

"Well, what do I know, but that's not the look of a guy who doesn't want you. I'd say he's pretty much eating you with his eyes right now." Jeff slid another soda across to Chris, who picked it up and downed half of it in one go. Dancing always made him so thirsty.

Samuel dropped his one propped-up foot from where it rested against the barstool to the floor and stood up. Chris's body, already primed with adrenaline from his fun on the dance floor, went into overdrive. His cock was hard as steel in his jeans, and his tight nipples almost hurt as they rubbed against the fabric of his button-down shirt.

Chris had never seen Samuel like this—almost predatory and so fucking huge. Samuel's quiet manner nearly made a person overlook his size, but there was no way Chris could miss it tonight. As Samuel made his way over to where Chris stood drooling, the man was wider and taller than most guys present in the club. The thick veins ran in heavy tracks all over his arms, his dark mocha skin shining like liquid caramel.

As Samuel's features caught some light, the liquid silver gaze burnt Chris as it ran over his body, like a physical touch setting him alight. Samuel moved right into Chris's personal space until he could smell the spearmint chewing gum on his breath.

"Making friends?" Samuel raised one eyebrow in question as he cast a quick glance toward Jeff behind the bar.

Chris instantly bristled but then realized Samuel wasn't asking him if he was interested in Jeff or if he'd gone from Samuel to Jeff so quickly. He was asking for an introduction, and that made Chris smile as he glanced between them.

"Samuel, this is Jeff. His little brother, Aaron, is around here somewhere," Chris said by way of a simple introduction. He turned on his stool to face Samuel fully and wanted to pull him between his thighs, to feel him against all the most sensitive parts of his own body. He practically needed it as he looked Samuel over and tried not to fucking drool like an idiot over how good he looked. Half the bar didn't have that problem, though, as he caught all kinds of men staring at Samuel, most of them not being discreet about it at all. While Chris didn't blame them, considering how damn good Samuel looked right then, he still wanted to put a giant trash bag over Samuel and run him out of the bar so that none of the other men could stare at Samuel like he was.

"Hey," Jeff said, leaning over the bar to shake Samuel's hand.

Chris watched the movement out of the corner of his eye and felt ridiculously, stupidly jealous as they shook hands because he wanted Samuel's hands on him. He was high on adrenaline and burning up from dancing for at least an hour already. Those two combined left him practically begging to be touched by Samuel. Anyone else he would have kicked in their dick, but he wanted Samuel's hands on him.

Going from needing space from him to seeing him there and feeling this desperate to have him was a mindfuck for Chris, but he was glad to have him there. "Did you come to dance or to make sure I didn't do anything stupid?" Chris asked him. Part of him loved the idea that Samuel wanted to look after him, if he'd come to Renegade for that. The rest of him, though, that bit of him felt a bit defensive and maybe even paranoid about Samuel showing up there. He tried to quash that annoying part of him as quickly as possible.

Before Samuel answered him, though, Aaron spoke up from over his shoulder.

"Wow. Uh. Hi."

Chris glanced back to see Aaron openly staring at Samuel. "Put your tongue back in your mouth. He's off limits."

"Because I'm twenty-two?" Aaron asked, sounding pissy.

Chris turned back to Samuel. The real answer was because he wanted Samuel and he needed another chance with him. But he'd screwed that up as far as he was concerned, and Samuel didn't want him anyway. Not as he was.

Aaron poked him hard in his shoulder, and Chris forced himself to look away from Samuel long enough to glare at Aaron.

"He's not available for you. Leave it at that."

Aaron huffed and moved away from him, which left Chris rolling his eyes. "Why are you here?" Chris repeated himself and hoped there would be no further interruptions while he waited for Samuel to answer him.

"I was curious," Samuel admitted.

Chris stared at him in disbelief. "Curious about what? There's not much about me you don't know already."

Samuel grinned, reached out and took his hand while pulling him toward the dance floor. "To see if you could dance."

Chris grinned devilishly. "Can I dance? Why the hell would I come to a club to dance if I can't do it?"

Samuel laughed. "Look around—not everyone who thinks they can dance can actually pull it off... ahhh—" Samuel seemed to scramble for the right word. "—gracefully."

Chris laughed out loud. "No, you're right. But they sure do have fun being ungraceful. So I must show you whether I can dance or not? Is it a challenge?"

Samuel shook his head. "No, mere curiosity. If it's anything like Bran's lap dancing, I'm going to have to kick my own ass, if I can reach it."

"If not, I can kick it for you," Chris offered as he advanced on Samuel, using his body to push him into the crowd of writhing people on the floor. "But for now, we dance."

Chris knew the evening wouldn't end up the way he dreamed of, but he forced himself to forget about the fact for the moments he had with Samuel. He let his concerns, pain, and disappointment drift away and immersed himself in the flow of the music, and his body became an instrument of seduction. For one man only.

A sensual beat pumped out from the speakers and echoed under his feet as he moved, coming up flush with Samuel's body as he rubbed against him. Samuel's eyes flashed bright with the disco lights as Chris watched his reaction, and then Samuel started to dance too. Chris's heart pounded, and sweat broke out in the palms of his hands as the gorgeous man matched his rhythm sensuously with practiced skill. The common ground exhilarated Chris, and his body welcomed the steamy distraction.

As Chris inserted his legs between Samuel's to rub against his crotch, Samuel grabbed his ass and pulled him right in there. The size of Samuel's erection almost made him drop to his knees to have a closer look, but he resisted making a fool of himself. Samuel seemed to like rejecting him, or at least nearly so since Chris was pretty sure Samuel didn't have any kind of malice in him like that. But asking, again, to be able to give Samuel pleasure would only end in the same answer. Chris was sure of it.

Knowing he was there and that his reaction was just for him was enough for Chris. With so many people around him, making the club heat up exponentially, Chris was quickly overheating. He stripped off his shirt, the button-down annoying him as his sweaty fingers fumbled with each of the buttons, until he was able to pull it off and tuck it into the back of his pants so that his arms were once again free.

As soon as Samuel reached up to touch his chest, though, Chris remembered why he hadn't been okay going around shirtless in front of Samuel, and he felt stupid for forgetting the last of the secrets he'd been trying to hide from Samuel. He hadn't even made it a few days without showing him his tattoo.

"Don't ask," Chris said, hoping Samuel would listen to him just this once, even as his fingers brushed over the curling tip of the tattoo, right over his heart.

Samuel leaned closer. "When did you get this?"

"Seven months ago. And I said don't ask." Chris wanted to put his shirt back on and take back the moment, but he knew it wouldn't do any good.

Samuel looked at it again and stroked a finger down his side. "It's fucking sexy. I love it." Samuel reached down, pulled his own shirt over his head, and tucked it into the back of his jeans. Then Chris was flush with his body and they started dancing again.

Chris tentatively wrapped his hands around Samuel's tattooed biceps, for the first time having the luxury of touching the man at leisure. Samuel's reaction to his tattoo hadn't been quite what he'd been expecting, but he was glad for it. He'd expected anger, or at least a lot of questions about why he had a Maori design stretching from his chest to his left hip, but Samuel thankfully had brushed it off. Chris was grateful for the minimal reaction.

"I love getting to touch your tattoos," Chris said.

Samuel might not have been able to hear him, given how loud it was in the club and how many people were talking around them, but that was okay with Chris. It was enough that he was getting to touch them. If it wouldn't have been too weird he would have tried to put his mouth on them too.

"You have never allowed me to really touch you."

Samuel's eyes were serious as he watched Chris speak. "Then touch me."

Chris inched closer and did what he had wanted to for so long—he kissed Samuel's shoulder where the dark ink curved around his deltoid. He licked his tongue over the warm flesh and groaned at the taste of this man on his lips. Moving in, he took Samuel's left nipple between his teeth and sucked it in, hearing the man hiss above him as he took advantage of the offer to explore.

He tortured the little bud some more before lavishing the same attention on the other, but his control was slipping. Releasing the tempting nipple, he licked a path up to Samuel's chin, where he reached up and pulled him down for a kiss. Samuel wrapped his arms around him, yanking him close, and with his heart pounding in his ears, he brought his right hand to the front of Samuel's pants. He went as slowly as he possibly could, waiting for and expecting Samuel to push him away. But he didn't. Instead he deepened the kiss between them, pushing his tongue between Chris's teeth as Chris unbuttoned Samuel's jeans and slid his hand inside. Without undoing the zipper, he wouldn't have much access, but it was enough to be able to graze his fingertips over Samuel's thick cock and feel wetness waiting there for him.

He groaned into Samuel's mouth, wishing he could do more and that they weren't surrounded by people on all sides. He'd been thinking about giving Samuel head since minutes after he met him, and if they were alone, he would have already been on his knees for him. He loved giving pleasure just as much as taking it, and he needed to do that for Samuel.

"I want you," he mumbled against Samuel's mouth. And the evidence of how much Samuel wanted him too was right there against his fingers. It was undeniable now.

When Samuel didn't instantly take him away from the crowd, Chris suddenly pulled away instead as he remembered that this was only a dance and just for fun. He didn't need his heart broken by Samuel twice in one day. He backed up, putting some space between them, and that helped him clear his head a little.

"I'm going to get another soda, then head back to my hotel. Thanks for the dance." Releasing him physically hurt, but he couldn't hear Samuel tell him that they were just going to be friends again, that just a friend was all Chris would ever really be for him.

He shook as he made his way back to the bar, where Jeff was already putting a new soda down in front of him, as if reading his mind. Samuel had said they could be more, maybe, if Chris was better, but he was pretty sure that this was his best, and realizing that fucking sucked.

"That was hot as hell," Aaron piped up from beside him.

Chris nodded. It had been hot. He'd felt alive and wonderful for the first time since Montana. He downed his soda and put more money than necessary on the bar. "See you later," he said to both Jeff and Aaron before turning around and coming face to face with Samuel.

"You leaving now? Just like that?" an obviously annoyed Samuel almost growled at him.

"I am. Just like that. The same as you rejecting me at every opportunity while insisting I get better. You said you're not interested in me unless things change with me, and I respect that. But it's cruel doing what you did tonight if you're just leading me on and you don't plan to ever let us happen. So, like you, I'm protecting myself. Because I deserve better than someone who hovers between yeah and nay and can't make up his damn mind." Where his anger came from, he didn't know, but he had to get out of there.

Bursting through the door, he gasped as the cool night air hit his heated skin. Seeing a taxi parked at the curb, he walked right over, and when the taxi indicated he was in service, Chris gave him the hotel address as he climbed in the back. Chris didn't try to see if Samuel had followed him outside. It would've been too much.

CHAPTER SEVEN

EXPECTING SAMUEL to be beyond pissed about the night before, Chris stared in surprise at the text on his phone the next morning. He was exhausted and possibly delusional from his lack of sleep lately. That had to explain the text.

I have the day off. Do you feel like going out somewhere?

Chris blinked to wake himself up fully. *What did you have in mind? Still in bed.*

No rush. Somewhere local. Some wildlife. Coffee shop for lunch.

Chris's stomach rumbled at the mention of food, and somewhere in the back of his mind he remembered New Zealand's wildlife were of the nonthreatening, noncarnivorous kind, so Samuel's idea didn't sound half-bad.

Sounds like fun. What time? he typed back, and also included the address of the hotel he was staying at.

I'll pick you up in an hour.

When the text came back, Chris rolled out of bed and headed to the shower. He dressed in comfortable khaki shorts and a T-shirt with sneakers before heading down to the lounge, where he had a cheese scone and coffee before Samuel arrived.

Coming around the corner into the lobby when he finished eating, he was just in time to see Samuel walk in the hotel door. He stopped and smiled when he saw Chris walking his way.

"Hey," he said, coming up to Samuel.

Without the dance music bouncing around in his head and overriding everything inside of him, Chris realized how very hard it would have been to live even on the same continent with Samuel and not have a chance in hell with him.

"Hey, you look good. Let's go." Outside, Samuel led him to a large truck and opened the passenger door for him to get in.

"Thanks." Chris huffed as he pulled himself into the high seat.

Samuel walked around and got in next to him. "How did you sleep?" Chris asked him.

"I have two days off a fortnight, and this is one of them, so I slept more than usual. How about you?" Samuel started the vehicle and drove them into the traffic, heading toward the outskirts of town.

"The hotel is comfortable, so that's nice. They've got a great pool if you want to go swimming before I leave." It was almost… pleasant talking to Samuel like this, as if they were friends. As if he hadn't been touching Samuel's cock the night before. Thinking about that made him blush, and he tried not to focus on it for long. "Where are we headed?"

"There's this butterfly sanctuary northeast of here. I've never been there, but Kaden took Bran there a few weeks ago, and he loved it. It's also safe taking you there, because they won't visit it again so soon. I understand there's an amazing little coffee shop on the premises with the best coffee and tiramisu in town."

"Okay, as long as it's safe." Chris couldn't imagine what he would do if he ran into Bran today. He wasn't ready, but then again, would he ever be prepared for it?

"Common sense tells me people won't visit the same attraction twice in a few weeks, but that's my best guess right now. Would you rather not go there?" Samuel slowed down, as if waiting for Chris to change his mind.

"No, keep going. What you say makes sense, so it should be okay." Chris settled back in the comfortable truck and watched the beautiful scenery pass by, the radio playing softly in the background.

"I'm sorry about last night. I didn't mean to lead you on, and I apologize."

The words caught him off guard, and he didn't know what to say for a few seconds.

"Thanks." Chris settled his arms across his chest and cast a sidelong glance at Samuel. "Bran's happy here? Isn't he? We talk all the time, but you know how good of liars we both are when we can't see each other. I miss him so fucking much."

Samuel laid his hand between them, and Chris brushed his knuckles against the back of Samuel's hand. "He smiles all the time, so yes, I'd say he's enjoying himself. And I've never seen Kaden happier than he is with Bran. It's a bit sickening, actually."

Snickering, Chris shook his head and slid his fingertips against Samuel's palm. He wasn't holding his hand, not yet, but he was close to it. And Samuel hadn't pulled away from him yet.

"Have you ever hit anyone? Like Richard did with Bran and I?" That night had hurt to talk about for a long time, but now it was just something he'd been through, like anything else in his fucked-up existence.

Now Samuel did take his hand. "No. And I never would. I think men like that are cowards."

It was good for Chris to hear the words from Samuel. He'd known Samuel wouldn't be abusive to him or anyone else, but it was still good to be told that out loud.

"Is that your only tattoo?" Samuel surprised him by asking.

Chris put his free hand against his side, touching his tattoo without even thinking about it. "Yes. For good too. It hurt a lot to get done. Do you really think it looks sexy on me?"

Samuel pulled them off the road and into a large parking lot. "Absolutely. Could I see it again sometime?"

Chris laughed and fought hard not to blush but failed miserably. "Sure. If you want to."

"How about now?"

He stared at Samuel for a long few minutes, not knowing what to say. "Here?" They were in the middle of the parking lot. Sure Samuel's windows were tinted, and being even partially naked in a vehicle wasn't exactly new to Chris, but it still seemed to be a strange request. Samuel slowly nodded, and heat began to flare over Chris's skin. He undid the seat belt and turned toward Samuel so Samuel could see the tattoo. He loved everything about the intricately carved design, especially how it reminded him of Samuel every time he looked at it.

In one quick motion, he pulled his T-shirt over his head, then leaned back against the door, giving Samuel a full view of the tattoo that stretched from his chest, down the left side of his body, over his ribs, to end at his hip just above the waist of his pants. Samuel's gaze traveled over the swirls and fine lines. Unlike many tattoos he saw in the States, Chris designed his tattoo with the short strokes and delicate markings of the Maori tattoos he'd spent hours looking at before deciding to get it.

"It's beautiful," Samuel said, making Chris smile.

"Thanks. I like it." Chris put his shirt back on and looked at Samuel. "We going in?"

Samuel opened his door. "Yep, let's go walk around and look at all the pretty butterflies and flowers."

"How many guys have you brought here?" Chris asked him as they got out of the truck and headed in.

"None, actually. I told you I've never been here," Samuel reminded him as they stopped at the ticket booth to pay the entry fee.

Chris grinned at him. "I find it awesome that you're actually honest, and you remember what you've told me. It's a nice change."

"I've got nothing to hide, mate. I'm a very good boy."

Snorting, Chris shook his head and chose not to argue with Samuel on that point. A good boy would not have let him put his hand inside his pants on a crowded dance floor the night before.

"How often do you see Bran? And Kaden and Trent too. But mostly Bran. Fuck, I miss him. Never thought it would hurt this much to be away from him for eight months."

They studied the hand-painted map of the sanctuary and chose which path to follow first. In between the trees and plants, it felt hotter and very humid, but Chris didn't mind it as he kept his eyes open for the butterflies and orchids.

"I see Trent almost daily because we work on the same farm, even if it's just in passing, but we all get together at least once a fortnight for a meal or drinks. Sometimes we meet up on Fridays at the school sports field to play a bit of footy." Samuel spoke softly, also looking around for the beautiful insects.

"Footy?" Chris had to ask.

"Football or rugby. We call it footy for short," Samuel explained with a smile.

Chris gave him a heated look. "Do you still take your shirts off to play while you run around and get all sweaty?"

"Absolutely. If you have a shirt on at the end, you're not playing hard enough."

Samuel winked at him, and Chris blushed.

"Someday, when Bran forgives me for coming here without telling him, because I'm sure he'll find out eventually, it would be fun to see you all play. I won't be joining you, but I'll clap and cheer from the sides."

Samuel frowned. "Oh, come on. Of course you've got to play. At least try. We won't tackle you. I promise."

A cheeky grin followed the words, and somehow Chris doubted the sincerity of the vow.

Chris turned and ran one of his perfectly manicured fingertips across the side of Samuel's jaw. "I'm actually more worried about breaking a nail than I am about being under you. The girl that does my nails is nearly impossible to get an appointment with on short notice." Before dropping his hand, Chris lightly brushed the pad of his thumb over Samuel's bottom lip. The next moment the bushes to their left rustled and out walked a woman and two small kids, so Chris dropped his hand from Samuel's face. No need to cause any drama in public.

"Come, let's go try this trail…. Hey, Samuel!"

The exclamation had them both spinning around in surprise.

Chris stared at the petite brunette woman, wondering who the fuck she was to Samuel. Ex-lover? Best friend no one had bothered to tell him about? He stared at Samuel, waiting for him to say something, but he looked stunned.

"Samuel?" Chris prompted him. "Aren't you going to introduce me to the nice lady with the two little kids that could pass for your own?"

"Uuuum, hey, Kylie."

Samuel had gone as white as a sheet when he looked at Chris. Where had all the beautiful Maori gone?

Kylie…. Kylie…. Where in the hell did he know that name from?

"This is Kylie—Kaden's sister." Samuel addressed her again, "Kylie, this is my friend…." Samuel trailed off, not knowing what to call him.

"Eddie." Chris remembered his manners and stepped forward to shake her hand. "It's cute that he forgets whether I like people knowing that my full name is Edward. It's so old-fashioned. So you're Kaden's sister. Nice to meet you. And who are these two adorable children?" He was surprised he sounded so calm, given how panicked he felt. Kaden's sister? Fuck.

Kylie smiled back at him. "Nice to meet you too, Eddie. Wow, Sam. It's been a while, hasn't it?" she added with a sly look at the big man. "Eddie, these are my two angels, Liam and Leilani."

"Are all the kids in your family named alike, or did that start with you two? It's cute, don't get me wrong, I'm just curious," Chris quickly said, in case he was about to piss off his best friend's sister-in-law. Assuming Bran ever married Kaden. Chris was pretty sure he was close to saying yes most days, if Kaden only had the guts to ask him.

Kylie laughed, and the sound reminded him of Kaden, as did her open, strong personality. It made him miss Bran so much more.

"I think my parents started it, but when I saw each of them, the names just came to me. They both ended up starting with an *L*, but it wasn't intentional." Looking at her kids, she grinned at them where they were studying a blue butterfly hovering over a hibiscus flower. "I think it fits them, anyway. And how long have you two been together?"

Chris decided to speak up before Samuel could say anything. "Oh, we're not dating. Just friends. Met last night. That's it." Shit. He should have let Samuel come up with something; at least it might have sounded believable.

Kylie pulled a face, clearly not believing the bullshit he spouted. "No! Really? Never mind, then. I think you Kiwi guys love the Americans. Is it coincidence that Bran's also from the States, Samuel?"

"It's a big country," Chris said defensively before he remembered to ask, "And who's Bran? Also, I'm from Canada. Not the US. Want to hear my French? Or should I make a French demonstration on Samuel here? With my tongue?" He realized a second too late that he had entered full bitch mode, which was never a good thing. "Or how about Russian? I'm also fluent there."

Kylie's bright smile diminished, and she beckoned her kids closer, away from the bitch-man in front of her. "Hey, no worries, mate." She gave Samuel a concerned glance and whispered loudly as she stepped away, "Geez, and I thought we were uptight about being called Aussies." Her kids ran ahead, and she waved awkwardly. "See ya later, Sam. Nice meeting you… Eddie."

"I owe her chocolate. That was really bad. Like volcano blowing up and killing the villagers bad." Chris shook his head after she'd gone. "When the fuck did I get to be such a bitch? And before noon too? Shit. Coffee! I need coffee."

Samuel looked at the toes of his boots and shook his head in disbelief. "That was awful. And may I add that she's everything but stupid? She's cunning and sneaky as hell. I'm sorry. Maybe it wasn't such a good idea to come here after all."

Sighing, Chris knew Samuel was probably right. "I'm not fit for public consumption. Take me back to my hotel? Or did you want to do something first? And you shouldn't be sorry. I'm the one lying to the only person in the world that truly loves me. It's not your fault I'm being stupid. Before we go, though, can we go through and see the butterflies? It is sort of our first date." He blushed deeply when he remembered a few key details. "If we were actually dating. If, you know, we could be that way for each other."

Samuel laced their fingers together and started walking down the track again. "Sure. I'm positive enough to believe bad luck can't strike us twice in one day, in one place."

Chris laughed humorlessly. "Then you haven't hung around me long enough."

"Come on. It's not that bad." Samuel smiled at him, and they continued to wander around different paths and found little hidden gardens with birdbaths and even a small-sized waterfall in one spot.

"I'm glad you brought me here," Chris said, leaning against Samuel's shoulder. "Like everything else about New Zealand, this place is beautiful. And quiet. I enjoy being here with you."

"I like having you here."

Chris knew this wasn't the time or the place to ask what he wanted to know, but he did know he needed to see what Samuel would want from him. "When I'm back in Manhattan, and things aren't going great, do you want me to call you when I get my kit out? Or would you rather not know?" It sucked talking about something he wasn't proud of but tried to normalize anyway, and it hurt to know that, as good as things were right then, they wouldn't be staying that way, especially not when he was back home.

"I'd prefer you not do it at all, but if you are going to, call me," Samuel said gravely.

Chris nodded. "Thanks." In a way, it was nice to know that Samuel would be with him. He was always alone when he did it, and it had always been such a source of shame for him. Samuel might not have wanted him to cut himself, but Chris felt better knowing that he'd be safe while he did what he had to do. Because Samuel would be there with him. He turned his head to give Samuel's shoulder a light kiss.

He felt Samuel's lips touch the top of his head, and the gentle kindness made his heart ache. "Let's go eat something, hey?" Samuel suggested.

"Yeah, I'm starving." Chris followed him as he walked ahead. "Where do you want to go?"

"Let's eat here."

Samuel led the way, and when they ordered, Chris stopped him before he could pull out his money.

"I'm buying us lunch. You're the one driving me around here," Chris said. And if they were together, this would have been their first date. He was glad Samuel didn't argue with him about who would be paying.

They talked comfortably about everyday stuff as they ate, and Chris wished it could always be this way. When would he accept the fact that Samuel would never be his?

CHAPTER EIGHT

SAMUEL DROVE back to the hotel in amicable silence. Chris appeared deep in thought, and Samuel had noticed him to be that way sometime during their lunch. He hated it when people prodded him for information when he wanted to be left alone, so he granted Chris the same privacy. Knowing Chris, he would talk if and when he wanted to.

"I'm glad we got to hang out so much during my trip," Chris quietly said.

"Me too, because I like spending time with you," Samuel admitted.

Chris gave him a small smile, but he still seemed distracted by something. "I head back to Manhattan tomorrow. When should I pick up my kit?"

"What? Tomorrow already? You just got here!" Samuel exclaimed.

"You thought I was moving here?" Chris replied, smirking at him.

But now seeing the mask was easy, and Samuel knew he didn't mean the sarcasm.

"Especially since you won't put out?"

"I'm serious, Chris. I really don't want you to go back. Not yet. Why don't you stay a bit longer? You need the rest." Samuel tried to reason with him.

"I need to work. I have clients. They have divorces, secret babies, and mistresses to please. I won't be gone forever. You'll see me at Christmas and stuff. Assuming Bran is still speaking to me after he finds out." Chris shrugged, but he looked incredibly sad.

"Work can wait. You need time to recover and get much-needed sleep. Why don't you consider coming clean with Bran? I'm sure he'd love to hang out with you too, and I know he'll definitely lift up your spirit."

Chris pressed his lips into a hard line. "I'll consider it. But I'm still leaving tomorrow night. So… about my kit?"

Samuel frowned. He hated the bloody kit and wished he could melt it and make a bloody innocent-looking trinket out of it. "I'd love to keep it, but it's yours until you no longer need it."

"I'll need it within the next few days, probably." Chris drummed his fingers over his knee.

"Why in hell are you going back to that place if you know this in advance?" Samuel growled in frustration.

Chris gave him a sideways glance before focusing back on the road. "Because I live there. This is my hotel up here on the right. In case you forgot since this morning."

Samuel sighed and pulled into the parking lot of the hotel before switching the engine off. He didn't want to look at Chris, because he was on the verge of begging him not to go back to Manhattan, but he knew it wouldn't make a difference.

The ringtone of his phone sounded harsh in the silence between them, and he pulled it out of his pocket to look at the screen. "Shit! We've got trouble."

Chris looked over at him, surprise clear in his expression.

Pressing the speakerphone button, he answered it. "Hey, Kaden."

Chris closed his eyes and banged his head on the headrest.

"What the hell are you doing, Samuel?" Kaden's voice barked over the line.

"It's complicated." Samuel looked at Chris in concern.

"Yeah, that's what they all say. What are you and Chris thinking, doing this to Bran? Do you have any idea what will happen if he finds out Chris is here in New Zealand and hasn't bothered to tell him? You two better have a bloody good reason for the lies." Kaden was clearly furious.

"This doesn't exactly have anything to do with you, Kaden. Try minding your own business," Chris snapped angrily.

"Oh, come off your damn high horse, Chris. This has plenty to do with Bran, and his well-being is my fucking business, and this time it involves you."

Chris had never heard Kaden speak like that before.

Chris looked over at Samuel. "What the hell is with you Kiwis and your damn protective streaks?" He shook his head and turned back to the phone. "Why does it matter to you if I want to have sex with Samuel? I'm in town for a hookup. That's it. Not your business, like I said. Unless you two suddenly became swingers."

Kaden snorted in disgust. "That's a damn long way to come for a fuck, Chris. Don't bullshit me. I'm not a child."

"You couldn't handle the truth," Chris practically growled at him.

"You don't know what I can handle, so just spit it out! What the hell is going on? Thank fuck Kylie got me when Bran wasn't around, because you'd be in shit up to your eyeballs this second if he overheard that conversation. Not many people look like you... Eddie!" Kaden replied angrily.

Chris snorted and turned in his seat to look at Samuel. "I'm going to take that to mean I have a unique look. That's kind of sexy. So, Samuel, should I tell him my dirty little secret?"

Samuel was at once relieved the deceit was over but also upset on Chris's behalf. "It's yours to tell. Not mine."

"True. But I think Kaden's being a pissy bitch enough about it to bother us until he gets the truth. And personally, I love your truck and all, but I'd rather have you in bed." With a sigh Chris looked back at Samuel's phone. "I had a self-destructive episode and needed some safety. That's all you're getting out of me, asshole. And if you tell Bran that, I will personally gut you. Also! Don't you blame Samuel for me not telling Bran I'm here. I'm blackmailing him. I'm doing the same thing to Trent too, if it matters. Oh yes, if Daniel counts, him too."

Kaden hissed. "What the fuck, Chris? Bran is going to kill you with his bare hands. You needed help, you were in trouble, and you didn't let him know, but everyone else and their mates know about it. Are you insane?"

"Do you even remember Montana? About how your little love fest got so fucking off track because of me? And you expected me to do that again? Fuck you, but no. I love him too much for that. He doesn't get to know about this. I'm fine now. I'm going back tomorrow. And you will keep your mouth shut." Chris shook his head and crossed his arms over his chest. "Turn it off. I don't want to hear him anymore."

"Don't you dare threaten me, you cow! You two have twenty-four hours before I spill the beans to Bran. He needs to know about this, and I'm not standing by while you fuck with him. You're on your own."

"I'll be gone within twenty-four hours! And moo!"

When Chris stopped speaking, Samuel held the phone sideways so Chris could see Kaden had ended the call on them.

"How rude!"

Samuel sighed and shook his head. "I've never heard him swear so much in one day since... forever, actually. He is royally pissed."

Nodding, Chris pulled his knees up to his chest. "Yeah. I got that. Sorry you're going to have to deal with him on your own."

"Once he knows the truth, he will understand. Eventually. Hopefully." Samuel didn't really know what would happen, but he thought Kaden would get over it.

Chris shook his head. "I'm sorry. Again. Fuck. Even more proof I really shouldn't have come here. Should we go up? Or are you just dropping me off?"

"Let's go up and have something soothing to drink. What do you say?" Samuel let Chris decide what he wanted to do. He didn't want to push right now.

"Tea for me. Or water. I don't really drink anymore." Chris turned around and got out of the truck.

Samuel opened his door too. "I really need a shot of brandy after that, but a cup of tea would do."

"You don't have to not drink just because I'm not," Chris said, coming around to the front of the truck to meet him.

"I'm not, believe me. I don't like drinking before four in the afternoon," Samuel assured him as he locked the truck, and they walked into the hotel lobby, heading to the elevator.

Chris gave him a small smile as they entered the elevator. "I don't like drinking without Bran there to stop me from making stupid decisions. Seems even without the alcohol, I manage to fuck things up just fine all on my own, though."

Samuel touched Chris's lower back, giving it a soft rub. "Don't be so hard on yourself. Life hasn't been easy for you, and you found ways to cope. I may not approve of your ways, but for you, it worked. At least you're managing."

"It's better than random sex to block out the pain. Less dangerous too, I think," Chris admitted, his voice low as they exited the elevator on his floor. "And thanks for saying that. I wish I didn't need it, that I could be perfectly happy like you are. But, bonus for me, at least I'm not suicidal."

Samuel smiled despite the serious nature of their discussion. "There is that. We all have our issues as a result of life's knocks, Chris. One of mine is that I'm not too generous with my affections, as you've probably noticed. I also have shit to work out."

Chris shook his head. "I'm too easy and you're too hard to get. Would be fun if I could handle being just your friend."

He opened the door to his room, and on cue, Samuel's phone started ringing.

"Oh, fuck me twice! It's Bran, Chris. What now?" Samuel groaned as he kicked the door shut behind them.

Chris looked petrified as he stared at Samuel's phone in horror. When he didn't answer Samuel, Samuel just put the call on speaker and braced himself for the shit storm.

"Hey, Bran! How's it going?"

"Don't you 'how's it going' me, Samuel. How could you?" Bran's yell boomed over the phone.

Samuel saw the nonspecific question as a possible cop-out, so he used it. "Uuuum, how could I do what, exactly?"

"Don't play the idiot with me! We both know you're too smart for that. What the hell are you doing messing around on Chris with this… Eddie?" Bran managed to make the fake name sound like a curse.

Samuel looked at Chris, and despite the terror in his eyes, Chris smiled at his friend's tirade. Probably because he was so happy to hear his voice, Samuel guessed. Too bad he was taking the brunt of Bran's anger, or he would've found it damn funny too.

"Oh, him?" Samuel muttered.

"Yes, him! Stop stalling and tell me the truth. I thought you cared for Chris and you were waiting for him to visit here to see if things could work between you two. Have you just given up now? Is it somehow not worth your time anymore?"

Despite Bran's anger, Samuel could hear the underlying concern for Chris in his words.

"Bran, calm down. Eddie is just a friend, okay?" Samuel tried to soothe the man's ruffled feathers.

"The fuck he is!" Bran yelled back. "Kylie apparently saw him stick his finger in your mouth! That's not something a friend would do, or if it was, it's not something you would allow a friend to do!"

"Uhh." While Samuel tried to come up with something to say, Chris took out his phone and started typing.

Tell him not to worry. Everything will be explained tomorrow, Chris had written.

Samuel frowned. "Bran, everything will be explained to you tomorrow," he tried.

"The hell it will! What are you doing?" Bran demanded.

Samuel looked to Chris for help, as he had no idea what to say to Bran, and Chris, as his best friend, should have been able to help more. But Chris just smiled at him, and as Samuel watched, his smile turned wicked. *Tell him you have to go*, Chris typed on his phone, then held it up for Samuel to see.

"I'll see you tomorrow. I need to go," Samuel tried, hoping Bran would let him hang up.

Bran huffed angrily. "I'm not done with you yet."

Chris gave no warning before he reached forward and cupped Samuel through his pants, making him jump. He kept squeezing, making anything Samuel had wanted to say impossible. Chris winked at him before taking Samuel's phone out of his hand and hanging up on Bran. Only then did he step back, releasing him, and Samuel took a breath.

"What was that?" Samuel demanded as heat flared over his skin.

Chris laughed. "I know him when he gets like that. You weren't going to be able to hang up on him." Samuel's phone started ringing in Chris's hand, but he ignored the call. "Bran again."

He tossed the phone onto the couch, quickly followed by his shirt as he stripped it off, giving Samuel a good view of his back, followed by his chest and the tattoo Samuel still couldn't believe Chris had gotten. It was stunning over his tanned skin, tempting Samuel to touch him.

Chris bounced on the balls of his feet as if he was nervous before kicking off his sneakers. "So... I'm seeing Bran tomorrow. My flight leaves at 10:00 pm. I'll need two hours to get through the airport, add another hour for travel. I'll need to stop by your house, and I'll need some time to actually talk to him. But I have to go to the store first to get him something to make him a little happier so he doesn't kill me. I'll plan on two, then. Is he normally free around then?"

Samuel didn't keep track of him and definitely didn't know Bran's schedule by heart. "If he's not, then he won't be too far away."

"Are you available to be there?" Chris asked him, sounding unsure of himself.

Samuel nodded, then went to him. He gave Chris a gentle hug. "I can be. If you want."

Chris nodded against his chest and rested his hands on the back of Samuel's shirt before tucking his thumbs into the top of Samuel's pants, right through the belt loops. The intimacy felt good to him, warming him from his core.

"I don't want you to go back to Manhattan tomorrow."

"I know you don't. I'll call you when things get bad."

That wasn't good enough, not by a long shot. But Samuel was starting to realize Chris might not be that easy to convince to stay.

Chris pulled away from him and bounced a little as he walked to the window. "I'm on edge and worried about tomorrow. Feel like distracting me for a while?"

"That depends on what you have in mind."

Chris was smiling as he turned around and faced him. "Were you serious about spanking me before? I could probably go for something kinky right about now."

Samuel stared at him, and as the seconds ticked by, he began to see Chris's mask crack open. He could be the sexy, sassy man he pretended to be all the time, but he wasn't that way now. He was angry and hurt, and Samuel went up to him to pull him into his arms again.

"It's going to be okay tomorrow," Samuel promised him.

Chris laughed humorlessly. "You've never seen Bran extremely pissed. I may need body armor and full-on riot gear to get through it."

Samuel doubted that very much. "If he's angry at you, it's for the same reason I am, because he cares about you and is worried over whether you'll hurt yourself again or not."

"That's guaranteed, so let's not focus on that too much, since worrying won't change anything about it," Chris said dryly as he pulled away and Samuel looked down at him. "Now, about that spanking…?"

Samuel had no idea what he was doing as he spun Chris around and had him facing the wall. "Do you really want to be spanked?" he asked as Chris practically vibrated under the hand between his shoulder blades.

"Yes. Please."

Chris's voice had already gone soft, and Samuel felt his body responding to him instantly.

Samuel shook his head. "Too bad. You're not getting that tonight."

He let go of Chris, who instantly turned around with a pout marring his perfect full lips.

"Damn. I was looking forward to having your hand on my ass. So, mister not-so-kinky, what do you want to do instead?"

"I'm going to give you a massage." He took Chris's hand and led him over to the bed, where Chris easily lay down on his stomach without having to be told. "I may not be a master at it like you, but I can give a good rubdown. Do you have some oil or cream around here somewhere?"

Snorting, Chris looked over his shoulder, and Samuel smiled at him.

"Baby, you can rub me wherever you want to, whenever the mood strikes you. And there's tiny bottles of hotel lotion in the bathroom. It seems like lemongrass, which is kind of nice."

Samuel left to fetch a couple of them. Once back, he rested a knee on the bed and sat across Chris's ass, running his hands down Chris's back. He'd lost a lot of his muscle, but Chris wasn't skin and bones either, simply under what Samuel would have considered healthy.

"How long until you can come back here?"

"Assuming Bran doesn't try to kill me tomorrow? A couple of weeks. Maybe a month. I might not make it back until Christmas, assuming I still have a best friend after tomorrow. I haven't decided yet. Have you given up trying to keep me here past tomorrow night, then?"

"I know when to admit defeat. You're more stubborn than Bran." Samuel opened one bottle and squeezed the contents onto his palm, then rubbed his hands together to warm it up before applying it to Chris's skin.

"Yes, I am. And more patient too. Were you really waiting for me to come here to see if we could have something, like Bran said?" Chris quietly asked him as Samuel watched him close his eyes.

"I was hopeful you would so we could explore the possibility, yes," Samuel admitted softly as he concentrated on spreading the lotion all over. He started doing full-palmed strokes up and down Chris's warm back.

Chris sighed. "That feels really good. I should have come here four months ago, when Misha first left. Back when I was better and not nearly as stressed. Maybe then we could have had something. Have you dated anyone since I last saw you? And I'll use that term loosely to include random hookups and glory holes."

"No, I haven't. We went out to the club a few times, all of us together, but just for some drinks and dancing. We sorta share Bran a bit on the dance floor." Samuel found a tight spot by Chris's shoulder blade and worked it a bit harder with his fingertips, making Chris groan.

"Now, when you say that you share my best friend, if you mean that you dance with him the way I danced with you at Renegade, I will kick you in your dick."

Samuel chuckled. "Do you honestly think Kaden would allow that? So, no. Just dancing, in a purely fun and innocent way. I think Bran keeps those special moves for behind closed doors, you know? Or should I say when they're alone, but knowing about Kaden's kink, I'm not sure that's the truth."

Laughing, Chris reached back to touch Samuel on his thigh, momentarily distracting him. "Yeah, I remember that kink. Not the most fun thing in the world to see my best friend having sex in the kitchen we were eating in only an hour or so later."

He shivered, and Samuel smiled down at him.

"Now a question for you. Why did you get the tattoo?" Samuel asked.

Chris took a long time answering him, as Samuel continued to work away the tension in his back. "The short answer? Because of you."

Samuel knew it had something to do with him or his heritage, but a tattoo was something permanent and lasting. Chris hardly knew him, and they hadn't even determined whether things would work between them, and if they didn't, the tattoo might become an unpleasant reminder of things Chris might rather forget a few years down the line.

"I'm going to need more than that."

"You were the first person to really tell me that I was worth more than what I'd let myself become. At first I started reading about Maori tattoos to find out what the hell yours might mean. I never did figure that out, by the way. But a few weeks into reading about the tattoos, I decided I wanted one, to remind me of what you said. I see it every morning, and it tells me that I'm supposed to be better. No random sex, no getting so drunk that I pass out with some guy's number written in marker across my hip. Just me, trying to be normal. We aren't even really friends, and so it's not like I got it because I'm in love with you. I got it because it's a reminder of how I can be. And it looks damn pretty on me."

Samuel nodded as he listened to Chris explain it to him. "We are friends, in my eyes anyway. You know much more about me than most people around me. And you're right. The tattoo suits you very well. It tells your story."

"Friends might be impossible," Chris quietly said.

"Why is that?" Samuel had a good idea, but he wanted Chris to speak his heart.

"Because friends don't get jealous when their friend shakes the hand of another guy. I wanted to smack Jeff's hand off yours when you two touched. If anyone had actually rubbed up against you at the club, I'm pretty sure I would have clawed their faces off. I want you, but we aren't like that, and I can't imagine seeing you with someone else. So friends is a complicated, likely impossible kind of idea. Maybe someday when we've both moved on, but right now I can't picture it."

Samuel leaned back a bit and reached below Chris, encouraging him to lift his body away from the bed so he could unfasten his shorts. He wiggled the fabric down some until the top of Chris's crack showed and took a seat across his upper thighs.

"I understand better than you think. Remember in one of our many games of crazy truth or dare, I told you I don't share very well, but a handshake? That's pretty harmless."

"Did you see what you were wearing? I thought I'd come just looking at you," Chris said with a snicker. "And why are my shorts down? Not that I'm complaining. I've got condoms in my bag if you want them."

Samuel gave his ass a light smack. "Get your head out of the gutter. I'm just moving my massage farther down. Your ass consists of muscles, did you know? And they're tight too."

"I'm very tight, if you want to check," Chris teased him.

"I have no doubt of that, believe me." Samuel's cock felt uncomfortably confined in his own shorts after seeing Chris's suntanned butt. Who tanned their buttcheeks? Obviously Chris Romanoff, and it was damn sexy. "Please tell me you don't sunbathe in public, because remember how I said a handshake was harmless? Well, baring your ass in public is not."

"You're not going to like that answer, actually. I belong to a private nudist beach. All naked, all the time."

"Let's just say if you end up here, there'll be no more of that shit. If you're mine, you're mine alone, and no one sees your ass but me."

Chris chuckled and squeezed Samuel's thigh. "Sure thing. Of course, if you were mine, then I'd get to have you naked all day sometimes. A complete no-clothing day, and if you get dressed at all, you have to do the laundry or some other horrible chore I can't stand doing."

Samuel laughed. "And if I'm yours, you can slap anyone's hands off me." He wiggled Chris's pants down some more until they rested under his cheeks and applied more lotion, starting to rub it in and massaging the tight glutes.

"I wish. I'd have to read up on the laws here to see what constitutes assault, because I don't think I'd be good at stopping with just a slap. I can be a violent little thing when I want to be, as Kaden heard earlier. I really shouldn't have been so mean to him. He was just yelling at you, and I couldn't stand that. Question, though, what do you think of my ass?"

Samuel grinned. "I'm speechless. And if we're strictly friends, then don't ask such questions."

Chris propped himself up on his elbows and looked back at Samuel. "I'm not the one that said we had to be just friends. You set that boundary, not me, so I'll ask you about my ass all day long. And I'll show it off and parade around in front of you all I like. In fact, get off and I'll do a little of that for you right now."

Samuel planted both palms on a buttcheek and pushed down. "Stay right where you are, because if you turn over, we won't stay just friends. I'm not made of stone."

Chris just grinned at him. "That was kind of my point. A bit of fun before I go, something to remember me by. It sucks that I'm leaving tomorrow. New Zealand isn't my home, and I really do have stuff to do back in Manhattan. But I'm going to miss you. And I wish I had been what you wanted. Maybe I was before I started cutting again. But it's crap that you waited for me and I waited for you, and I'm not good enough to deserve you. Kind of a waste of time. It was good to see you, though."

Samuel reached down and pulled Chris's pants up halfway. "Turn over." When Chris complied, Samuel zoned in on the fabric where it got caught on Chris's very erect cock. He made eye contact with Chris. "Before I deal with that problem, you need to stop saying you're not good enough for me. That's a lie. I want you healthy for you first and foremost, and I come in after that. And you didn't waste your time coming here and neither have I, or will I if you go back to Manhattan."

Chris rested his hands behind his head. "How's that just-friends thing working out for you now? Also, do you like shaved guys or a bit of fluff? I feel cleaner without the hair. And fine, I get what you're saying about me being healthy. But my problem with that is: this is my healthy. So to me it is like I'm not good enough. And there's no *if* I go back. I'm going to be on a flight to New York tomorrow at ten. That's just how it's going to be. And in a few days, I'll call you, and if you pick up, you'll get to talk to me while I cut. That's my reality. I'm sorry it's not better, but this is me being healthy."

"This healthy can still hurt you badly or even get you killed, so I beg to differ. But I'm not arguing with you right now. I have better things to do." Samuel once again pushed the annoying fabric out of his way to expose Chris's cock. He had spent hours and probably days wondering what Chris would taste like. It was time to find out.

"Yeah, you do. Rules about holding your head?" Chris asked him. "And when are you going to let me help you out? I can see how hard you are from here, and you weren't that discreet when you were rubbing against my ass with your cock a few seconds ago."

Samuel licked his lips, moved back, and lowered himself onto one elbow while wrapping the fingers of his other hand around Chris's girth to lift him toward his mouth. "You can touch my head. Just don't force me."

"As if I could make you do anything you didn't want to do."

Chris choked on his last word as Samuel slid him into his mouth, taking him down halfway before withdrawing to the tip and going back down all the way. He felt Chris lay his hand over the top of his head and rest his other on his left shoulder, lightly squeezing him.

"I've wanted in your mouth for so long or you in mine, this is like the best feeling ever," Chris moaned as Samuel flicked his tongue over the tip, enjoying the moisture Chris's body gave him.

Looking at Chris's groin area, Samuel felt his own body heat up even more. The whole area was clean of hair and tanned to perfection.

Chris pushed him down a little, then quickly removed his hand. "Sorry. Don't stop. Fuck, don't ever stop this. Sure you don't want to move to Manhattan and live in my bedroom? It's got a decent view."

Samuel reached down, took Chris's waxed balls into his palm, and rolled them gently while loving on him. His saliva wet the area, and it was all Samuel could do not to reach down and touch Chris where he longed to most, to use the lubrication to ready him for Samuel's possession, but he held back, barely.

"I'm close," Chris gasped, sounding miserable about it. "Not yet. Shit."

Samuel pulled off and released him. Turning his head, he kissed the smooth skin around his cock, licked his tongue over the softness. Pushing up, he lavished the same attention on the gorgeous ink staining Chris's torso. He'd craved to do so since the first moment he laid eyes on it.

"Where do you want me to come?" Chris asked, his voice coming out like a hiss as he dug his fingers into Samuel's shoulder.

"In my mouth," Samuel murmured against his nipple as he kissed it.

Chris reached down, and while Samuel thought he was going to stroke himself, he ended up grabbing Samuel instead, startling him. "You can't tell me you don't want to fuck me when you're that hard," Chris said huskily as he gave him a squeeze through his shorts.

Samuel hissed at the rough pleasure, so tempted to say to hell with his reservations and go for it. "Oh, I want to all right. But it's not time yet." He returned to his original spot, dragging his lips down over Chris's sweaty stomach before taking him into his mouth again.

"You let me know when it is," Chris ordered.

"You'll know," Samuel managed to mumble before getting serious about blowing Chris's mind. Sliding down the length of Chris's dick, Samuel applied gentle pressure with his teeth on the upstroke, and as he suspected, Chris went wild at the rougher touch. It wasn't long before anything Chris was trying to say became little more than mumbled, unintelligible cries peppered with the sounds of Chris begging Samuel for more.

Samuel welcomed the dribbles of precome into his mouth, and he used the tip of his tongue to tickle the hole where he loved to be touched too.

Chris gasped, and his back lifted off the bed as he scratched over Samuel's shoulder. "Fuck," he hissed, his hips jerking and his cock bobbing wildly in Samuel's mouth.

Samuel covered Chris's hips with his hands, steadying him as he took him deeply, his lips pressing against Chris's base. Hot come sprayed against his tongue and the back of his throat seconds later as Chris shook beneath his hands.

Samuel took his time cleaning him up, running his tongue gently over him as Chris's body slowly stopped trembling. He was still breathing heavily, though, and barely had his eyes open when Samuel did release him. He didn't get far before Chris sat up too and grabbed him by the front of his shirt to surprise him with a rough kiss.

Many men didn't like the taste of their own come after getting head, but personally, Samuel thought it was very intimate sharing it. Obviously Chris liked it too, as he devoured Samuel's mouth as if trying to get it all back.

He flipped Samuel onto his back and separated long enough to position himself over Samuel's hips and grind into him. "Is it time yet?" Chris asked him, leaning back as he rubbed himself over Samuel's aching cock.

Samuel lifted up at the wicked pressure on his erection. It would be so easy just to let it all go and have Chris, but his conscience screamed at him to be fair. Chris didn't need him to complicate things in his life any further and make his decisions harder. Samuel knew what he wanted, and he needed to let Chris have the same freedom to decide without any strings.

"Sadly, no. And if you rub against me much longer, I will walk out the hotel lobby with a big wet spot on my shorts." He tried to laugh, but it was hard when his balls were turning blue right there.

"I have extra shorts you could borrow," Chris offered, but he stopped anyway and moved off to the side.

Samuel snorted. "As if they would fit me. They would hardly wrap around one of my thighs."

"I'm going to go shower and get the sweat off me. Want to come? Silly me, of course you do. But if you want to shower with me, conserve water and all that, I promise not to jump on you and screw you into the wall." Chris blew him a kiss as he got off the bed and went to his bag to pull out what looked like a fresh pair of shorts. "Be here when I get out. That's not a suggestion."

"Yeah, your invitation is purely innocent." Samuel closed his eyes and groaned in agony when Chris shut the bathroom door, muffling his laughter. He felt like rutting against the duvet just to relieve the pressure in his dick but reminded himself he was forty, not fourteen.

When Chris came back out of the bathroom, he'd changed but hadn't put a shirt back on. And Samuel had only partially been able to get himself under control. "Are you staying here for a while?" Chris asked him as he came to kneel next to him on the bed.

"If you want me to."

That made Chris smile. "And if I insist that you spend the night here, in a completely nonsexual manner, because your national bird is weird and kind of freaks me out, would you?"

"I would probably say yes, but I'd be in agony by morning," Samuel admitted his dilemma.

Chris tapped his finger against his bottom lip as if he was deep in thought. "Well… you could fuck me. Or you could use your hand. Or you could just suffer for the sake of me feeling safe with you here. Seriously, the bird is scary. I don't care that you all call yourselves Kiwis. That's fine. Just, couldn't you do it after the fruit?"

Samuel closed his eyes again and thought of a solution that would work for both of them. "Okay, give me a few minutes." He rolled off the bed and went into the bathroom, where he took care of himself and washed his face and hands.

Slightly calmer, he walked back into the room and switched off the lights before climbing onto the bed beside Chris, even though it was still early.

"Good night," Chris whispered, pressing himself against Samuel. "Wow, you're warm. You can be my permanent blanket too. Manhattan gets damn cold in the winter." He yawned loudly. "I'm gonna steal your sunshine as well."

Samuel pulled Chris into his arms, satisfied when Chris laid his cheek on his heart. It was painful the way Chris fit against him so perfectly. Samuel wouldn't allow himself to lose the hope that things would work out for them. If he did, his heart would take a long time to recover. That's why he never fell into relationships haphazardly. His heart always led the way, and most times it didn't end well for him.

As he expected, Chris's breathing evened out within a few minutes as he fell asleep. The man was so exhausted he didn't stir as Samuel extracted his arms from around him and covered him with the blanket. He couldn't resist laying a soft kiss on his cheek before heading to the door, where he stopped to look back at the figure on the bed.

Why did life have to be so bloody hard?

CHAPTER NINE

WAKING UP without Samuel next to him sucked, but once he realized he'd slept for over twelve hours, Chris figured that was to be expected. It was nine before he rolled out of bed and headed for the shower. He chose his clothes carefully, or more accurately, his underwear. Bran wasn't Samuel, in that he wouldn't be fine simply taking his word that he was back to cutting. Chris expected that he'd want to see the scars for himself.

Which meant he needed to wear underwear. That wasn't normal for him, but he found some buried in his duffle anyway. He was actually surprised he'd managed to pack anything useful at all, given what a mad rush he'd been in to simply leave before deciding on coming to New Zealand.

And now he was going back. He shook his head and finished getting ready for the day. There were things he had to focus on first, like what in the hell he was going to say to Bran when he saw him again. He was drawing a blank, and coffee and some fresh fruit from the hotel lobby didn't help either.

It was nearly eleven when Chris turned off the TV and decided to text Samuel. *Can you bring my kit to Bran's house so I can pick it up there?* He frowned down at his phone, wanting to say more. *Thanks for the blowjob.*

He sent it off before he could change his mind about what to say and rolled onto his back to stare up at the ceiling. When he had more time in New Zealand and wasn't hiding from his best friend, he'd have to do more. The pamphlets of everything he wanted to do near the hotel were already in his duffle bag, ready to go back home with him.

Back to his tiny apartment in Manhattan that was barely bigger than Samuel's living room and kitchen put together. He sat up and pulled his knees to his chest as he stared across the room at the black screen of the TV he'd grown tired of watching. This royally sucked.

He pulled out his phone and tried to distract himself. But his gaze locked on his last text message from Bran. He'd sent it the previous morning, before going down to breakfast. A quick *hey* was all he'd said. And Bran had texted back about how sunny it was and how he wished Chris was there.

Missing you, he texted now. He'd be seeing Bran in a few hours, and he couldn't wait, but he was scared too. They didn't keep anything from each other, especially not after their blowups in Montana. And Chris had broken the promise they'd made to each other about how there wouldn't be anything between them again.

His phone beeped, and he looked down at it. *Samuel's over here. I'm so fucking pissed at him right now. I'm sorry, hon, but it seems that he's with some asshole named Eddie or some shit. Want me to kick his ass for you?*

Chris laughed. Damn, he loved Bran. *Nope. But thanks. He was never expected to wait for me.*

He got a text back almost immediately, which wasn't all that much of a surprise since it was from Bran, who did like to text. *I wanted him to.*

There was nothing good that Chris could say to that. He'd wanted Samuel to wait too, and Samuel had. Samuel wasn't the problem here, though. It was all him. *I know*, he finally decided to text back, since Bran would be expecting him to say something.

Samuel still hadn't texted him back an hour later when Chris checked himself out of the hotel and headed across the street to the grocery store. Knowing he was at Bran's, though, Chris figured he was probably busy or something. And it wasn't like there was some expectation that he'd text Chris back right away. As long as he brought the kit so that Chris could pick it up, Chris would be fine.

He felt a little weird carrying his duffle bag around the store with him, but it wasn't as if he had a car to stash it in, and the checkout time for the hotel had been noon, and he didn't want to be rushed at the store. Especially when he had no idea what he was even looking for.

"Something to make Bran forgive me…," he mumbled to himself, heading straight for the alcohol.

The whiskey made him think of the bourbon they'd all shared in Montana, and he smiled. Bran had always liked vodka, unless his tastes had dramatically changed in the last eight months. Chris felt like shit for not even knowing what his best friend liked to drink anymore.

Fuck it. Alcohol was hard. Chocolate was much easier. That aisle proved to be a lot more fun as he read the labels of chocolate makers he'd never heard of before and definitely couldn't get in the States. Maybe Bran had a new favorite chocolatier to go with his life in New Zealand. Anything was possible, Chris knew, since Bran had so easily managed to assimilate himself into farm life. How he'd managed that one, Chris still wasn't sure. He just knew that he couldn't have done it so easily. Trent's goat was more than enough farm exposure for him for a while.

With a dozen or so chocolate bars in his arms, from all different makers and containing as many various flavors as he'd been able to find, he headed up to the registers. He was nearly checked out, the next person to be rung up, when he turned his head and found Bran staring at him.

"Um. Hi?" Chris tried weakly.

"You're so fucking dead!" Bran practically screeched at him, the box of cereal in his hand falling to the floor as he rushed at Chris, who was already bolting toward the front doors. There was no plan past that, just to run around the parking lot and hopefully keep running while Bran chased him. Eventually Bran would get tired, and by then Chris hoped to have an explanation that made sense.

But his duffle bag slowed him down and made him clumsy. Bran caught him on his second lap around the outside of the parking lot and tackled him to the grass. "You're Eddie!" Bran cried, jumping on him and pinning him to the ground.

As far as things Bran could have been mad at him for, that hadn't even crossed his mind. "I am. Hi. I missed you."

Bran sat on his hips, keeping him there, and smacked him hard across his cheek. It fucking hurt, and Chris wasn't at all happy that their spectacle was starting to draw attention.

"How long have you been here? And you didn't bother calling me and letting me know!"

Bran tried smacking him again, but Chris grabbed his hands and rolled him over, having Bran lying under him instead, even as Bran kicked out at him.

"A few days. I was going to tell you. Today, actually. I was getting stuff as a peace offering. Chocolate. You like chocolate." Seeing how furious Bran was at him, though, he knew chocolate wouldn't have cut it. Not this time. A dozen naked Kadens might have done it, but unfortunately Chris was fresh out of cloning machines.

"Who else knew you were here before me?" Bran demanded, sounding more hurt than angry now.

Chris frowned and sighed loudly. "As Eddie or myself? I'm sorry, but a lot of people. Starting with Samuel, then Daniel, Trent, Kylie, Liam, Leilani, and Kaden."

Bran scowled at him, and Chris didn't know what to say to make this any better. "I am sorry, if that matters," Chris quietly told him. He moved back, letting Bran have some space since he was pretty sure Bran wasn't going to try to hit him anymore. When he offered Bran his hand to help him up and Bran smacked his hand away, that hurt more than being hit, though.

"Everyone fucking knew before me. Everyone." Bran shook his head. "You're my best friend...."

"And you're mine too. That's why I couldn't go right to you!" Chris clamped his mouth shut as quickly as he could, but Bran was already staring at him.

"What, exactly, is that supposed to mean?" he spat.

Chris really didn't want to do this in a parking lot, with people watching them as if they were some kind of circus attraction. "I did something bad. And I went to Samuel for help."

Bran flinched back, and when Chris reached for him, he took a step away. "You went to Sam? Instead of me? You barely even know him!"

Bran rushed him again, and this time it was a punch instead of a slap that caught Chris by surprise and had him stumbling back.

"When did you become such a violent fuck?" Chris snapped at him as he rubbed his chest where Bran had punched him.

"When did you start trusting him more than me?" Bran shot back. He started walking away, and Chris was quick to go after him, grabbing him by the sleeve of his light jacket.

"Wait, Bran, c'mon. Talk to me," Chris pleaded.

Bran pulled his arm out of Chris's grip. "Oh, we're not done. You're getting in the fucking car, and we're going back to my house, where I'm going to interrogate the fuck out of you and find out what the hell is going on with you."

"Okay." Chris could deal with that. At least Bran was talking to him. That was better than the alternative.

Bran led him to a sleek white sedan. It was completely practical, but it looked fast. Living in Manhattan, neither of them had owned cars. There hadn't been a need to, and even though Bran's apartment had come with a parking spot, Chris's certainly didn't.

"Nice car," he said. "Kaden's?"

Bran shook his head. "Mine. I got it once I decided to stay here for good."

That made sense, Chris realized. Bran probably needed his own car to get around, and he'd known Bran wouldn't be coming back to Manhattan, ever. Not when he'd gone from simply subletting his apartment to outright selling it a few months after moving to New Zealand.

"I'm glad you're happy here," he said, meaning every word of it. He wanted Bran happy. He wanted to keep him that way for good.

"What did you do? That thing that was so bad you couldn't come to me for help?" Bran asked him, his voice ice cold as they stood beside his car door.

Chris took a deep breath and wished Bran would look at him. "I'm cutting again," he whispered, knowing Bran was likely about to blow up again.

Bran opened the car door so fast he hit himself in his lower lip, splitting it open. "Fuck!" he gasped, and Chris came closer to look at it.

"You'll need ice on it when you get back home. Right away or it'll start swelling." Shaking his head, he stepped back, giving Bran space to get into the car.

"Sit your ass in my car," Bran snapped at him.

Chris quickly went around to the other side of the car, tossed his duffle onto the backseat, then slid in next to Bran. The car was even nicer on the inside, with black leather interior and bright blue lights that wound around the dash, illuminating everything.

"You always did have really good taste."

"Shut up until we get home. Not one fucking word, Chris. I'm too fucking pissed at you right now to hear any more of your bullshit and lies. You're cutting? Again? What the absolute fuck—no. Don't answer that. And don't you dare fucking tell Kaden about how fucking much I'm cussing right now. I'm trying to get better about that."

Chris snorted. "You must really love him, then, to try to tame down that mouth."

"What the fuck did I just tell you?" Bran snapped at him, and Chris instantly shut his lips.

They were pulling up in front of Bran and Kaden's house a while later, and it was even nicer than the pictures Bran had sent him suggested. Though far more traditional in style than Samuel's lavish log cabin built of old wood and natural stone, it was no less beautiful and just as large. It suited Bran, in a way he'd never thought his big apartment in New York had. Bran had always seemed more like a house person, and he certainly had one now.

Trent was coming out of the front door as they were coming up, but he quickly started retreating as he caught sight of them.

"Running away won't help you!" Bran called after him.

"Don't be mad at Trent. I blackmailed him," Chris revealed as he slung his duffle over his shoulder. Bran shot him a dark look.

Everyone stopped talking in the kitchen once they came into the house, and Chris briefly met Samuel's gaze before Bran grabbed him by the front of his shirt and pulled him into the living room, which was right off the kitchen but would give them some privacy.

"Sit," Bran ordered, releasing him in front of a comfortable-looking leather sofa.

"No. You sit. I'll be back in a second," Chris said, heading back into the kitchen. He ignored everyone in there, or would have if Kaden hadn't gotten in his way. "What?" he snapped at him.

"I told you that your lies were going to be—"

Chris walked around him, cutting him off midtirade, and went right to the freezer to pull out two ice cubes. He didn't feel like looking for a towel to wrap the ice in and really didn't want to be around Kaden, with him glaring at him like he was, any longer than he had to be. He dragged his fingers across Samuel's stomach as he walked past him and back to the living room, where Bran was looking murderously at him. Chris popped the ice into his mouth, since he hadn't taken the time to grab a glass for the cubes and didn't want to get water spots on any of the furniture, then stripped off his shirt without thinking about his tattoo until he saw Bran staring at him, his mouth open.

"When the hell did you get that?"

He spat the ice cubes into his shirt, wrapped the material around them, then pushed Bran onto the couch. Bran had gained a lot of muscle working on the farm, but he was still easy to maneuver when he was in shock like he was right then.

"Seven months ago," Chris said offhandedly as he sat down on Bran's lap, putting his knees on either side of Bran's hips and keeping him trapped on the couch as he pressed the ice to Bran's swelling lip.

"It looks Maori."

Chris nodded. "It is. Stop talking. I'm trying to fix your lip."

"I can do this myself," Bran argued with him.

He was sure Bran could. They weren't children, after all. But it was nice to be doing something, to feel like he was helping Bran for once in their lives, instead of just causing him more trouble. Samuel, Kaden, and Trent began filing into the living room, all of them staring at him and Bran. Chris tried not to feel like he was a bug under a microscope with their scrutiny.

"If you hit him…," Kaden warned.

Chris rolled his eyes. "He hit himself with the car door. And I'm the one that got smacked and punched, thank you so much for your concern."

Bran glared at him, though he didn't say anything, and Chris slowly nodded, understanding Bran's look. He couldn't talk to Kaden like that if he ever wanted Bran to forgive him. He looked over his shoulder at Kaden as he saw him sit down between Samuel and Trent.

"Sorry. I'm kind of an asshole when I'm upset. And sorry about yesterday too. I shouldn't have talked to you like that," Chris muttered.

His apology done, he turned back to Bran and pulled the ice off his lip, not wanting to keep the cold on there for too long. "There, you'll live. Keep ice on it, on and off. You know the drill." He tried getting off Bran's lap, but Bran put his hands on Chris's hips, stopping him.

"Are you really cutting again?" he asked, sounding so scared and making Chris wish he'd done anything but that.

Screwing around would have sucked, but Bran wouldn't be looking at him like he was right now if Chris had just gone back to being a slut. He'd be disappointed, Chris knew, but he wouldn't be afraid.

Slowly nodding, Chris felt sick as he looked down at Bran and saw only fear in his expression. "I am. I have been for the last four months."

"Misha was supposed to watch you."

He wasn't a child that needed supervision, but given what he'd done to himself the same week Misha had left, maybe, in a way, he did need someone around to look after him and make sure he didn't screw up.

"He's been in the Middle East since about the same time I started hurting myself again."

"Strip," Bran demanded, his voice suddenly cold.

Chris laughed dryly. "Want to give your boyfriend a show, then?"

Bran slapped him again, and Chris knew he deserved it, but it still fucking stung. He rubbed his cheek and met Bran's gaze. He looked shocked.

"I've never once hit you before today. And now I've done it a lot. Shit."

"Yeah, but in all fairness, I kind of have them coming. And they sting, but it's not like you're really hurting me, so I'm not complaining. Can we go somewhere? For me to show you what I've been doing?" Instead of in the living room with everyone silently watching them and making him uncomfortable.

Bran shook his head, and Chris knew he wasn't going to get off that easily. "Nope. Right here. And you better have worn some underwear."

"You're in luck," Chris said, rolling his eyes as he leaned back to undo the button, then the zipper, of his shorts. Once they were open, he pulled the waistband of his underwear down just enough for Bran to see the scars over his hips. He looked at Bran, watching his expression as he looked down at the dozens of small cuts. The fear had turned into worry, and a sadness so deep Chris wanted to cry right along with him as Bran touched each small scar, as if he was trying to count them.

"How many of these are new? Since college, I mean?" Bran quietly asked him as he kept tracing the faint marks with his fingers.

"Fifty-seven," Chris instantly responded. He'd always kept track of them. Sometimes he'd been able to go for a week without cutting. Sometimes it had been a few times a day. Workdays and Saturdays after lunch with his parents were always the hardest.

Bran just sat back and shook his head, looking miserable. "I want to strangle you right now. If I didn't love you so much, I probably would."

"I know." Chris took the chance of being hit again and leaned over him, wrapping his arms around Bran's shoulders and laying his forehead against Bran's neck. "Believe me, I do know."

CHAPTER TEN

CHRIS WANTED to cry as he felt Bran wrap his arms around him to hold him tight. His heart pounded in his ears, and he battled to hold back the tears as the intense fear and emotion of the last few months burst forth.

"I missed you so much," Chris whispered to him as he hugged Bran tighter. He knew the other guys were still there, silently hanging out less than ten feet from him, and he was thankful that they'd stayed so quiet, but he knew that likely wouldn't last.

Bran withdrew, and a deep frown creased his forehead. "What the hell was Misha thinking by leaving you on your own? He promised to keep a close eye on you, and you also promised to ask if you needed help. Why, Chris? We're your friends, and if that's not what we're there for, why call us that?"

Chris pulled back and fixed his shorts before sliding off Bran's lap and sitting down next to him on the couch. He could see Samuel if he turned his head to look at him, but he was trying not to see his face and desperately needed to resist the urge to crawl into his lap.

"You wouldn't understand," he said with a loud sigh.

"Of course I wouldn't," Bran snapped at him. "I'm not the one hurting myself all the time. Tell me something. Anything. Help me figure out why you're doing this again. Maybe we can come up with a solution together."

"I don't like doing it, but in some sick, twisted way, it helps. If you don't have the same problem, you won't get it." Chris looked at the rug on the floor, feeling very exposed in front of them all as the weak freak. "Can we talk about something else? Like, Trent, how are the cows?"

It was a desperate attempt at getting out of answering Bran's questions, and Trent absolutely did not look like he wanted any part of helping Chris at that moment as he glowered at him from across the room.

"Don't you do that," Bran growled. "Don't try to distract me. Give me one good reason why you need to slice yourself open all the damn time."

Chris looked Bran straight in the eye without backing off. "Because as the flesh opens up and blood flows, so does the pain. It flows out and lessens the pressure inside. It's an amazing relief, euphoric almost. And there, right there in your eyes, is why I couldn't tell you this. Because you won't get it and you will worry yourself sick. Over me. Again."

"You sound like an addict," Bran accused him.

Chris only shrugged. "Maybe I am. But this is better than ruining someone else and destroying relationships and marriages like I did when I was having sex with strangers. I'm lucky I'm not dead for how many guys I've been at the mercy of. This way there's only me and I'm in control over everything. It's the only thing I've ever really been in control of. So excuse me for being screwed up and needing this. I never said I was perfect."

He took a shuddering breath and dragged his fingers roughly through his hair. "And I didn't come to you because you would have jumped on the first plane back to Manhattan, and your life is here now. I didn't want you to help me because it would have meant messing things up for you here. I've never once put your needs above my own, and I decided to this time. You want the truth? There it is. I cut myself, I freaked out, I called Samuel, I got on a plane, I came down here, and then I ran into you while I was buying you a whole ton of chocolate in the hopes that you'd forgive my sorry, lying ass."

Chris's heart broke some more when Bran pushed him off and walked to Kaden, where he climbed into his lap as Chris wanted to do with Samuel. Their intimate connection and love was tangible across the room, with Bran fitting into Kaden's arms easily for comfort. Chris shook his head and had to look away before he really did start crying.

"I should go," he quietly said.

"But you just got here," Bran complained.

Chris forced himself to look at Samuel and meet his gaze. He looked worried, and Chris knew he had every right to be. "Did you get my text?"

Samuel nodded sadly. "I did."

"And? Did you bring it?" Chris nearly whined. He needed it before he could go back to Manhattan. He had kitchen knives at home, of course, but they didn't cut like that one did, and he didn't trust them to work properly.

Samuel sat forward on his seat. "It's in my truck outside. Do you want me to get it?"

"What are you two talking about?" Bran interrupted them.

Chris glanced away from Samuel to focus on Bran again. Knowing that his kit was there, within easy access, was some relief. "The knife I use to cut myself. The one we got in Colorado when we went snowboarding a few years ago. Samuel was hanging on to it for me."

Bran frowned at him. "Why in the hell would you need it now?"

Chris pulled one of his knees up to his chest and locked his hands around his ankle. "Because I'm going to need it when I go back to Manhattan." He turned back to Samuel. "Right now isn't necessary, but before I go I'll need to get it."

Bran openly stared at him, and Chris flinched under his gaze. "What?" He tried not to snap, but his nerves were wearing thin.

"You're going back. Seriously? You tell me you've been cutting for the past four months, and now you're going back to Manhattan? Are you insane?" Bran yelled.

Why everyone assumed he'd be leaving his home was beyond him. Maybe they were the ones who were crazy, not him. "I live there," he slowly reminded Bran.

"Maybe you shouldn't," Bran snapped. "Maybe you should move away from your controlling, homophobic father and figure out your own damn life for once!"

"Where should I go? Here? What is there for me here? Seeing as I'm the freak no one wants and thinks belongs in a mental institution." Chris felt completely outnumbered. "Screw this. Actually, Samuel, I do need my kit. I'm going to the airport now."

Bran jumped up and tackled him before he could get two feet away from the couch. "Not if I say you're not."

Chris loved him for his stubbornness and his determination. But he wasn't going to win. Not in this. "Kidnapping is illegal here too. Seriously, Bran. I'm okay. Cutting is normal for me. And I don't feel like shit after it like when I'm with strange men. I honestly did stop drinking, and I haven't had a dick in my ass since before Montana. You can let me go and not worry about me. Everything is fine. I just cut. It's not as big of a deal as you're making it. Or as Samuel makes it, for that matter. Think of it like smoking, which is actually a lot more dangerous."

Bran watched him in horror. "Samuel, I guess you were right back in Montana. He is intent on killing himself, and I never saw it."

Chris had no idea what he was talking about, but he was scowling as he turned to look at Samuel. "You thought I was suicidal? I've never once tried to kill myself."

Samuel glared at Bran before looking at Chris. "No, I said you were both so destructive and that you are gonna get hurt if you carry on the way you were. I was right, because you are hurting yourself, aren't you? When is a little, shallow cut not going to be enough, and it gets deeper to help as your stress levels fluctuate with your useless parents? When is enough, enough?"

Chris didn't have answers for him, and he didn't like being put in that position either. Especially while everyone kept staring at him.

He shook his head and turned back to Bran, who was still sitting on him. "Get off. I'm going now."

Bran stubbornly shook his head. "No, you're not. I'm not going to let you go until you see just how much you're hurting yourself. Until you get how scary and dangerous this is. When I first caught you cutting, I was sixteen and stupid. I'm thirty-three now and sane, and it's not okay that you do this to yourself. Not at all. I won't watch you die. I can't."

Chris blew out an irritated breath. Arguing with Bran was apparently going to go nowhere, but he needed to get Bran off him so he could get going. Using one of the tricks Misha had showed him over the years in case he was ever in trouble with a guy, he planted his feet and lifted up his hips, throwing Bran forward and off balance so it was easy to roll him over and get on top of him.

"I'm not fucking suicidal. You think I need to understand that cutting is dangerous? Maybe you need to figure out that I have some self-control and know when to stop," Chris spat at him as he got to his feet, leaving a surprised-looking Bran still lying on the floor.

He stopped to get his shirt on and frowned as the icy wet spot touched his back. "Do you want to let me borrow your keys, or are you coming out with me?" Chris demanded from Samuel.

Samuel got to his feet. "Chris, listen to us. We're only trying to help because we care. We're not the enemy. Your ass of a father is. Cutting yourself is not the problem. Get rid of the source of your heartache and the cutting will stop. I believe that with my whole heart. This is not you.

You are so much stronger than this, but that father of yours would drive me to the brink of stupid too."

Chris groaned and ran his hands roughly through his hair. They were all so very frustrating. It was like some intervention on the TV and one he absolutely did not need. There was nothing wrong with him, and he was fed up trying to make them see that.

"You said you'd give it to me when I wanted it back. It's not yours to have. It's mine. Give me back my knife, Samuel." He crossed his arms over his chest and hated to see the pain in Bran's eyes as he got up and went back to sit with Kaden.

Samuel squared his shoulders, and Chris saw the anger in them.

"There's no help for the sick if they can't admit they're sick. No one can help you until you decide you need help. Until the alcoholic admits he's an addict, you can do nothing for him. You're in that same boat. You think you're so tough and you're in control. I've got news for you—you're not. That man that donated his sperm for your existence is in control of you! He's got you right where he wants you, and you're too bloody blind to see it. This here—your unwillingness to even listen to us, your friends, your real fucking family—is why I won't have a relationship with you. Your asshole of a father and your precious knife are more important to you than any of us. And I'm not signing up for coming home to a bled-out lover one day. I've seen shit like that as a kid, and I've decided not to ever put up with it again. The truck is open. Go fetch your piece of gold you love so much." Samuel spat the last few words out in disgust as his gray eyes flashed heat at Chris.

Chris tried not to shake or break down crying as he stood there listening to Samuel. He wasn't right. Not at all. Not about him and not about his dad. He knew who he was and what he was doing, not Samuel, who hardly even knew him. He couldn't get a single word out, so he simply turned, though his movements were stiff, and headed back to the front door.

He heard someone running up behind him and expected Bran but not the anger in his expression.

"If you leave right now, if you choose him over yourself, just like you always do, then don't expect to be welcome back here. At all. You walk out that front door and you don't get to come back to New Zealand. And I don't want to have a best friend that can't see that he's dying."

Chris couldn't hold back the tears anymore, not when Bran was there, telling him he was done with their friendship and that Chris was so easy to throw away. He hugged Bran close, holding him as tightly as he could before letting him go and bending down to get his duffle bag. Walking out the front door and hearing it slam shut behind him, followed by the sound of Bran's howling sobs, nearly broke him.

He had this. He didn't need any of them. If they couldn't see he was fine, he could manage without them. Or die trying.

CHAPTER ELEVEN

THE SOUND of the door slamming reverberated through the house, and Samuel couldn't help flinching. Adrenaline still pumped through his body from his anger at Chris, and it took him a few seconds to comprehend that Chris was gone. He'd just left. Without them saying good-bye properly.

He hurried to the front door, jerked it open, and looked down the winding driveway. A lone figure stood by the postbox, but before Samuel could get to his truck, a white taxi stopped and Chris got in and drove off.

"Fuck!" he yelled in frustration and kicked at his truck tire, the action giving him no relief from the torment in his soul. When he turned around, his friends stood on the wooden deck, Kaden and Trent's expressions filled with worry and Bran's completely ravished by his grief. His heart beat a fast tempo in his chest, and every instinct in him commanded he run after Chris, but his common sense told him it would achieve nothing, but cause another argument. Another dead end.

He clenched and unclenched his fists, the desire in him to break stuff so great that denying it freedom made a sweat break out on his skin. In high school he had learned to box, then wrestle, and eventually he ended up in kickboxing. His training would prevent him ever becoming a victim of violence or abuse again. At home he had a gym where he stayed fit and practiced, but never once had he needed to use his skills. But today, if he could get a hold of Pavel Romanoff, he would break his neck with his bare hands and enjoy the hell out of the brutal act.

Holding back from acting out was painful, but he managed. He stomped up the stairs and walked past the other men to go back inside, where he slumped down on the couch and closed his eyes. Soft footsteps and the door closing told him they were all in the room, but he stayed quiet. What was there to say?

Bran still cried softly, and Samuel's own eyes stung with repressed emotions. Kaden said nothing, but when Trent spoke, it surprised Samuel so much his eyes popped open.

"May I be the bearer of bad news to tell you all how royally you just fucked things up?"

Bran's spine stiffened, and he stopped crying. "Excuse me?"

Trent sat forward on his seat and rested his elbows on his knees, making his long limbs appear even lankier. "You heard me. What were you lot thinking, man? Ganging up on Chris like that? We all know he has a problem, and deep down he knows it too. But what happens when you corner an addict?" Trent's voice got louder with every word he spoke.

Bran stared at Trent like he'd never seen the man before. "We were only trying to help him. Talk some sense into him."

Trent laughed humorlessly, the sound completely foreign from his usually calm and jovial friend. "Helping? How is it helping him to tell your best friend that he's not welcome back here at your house or even in New Zealand if he doesn't do what you say, Bran? Who the hell are you? You don't own this country and don't speak for everyone. Not for me, anyway."

Trent's green eyes flashed in outrage. Samuel had only ever seen Trent this angry once, the time they'd found him lying wounded in the grass by the creek. Trent didn't do angry. Until today.

Bran tried to retaliate but looked like a goldfish with nothing coming from his mouth.

Trent dragged one hand roughly through his messy long blond hair. He pinned each one of them with a disgusted look. "I know you guys are my friends, and I love you to bits, but I'm so disappointed in you right now. The only thing you geniuses managed to accomplish was to confirm what Chris had feared his whole life—rejection, abandonment, and ridicule."

Samuel knew Trent was spot-on. They might have all been well meaning with what they had said to Chris, but pushing too hard, too fast all at once might have done more damage than good. He nodded at Trent to acknowledge his agreement.

"Now Chris is on his way back to a nightmare of a life with no support structure. Until now he never went off the edge, because despite the shit in his life, he had you, Bran, and Misha. And us for the last eight months. He knew he had us to fall back on if all else failed. What does he have now? A possible lover who wants him fixed before he'll love on him? A brother who is in bumfuck who knows where shooting people for a living, and friends who told him his head is so fucked up that, unless he sorts himself out, he's not welcome back. So he's all alone. In his current state, Chris becomes a man who plays Russian roulette with a fully loaded gun, and he'll smile every time he pulls the trigger." Trent's skin appeared very pale as he glared at them all.

"I'm so bloody disappointed in you all right now. I can't even text Misha to give him a heads-up on Chris's mental state, because the prick won't answer me! If anything serious happens to him, then you've got only yourself to blame. Later."

Trent left the house with another slam, and under different circumstances Samuel would've felt sorry for the piece of wood.

Trent's words hit home, because Bran burst out in fresh tears while Kaden tried to calm him down without success.

"I've got to call him. To apologize and tell him I didn't mean it."

He grabbed his cell phone and walked into the kitchen, where they could hear his voice but not the words he spoke. A few minutes later, he appeared from around the wall, still very upset.

"He's not answering. I left a message." Bran climbed on Kaden's lap and started crying against his neck.

"Bran, don't take this all upon yourself. I've let Chris down too." The guilt lay heavy on Samuel's soul.

"I'm his best friend, Sam. Best friends don't do what I did today. They stand by their mates, no matter what. For him to hide something from me like his visit here, I should've known it was serious. I behaved like a selfish child. I've failed him so badly."

Bran's pain echoed through his own heart.

"Me too. Look, I'm gonna head on home and try to get some rest. I don't know what we're gonna do right now. Going after him will only push him farther away. I need time to think. See you guys later." Samuel let himself out of the house and closed the door softly, despite wanting to punch a hole in it or rather break his hand against the solid wood.

Exhaustion weighed him down as he drove the short distance home, and when he walked into the house, he wanted to cry. Even with only a short stay there, Chris had left memories behind for Samuel to revisit. The couch was no longer just a seat to relax in—it was a piece of furniture reminiscent of heartbreak, affection, comfort, and desire.

The kitchen came across empty without someone sitting at the table keeping him company while he cooked something to eat. Hearing

Chris's voice behind him would've been a hell of a lot better than the still emptiness now surrounding him.

He drew the curtains and toed off his boots before lying down on the couch despite the ache it brought to his heart. An arm over his eyes somehow relieved some of the pressure behind them and the throb in his head. His concern for Chris in his current mental state had him on the edge, but he knew there was nothing he could do about it right now. Chris was probably at the airport or already on his way back to Manhattan. Phoning him or texting him wouldn't get an answer after what went down that afternoon.

If he was Chris, he would never speak to them for the rest of his life. Where Chris had needed if not support then understanding at least, they had given him nothing to work with. No encouragement or kindness, and although Samuel had meant every word he said to Chris, his timing had sucked so soon after Bran going apeshit on him for lying and hiding his problem.

Trent had been spot-on, they had fucked things up badly, and Samuel honestly didn't know if Chris would let them make it up to him. He was not so sure he would have given them a second chance if he'd been the one on the receiving end of their selfishness. His best guess was that he'd probably blown his chance to ever have a relationship with Chris. Since day one, all Chris had wanted was to be with him, and he had to go and put some conditions on them being together. Like hoops a dog had to jump through to get a treat. What an ass he had been. He deserved to lose Chris, if he had to be honest, because if anyone had told him he had to do this or that, or attain certain things before they'd be with him, Samuel would've told them to go to hell. Plain and simple.

The few relationships he'd had before were all of the serious kind, but Samuel hadn't meant as much to those guys as they had to him. He gave his all and received second best in return. In his opinion, a relationship took hard work, and unless both parties were willing to give it, they didn't have a fighting chance to make it succeed. So why even try? None of those guys had looked at him and treated him the way Chris did, but he had treated Chris as if he was the type of people they were.

If he had learned anything about Chris, it was that the man was the most self-sacrificing guy he knew. His life was a mess because he cared more about his parents than he did for himself. Chris had hidden his issues from Bran to protect his friend and not burden the new couple with his problems. Samuel should've seen Chris was sincere, despite his emotional baggage. Chris might be broken, but he was loyal, hardworking, dedicated, and loving. Not the self-seeking jerk Samuel had treated him like.

As he replayed the whole mess in his head, trying to figure out how the hell he could make things right, the tiredness caught up with him and he succumbed to a restless sleep.

CHAPTER TWELVE

CHRIS HAD turned his phone off while he was on the planes and didn't turn it back on until the taxi had dropped him off in front of his apartment building. But once he did, he could only stare at his phone as a voice mail notification from Bran blinked up at him. He couldn't handle being yelled at by his ex–best friend again, especially not so soon, and quickly shoved his phone back in his pocket before getting out of the taxi.

His building was the most modern on the block, all light gray cement and steel beams. And he'd missed it, right down to the coffee house music on the elevator up to the third floor. There were only four apartments on each floor, giving them all their own little corner of the building. His views weren't great, but they were something, and sometimes the yoga studio across the street left their blinds open and he could watch the cute guys stretching from his couch.

He was so tired, so completely out of it, that he nearly ran over a boy sitting in front of the door to the apartment next to his, a soccer ball held tightly between his crossed legs.

Chris crouched down to get Mikey's attention and waved his hand in front of the little boy's face to say hello. Mikey smiled at him, then pulled out a pen and pad of paper, something he always had with him, ever since he and his mom had moved into the building two years before.

How was New Zealand? Mikey wrote, then showed it to him.

Chris stood and motioned Mikey up as well. If he was going to have company and force himself to interact with someone, then he sure as hell was going to do it while being comfortable. Mikey followed him into his apartment and plopped down on Chris's sleek black sofa. It was his usual spot. Chris dropped his duffle by the front door and poured himself a glass of soda before coming over to sit next to him. He desperately needed the caffeine, and the sugar would help perk him up. Mikey knew where everything in his kitchen was if he wanted to get himself something.

He pulled out his phone and typed back to Mikey, holding it up for Mikey to see as soon as he was done. *Far away. Glad to be home.*

Mikey nodded as if he, being only twelve, had any concept of what the hell a thirty-hour trip felt like. To Chris it was like being dead, then left somewhere in a tiny compartment filled with a bunch of other dead people. He desperately needed a shower to get the airplane funk off his skin.

Where's your mom? Chris asked him before Mikey could write anything else to him.

He wrote quickly. *Work.*

Chris really didn't need this right then, especially when he only wanted to crawl into bed and forget about all the shit of the last few days. On Monday he'd still had Bran, still had a chance with Samuel and a place to go if things ever got bad. By Friday he'd destroyed it all and his friends had turned against him. *Sitter?* Chris typed back.

Mikey shrugged, and Chris quickly dialed the boy's mom.

"Chris? What's up? I didn't think you'd be back already. But maybe I'm getting my days mixed up."

He could hear the sounds of the hospital where she worked as a nurse in the background. "Hey. I found Mikey in the hallway. Mind if he hangs out with me for a bit?"

She sighed loudly and mumbled something he wouldn't have expected the petite, pixie-like woman to know how to say. He felt like laughing and probably would have too if he didn't feel so miserable.

"I'm firing that babysitter. I know he's old enough, at twelve, not to need one, but I feel better with him having someone there with him. Maybe his dad can take him tomorrow. Or I'll try to switch my shifts to overnights while he's mostly asleep. Something. Are you really okay if he stays there with you? Just for an hour? I'll call my sister to pick him up today. I'm pretty sure she has the time off."

Mikey wasn't any trouble for him, and in a way, it was nice not to be so alone for a little while. "Yeah. It'll be fine. I'll give him beer and take him to a strip club."

She snickered. "Of course you will. Make sure he doesn't spend all of his allowance."

Chris liked that she didn't take him too seriously. She was a good neighbor like that and a great mom for Mikey as far as he was concerned. Not that he had much experience in the parenting department.

"Thanks for letting him hang out with you for a little bit. I promise it won't be more than an hour. At the absolute most. And I'll pay you for watching him."

"I'm not taking your money," Chris told her. He'd never let her pay him for watching Mikey before.

"You're a good guy, Chris. Find a husband and adopt a lot of kids someday, okay?"

That definitely wasn't happening. "I'd rather have a dozen deadly spiders attacking me in my sleep."

Miranda laughed like she thought he was joking. Too bad he wasn't.

"Sure…. Whatever you say. I have to get back to my rounds. Take care. Thanks for being a lifesaver. And tell my kid I love him."

"See you." Chris hung up, then looked down at Mikey, who was watching him intently. He typed quickly so the kid could get caught up. *Talked to your mom. Your aunt is coming to get you in a bit. Mom says she loves you.*

Mikey grinned and nodded, letting him know he understood. Chris erased the words and wrote another message. *I need a shower. Food's in the fridge. Order a movie if you want.*

He showed Mikey the text, then got off the couch while the kid got the remote and started going through the animated movies. There was a whole section of movies that came with text, something that hadn't cost him more than a few dollars extra on top of his already expensive package. He figured it was worth it so that Mikey could see the new movies his friends had, and Miranda couldn't really afford what he paid to be able to watch TV in his limited downtime.

He headed into his bedroom, making sure to close the door behind him, and ignored his phone when it beeped. He couldn't stop his curiosity for long, though, and before he got into the shower, he was looking at a text from Samuel.

Did you get back safely?

Chris shook his head and deleted the text. Samuel didn't get to ask that, didn't get to care about him. Not anymore.

The shower felt good and helped him feel human again. So did changing into slacks and a button-down shirt. Shorts were for vacations and going out with friends. He'd have a vacation again in a few months, but friends were off the table for him, at least for right now. When he came out of his bedroom, Mikey had finished off the rest of Chris's soda and made himself some microwave popcorn. Chris tried not to care about the mess Mikey was making with the loose kernels as he sat down next to the kid on the couch.

Mikey's aunt showed up about ten minutes later, looking a bit frazzled with her hair in a messy bun and her mismatched socks, but she seemed happy to see Mikey as he ran to her, dropping popcorn after him. He signed excitedly to her, and she was just as fast with her responses. Chris wished he'd been able to pick the language up easier. His sign language skills were limited to hello, good-bye, I love you, and fuck off. The last one he'd learned by accident when he'd been trying to copy Mikey's movements and done one of them wrong.

"Hey, Stephanie," Chris said, holding the door open for her if she wanted to come in.

She patted his shoulder. "Hello. I somehow thought you'd look better after your trip to…. Now, don't tell me. Miranda said you were visiting friends in… New Mexico?"

That would have been a much easier trip. "New Zealand."

Her eyes got big. "World traveler. That's nice."

"Not so nice on my back. Airports are not the most comfortable places in the world. Thanks for coming to get him. I'm probably going to head into the office in a bit."

She shook her head at him. "You just got back. Relax for a few days. And don't thank me. You should be getting all the thanks for letting him stay with you for a little while."

It really hadn't been a big deal, as luckily Mikey was pretty self-sufficient. "I won't be working too late," he promised. He had things to do, though, notes from meetings to catch up on, probably a whole pile of paperwork, and hundreds of e-mails from clients, all demanding attention at once. That last bit always took the longest and drove him completely nuts.

Stephanie smiled at him. "Good. Also, there's a new guy at the art studio I work out of on the weekends. He's pretty cute. I can get you his number if you want."

Chris appreciated her thinking of him, but he shook his head. "Thanks, but I'm off dating for a while. Too much work to do," he added quickly, in case she thought to pry. They were good people, but the sisters spent far too much time thinking about hooking him up with the guys they knew for his taste.

"Poor baby. But okay. Go be whatever the gay version of a spinster is when you're sixty and only have your career to keep you company."

He rolled his eyes and waved at Mikey. They bumped fists, something that made Mikey smile, and minutes later he was alone in his apartment. He sighed and started the laundry, took stock of his groceries, and cleaned up the popcorn. An hour later he was bored and staring at a picture on his phone of himself and Bran from their trip to Key West while he tried not to cry.

"Get it together, asshole," he grumbled to himself. He needed a distraction, and work would be perfect. It was usually easy to get lost in the problematic lives of his clients while he tried to forget about his own.

The office was a quick five-minute taxi ride from his apartment when there wasn't snow everywhere. That afternoon it took him nearly twenty. He didn't have a set time to be there and wasn't even expected to come back until Monday, so that only left him staring at the hundreds of pictures he had of himself and Bran as he waited for the traffic to clear. If anyone looked through his phone they would have probably thought he was with Bran, judging by how many pictures he had of them with their arms around each other. And in every damn one, they were both smiling. Because that's what best friends did when they were together.

He exited out of his pictures and shoved his phone back into his pocket. Screw that. If Bran didn't want him in his life anymore, then Chris wasn't going to mope either. Over a decade of being friends and Bran was the one that had thrown their friendship away, not him. He was a stupid, mean…. He was Chris's best friend, and now he was gone, and Chris felt completely alone.

He texted Misha and gave him an update, knowing Misha would want to know the latest happenings in his life. *You got your wish. Bran is out of my life. He threw me away.*

Misha wouldn't be texting him back until tomorrow, as was his pattern over the last few months. And it was only ever one quick text to let him know Misha was okay. He needed those texts more than he was sure Misha was aware.

After getting out of the taxi in front of the historical brick building in the heart of Manhattan, Chris quickly made his way up the half-dozen steps and into the lobby, where the receptionist gave him a nod. And he walked up another set of steps to his office at the end of the row of offices completely identical to his own. The only thing that made his office different was the brass plaque on his door that said his full name, followed by the shiny italic title of Attorney at Law.

As predicted, there were files stacked on his desk, but instead of letting that pile of work fill him with dread, he welcomed the distraction from thinking about the mess he'd made of everything in New Zealand. It wasn't even like Bran and everyone being mad at him was his fault. They were the crazy ones, not him.

He sat down at his desk, started some low, soft music, and got started. He wasn't even through answering his first page of new e-mails when his dad came into his office without knocking.

"Hi," Chris said, moving back from his desk and getting to his feet to greet him.

"I see you're back. I wasn't happy about hearing the news from my assistant, though. You're expected to come straight to me. We have cases to go over."

Chris nodded and retook his seat as his dad sat down too. He went on vacation so rarely he'd completely forgotten what his father wanted from him as soon as he was back in the building. He'd only been focused on getting to his office to see how much work had piled up in the less than a week he'd been gone.

"Where did you run away to this time?"

Running away was a pretty appropriate description, unfortunately. He wouldn't be going anywhere for a long time, though. Vacations were lonely, boring things without a best friend to take them with.

"New Zealand."

His father's expression turned sour. "To be with that faggot, no doubt. When are you going to grow the hell up and figure out he's a toxic disease for you? He's a horrible person, and he threw his whole future away last year. I should have dragged you out of that damn college the moment you told me about him. If you'd never met him, I could have grandchildren by now. Lord knows your brother isn't giving me any with that woman of his."

Chris sat back, the chair squeaking under him as he shifted his weight over the springs. "Bran didn't turn me gay. I've told you that before. That's not how it goes."

His father's expression turned sour. "That faggot brainwashed you into believing that. I know how their kind works."

Normally he would have just brushed all of his father's hateful words aside. He was a mean man, but he was his father, and Chris only had one of those. And after losing Bran and Samuel, he really didn't have anyone else left but his dad. Misha certainly wasn't coming back home anytime soon, his mom was always busy, and Chris liked being around people.

But maybe it was being in planes and airports for thirty hours or losing the people who had meant the most to him, but he couldn't simply ignore his father's words as easily as he usually did. It just didn't work like that.

"I have piles of work to do," Chris said pointedly, hoping his dad would get on with whatever he was going to say.

He didn't, though. Instead he got up and started pacing around Chris's office. Going on about how the gays were ruining the country and his family. It was nothing Chris hadn't heard before, at least a hundred times, especially the parts about curing the world of all their influence, but it was as if he was hearing it all and seeing his father rant about all the horrible things his people had done but not actually being a part of it. Not this time at least.

He must have been far too tired to be having this conversation and likely shouldn't have come into work at all, because all he could think about while listening to his father go on and on was how absolutely ridiculous he sounded. He was a crass old man, and Chris really needed some time away from him right then before he said something he didn't actually mean.

"I need to go," he said, getting to his feet.

"I'm not done speaking with you."

Chris shook his head and gathered his things. "I wasn't really listening anyway."

His mouth agape, his father simply stared at him. "Why you disrespectful, ungrateful little faggot."

The word hurt, but it didn't make him want to kill people like it did with Bran. Maybe because he'd been hearing it most of his life, often directed right at him. It was a normal part of everyday conversation when his father was involved. Still, it was wrong of his dad to say it, and Chris had been asking him not to.

"I'd prefer that you not call me that."

"Well I'd rather have a son that didn't disgrace the family with his ridiculous affairs."

Chris took a deep breath to calm his nerves and tried really hard to hold back what he wanted to say. And it worked, at least a little. "You have that with Misha. And if you mean me, well, I've never once been portrayed badly in a paper, or been in a tabloid, or had a sex tape released. There is no shame in who I am and what I do. Now, I really do need to go."

"I will dismiss you when I'm done talking to you," his father snapped at him.

Chris's headache pounded against his temples, and he wasn't sure how much more of this he could take. He loved his father, and he wasn't a bad man, but some of the things he said were not appropriate.

Chris stepped around him and headed out of the office. Getting outside helped some, but he hoped seeing his mom would be even more beneficial. He'd be seeing her at lunch the next afternoon anyway when they had their weekly lunch date at Diamino's, a small upscale cafe that served twenty-dollar salads along with pretentiousness. But those lunches were always with his father in attendance, and he wanted some time with only her.

His parents lived within walking distance of the firm, on a tree-lined street with bright yellow and red tulips planted along walkways. It was lovely, or it would have been if he wasn't slushing through three inches of snow and wet gray junk that clung to the cuffs of his pants. He worried about being presentable for her, especially when he saw a few extra cars parked in front of his parents' house and hanging out in their driveway too.

His mom had company, which wasn't rare, but he'd been hoping to catch her alone that afternoon.

"Welcome back, Mister Romanoff," George said, opening the door for him when he started up the walkway. He hadn't even reached the first step.

Chris gave his parents' butler a small smile. "Hey. My mom busy?"

"She has campaign visitors, but I'm sure she can find time for you," George said, letting him in and showing him to where his mom sat, surrounded by envelopes and letters apparently waiting to go in them.

"Hey," Chris said, sitting down across from her. At least she was alone now, though she hadn't even looked up at him when he'd joined her at the table. Instead she was focused on her phone. "So… I'm back from New Zealand."

"That's good. Be a dear and help me get these campaign contributor letters ready."

Biting back a sigh, Chris got to work. "I was visiting Bran."

"No. Not like that. Get your creases better. Don't you remember anything? Honestly, how many times do I need to show you this?"

It took him a second before he could continue on to his fifth envelope. He was folding the letters the same way she was. He could hear people talking in the rooms nearby and saw George carrying around a bottle of wine, ready to refill everyone's glasses. Just as he'd been doing for the last seven years whenever Chris's mom and her senate friends got together at one of these campaign things. He didn't even read what he was helping to send out. He hadn't been reading the letters for years.

"He's in love, with a dairy farmer, if you can believe that," Chris continued, trying to get her attention. Even thinking about Bran hurt, so talking about him was much worse. But it was something his mom should have been able to talk about. It wasn't as if he and Bran had just met or anything like that.

When his mom didn't say anything to that, he tried a different tactic. "Dad and I had a spat again."

She sighed and shook her head at him, clearly disapproving of whatever he'd done to upset his father. "You know how important family is in this house. There is nothing else. You'll apologize to your father immediately." With that reprimand she was back to folding the letters and stuffing the envelopes.

"He called me a faggot," Chris tried to explain, wanting his mom to actually understand what had happened between them and why, as usual, it wasn't his fault. He'd reacted badly, but he didn't believe that he ever started the arguments.

She didn't turn away from her busy work. "Well, that's what you get for having relations with men. Honestly, where you got that idea in your head is beyond me. Certainly your father and I never had anything like that in our families. Now, enough talking about your ruined life. You'll apologize to your father at lunch tomorrow and that will be the end of it. Maybe one of these days, you'll realize the error of your ways and take that nice woman who lives next door to you out for dinner. Her son, though, he's a predicament, isn't he? But I suppose at your age a woman with a peculiar son is still a catch. You aren't getting younger, and I do want grandchildren to spoil."

Chris forced himself to go slow as he slid back from the table. He'd had quite enough of his family for one day and desperately needed to be away from them. It wasn't anything he hadn't heard before, but this time he couldn't get Samuel's voice out of his head, and it was starting to bother him. These were his parents, and he loved them. A good son would have been able to sit and listen to them, even when he didn't agree with them. But Chris wasn't feeling very good in that moment as he came around the table and kissed his mother on her wrinkled cheek.

"Are you leaving? But there is so much left to do!"

And he wanted no part in any of it. "I'm not feeling well. I'll see you and Dad tomorrow for lunch."

George showed him out, not that he needed help finding the front door to the house he'd grown up in, but it was customary.

"I do hope you'll be more on your feet tomorrow," George told him as they parted.

Chris nodded to the elderly man. "Me too. I'll be ready for the car at eleven thirty, as usual."

"Very good, Mister Romanoff. Take care."

Pulling his jacket closer around himself, he headed back to the sidewalk. A taxi would have been faster and would have saved his shoes from the snow, but he wanted to walk home. It would help him clear his head some of all the racing thoughts.

Back in his apartment nearly an hour later, since he'd taken the long way around and been slow about it, he sat down on his couch and pulled out his phone. His first choice of someone to call would have been Bran, followed then by Samuel.

Since neither of them were an option, he considered texting Misha. But what was he supposed to say? That he'd had an argument with their dad and his mom thought it was his fault, as always? With a sigh he put his phone down and went from the couch to the middle of the floor where he could see the evening sunlight coming in through his big windows.

The first shreds of uncertainty and doubt began creeping into him, and he shuddered at the questions they raised. He was scared, he could admit that to himself, but it didn't help anything for him to realize that. Bran and Samuel couldn't be right. They didn't know his dad like he did.

They didn't see the good in either of his parents. They had no idea what they were talking about. He was sure of it. But somehow he couldn't get their words out of his head.

In the end, he did text Misha, a simple one-liner to say, *I'm not doing okay.* His brother was all he had for now, and he hoped to God he got a reply. He needed to know he mattered to someone.

CHAPTER THIRTEEN

TWO DAYS later Samuel felt like climbing the walls in his house. There was only so much he could do on a farm that they kept in a tidy condition, because the general rule was if something broke, you fixed it straightaway or told the staff member who could see to it. Despite searching high and low for jobs to keep his hands and mind occupied, once these were done, there was nothing much to do but daily milkings and the odd fencing problem.

After the way things fell apart at Kaden and Bran's house, he hadn't seen them since, and he would never admit it to them all, but he had been avoiding Trent like the plague. His kind friend turned awfully nasty when he got riled, and he'd rather avoid another tongue-lashing so soon.

He looked down at his phone, and his heart sped up as he hoped the call would be coming from Chris, but instead it was Bran's number that lit up his screen. "Hello, Samuel speaking," he said softly, expecting to hear bad news from Bran about Chris. He hadn't heard from Chris at all, but if he would call anyone, Samuel was sure he would have called Bran.

"Hey. Has he called you?" Bran asked him, the worry thick in his voice. He also sounded as if he'd been crying again.

Samuel frowned and ran his hand over his head. "No. You?"

"I wish. But no. I haven't heard from him. You'd tell me if you had, though, right? Even if he asked you to lie to me again? I need to know he's okay, and he's not returning my calls, my texts, or my e-mails. I've tried dozens of times now, and just… nothing."

Samuel sighed, completely worried out of his mind. "Bran, you know him better than anyone else. Would he do something stupid? Is he really that unstable? I'm trying to calm myself down by believing he would need some time to think and get over some shit spoken in anger, but it's not working so well."

Bran was quiet for a long time, which only made Samuel worry more.

"Honestly, Sam, I'm not sure. I mean, I'd love to say that he's completely fine and just pouting in his living room and watching some of our favorite movies. But two days ago, I would have said there was no way in hell he would have been cutting again. I saw the scars, though. I touched them. And now I don't have any idea what he would do. Look, will you come over? Trent's here. Kaden's sitting across from me. He bought four types of ice cream, including Swirly Caramel and Goody Goody Gum Drop, to cheer me up. If I eat much more of this alone, I'm going to have to go shopping in Thames for new pants. Don't make me go shopping again. You know how much I hate to buy clothes for myself when I'm alone, and Kaden says he doesn't want to go with me just to get me more junk I don't need. Please? Come be worried and miserable over here with the rest of us," Bran practically begged him.

Samuel looked at his timber walls again and thought it a better idea to get out of there. "Okay, I'll just have a shower and head on over."

"Great. I'll save you some of the chocolate. You could come over stinky if you wanted to. We're all so screwed up over here that no one would mind. Or, you know, shower. Whatever you want to do. As long as you come over and we can all be together. I wish he was here, though," Bran said. He sounded like he was trying to be happy and normal, yet failing miserably.

"I would rather clean up. I've been working out, so I'm sticky and I stink." His boxing bag had been kicked and beaten harder than ever before, and still the damn thing didn't break on him. Samuel had been tempted to douse the bag in fuel and burn it. Outside, so he didn't burn down the rest of his house.

"Ew. Yeah, get showered. We'll see you soon. Bye."

Bran hung up quickly, leaving him alone once again.

He dragged himself upstairs and had his shower, putting on a pair of comfortable jeans and an old T-shirt before heading to the front door. He put on his flip-flops, which lay on the deck, and got in the truck. Even the vehicle brought back sweet memories of Chris, and he swore as he started the engine and drove to Kaden's farm.

As soon as he was parked, the front door flew open and Bran came toward him. He'd barely been able to get out of the truck before Bran was hugging him.

"I'm glad you came over. I'm so scared and want my friends close right now. Come on in."

Bran brought him inside, where Kaden sat next to Trent in the living room, both of them looking miserable.

"Hey," he said to them but focused on Trent. They both greeted him back the same as always, and he relaxed a bit, knowing Trent was back to normal.

Kaden shook his head sadly. "You look like shit."

Samuel smiled a little. "So do you. I guess none of us have slept well or stopped worrying since he left."

Kaden looked to Bran, then back to Samuel. "He absolutely hasn't. That's for sure. Most of the time, I can't get him to let go of his phone just in case Chris texts. He lays there holding it and jumping every time he gets a spam e-mail, even when I'm trying to get him to sleep."

Not denying what Kaden had said, Bran disappeared into the kitchen, where Samuel could hear him getting dishes down from the cupboards.

"Everyone is having ice cream," Bran called to them. "No exceptions. Anyone want a drink? Iced tea? Water? An entire bottle of vodka?"

"Coffee for me, please," Samuel said, then instantly regretted it because coffee made him think of Chris and the sweet smile Chris had given him when he'd discovered the coffee machine in his house.

Bran came into the living room with four tubs of ice cream piled on top of each other in his hands and placed them on the coffee table in the middle of the room. He went back into the kitchen and returned with the dishes and cutlery, which joined the dessert on the table. "Help yourselves."

Trent got on his knees on the carpet and helped himself to a large serving of Swirly Caramel and Strawberries and Cream. Bran returned a few minutes later with coffee for each of them. After they had a cup in front of them, he bounced around a bit on his feet as if he needed something to do, some way to keep busy or else risk going mad. It was a familiar feeling for Samuel as well.

Kaden tapped the seat beside him. "Sit down, babe. Do you want more ice cream?"

Bran bit his bottom lip and shook his head. "Maybe in a bit. I keep going between feeling sick and hungry."

He curled up next to Kaden, who put his arms around Bran. As much as Samuel was happy for them, he couldn't watch them for long.

Averting his eyes from them, he crouched down to get himself some of the frozen dessert when Bran's phone rang loudly, startling him. Bran was quick to grab it out of his pocket and answer it.

"Misha? What's wrong? Is Chris okay?" he demanded, his face losing all color. He looked to them all, then put his phone down before putting it on speaker.

"I have nothing to say to you. If Samuel is there, put him on the phone. Otherwise, give him my number and tell him I expect a call back."

Misha sounded so cold, so angry, as they all stared at Bran's phone.

He was silent as he brought it over and placed it on the coffee table in front of Samuel.

"He's here. Will you tell me if Chris is okay?"

But Misha ignored him. "Samuel?"

Readying himself for the worst, Samuel spoke. "I'm here, Misha."

"If you still care about my brother at all, as you swore to me that you did in Montana, then you will keep that one away from him. This isn't a request. It's an order. Bran is not to have any more contact with Chris. I don't even want him breathing my brother's name. Not after what he did. Can you do that?"

Bran sat down heavily beside the coffee table, and Kaden was quick to join him, putting a hand on Bran's back.

"I told him I was sorry."

"Apparently you saying that, if you ever did, doesn't make up for throwing him away. Now, not another word from you. Samuel?" Misha barked at him.

Samuel looked at the anguish on Bran's face and the anger on Kaden's, and he felt like screaming until his lungs bled. "Misha, that day when he left, things were really messed up. We were trying to help him, and tempers were flying. We all said stuff we shouldn't have. We're all sorry, but Chris isn't responding to any of our texts or calls."

Misha sounded far less angry this time around. "I knew he was avoiding Bran, because why would he want to be rejected again, but he didn't tell me that he was also refusing to respond to you. I'll talk to him about making sure a line of communication is kept with you. I should be there in twelve more hours. Unless there's some reason you're not telling me that you shouldn't be allowed near him either?"

"I'm not sure actually how to answer that, because he's avoiding us all. Do you have any idea what happened?" Samuel had the idea if

Chris kept the cutting a secret from them, then Misha was probably in the dark too.

"He told you something, and you all rejected him. I didn't care what it was at the time, as it can't be any worse than the things he's forgiven Bran for over the years, or even in Montana. I need to go. My next flight is leaving. Keep Bran away from him, or I'll shut down his communication with all of you and take him so far away that none of you will ever be able to find him again."

The call ended, and Samuel simply stared at Bran's phone as he delicately took it back.

Trent got up and carried his empty bowl to the kitchen. "My knees still turn to fucking jelly."

If things hadn't been so serious, Samuel would've laughed at the dry comment.

"Shit. He's right," Bran mumbled. "He forgave me for everything. Always." His phone beeped, and Bran looked down at it. "Samuel, Misha wants your number. Can I give it to him?"

Samuel nodded his answer, and Bran's fingers tapped on the screen as he gave the number to Misha.

Samuel's phone was next to make a noise, and he looked down at it to see he'd received a text message from an unfamiliar number. *My brother's address is below. I won't be able to stay more than a few hours with him, but if you intend to show that you care in any way, I expect you to be on the first flight out. If Bran is with you, Chris won't be there.*

He responded with a simple, *Arrangements to make. Will keep you posted.*

"Was that Chris? What did he say?" Bran asked him excitedly.

Samuel looked up, and they all stared at him in anticipation.

"No, that was Misha telling me to get my ass on the first plane to Manhattan if I meant it when I said I cared for Chris."

Bran jumped to his feet. "I'm going with you. I can be packed in twenty minutes while Kaden makes the flight arrangements for us."

"I'm sorry, Bran, but no. If you are anywhere near me when I arrive, Misha promised to make sure we never see Chris again. You heard him." It broke Samuel's heart to deny Bran, but Misha wouldn't issue an empty threat, and right now the man clearly hated Bran with a passion.

Bran's bottom lip trembled. "But… he's my best friend. I should be there. I have to be."

"If Misha thinks I can make a difference by going after Chris, then there is also hope that you two can patch things up in the future. You were much closer than he and I have been." Samuel tried to comfort Bran with the words, because it was all he could think of right then.

Bran slowly nodded, though he hardly looked convinced. "You'll let me—us—know when you see him again? Texts and calls. And video calls. Then you'll tell him to come back here? Convince him somehow?"

Samuel nodded to him, giving him a silent promise that he'd do his best.

CHAPTER FOURTEEN

FOR CHRIS, lunch out with his parents each Saturday afternoon was less about spending time with them and more about being seen as the wholesome, all-American family that they were. If Misha had been in town and wearing his old Army uniform, Chris was pretty sure their dad would have acted like he'd hit the jackpot if any reporters were around to snap a family photo of them.

The car was prompt picking him up, and Chris relaxed in the warm backseat, the fine cream-colored leather cradling him, as he did some last minute adjustments to the nearly black but still plenty blue tie he wore. Ties weren't an option, just as having his shoes shined before he arrived was something that was expected of him. He was an adult and as such had to look presentable when going out in public.

The car dropped him off in front of the restaurant, and Chris was led to his parents' favorite table, one that offered them a perfect view of Central Park. Bran's old apartment wasn't far from the restaurant, but even though Bran could have easily afforded to eat there a couple of times a week, the food actually wasn't all that good, despite the high price tag. And so they had skipped it, letting the restaurant remain a favorite spot for his parents and not any place he took his best friend, or any guy he was interested in.

Thinking about Bran was a distraction, and normally a welcome one at that, but when thoughts of Bran only made him depressed, he couldn't afford to have them clouding up his mind. Family lunch wasn't supposed to have any sort of drama in it.

"Christophori!" his mother called happily to him, spreading her arms wide to take him in.

He kissed her cheek, tried not to suffocate on her heavy perfume that smelled like decaying roses, and stepped back. Shaking his father's hand came next, and the host pulled his chair out for him. There was no mention of the words they'd thrown around or of how he'd left his father standing there in his office when he'd walked out.

There was only the quiet talk of elections and issues at hand, of ladies' parties and who would be attending. His mother was a good senator and mostly well liked, but Chris knew how much of an act her performances really were while she was in that arena. She liked the attention and the power, but he was well aware that her idea of social change stopped well before it ever actually mattered. She was a pretty act, a painting to keep behind glass and never look at too closely because of the cracks in the old paint. It bothered him that he was thinking of her in that way. A good son never would have done so.

"I expect you to be early on Monday," his father said, finally deciding to talk to him at least ten minutes after lunch had actually begun.

Chris had barely touched his salad, but the lobster bisque he had next was likely the only thing he actually enjoyed on a menu that was devoid of anything even remotely fried or greasy. He could have killed for a bacon cheeseburger with extra cheese and no pickles anywhere in sight right about then.

Chris nodded to him. "Of course. There is plenty to do."

"Especially when you leave your office like a child in the middle of a discussion. That was a poor performance, and I expect you to behave better than that in the future."

His father gave him a level glare, and Chris looked away.

"Yes. That was a mistake." He should have stayed to listen to what his father said instead of leaving. "I spoke to Misha this morning." He was eager to change the topic and get the focus away from himself for a change. "He says hello."

His father straightened a little at the mention of Misha's name. "When you speak to him again, tell him he is expected to settle down with that woman of his sooner, rather than later. His time to start a family is running out, and as proud as I am of him in his retirement, he should do something better with his life now than traveling around Europe. It is unseemly for someone at his age to be unmarried."

"The ladies are beginning to talk," his mother added.

Chris wanted Misha to come out to them, if only to get them to stop talking about his brother like he had some kind of time bomb attached to his hip that was quickly approaching detonation.

"People are getting married later in life," Chris spoke up. His attempt at covering for his brother only earned him a glare from his father in reprimand, however, and Chris knew not to speak on it again.

Without looking away from him, his father lifted his hand, signaling the nearest man with a shiny silver water pitcher held tightly in his hands.

"More water, sir?" he asked them as he came over to the table.

Chris looked away from his father to see the guy giving him a little smile, and he blushed. He should have known better than to have sex with one of the waiters at his parents' favorite restaurant. It'd been over a year, but Chris was bad at hiding what they'd done as the memories made him darken even further.

"Is he gay? Is that why you're staring at him?" his father demanded, as the man was still standing there with the water tipped over his mother's glass.

Clearly startled, he splashed the water a little and stepped back quickly.

Chris looked between his father and the waiter, whose name might have been Byron or Brian. Maybe Ben. He couldn't really remember. Nodding, he sipped some of the icy water out of his glass and hoped his father would leave it at that. Of course not, though. That would have been asking too much.

With a disgruntled huff, his father rose from the table, nearly colliding with the waiter whose name Chris wished he could remember, because he'd actually been a pretty nice guy for the few minutes Chris had spent on his knees in front of him, and he hated not being able to remember something. Without a word to any of them, his father headed directly to the manager, a man dressed all in black and one of the few people wearing a name tag in the restaurant.

"That man is a faggot!" his father declared, causing a scene and making Chris blush again, but this time with shame. His mother appeared unbothered as she took out her compact and checked her makeup.

Figuring that it was up to him to defuse the situation, Chris got up and walked over to his father as quickly as he could without drawing even more attention to him.

"Dad," he said, laying his hand gently over his father's arm. "People are watching."

"I don't care," his father said, jerking his arm out of Chris's hold. "Let them see what a man does with one of them. He cannot touch my food. I will not have his disease coming near me."

"Dad!" Chris tried again, louder this time. "This is completely inappropriate behavior."

His mom turned around in her seat to face him. "Oh, Chris, honey, come sit back down. Your father is only doing what's right. You know how they spread their filth."

Chris violently shook his head. It was as if he was seeing them both for the first time and hating everything about them. The judgments, the ridicule… he'd put up with it all only to please them. And he'd been doing it for the past thirty-five years without ever once really being heard.

"I'm gay," he snapped at her, far more loudly than he'd meant to. By this time most of the other patrons had been moved to a different section of the restaurant, either to avoid the noise or to keep the owner's most profitable customers from being embarrassed in any way.

His father shook his head at him. "You think you are, and it is by far the most disappointing thing about you."

That was news to Chris, who had always tried to be perfect for his parents, even now. "What else is there?" He was nearly afraid to ask, but some part of him felt like he really needed to know. Was it how long he kept his hair? That he liked getting manicures? What could it have possibly been that made his dad look at him with such disgust right then? As if he couldn't stand to be near Chris for another minute because of how awful he was.

His father simply shook his head. "Go sit back down. This doesn't concern you."

Chris wasn't so sure about that. "Seeing as how I'm gay, and you're upset because a gay person might come within ten feet of your precious, overcooked pork chop, I kind of think it does." It was a tone he never used with his father, but he couldn't have stopped himself right then as the words tumbled out.

His father turned his anger on Chris, which was nothing new for him, but the backbone he currently felt holding him up was. And surprisingly, it felt good.

"You are a disgrace. At least Misha made something of himself. They had an entire ceremony for him. If he'd chosen to be a lawyer instead of some soldier, there would have been no limit to what he could have done. But you, you're a waste. You had such promise, such talent, and you let it all go. You're not a partner at the firm. You aren't trying cases in the national news. No, instead you listen to pathetic people whine about their horrible little lives as they complain about divorcing people they never loved anyway."

The problem was that his father was pretty much spot-on about what he did at the firm. He handled divorces, and a lot of them. They weren't glamorous, but they paid damn well. Apparently he should have been trying to achieve more in the last dozen years he'd been working for his father. Too bad no one ever told him that doing everything he thought his parents had ever wanted for him hadn't actually been good enough.

He took a step back, suddenly needing to put some distance between them. "Actually, you're right. I am a divorce lawyer. But if that doesn't work for you, then I guess I won't be one anymore. Since I'd kind of thought you would have realized that my entire fucking life has always ever been just about pleasing you and Mom. Bran was right." He laughed and had to wipe at his eyes. Shaking, he then loosened the tie that felt like it was strangling him. "Fuck. All these years. And Bran was fucking right. He should get a fucking trophy or some shit for that."

"You won't use that language around your mother," his dad scolded him sharply.

But Chris just laughed and kept moving backward until he ran into a table. Then he walked around that and kept going toward the front door. "Fuck you. And fuck this. And fuck being a lawyer at the prestigious Romanoff firm. Fuck being your disgrace of a son. I quit. That pile of papers on my desk? You can have them. The bitchy people and their whiny mistresses? Take them all. You are welcome to them. I quit. Quit. Quit. Quit."

Damn, that felt good, almost like he was high, and he couldn't stop laughing as he went to his parents' car and helped himself into the backseat. "Take me home, please," he told the driver.

"Are your parents coming too?"

Chris shook his head. "Not this time."

The driver nodded to him, and less than a minute later, Chris was being driven through the crowded streets of Manhattan and back to his apartment. It was good to be home when the driver dropped him off in front of his building. But it was so much better when he opened his front door and found Misha standing there in his living room with his hands clasped behind his back as if he'd been standing at attention and could have continued to stay right like that for as long as he needed to.

"You're here!" Chris said, practically running toward him before he folded his arms around Misha's much bigger body. A lifetime in the Army had made him muscular, and though he could have easily crushed him, Chris was sure, Misha only gave him a light hug.

"Dad called me from the restaurant. Seems you had a breakdown. He's blaming it on you spending too much time with Bran." Misha pulled him over to the couch, where they sat down together.

Chris just grinned. "More like too much time around our dad." He lost some of his smile as he shook his head. "I just snapped back there. Bran's been telling me how awful he is for most of my life, and I think I saw that a little."

Misha shook his head and laid his arm around Chris's shoulders. "I'd prefer not to talk about Bran right now. When we spoke yesterday, you sounded miserable, and that was because of him."

"Actually…." Chris bit his bottom lip and leaned forward on the couch. "That was more my doing."

"Don't you take the blame for him. Not again. He's an idiot, and I'm glad to see you getting some space from him."

Misha sounded angry, and Chris sighed as he turned his head, propped his cheek up on his fist, and looked over at his brother. "Bran, and Samuel too, and maybe even in a way Kaden as well, though probably just for Bran since he and I aren't friends at all, but they were mad at me for doing something pretty bad."

Misha froze and gave him a dark look. "I thought you'd finished being a slut."

If only it was that simple. Chris gave him a weak smile. "I did. That's not what this is about. You see… there's this thing that I do sometimes, and…." He shook his head. After confessing to everyone else that mattered to him, telling Misha about his self-harming behavior should have been easy. But Misha was his big brother and someone Chris had always looked up to. It was hard to know that he'd be forever flawed in Misha's eyes after revealing his darkest secret to him.

"What is it?" Misha asked him, his voice going low, dangerous, like he expected Chris to tell him something awful, like when Bran's abusive ex, Richard, had beaten Chris up the year before.

"I cut myself. It's a self-harming behavior I use as a coping mechanism. I've been doing it since I was a kid and stopped for a long time, but I recently started up again," Chris admitted in the most casual, matter-of-fact way he could manage. He hoped presenting it like that to his brother would make him freak out less. He watched Misha, expecting the worst from him, like he'd gotten from Bran. Shit. Bran. He hadn't even stopped to wonder if Misha would be just like him, if he would throw Chris out of his life too.

He didn't have long to think about that, though, before Misha surprised the hell out of him by wrapping his arm tightly around Chris's shoulders and pulling him close against his side.

"You need to stop that, and I want you in therapy. No arguments. You get your ass in therapy or I'm putting someone on you to make sure you go. They will drag you there if they have to. I've still got some old Army buddies in the area that would help."

Chris smiled and rested his head against his brother's chest. "I'll go to therapy in a while. I have a few things to figure out first. Thanks for not hating me like Bran did."

"Never could hate you, but don't for a minute think I'm not pissed off at you."

That was a fine compromise as far as Chris was concerned. "I quit my job today."

Misha let him go, and Chris sat back up and smoothed his hair away from his forehead.

"I know you did. What are you going to do now?"

"I don't have the slightest idea. Maybe I'll travel for a while, like you did," Chris said with a shrug. Not having a plan, or even the slightest hint of what he was going to be doing even the next day, was a whole new experience for him. In a way it was terrifying, but he was also excited. "Before I do anything, though, I need to go back to the firm and get a picture of Bran and Kaden that's sitting on my desk. The rest of the crap Dad can do whatever with. I can't believe I quit. I've never quit a job in my life. And now I quit the firm? What the hell was I thinking?"

Misha shook his head. "Regretting your choice already?"

Maybe he should have been, but that wasn't really how Chris was feeling right then. "No. Actually, I'm scared out of my mind, but I don't regret what I said or did or how I quit. I guess the only thing is that I wish I'd done it sooner. And I kind of wish that I could call Bran and tell him what happened, except I'm still so damn mad at him."

"Good, let him know you're angry for a while." They shared a smile. "Hey, so, about traveling. Think you could go down to New Zealand for me?"

Chris stiffened. "Why…?"

Misha reached into his shirt and pulled out a long beaded silver chain with one of his dog tags dangling from the bottom. Looking back at his neck, Chris could see he still had another chain on, identical to the one he'd just pulled out, which had to be the other copy.

"I want you to give my dog tag to Trent."

Chris could only stare at him as Misha pulled the chain over his head and took his hand, opened it, and dropped the chain into his palm.

"That's massive," Chris said, wondering what the hell his brother was thinking. "You don't even know him. Not really anyway. You've spent, what? Three days with him? Total?"

Misha laughed and ruffled Chris's hair. "Like you know Samuel all that much more than I know Trent. Give it to him for me."

He didn't think Misha had any idea what he was doing, but when he sounded as serious as he was right then, Chris knew better than to argue. "Why can't you do it?"

He looked a bit sad, or maybe that was just exhaustion on his brother's face.

"Because I have to be in Kuwait tomorrow. Do this for me. I want him to have it."

"I will."

Misha gave him a soft smile and rubbed his back. "Thanks." He got up from the couch. "Stay here for a while. Lay low and don't be stupid. I'll be back in a few hours with the picture."

Chris frowned up at him. "You're going to the office just to get my picture back for me? But I can do that myself. You don't have to."

"You in the same building as Dad sounds like a disaster right now. No, you stay here. Take it easy. Think about what you want to do next after you visit New Zealand for me," Misha said, heading to the door with Chris following him out. They said good-bye, and Chris went into his kitchen to see if he had any soda left.

Misha was right. Chris would have probably gone off on his dad again. Or worse, apologized when he felt no real need to. He felt guilty for what he'd said, especially since he'd done it in front of his mom, but he wanted this to be the one time that he didn't go crawling back to his dad, apologizing and begging for forgiveness for causing a scene and hurting the family.

His behavior had been far from great, but he wasn't sorry. He was ashamed of how his father had acted and couldn't believe he'd come from the two of them. Maybe Samuel had been right. Maybe his family was back in New Zealand and these people were just in his way. While that thought would have been welcome and comforting any other day, while he wasn't speaking to any of them, it just made him miserable.

CHAPTER FIFTEEN

FOR SAMUEL, the next few hours were a blur—booking his ticket, packing, and informing his staff of his leaving, how long he would be away, and what he required of them in his absence. The drive to the airport took him just over an hour, and he found himself checked in and standing in queue to board before the lack of sleep and constant worry became tangible.

As his turn came for the gate attendant to check his ticket, her smile faltered when she focused on his face. "Are you all right, sir?"

Samuel tried his best to smile back to reassure her. "I'm fine, just extremely tired."

She scanned his face, and he was damn sure the crew on board would be notified about the big man who could possibly be hungover, drunk, or drugged. He must look pretty bad.

"Oh, I'm sorry. I hope you get time to rest during your flight."

She handed back his ticket and ushered him through. He walked through the loading bridge, and another attendant guided him in the direction of his window seat.

He sighed in relief when the Airbus started moving twenty minutes later and he saw the middle spot between him and the aisle seat was empty. No elbows to contend with for space or someone falling asleep on his shoulder by accident. A good thing, because other than eating his meals, he intended to sleep the whole way.

Once airborne, he put the pillow between his head and the wall to sleep. The crew woke him up half an hour before landing to eat his dinner, which he almost inhaled he was so hungry. They stopped over in Bangkok, and he wandered around in the airport for four hours and bought a few silly gifts for his friends. Kaden would have a beer mug with massive boobs, and he couldn't resist buying two ankle bracelets with fifteen copper bells each for Bran to do his lap dances with. He looked around for the perfect gift for Trent and settled on a container with a big red warning that said "May attract unwanted amorous attention from male elephants. Do not use in zoos, circuses, or the jungle," and had the title *Elephant Love Juice* scrawled in flowing script across the front of the bottle.

He found himself staring at jewelry through a glass cabinet and couldn't stop thinking he wanted to get Chris something. Their future looked very unsure right now, but even if they never got together, he would still want Chris to have it, because it would suit him.

There were plenty of studs, lots of nipple jewelry, and even some nose piercings, but he couldn't imagine any of those looking good on Chris. Oh, he'd look good wearing them; of that Samuel had no doubt. But they wouldn't be the best for him. He was nearly ready to give up when he spotted a simple silver ring with a ball on it that was a belly piercing. It wasn't very big, only about the width of his thumb, if that. And it was plain too, maybe too much so for Chris. But even when he looked away to consider the other options before him, Samuel kept coming back to that little circle of silver. Which was crazy, because Chris didn't even have a piercing there, but Samuel thought maybe getting it would inspire Chris to have it done.

In the end he picked that ring up and hoped Chris would like it. He didn't like Misha at the moment so he left his gift for another time when he had time to get over the mess of things first. With his purchases safely stored in his hand luggage, he had a cup of much needed coffee and some noodle dish with a pale meat in it, which he was too scared to ask about, before wandering back toward the boarding gate for his next flight to Dallas.

He was able to sleep much of that flight as well, which was fortunate, he thought, because it was the longest of his trip. Being back in America and knowing he was so close to seeing Chris again gave him some energy as he sat in the Dallas airport and waited for his next flight, along with dozens of people in cowboy hats and teenagers talking about spring break coming up next month.

He took out his phone and texted Misha. *I'm in Dallas.*

The return text was almost immediate. *Send me your flight details. I'll pick you up at JFK.*

Will Chris be with you? Samuel texted back. He hoped so, since that would be that much sooner that he could see him. His heart started racing at just the thought of spending time with him again. He had a lot to apologize for and hoped Chris would take the time to listen to him.

Not when I pick you up. You'll see him after. We need to talk first.

That sounded ominous, and Samuel disliked when people said that, as it put him on edge. *You and I? About what?* Samuel asked him.

How to keep my little brother from killing himself someday.

Samuel imagined Misha as angry as he'd felt the moment he'd learned that Chris was hurting himself and shook his head, knowing that must have been a scary sight. He and Misha were about the same size, and he guessed they had some of the same martial arts training. What made Misha dangerous, though, was how much he cared about his brother. He was good to have on their side, Samuel knew.

I hope we can come up with something, Samuel texted back.

He didn't receive another text from Misha before he had to turn his phone off on the plane, but he still had a few seconds as the flight attendants did last checks, so he sent off a quick text to Chris, saying, *Take care of you.* He'd said the same thing to him when Chris had left Montana, and even if he didn't respond to the text, Samuel hoped Chris at least read it and knew someone cared about him.

JFK airport in New York was a busy nightmare. At least it was to him. There were people everywhere, all of them talking quickly and moving even faster, seeming determined to run him over with their matching luggage. And he only wanted out of it all. He hadn't been able to sleep on the flight over from Dallas to New York, too excited to be in the same city as Chris again, and that adrenaline kept him going until he found Misha standing in front of a sleek black sports car in the passenger pickup area.

"Hi," Samuel said, coming up to him.

Misha gave him a nod and looked him over in his shorts and T-shirt. "You knew we were having winter here, didn't you?"

"This was more comfortable. I have warmer clothes to change into if I need to," Samuel explained. He didn't feel all that cold standing there, though most of the wind must have been blocked by the building, judging by how wildly the American flags were flying.

Shrugging, Misha moved away from the car. "Get in. We're going to the office first."

That was a surprise to Samuel. "We are? Why?" he asked as he got into the car and instantly sank into the heated leather seats with a soft sigh. It was a rental. He could see the sticker in the window and was glad Misha seemed to have a taste for upgrades.

Misha glanced at him sideways before pulling into traffic and getting them away from the airport. "I'm picking up a picture from his desk for him. I thought it would be better for me to go there instead of him, after what happened at lunch."

"What happened? Is he okay?" Samuel asked him as Misha drove along the highway. He tried focusing on everything around him, the water, the high buildings, of which New Zealand had none, but the only thing, the only person, he wanted to see was Chris.

Nodding, Misha changed lanes to get around a particularly slow car. The car's engine was a smooth purr that only something excessively expensive could have pulled off as Misha raced it down the highway.

"After how you two were in Montana, I'm surprised he hasn't said anything to you about it. But now that I know he was hurting himself, I can see why you would all be so angry with him. Not that I believe any of you helped him much from what little he's told me."

He got back into his original lane and then turned off the highway a minute or two later, pulling onto a residential street. "At lunch, though, he quit his job at the firm. Apparently it was a big scene, and our dad thought he was having a breakdown. I have him lying low in his apartment right now, hoping that keeps him out of trouble. He has snacks, movies, and cable, which should keep him entertained until we get there."

Samuel snorted a laugh. "If you think that will keep Chris out of trouble, you don't know your brother very well."

Misha laughed as well. "Maybe not. But have you ever seen him in the snow? He detests this stuff. Can't even be made to go get a good cup of coffee if there's more than half an inch on the ground. I bet he's either laid out on his couch watching some ridiculous movie or neck deep in his building's hot tub." Misha's smile dimmed a little. "Thanks for coming out. Now that I know why you were all upset with him, I'm glad you're here to watch him. I have to leave to go back in a few hours, and I'd hate to do that, knowing what I do now about what he's going through."

Samuel frowned. "When you left Montana, we assumed you would be around to keep a close eye on him, and once you took the jobs, Chris didn't let us know he was on a downward spiral emotionally with no support. So he left it very late to get in touch and ask for help. I'm scared at this point to leave him alone."

Misha paled considerably as he stopped the car in front of a brick office building on a busy, narrow street. "I didn't know that's when he started. He only briefly mentioned it to me. I told him not to do it again and that he needed to get into therapy. Then I had some things to do before I came to get you. That's been my afternoon with him so far, and that's not okay. I'll stop after the next few jobs. I have him going to New Zealand soon, so that should help him some. And not having our dad around him will be good for him too, I'm sure. How long are you able to stay? Assuming, of course, that he lets you near him at all."

"Why would he be going to New Zealand? I thought he would stay far away from there with the way things ended between us all. And I can only stay a week, sorry. My staff is running the farm without me right now, but I will have to go back to give them a break soon." Samuel stared out at the snowflakes drifting down to the ground. It all looked so beautiful, but wet and cold too.

"I have him taking something to Trent for me. You don't need to know more than that. And a week should be fine. I'll make sure he's down there not long after you. It'll be a nice vacation from the snow and cold for him. Why he never moved somewhere warmer is beyond me. He's never lived outside of Manhattan." Misha shook his head and killed the engine. "This shouldn't take more than a minute or two, I hope. Do you want to stay in the car, or do you want to see where Chris used to work?"

Samuel dug through his bag by his feet, pulled out a hooded puffer jacket, and put it on before looking at Misha. "Actually, I would love to meet your father."

Misha stared at him, then started to chuckle. "No, you really wouldn't. But let's go anyway." He got out of the car and headed over to the sidewalk, stopping there as if waiting for Samuel to join him, which he did.

Misha led the way, with Samuel following closely behind him, as they entered the building and headed directly for the stairs without stopping at the front desk, where a receptionist sat, eyeing them warily. They went to the second floor. Then Misha's pace slowed as he paused by each door, reading it, until he came to the one with Chris's name on it.

"I haven't been in this building in over a year. No reason to." He opened the door, which was surprisingly unlocked, and Samuel followed him in.

The office itself was neat, with plaques and degrees hung up on three of the walls. On the last wall, a heavy bookshelf sat, filled with law books and encyclopedias.

"So, this is where Chris has spent most of his life over the past ten years." Misha went to the only messy place in the office, the large desk in the middle of the room, which was covered with piles of manila folders.

Samuel took his time and absorbed everything he saw—the awards and qualifications on the walls, the neatness, the order, and the shitload of files on the desk. One thing was clear. The only orderly part of Chris's life had been in here, because his emotions and personal life had been like a storm. But when Samuel looked over at the corner of the workspace, he saw what mattered most to Chris—his friends and real family. There stood a framed photograph of Chris and Bran, taken during one of their many vacations together, with the ocean behind them and their skins tanned and dusted with sand. Another picture beside it was of Misha in uniform, giving Chris a crooked smile as he waved and prepared to walk off with an army duffle bag in his hand. A newer memory showed Kaden and Bran with their cheeks squished together and pulling tongues at the camera.

There was one picture, though, that really caught his eye, and it was of himself, taken while in Montana. Somehow Chris had managed to get a picture of him sweaty, dirty, and with his shirt sticking to his chest and stomach, the milking shed in the background. Samuel simply shook his head as he picked up the framed photograph and handed it to Misha as he was collecting the others.

"It feels a little weird being in here without him. Like I'm prying into his life," Misha confided.

"This wasn't his life. How a person with such a caring heart could've survived here for so long is beyond me. I think the only thing he wants in here are these and maybe those," he said as he pointed at the degrees and plaques.

Misha grabbed them down too, and his arms were overfilled by the time he was done. Fortunately there was an empty box that computer paper had come in, and he placed the things Samuel thought were most important to Chris in the box with care.

"Come on, then. You can meet Dad before I take you to see Chris. I'm fairly certain they'll both be pretty shocked to see you."

Carrying the box with both hands, Misha led Samuel back out of the office to the other end of the hall, where he stopped at a closed door. "He's in there. Door's closed, which means he might be busy, but if you knock—"

The door opened, and Misha stepped back so quickly that Samuel had to move out of the way to avoid being run over.

"Oh. It's you," the man Samuel assumed to be their dad said as he looked them both over. "Where's that useless brother of yours?"

Samuel couldn't get over how much like his father Chris looked. They had many features in common, but when Samuel looked into his eyes, he saw how different they really were. This man had a hard, unfeeling, unyielding gaze, and Samuel guessed it was part of being a successful lawyer, but Chris was excellent at his job, and his eyes were warm and filled with mischief. The moment the smaller man's words sunk in, Samuel felt his hands start to shake, and by the ticking muscle in Misha's jaw, the big man beside him was fast getting upset too.

"He's not here," Misha bit out.

"I can see that, you idiot. Get his worthless ass in a car and get him here. It shouldn't be that hard for you. And you." Pavel turned his attention to Samuel. "Unless you have an appointment, I'm a very busy man and don't have time for whatever it is you need right now. One of the many other lawyers that work for me would surely take whatever case you think you have."

Misha looked around nervously. "Dad, can we please take this into your office before we cause another Romanoff scene in one day?"

Pavel sighed, but he did step back to let them both into his office. "Am I to assume that you're a friend of Misha's, then? An old Army buddy wanting to see where he comes from? Good lines, I'll tell you that. Filthy rich good lines." He shut the door behind them both. "Now, talk."

Samuel glared at the man in disgust. "Actually, I'm Chris's friend, and you're spot-on to say your lines are filthy. No, you are the filth."

Misha openly stared at him while Pavel shook his head.

"You're one of those faggots, aren't you? What's my son giving you in exchange for coming down here for him? Misha, I thought you knew better than to bring their kind here. I only tolerate the one, barely, because of his money. This one certainly doesn't have that going for him.

Now, both of you, out of my office. And Misha, don't come back here without your brother."

Between one moment and the next, Samuel lost his temper. He saw the light, a red flash, and when he next looked around, he had Pavel pinned to the wall with his forearm on his Adam's apple with no idea when he'd moved.

"Listen, asshole. How your two sons managed to listen to the drivel from your conceited mouth their whole lives and not kill you is a mystery to me. Now you shut up, and I'll speak."

When Pavel struggled to try to dislodge him, Samuel used his forefinger and thumb on a pressure point in the man's neck. He stopped struggling immediately, and his eyes bulged, his face turning a sickly purple before Samuel let up on the grip of his fingers.

"You can make this difficult or spare yourself heaps of pain or possible paralysis. Up to you." Samuel waited for the barely there nod from the bastard before he continued.

"Your son, Chris, quit today by his choice. If it is up to me, he will never set foot in this building again. Ever. And if you or your useless wife try to threaten him, persuade him, humiliate him, or use any of your slimy methods you employ, I will personally make sure you will never be able to walk again. I know of over a hundred ways to do that, and if they won't suffice, the Maori tribe I come from are known for their very painful tactics of emasculation. Either way, you will lose." Samuel glanced at the quiet Misha a few steps to his left. He had no color left in his face, but Samuel would deal with that later.

"Help me…," Pavel hissed out, his gaze going to Misha pleadingly.

But Misha only shook his head. "What Sam just said, every last word of it, is something I've been wanting to say to you since I was thirteen. I've hated you most of my life, but luckily I had my mom to keep me away from you for the most part. I even had a plan and a gun I wanted to use on you, the first time I saw you spit on a gay man at a pride parade. I was thirteen, and I knew I was gay, and there was nothing I could do about it because I was so damn scared of you."

He took a deep breath. "Chris is so much braver, so much stronger, than I ever was. He had the guts to come out to you, and you've been calling him a faggot ever since. So no, Dad, I'm not going to stop Samuel. If he kills you right here, then at least Chris will be permanently free of you. Though for Chris, I'd rather he didn't. Visiting Samuel in jail would scare him, and I don't want to see him worry or hurt ever again. What is your problem, anyway? Chris only ever wanted to make you and his mom happy. That's it. He's like a puppy, only wanting to please everyone else. I've never once seen him do a single selfish thing. And you have the nerve to call him useless? And worthless? Like you're some kind of a saint? Thank God I didn't grow up with you over my head all the time. Maybe then I'd be just as screwed up as Chris."

Samuel removed his arm from Pavel's throat but kept him in place by planting his hand over his sternum, hard.

"Chris is more of a man than you will ever be. You use your status, money, and power to hurt and destroy other people. Instead of using all you have for good, you've become rotten from the inside out and lost both your children. What do you have to be so proud of? If Chris would have me, some day in the future, I would happily give him my name so your name could be wiped out in his lineage. Same-sex marriages are legal in my country, so there's nothing you can do about it." Samuel spat the last words out in disgust.

Pavel coughed hoarsely. "You two sicken me. I no longer have sons, and neither of you are welcome near me again. You've been erased from my life. Don't ever come to me asking for anything ever again." He fixed his gaze on Samuel. "And as for you, I hope you wither and die from the filth that he is. You want him, he's yours. I certainly will make no more claim to him if this is who he calls his friends. A violent savage and a man who wanted to kill his own father. You both have ten seconds to get out of my office before I start yelling for the police. Then we'll see how long you last in prison after the judge hears about how you came in and attacked me, unprovoked, in my own office."

The old man didn't see it coming, but Samuel had his testicles in a death grip in two seconds flat. Pavel coughed and gasped in pain.

"Before you have time to yell for the cops, these two raisins will be stuffed down your throat and you'll make no sound, because you'll choke to death on your own balls. And I'll tie your tubes into tiny bows for them to find. Just for the record, they won't claim you, and I and Chris's other savage friends from down south have our own fucking money, dickhead."

Samuel pushed away from the man but not before giving his sac an extra twist and then letting go. Pavel crumpled to the carpet and folded his legs like a girl as he mewled in pain.

"You remember your own words. I'm a violent, savage man, so stay away from Chris, me, and my friends. I have contacts who would smile as they take you out and bury you in a desert where no one will ever find your remains." Samuel shook with suppressed violent anger. "Misha, I'm done here, because if I look at his sorry ass any longer, I will break his neck. I'll see you outside." He opened the sandblasted glass door and let himself out into the hallway.

Misha was silent until they were out of the building. "So, how long have you been wanting to do that?" Misha asked him with a shaky smile.

Samuel's adrenaline-infused blood still raced through his veins, and he concentrated on his breathing to calm him down. "Months." He welcomed the cold blast of air as they stepped out of the building onto the pavement. So far he heard no sirens in the vicinity, so he guessed Pavel took his advice and decided against calling the cops on them.

Misha tucked Chris's things safely into the backseat, then got in the car, and Samuel was quick to follow him. "I'm glad you said what needed to be said. What I couldn't. Family is…. Growing up with him, even though I didn't spend a lot of time with him and my mom divorced him early, the one thing that stuck with me that he would always say is how important family is. But it's not in the way that I think other people consider family to be. For Pavel, it seemed like family was all there was, like if you weren't part of it, then there was nothing else for you out there. Whenever I've thought about going against him, I always get sick to my stomach and remember his words. I guess it took someone he had no power over to really put him in his place."

"My family has always been Kaden's and Trent's family, because my own birth parents loved partying and drugs more than their son," Samuel said gruffly, his emotions in turmoil because he wanted to see Chris right then.

Misha nodded but said nothing to what Samuel had revealed as he wound through the busy, snow-covered streets with ease. "Don't tell Chris what you did. I don't want him being worried about Pavel and wondering if he's okay. Pavel doesn't deserve that, and Chris doesn't need it. He worries about everyone else too damn much as it is."

"What are we stopping for here?" Samuel asked as Misha pulled into a drive-through coffee shop.

Misha looked over at him. "I need something sweet after all that. What would you like? My treat. I'm getting Chris something too."

"A cappuccino would be great, thanks." He hadn't had a cup since Bangkok, and he needed it to warm him up. Pavel's harshness had left him cold to his bones.

Misha quickly placed the order, adding a chai and a hot chocolate with peppermint. "The hot chocolate is for Chris. You ever want to get on his good side, that's how you do it," he said as he pushed the car forward.

As they sat in the car together, Misha drummed his fingers on the top of the steering wheel, as if he was as anxious to get back to Chris as Samuel was. "Did you mean what you said about wanting to marry him? Because you know he doesn't believe in marriage, right? He was, is, a divorce attorney. So if that's really something you're set on, you'll likely be in for an uphill battle."

Samuel thought about it for a minute. "Maybe he would be opposed initially, but I believe once he's far removed from his controlling parents and the superficial marriages he witnesses through his job, he may start believing in it again."

Misha paid for the drinks and handed Samuel his coffee before getting back on the road. "I hope so. I mean it. As far as a brother-in-law goes, you'd be a good choice for him. I'd like to see you two work out. Assuming he's actually willing to speak to you, but I guess we'll see in a minute or two. This is his apartment building." Misha found a parking space in front then backed the car in.

Samuel didn't know if Chris would see him either, so he stayed quiet as he followed Misha, his heart starting to race the closer they got to Chris.

CHAPTER SIXTEEN

CHRIS HEARD the front door open and smiled, knowing Misha was the only one, aside from Bran, who had a key to his apartment. And Bran wouldn't be coming to see him, not after their fight.

"There's pizza and Thai in the fridge. I couldn't decide, so I got both delivered. Help yourself. I'll be out in a second." As soon as he figured out if the swimming briefs he'd found buried at the bottom of a drawer covered enough of his ass to wear them to the hot tub. With a shrug he figured they were good enough. He had trunks, but he felt like being slightly sexier than that. He'd have to order something in between soon, though, because his trunks were completely unsexy, and these were barely on the good side of obscene. Oh well, it wasn't like anyone would really be looking when he was under the water.

"Hey," he said, coming out of his bedroom, his bare feet slapping on the polished hardwood floor that flowed throughout his apartment. "Come hang out in the hot tub with me, will you?" Chris asked him, then stopped cold as he came around the corner and saw Misha and Samuel standing in his kitchen. "Hi." He shot a look to Misha. He had to have been behind this somehow. Chris was sure of it.

"Change into something else. Right now," Misha demanded.

Okay, so maybe the briefs showed off a little more than he'd thought. But they looked damn good on him, and Misha didn't get to tell him how to dress. Especially not when he'd apparently brought Samuel back with him. It was gratifying to feel Samuel's gaze on him as he came forward, though, and even angry at him, Chris couldn't deny the attraction he felt to him.

"Did you get the picture from my office?" he asked Misha, ignoring his demand.

Misha nodded and pushed a box toward him. Chris picked through the things his brother had grabbed for him and, once he'd found the picture of Bran and Kaden together, took it out and walked it over to its new place on his mantel.

"Chris, you're practically naked. Go put on some clothes," Misha tried again. "And I'm not even going to tell you about your tattoo, which apparently you're trying to show off. I should have been blessed with an ugly brother. Then I wouldn't have to worry about you so damn much."

But he wasn't having it. "I'm going to the hot tub in a bit. Now, Samuel, why are you in my kitchen? And, side note, is that peppermint I smell?" Misha pushed a drink across the counter toward him, and Chris was careful not to get too close to Samuel as he moved to take it from Misha. As soon as he had it in his hands, he jumped back just as quickly.

Samuel stared at Chris when he shied away. What did the man expect—that he'd run back into his arms after what they had all said about him in Thames? Not likely. Misha's phone rang, and he walked away to deal with it, taking his drink with him. Chris was left alone with Samuel, and he was at a loss for what to say.

"In case it wasn't clear, I was avoiding your texts," Chris said, hating that he felt like retreating from Samuel when he was in his own home. He should not feel that cornered, that trapped somewhere that had always been safe to him. It still was, only Samuel was now standing in his kitchen and part of Chris never wanted him to leave. The other wanted to throw him out on his ass.

Samuel swallowed some of his coffee before placing it on the bench. He stepped toward Chris, but when Chris retreated, he stopped. "Chris, I had hoped we'd have some time alone to talk, but I need to get this out. I'm sorry for what happened. Not necessarily what I said, because many of those things were true, but because I didn't find a better way or opportunity to say them. We came at you all at once and pushed you away instead of supporting you. Bran is a mess. He tried to call you, minutes after you left, and Trent crapped on our heads for what we did to you. He's left messages upon messages, but you never responded, and it's driving him out of his mind with worry."

"I thought he'd just want to yell at me again," Chris quietly admitted. Frowning, he took a good look at Samuel. "Here, sit down on the couch. You look ready to fall over. I'll call him back, and if he's as worried as you say and not being an ass, I'll talk to him instead of just hanging up on him. Fair enough?"

"That's all I'm asking. Because Kaden told me he's not even sleeping and eating properly. He feels horrible for threatening you like he did, because that's all it was. Empty threats. Your friendship is far more important than this spat."

"With how hot Kaden is, I'm not surprised Bran isn't getting a full night's sleep. And I'm sure he's getting plenty of liquid protein," he joked, just as he would have with Bran. And instead of cheering him up, it only made him hurt. "I'm pissed at you, but I do understand what you were trying to do. I don't like how you did it, but I get what you were thinking. Sit. I'll call him." He nodded as Samuel took a seat on his couch, looking ridiculously good on it, and went to where he'd left his phone on the counter. When he glanced back at Samuel, Chris found him watching him too, and he leaned over a little more to tease him as he dialed.

"Hey. I'm glad you called. I missed you," Bran said before the first ring had even finished.

Chris tried not to think about how good it felt to be talking to him again. "First of all, I don't forgive you. And I'm so fucking pissed at you right now. But I wanted to say hi, I love you, and I'll see you in New Zealand in a bit. I need to do a favor for Misha."

For a long time, Bran didn't say anything. "I'm sorry. I didn't mean it."

Chris closed his eyes and tried not to scream at Bran, but also not to cry on the phone with him either. Both of those could wait until he was back there. "You did, though. I need to go. I'll see you later. Bye." He hung up before Bran could say anything else and left his phone on the counter as he came back to sit on the couch near Samuel. "Happy now?" he asked Samuel, a little bitterly.

"It wasn't to make me happy. It was necessary for you two to know you're okay. Knowing you have Bran means so much to you. You can have a go at me all you like, because I deserve it. Anything else you want to say?"

Samuel sat back, and for the first time, Chris noticed the lines of exhaustion all over his face.

There was plenty to say, but having Samuel that close to him, and for some reason not being on his lap, was more of an issue than how much he wanted to yell at Samuel for his stupidity back in New Zealand.

"I'll yell at you later. Promise. How long are you staying? I'd like you to stay here while you're in Manhattan. You can sleep on the bed. I'll take the couch. You look like you need a nap, and you're welcome to go take one." He shrugged, done saying what he'd wanted to as he pulled one of his knees up to his chest. Smiling, he saw Samuel watch that movement and let his gaze roam over him, and Chris knew he had no intention of changing out of the briefs anytime soon.

It was much more fun to know that Samuel wanted him, even though Chris had no intention of going back to the place they were at before they all ganged up on him. He needed time and space to figure out how he felt about what had happened once his anger went away. Right now it was still a burning, gaping hole in his gut that festered and bled each time he thought about Bran.

He wasn't as angry at Samuel, but he wasn't ready to just say it was all okay and they could move on and try to be together again either. He'd been hurt, and he felt betrayed. More than that, though, it was hard for him to admit that he'd been wrong, which he was starting to understand. His father hadn't been a good man, and Chris shouldn't have blindly followed him along. He was ashamed of his own behavior and felt humiliated over the fact that everyone else had been able to see his father for who he was first.

Chris had become so lost in his own thoughts that he hadn't realized Samuel had drifted off to sleep. He looked strong and powerful even while resting, and Chris didn't have the heart or the nerve to wake him as he got up from the couch as quietly as he could manage and went in search of Misha.

He found his brother in the bedroom, which wasn't strange since it was only a one-bedroom apartment and there was nowhere else to take a private call. "Hey," Chris said, keeping his voice soft as he came into the bedroom. "Samuel fell asleep on the couch. Everything okay?" He wanted to ask Misha why he'd somehow orchestrated Samuel coming to Manhattan and what in the hell his point in doing so had been, but those questions died with the worry he could clearly see cutting into Misha's face.

Misha slowly shook his head, and they sat together on the edge of Chris's bed. "I need to leave again, which I knew, but it seems we're doing something pretty heavy this time around. I can't give you details, so please don't ask, but it's important work."

"I'm sure it is. You wouldn't put yourself in danger for anything less." Chris knew his brother, and Misha wasn't some thrill-seeking adrenaline junkie with no sense of self-preservation. What he was, though, was a man who did the right thing when it needed to be done, and Chris was okay with that. Sometimes a situation could be worked out with words, sometimes not. He worried about Misha, but he wasn't about to wrap himself around one of Misha's legs and beg him not to go. "Shoot the bad guys before they shoot you. I mean it. Don't let the last thing you ever give to Trent be your dog tag. That's too fucked up for words."

Misha gave him a crooked smile. "Deal. But I do have to go. And for the love of God, will you please put on some pants?"

Chris laughed, then quickly covered his mouth, hoping he hadn't woken Samuel up with the sound. "I'm going down to the hot tub right now."

Misha didn't look pacified. "And Samuel?"

"He can nap. No reason to wake him when I'm just going to be up to my neck in hot bubbling water." Chris smiled. The hot tub was his favorite thing about living in the building, and he absolutely could not wait to indulge in it, especially since it had a window where he could watch the snow coming down as he relaxed.

"No. I mean what are you going to do with him now that he's here? Planning to throw him into a hotel until he quietly goes away, or what?" Misha asked.

Chris hadn't planned on that at all. "He'll stay here, with me. We'll figure it out." He shrugged, not really having anything definite in mind. Without a job to go to, there wasn't any sort of plan for the week in his mind, except for eating some junk food and sleeping in as long as he could each morning. It would be like his first break in college with Bran, when the most entertaining thing they did was play video games and throw popcorn at each other. That had been before they'd discovered the wonderful combination of alcohol, older men, and sex.

"I need you to promise to let someone know if you're going to be cutting yourself again," Misha said, his voice soft despite the ice running through his words.

Chris swallowed thickly and gave his brother a nod. "I will. Thank you for not just assuming I can turn this off like a light. I wish I could. I haven't cut today, but that doesn't mean I won't tomorrow."

"I figured it was something like that. I only want you safe. You have friends. Let them help you." Misha gave him a sideways hug before he got off the bed. "Come on. Show me out."

Chris knew he was right and intended to talk to Samuel if anything changed for him from his current state. Bran wasn't his go-to, not right now, but he was pretty sure that Samuel would listen to him and might not yell at him this time. If he could talk about what he was feeling, or if he could have some kind of distraction when his emotions and the stress got to be too much for him, then maybe he could get through the height of the need until it naturally tapered off.

There had been times, especially in meetings with his dad, that he couldn't cut on himself right when he became upset and felt most like he needed to. And the urge eventually lessened to a more manageable degree, so he knew it was possible. It was usually a tense couple of minutes where he shook and wanted to claw at his skin to lessen the frustration and hurt, but it could be done if he couldn't help himself get through it any other way.

As Misha gathered up the few things he'd brought with him, Chris found a notepad and a pen to write Samuel a quick note. He left them both by Samuel's left hand, which was on the couch, and hoped Samuel saw them before he started to wonder where Chris had gone. The building had towels down by the hot tub for them, so he didn't bother bringing any with him, only his keys and phone, as he met Misha at the door and they headed down the stairs together.

Hugging Misha at the front door to his apartment building was hard, because it meant that Misha would be leaving and he wouldn't be seeing him again for a while, and with him being places Chris would be afraid to step foot in, he couldn't help being constantly worried about his brother.

"Be safe," Chris told him.

Misha chuckled and ruffled his hair. "I'm more worried about you. Go soak and relax. Be nice to Samuel, don't stay up too late, and eat something healthy once in a while."

Chris snorted, then backed up so Misha could go and not hit him with the door. "See you."

"Tell me when you're in New Zealand and if Trent likes my gift."

"I will," Chris promised.

Misha gave him a wave, and Chris stood by the doorway, silently watching him, until Misha started driving away. When he could no longer see the beautiful black car Misha had rented, Chris headed into the small hot tub room, grabbed a towel from the metal shelf, and put his things on it a few feet from the hot tub so they wouldn't be splashed, but close enough that he could still reach them if he got a call.

Seconds after getting in, he was up to his chin in the hot water and had his eyes closed as he enjoyed the bliss. The hot tub room was perfectly empty this time of the evening, and in a few hours, it would be off limits to anyone under eighteen. He hadn't brought any bottled water down with him, so he couldn't really stay hydrated and cool himself off, but he didn't plan to be down there too long anyway.

Chris rolled his head to the side and opened his eyes. He smiled softly as he watched the snowflakes glitter as they were caught in the streetlamps outside. Winter in New York City could be exceptionally beautiful, as long as he didn't have to go out in it.

CHAPTER SEVENTEEN

SAMUEL DIDN'T know how long he slept, but it surprised the hell out of him that he'd fallen asleep on Chris like that. Looking around, he listened but couldn't hear anyone moving around in the apartment. Then he saw the note next to him.

In the hot tub. 1st floor, clear glass door.

A hot tub of any kind sounded amazing to him right then, and he went in search of his luggage to get out a towel and a pair of shorts appropriate for joining Chris. He kept a T-shirt on as he made his way down to the floor that housed the tub. He stopped in front of the door, looked in, and saw Chris deep under the bubbling water while he stared out the window at the snowy night. With the now longer tendrils of wet hair sticking to his neck and his skin flushed from the heat, Chris looked so tempting to him right then. Drawn to Chris by some seemingly irresistible force, Samuel pushed the door open to a room full of steam and heat.

"Stop staring and get in here," Chris called to him.

Samuel hadn't even thought his eyes were open, but as the door closed on its own behind him, Chris turned his head and gave him a soft, sleepy smile. "Hey. Glad you could join me. Sleepyhead."

"Well, it's snowing outside, and what's a better way to stay warm than this?" He pulled his T-shirt over his head and placed it with his towel close by before climbing into the warm water. He sighed in bliss as he took a seat opposite Chris and allowed his muscles to relax.

He watched as Chris slowly closed his eyes again.

"You're never allowed to wear a shirt again. I'm outlawing it. Fuck, you're beautiful."

He was flirting, clearly, but since Chris didn't make a move to come closer to him, Samuel was fairly certain he didn't actually mean what he was saying.

"Beauty is in the eye of the beholder and all that. To some people, I'd be too big or whatever, and someone like you would be considered stunning. Which you are. To me." Flirting was harder than he thought, but he meant every word he said about Chris.

Chris opened his eyes and tilted his chin toward Samuel. "The only people who wouldn't want you are lesbians. Everyone else will have their eyes clawed out by me if they stare at you. My neighbor is going to drool just as hard as Aaron did back at Renegade. I think you might like her. She's nice, has a kid that isn't obnoxious. By the way, though, you fell asleep before you told me how long you'd be staying here."

"My workers gave me a week off." Samuel smiled as he said it so Chris would know he joked about being allowed time away.

Samuel couldn't help staring at him as Chris stood up, long rivers of water running down his chest and over his flat stomach. He didn't have defined abs, not like Samuel himself did, and maybe that difference added to his beauty. Or maybe it had something to do with the sexy, tempting smile Chris gave him as he slid himself into Samuel's lap and laid his forearms over Samuel's shoulders.

"A whole week, huh? Anything you've ever wanted to do in New York that we can take off your bucket list? Assuming I don't have to stand in the snow for it, of course."

Samuel couldn't get over how right Chris felt in his lap, and he quickly wrapped his arms around Chris's waist to keep him in place. He was so content with Chris around him and didn't feel like talking about New York right then.

"Let's talk about that tomorrow. Can we just enjoy each other's company for now, and after what happened back home, I haven't slept much. I just want to chill out with you. Okay?" Samuel tightened his grip on Chris's hips and pulled him forward, making their groins touch.

He felt Chris shiver as he leaned forward and rested his forehead against Samuel's shoulder.

"Two things. First, not sure if Misha told you or not, but I quit my job today. It was pretty much a nuclear war zone in public with my dad. Not great. So I'm pretty worn out too. Second, and I can't believe I'm about to say this when you're holding me like you are, but I don't think we should have sex this week. And don't you dare push me off your lap because I said that. I will bite you, and not in the sexy way either."

Samuel groaned and let his head rest back onto the side of the bath. "Misha told me about you quitting. I'm really proud of you for doing that, because I believe that place was toxic to you. May I ask why you've decided no sex for us for another week?"

Chris wouldn't look at him, which bothered Samuel, but he wasn't about to start demanding anything of Chris. Not again so soon after what had happened back home.

"You said you didn't want to come home to a dead boyfriend, and you deserve not to have to worry about that kind of thing. Quitting felt good, but I'm in no way cured. You like to have sex with people you're actually with, and I don't want to be someone you feel like you have to call and check on every few minutes to make sure I'm still alive. So, as much as I want you, I don't want you to be with me right now. If that makes any sense. I don't want you with anyone else, though, either, in case you were starting to get any ideas. I'm a selfish bastard like that."

"Well, that's perfect, then, because I'm the same way. What's mine is mine, and with my head full of you, there is no space for anyone else at the moment anyway," Samuel teased him.

"What do you need from me to have something together?" Chris asked as Samuel slid him a little closer. The warm water bubbling around him felt amazing. "I'd want to be at a place where you don't have to worry about me all the time. I can't feel guilty for making you call me because you're afraid I've been cutting myself, rather than simply wanting to talk to me."

Samuel thought about it carefully before deciding on an answer. "I would like for you to throw away your kit, but I also don't understand what you're going through, so I may be completely unrealistic."

He smiled as Chris gently kissed the side of his neck.

"No more cutting at all, then. What about living on different sides of the planet?"

Samuel grinned now. "Well, seeing as you no longer have a job, you may soon have no place to live, so how about coming back home with me?"

Chris snorted like he thought Samuel had been joking, only Samuel hadn't been, so seeing the mirth in Chris's eyes put a damper on his good mood.

"And what? Come be a dairy farmer with you? No thanks. I don't get dirty unless it's with sex."

Samuel felt so relaxed. "Mmmm, sex is a brilliant way to get dirty. And no, you don't have to milk cows with me. You have amazing qualifications, which would be valued and recognized all over the world, so you can do anything you like."

"As long as I'm not cutting anymore." Chris sighed, and Samuel held him a little tighter. "The stupid part is that I should be done with this. I was fine for an entire decade. I don't need a babysitter. At least I shouldn't. And I don't want you to be that for me. I want you so damn much, but not like this. I don't even know if it's possible for me to cope at this point, since I've been cutting or using other people to help with that for so long."

He stroked his hands down Chris's warm back in comfort. "You will be fine, and I think you're stronger than you think. As soon as you're away from all the voices who made you doubt yourself, your head will clear and you'll be able to think straight, probably for the first time in your life. Maybe then things will all seem clearer to you."

"Is not living in New Zealand a deal breaker for you?" Chris asked, seeming to avoid what Samuel had said entirely.

"No, not necessarily, but it would be hard to have such a long-distance relationship. Look at it this way—at least we have Bran in common. He lives there." Samuel didn't want to put a damper on things, but opposite sides of the planet could make things incredibly hard.

Chris moved back like he wanted some space, and Samuel reluctantly let him go and tried not to blush as Chris got to his feet in front of him, the front of his briefs coming down a little and exposing the hairless base of Chris's dick.

"Don't look so surprised. It's not like you've never seen me naked." Chris laughed as he got out of the hot tub and started to dry himself off while Samuel still watched him intently. "We shouldn't stay in there too long."

He sat forward in the water and turned to get out. "I've seen you naked before, but this is something else. You tease me." Samuel started toweling off and pulled his T-shirt on.

Chris grinned. "Yeah. Want me to stop, or is a bit of playful flirting between friends allowed?"

Samuel shook his head. "Playful is good. Just don't be surprised if I pin you to the nearest surface, because my control is almost at its end."

"Having sex with me isn't off limits for you, then? Despite my issue? Or do you just want to tease me back and don't actually want to try me out?" Chris asked, the towel pressed against his stomach as he stopped drying himself off. "And also, telling me that someone I'm really mad at right now is going to be nearby isn't really an incentive. I know Bran's there. And I'll probably have to see him when I visit you and give Misha's present to Trent. Doesn't mean I'm looking forward to it, though. Enough about that. Back to sex." Chris dumped his towel in a bin and looked at Samuel as if waiting for his answer.

Samuel understood Chris was still mad at Bran. "He's your best friend, and this too shall pass. No, I don't like teasing you, especially if it goes nowhere, but I'm not gonna rush things either. You asked for space, and that's what I'll give you, all right? So calm down and don't be mad anymore. It's time to replace all those ugly memories with the good stuff."

Chris picked up a clean towel and threw it at him, hitting Samuel in the face. "You sound like my old therapist. It's not such a bad thing. I think what I'm worried about is that you'll forget all about how you want me not to cut anymore and settle for great sex and being worried all the damn time. Worry because I'm in New Zealand and hang gliding or something, not because I'm home alone and upset about something stupid. Deal?"

"Yup, I understand that, but remember, I'm not fifteen years old or even twenty-five. I know what I want, and great sex won't make me stupid enough to ignore when you're not doing well. And great sex also couldn't be a substitute for your health and happiness. So I'll never settle for something, as you call it. It's called working at it and making progress."

Samuel blushed as Chris came up and kissed him on his cheek before taking his hand and pulling him from the hot tub room. "You're a good guy, Samuel. Too bad I didn't meet you before I got all fucked up in the head. You said you'd only been with three guys when we were back in Montana. Right? Tell me who they were?"

"The first one was a high-school crush, and it was fleeting and quite awkward, because he couldn't quite figure out if he was gay or not. The second guy was someone I did martial arts training with. That time was more serious, until his father, our sensei, found out and threatened to send him far, far away unless he forgot about me. Which he readily did, of course. The last relationship I had lasted about two years, give or take a month, and the end came very suddenly. For me anyway. He felt a little bit like you about cows, actually—he hated living in the country and being so isolated from the big city life he grew up in. He took a position at a dental practice in Queensland but told me a week before he left. I didn't see it coming, and I'll be lying if I say I wasn't hurt, because I was. And before you go there, the answer is no, he doesn't pose any competition for you, and I won't take him back even if he came and begged me to."

Chris shook his head and opened his apartment door. "They all sound like assholes. Sorry if you still care about them at all, but they do."

He closed the door behind Samuel and let go of his hand, making Samuel instantly miss that simple connection as he watched Chris head in the direction of the bedroom.

"Shower's here if you want to get the chlorine off you. I'll be out in a minute. And I'm not that worried about competition from your exes. I was simply curious. The only person I ever thought was a threat to what I want with you was Bran when I caught you staring as he gave Kaden that lap dance."

He disappeared into his room, leaving Samuel standing there in the living room. Chris hadn't closed the door all the way, though, and Samuel caught sight of one perfectly toned and beautifully tanned buttcheek before he looked away.

A cold shower looked very attractive right then to get rid of the hard-on he had going since the hot tub, and seeing Chris's naked butt hadn't helped. He retrieved a change of clothes, something warmer and more suited for New York in winter, and a dry towel, then turned the shower on cold. The water was freezing for a few minutes before he turned the taps so it slowly heated up, and he sighed when it reached just the right temperature.

Chris had plenty of smelly bottles in there, and he made use of a couple to clean himself. It felt so good, if a little bit corny, to smell like Chris when he was done. He quickly pulled on a pair of thick track pants, a T-shirt, and a hoodie over that. After dealing with his towel and dirty laundry, he padded into the lounge on bare feet.

"Are you hungry at all?" Chris asked from the couch as soon as Samuel came into view. Samuel looked him over and smiled at the sight of him in jeans so dark blue they were nearly black and a soft-looking gray sweater. He was stretched out on the couch, the sweater riding up a little over his stomach and showing off the bottom curve of his tattoo. As he watched, Chris slowly sat up, and a bit of his brown hair fell over his forehead. It looked like he hadn't cut it since Montana, and the small curls that had been there before had lengthened into soft waves around his face and neck.

"I ate a meal in Bangkok, which freaked me out because I couldn't figure out what it was"—he shivered again in horror—"and again on the plane, but I have no idea how long ago it actually was. Going by what my stomach is saying, yeah, I'm hungry."

Chris laughed, and Samuel shivered for a completely different reason as he dragged his palm across Samuel's stomach before going into the kitchen.

"Cold pizza, Thai, milk that might still be good, or let me take you out? Or there's always the option of ordering food in...." Chris leaned his back against the fridge as he waited for Samuel to decide.

Samuel turned up his nose. "How about ordering something nice and warm? I'm not quite up to going out tonight. If that's okay with you?"

Chris smiled at him and gave him a quick nod. "Sure. Anything you want is fine with me." He reached into a nearby drawer and pulled out a stack of delivery menus, along with a credit card. "Pick something out. All my favorites are circled. It makes things easier for me when I can't remember what I like from where."

He pulled the menus closer and scanned through them before deciding on spicy Indian curry. Back home he didn't eat it often, but reading the descriptions of the delicious food, he felt a sudden craving for it tonight. He stiffened, only for a moment, as Chris came up behind him and rested his forehead against Samuel's back.

"Remember the first time I ran my hand down your back? You got so stiff. I thought you were going to turn around and punch me," Chris said. He sounded like he was smiling.

Samuel frowned as he recalled the moment. "Ten years ago, I probably would have."

"You wouldn't have hit me." He seemed so sure.

"Maybe, but it would've been a reflex if I did. Let's just say, as a kid, my dad came from behind." It wasn't much of an explanation, but he didn't want to talk about it anymore.

Samuel felt it the minute Chris pulled away from him, backing up abruptly.

"I'm sorry. If I'd known, I wouldn't have done it. I wanted you to want me as much as I did you."

Samuel watched him as he came back around and stood beside him against the counter, giving Samuel his shoulder.

"I did want you. From the start, but I don't like rushing into anything worthwhile." Samuel thought admitting that much would help Chris.

CHRIS GAVE him a soft smile and put his phone on the counter. "Back in Montana I thought the definition of worthwhile was an hour with you under me. Use my phone to call. No reason you should get charged for an international call for dinner."

Samuel nodded and took Chris's phone to dial the number. The chirpy guy on the line took his order and promised delivery within half an hour.

When he disconnected the call, Chris smiled at him. "Would you like something to drink? Coffee, tea, ice tea, wine? Sorry, I don't have anything stronger, because I've stopped drinking. The wine is left from then, if you're interested?"

"Ice tea would be nice, thanks. The hot tub made me thirsty."

Chris busied himself pouring them each a tall glass and added a slice of lemon. He placed one in front of Samuel where he sat at the small dining room table and took a seat.

Samuel could see the strain of the day taking its toll on Chris. Dark rings framed his slightly red eyes, and small tension lines pulled at the corners of his lips.

"You are exhausted, aren't you?" Something in him wanted to take care of Chris. So badly.

Chris tried to laugh it off. "I'm fine."

Samuel frowned at him. "I am the one person you don't have to lie to, so don't. Tell me where the cutlery is, and I'll set the table for us. Our food will be here soon."

Chris let the mask drop. "Deal. Second cupboard on the left for plates. First drawer for knives and forks. The next drawer holds the napkins and place mats."

He ended with a deep yawn, and Samuel smiled.

If they could be honest with each other, and it appeared Chris wanted that, he had hope for them yet.

CHAPTER EIGHTEEN

SAMUEL USED the last piece of garlic naan to mop up the butter chicken sauce on his plate. Before them the table looked like a disaster zone… well, on his side anyway. Chris had long since finished eating and watched Samuel clean out the rest of the food from the takeout containers.

He sat back with a sigh and drank the last of his second glass of tea. "Wow, I didn't realize how hungry I was."

Chris stared at him with wide tired eyes, which he blinked very slowly. "I can't believe you just ate all that." He tipped the empty containers toward him to see if they were completely empty, which they were.

"Hey, I traveled many, many miles to be here, and the trip sapped all my energy, so be nice," Samuel joked as he got up and took their dishes to the kitchen, where he rinsed them before stacking them in the dishwasher.

"I'm about to fall asleep on my feet. The day must have taken a bigger hit on me than I thought. Imagine that. I woke up this morning like every other day and did some work. At the end of five hours, I had no job and no parents left."

Chris gave a weak laugh, but Samuel heard the sadness anyway.

He stepped closer to Chris and rubbed his palms over his upper arms and shoulders. "I know it must have been damn hard to stand up against your father like you did, but give it time. As soon as the cloying fog of his intimidation and abuse fades, you will be a different person."

Chris dropped his head back limply as he looked up at Samuel. "I hope you're right." He leaned closer and kissed Samuel softly on his mouth. "Yuck, you smell like garlic."

Samuel laughed as he switched off the kitchen light. "So do you. We ate the same food."

Chris smiled crookedly. "Your fault. I'm gonna go brush my teeth and crash, or I'll end up passed out on the floor here."

"Where are you sleeping?" Samuel looked around.

"On the couch… and before you object, it's really comfortable, and I sleep on it plenty of times for that reason."

Chris disappeared into the bathroom, and Samuel waited his turn.

When Chris came out, he went into the bedroom. "I'm just changing into more comfortable clothes."

The door stood open a crack, and Samuel forced himself not to peek.

In the bathroom he cleaned his own teeth and used mouthwash twice before feeling satisfied. He came out to see Chris dressed in soft sleep shorts and a pale yellow T-shirt as he prepared his bed on the long sofa.

"I'll be fine. Go to bed. You're as tired if not more so than I am. See you in the morning. Good night."

"Okay. G'night." In the bedroom he left the door half open and took off his shirt and hoodie before sliding under the covers of the large, comfortable bed. The bloody thing was massive and had more than enough room for both of them, but Chris needed his space, so he wasn't going to push.

Knowing Chris was near worked better than any sleeping tablet Samuel had ever heard of, because he didn't remember falling asleep. About an hour later, even his complete exhaustion couldn't suppress his sharp reflexes, because the moment Chris pushed the door open farther, he woke up.

"Are you okay?" His voice sounded groggy, but he was wide awake.

"Can I please sleep in here with you?"

Chris's voice sounded pretty normal, but Samuel knew something was wrong.

"Of course you can. It's your bed. Come here." He lifted the bedcovers to his left so Chris could crawl under them. He slid right up to lie beside Samuel, their skin touching as Chris made himself comfortable and wound his legs around Samuel's.

"I guess the couch wasn't as comfortable as I remember," Chris said softly against his shoulder, but Samuel could feel the twitches in his muscles. Samuel knew it to be a lie, but he said nothing.

Chris placed the palm of his hand on Samuel's chest and rubbed it back and forth while he tried to push the other underneath his back. "That's a lie. I'm sorry. I'm not doing too well."

The relief at the honesty washed over him. "What can I do to help?"

Chris's body shook a bit harder. "Please hold my wrists for me. The craving to cut is almost overwhelming, but I don't want to. I want to stop hurting myself, but I'm afraid I'll scratch my wrists to let out the pain, the disappointment. It hurts inside. So bad."

Samuel rolled onto his side and pushed Chris over too until he spooned him. He wriggled one arm around Chris's neck and reached the other over his body to take both his wrists into a strong grip.

"I'm here for you. Whatever you need." Samuel kissed the back of his neck where Chris's hair fell away to reveal soft, warm skin.

Chris's teeth started chattering, and he curled his fingers into tight fists as he took deep breaths, which released as small sobs full of deep agony. "I'm so freaked out by all that happened today. I've always had my job and my parents. They may have been shit at having kids, but they were a constant in my life. Bran too. Now it's all gone, and it scares the fuck out of me. What comes next for me? Bran's in New Zealand. Misha is God knows where. My career is shot to hell if my dad has anything to do with it. And my mother and father have finally written me off. Torn me out of their lives like a dirty page in a book."

Samuel squeezed him tight against his chest. "They wrote you off long before today. Emotionally anyway. And I promise you, you haven't lost Bran, and Misha will be back before you know it."

"I tried to call my dad a couple of times, but he's not answering, and his receptionist refuses to put me through to his office. My mom hung up on me, several times. I guess it's really over." Chris's tears wet Samuel's arms where his cheek rested. "The need to cut and let the pain flow out and drift away became unbearable earlier. I got the knife out but thought of you in here believing in me. It felt like I would be betraying you if I did it. So I stopped and came in here instead."

"I am so glad you did and proud of you for saying no to yourself. The only loss in this situation is theirs, babe. You are worth so much more than what they've given you. Instead of being proud of you, loving and nurturing you, they've done all they could to destroy your heart. They don't deserve you in their lives. You may have lost part of your family, but you've gained three more in us. And once Kaden's mom meets you and Kylie forgives you for lying to her, you'll have a much bigger family than you've ever dreamed of." Samuel hoped his words would hit home for Chris, the realization he wasn't alone anymore.

The shaking and sniffles continued for another ten minutes or so, but eventually the tension eased from Chris's body as he relaxed completely into the shape of Samuel's position. He loosened his grip around Chris's wrists but didn't release them yet.

Chris stretched his legs after a while. "You can let go now. I think I'm over the worst. You being here helps."

Samuel let go and rubbed his thumbs up and down to get the blood circulation going again, and Chris hissed at the sensation.

"I'm sorry. They must tingle," Samuel apologized.

"If you hadn't done that, the damage would've been way worse. Thank you." Chris turned over and pushed him onto his back before wrapping one leg and an arm around Samuel's body. He placed his head onto his chest and sighed deeply, slight tremors still echoing through his limbs. "I think I can sleep now."

He followed it with a yawn, and the next Samuel heard was soft deep breathing.

He closed his own eyes and tried to grab a hold of sleep again. The storm had come and gone, and they were still standing.

CHAPTER NINETEEN

WAKING UP, Chris struggled to untangle himself from the rumpled sheets twisted around his legs. Bright light hit him in the face as soon as he turned over, and for one panicked moment, he thought he was late to work.

But then he remembered the day before, and especially that night, and shame darkened his cheeks as he slowly sat up in bed, trying to make as little noise as possible. He heard Samuel moving around in the kitchen, and Chris knew he'd have to go out there and see him at some point. It might as well be right then.

He got out of bed and stopped by the bathroom to go through his morning routine. He skipped the shower for now, and couldn't help looking at his wrists, where Samuel had held him. There were faint pink lines, but Chris hardly minded them. He'd let Samuel into a place that no one had ever been with him before. As far as he could remember, no one had ever cared enough to be there either. Bran loved him, but they were different from that. Chris would have never allowed Bran to see him as vulnerable, as absolutely fucked up as Samuel had seen him last night.

His kit wasn't on the sink where he'd left it the night before, but after a quick look through all the drawers, Chris found it next to his supply of condoms. Samuel had put it away right where it belonged without even realizing it. His two vices, neatly packed together in one seemingly innocent drawer.

Samuel was still in the kitchen when he came out of the bathroom, and Chris gave him a weak smile as he slid onto one of the barstools at the island. "Hey."

"Hi. I'm glad you were able to sleep."

Samuel slid a cheese omelet onto a plate in front of him, and Chris frowned. The breakfast clearly wasn't for him, as Samuel couldn't have known what time he would be getting up, but before he could say anything, Samuel was already moving on to the next.

"Thanks," Chris said, taking a bite and slowly starting to eat. Breakfast wasn't usually a big deal to him besides a piece of fruit or maybe some yogurt, both from the break room at the firm. Eggs in the morning were a nice surprise and one he couldn't have anticipated since he didn't have any eggs in the apartment. Or he hadn't until Samuel had gone down to the convenience store at the corner. The shopping bag was still on the counter.

"About last night...," Chris began, though he quickly lost his nerve as Samuel looked at him over his shoulder. "Never mind." He went back to eating.

Samuel finished cooking his breakfast and came over to sit next to him at the island. "I'm glad you came to me when you needed help."

"I'm sorry I had to at all," Chris said quietly. He didn't like getting to that place, especially not with Samuel around. His hand shook, and he put the fork down before it could make a lot of noise and draw Samuel's attention.

Samuel kept eating, but he did glance over at him. "Will holding your wrists until it passes always work?"

"Cutting is the easiest and fastest way to stop the pressure. Sex does help, but it needs to be rough, and it takes longer. I've scratched or pinched myself when I couldn't do either of those, but I end up bruising more than anything else. I have gloves in my backpack that I put over my hands when I can't scratch but still need to release."

He went back to eating and was glad his hands were no longer shaking. "But no one has ever held my wrists before. It worked, though it did take a long time. I'm not used to being in that space for that long. It was just a guess that it would work at all, but I figured not being able to use my hands would make hurting myself impossible. I didn't mind it, though." Explaining everything to Samuel, talking about it like the normal thing it was for him, was liberating in a way. He wasn't delusional in thinking Samuel accepted what he had to do, but it was nice that he was willing to listen anyway.

"What would you like to do today?" Chris asked. There was so much to see and do in New York City, and if it was warmer and not snowing, there was plenty he would have wanted to show Samuel, from the Statue of Liberty to Times Square, Grand Central Station, Central Park, and the New York City Library. They were some of the biggest tourist spots, but that made them no less interesting to him, and it didn't stop him from wanting to share them with Samuel in any way.

Samuel took a long time answering him, and Chris waited for him to make up his mind. When he did speak, though, what he said had Chris freezing beside him. "I'd like to go to the September 11 Memorial. Do you know where it is?"

He had to remember to breathe as he gave Samuel a slow nod. "I've lived here all my life. I know where it is. You sure you want to go there?"

"I do. Would you rather do something else instead?"

There were probably a hundred places Chris would have rather gone that afternoon, but if Samuel wanted to see the site where the World Trade Center had fallen, he'd take Samuel there. It just wasn't his favorite place to go, not by a long shot, and Samuel must have realized that somehow because he stopped Chris with a hand on his arm before he could finish standing up.

"We don't have to go there."

Chris leaned forward and kissed Samuel's cheek. "Get your shoes on. And wear something warm." He pulled out his phone and ordered a cab. When he was done, he looked back at Samuel, and when he didn't see him getting up to get ready to go, he frowned. "What's wrong?"

Samuel gave him a soft smile. "I was about to ask you the same thing."

Chris forced a smile, but it felt wrong, so he quickly let it go and decided to tell Samuel the truth instead of playing it off like he would have done with nearly anyone else. "The attack felt as if it physically damaged us all, if that makes sense. It's hard to think about, to remember, and many places in the city still close each year on September eleventh. But it is important not to ever forget what was done to us. I'll take you there—I'm not saying I won't—but I'm not saying I want to go out for ice cream and cotton candy afterward either and pretend being there doesn't affect me deeply. It'll be a hot chocolate kind of thing. I ordered the cab to be here in half an hour so if you want to go, get ready."

He headed off and got a shower as quickly as he could. Even if Samuel decided he didn't want to go to the memorial, Chris still wanted to feel clean. He came out of the bathroom with a towel tucked in loosely around his waist. Not really having any sort of hips to speak of and only his ass to hold his pants up, the towel started to slip a few times before he managed to get himself into his bedroom.

"Are we going or not?" Chris called through the closed bedroom door. A few seconds later, he heard the shower start up.

"Yes, please!" Samuel's muffled voice answered.

Chris dressed warmly in jeans, a thick sweater, and boots. He placed a woolen beanie, scarf, and his windproof jacket on the foyer table just as Samuel emerged from the bathroom in a similar outfit. He was so damn sexy Chris found it hard to drag his eyes away. Instead of a sweater, Samuel wore a thick hooded sports jacket, and knowing what he hid underneath made Chris want to rip it off him to expose the wicked tribal tattoos.

"You look good," Chris said, grabbing a handful of Samuel's ass as he walked behind him.

Samuel pulled his butt in a little and laughed. "Hey, don't abuse the merchandise! Come on. Let's go."

Chris stopped in front of the door as soon as he'd opened it and went over to tap Mikey on his shoulder. Finding the kid in the little corner between their apartments wasn't that unusual since he wasn't allowed to play on the street by himself, but as much as he sometimes wanted to, Chris couldn't just leave Mikey there to entertain himself.

He waved to Mikey, got a wave and a smile back, then held up one of his fingers, asking for a second. Mikey nodded, and Chris turned to Samuel. "This is my deaf neighbor. His name's Mikey. His mom is Miranda. He says he can't read lips, but I don't think that's true. I don't like leaving him in the hallway, so if you're okay with it, we can take him with us, if his mom says yes, or he can stay in my apartment and watch movies like he usually does. Which would you prefer?"

Before Samuel could even form an answer, Mikey grabbed Chris's hand, pulling his attention away from Samuel. *Can I watch Zombie Kids Undead Three?* He'd written down. That settled things for Chris at least, and he pushed his door open wide enough for Mikey to rush in.

Before they left he sent Mikey a text saying, *Lock up when you leave* and another to Miranda saying, *Mikey is watching some zombie movie on my couch. I won't be home until later.*

"All done," he told Samuel.

THE CAB ride through midtown and down to the memorial was spent in silence. For Samuel it might have been comfortable, and Chris hoped it was. For him, though, it was anything but. Going back there brought up memories he didn't choose to visit often, if ever, and it wasn't a good feeling.

They arrived and Chris let Samuel lead, not wanting to rush him along. He stayed close enough to answer any questions Samuel had, but he didn't want to hover either. In the concrete plaza, there were thousands of trees, one for every person who had died, and in the midst of those trees were two massive pools of water. He wasn't one to pray, but he did bow his head when he followed Samuel close to them.

"You look miserable here," Samuel said, putting an arm around his side. The contact helped shield him from some of the wind and also chased away the cold tightness in his gut.

He nodded and laid his head against Samuel's chest, coming fully against him and grabbing the front of Samuel's jacket. As Samuel wrapped his arms around Chris's shoulders, Chris began to relax.

"I'm just remembering. This day was hard for a lot of people."

"What was it like for you?"

Chris closed his eyes and focused on Samuel and the feeling of being held as he let himself remember that morning and the hours after it. "There was a lot of panic. That's what I remember most. Back then Bran had his office only a block from the towers, and at first no one knew anything. We were supposed to meet for breakfast like we always did, and I was walking along to get to this little cafe with the best eggs Benedict I'd had up to that point. I was running late, and I'd texted him, but he hadn't texted me back yet. Then I started to see people staring up at the sky, and before I could even begin to register what had happened, I heard the sirens."

He wiped his eyes on Samuel's jacket, refusing to let go of him to wipe the tears away himself. "I started calling Bran. Misha was deployed, and maybe I should have called my parents, but Bran was the person I called. Only the lines were all busy and I couldn't get through. So I went to his apartment, and he wasn't there. He wasn't at the cafe either, and I couldn't get to his office because that had all been blocked off. I was panicking as I stood there on the corner, looking at the destruction and listening to people wail and not knowing if he was alive or not." He was shaking by then. So many people had experienced loss and real terror that day, and he felt like he shouldn't have still been so affected by the few hours that he could not reach his best friend, but he was.

"When did you find him?"

Chris loved that there was no judgment in Samuel's voice, only quiet understanding, like he'd been through that kind of panic before and knew how bad it could be. "A few hours later, he found me on the sidewalk. I was still dialing him, trying desperately to get a call to go through, and he walked up to me and held my hand, and I'm pretty sure I cried then too."

He pulled away but didn't go far, keeping one hand wrapped in Samuel's shirt as he pulled his phone out of his pants pocket with the other. Bran answered on the first ring, and Chris smiled, glad to hear his voice.

"Hey. We're at the memorial. You remember that morning?"

"Of course. I've only ever been that scared when Richard beat the shit out of you. When are you coming back to New Zealand?"

Chris pressed himself back against Samuel. He was glad to have them both, even if he was mad at Bran still. But that anger was beginning to wane as well. "Next week."

"Good. We should go out. All of us. We'll do something fun. It won't be anything like last time."

Chris could have said something mean, but he didn't have it in him right then. "Okay. See you later."

"You need to go?" The disappointment was clear in Bran's voice.

Some days Chris might have reconsidered, but he was still too raw from the botched intervention they'd all tried to do, and his guilt and shame were far too raw on top of that, for him to be able to carry on a normal conversation with his best friend right then.

"Yeah. Later." He hated hanging up on Bran like that, when they'd always been so close, but he couldn't pretend everything was fine. Not when talking to Bran brought up such anger and so much resentment within him.

He put his phone back into his pocket and looked up at Samuel to find him watching him.

"I'm glad you called Bran."

"Me too. I wish I wasn't so angry at him, though. We'll work that out in New Zealand."

Samuel nodded. "When I hear and see tragedies such as these, they make me forgive much easier, because I wouldn't have wanted to lose those people in these moments, no matter how angry I was with them." He took Chris's hand and began leading him toward the front of the museum, where a long line of people already stood, waiting for their chance to see what was left of that terrible day.

CHAPTER TWENTY

SAMUEL STARED at the memorial grounds around him and shook his head at how clean and tidy it appeared, compared to the devastation of the terrorist attack. He remembered getting home from the milking shed and switching on the television after getting a text from Kaden and Trent. About to go make his dinner, he watched in shock as the events unfolded and sat there until the early hours of the next morning. Dinner never happened because his appetite disappeared and sleep never came that night.

"We should go back to New Zealand earlier than next week," Chris spoke up from beside him. "Would you mind?"

Samuel turned and wrapped his arms around Chris's waist and looked him in the eyes. His cheeks were red from the cold air, and wispy bits of his fringe twitched where they poked out from beneath his beanie.

"I don't mind at all. I miss my friends when I'm far away, but you're a good distraction from that. If you really want to go, we can go. It means I can get back to work sooner than I thought, but it's completely up to you."

Chris groaned. "No. Not so that you can get back to work. So that we can do something, all of us together, like Bran suggested. Now that His Majesty has decided I can be let back into his country after all." He gave Samuel a wink.

Samuel had to grin at Bran's new nickname. "Well, if you put it like that. Maybe we can go fishing. For that, I'd take off another week if I could."

"And I can always bring you back here and show you more sights when it isn't fucking freezing." Chris shivered and burrowed in against Samuel as if there was no getting warm for him.

"Deal." Samuel rubbed Chris's back through his thick clothing. "Let's get out of here, then."

"I'd love to."

As Samuel watched him, Chris took out his phone, and minutes later a cab arrived for them.

"Thanks for being okay with killing your trip early. I do like hanging out with you, but the cold is getting to me, and being here isn't fantastic. I felt better in New Zealand."

"The reason I'm here at all stands right in front of me, so if you're no longer here, I don't want to be either." Samuel did something he rarely ever did, but now might be a good start, because he kissed Chris full on the lips. A quick one but nice nonetheless.

"You're crazy for coming across the planet for someone you'd barely spoken to recently. Sorry about that too. I wanted to be at my best, even had a plan of showing up on your doorstep, all perfect and not cutting at all, and we'd be okay somehow." Chris shrugged and looked away from him as the cab driver took them back to Chris's apartment.

Samuel tapped him on his thigh. "Hey. Let's forget about that for now. I want you to stop apologizing for surviving the best way you knew how, okay? You are already much better even though you don't see it yet. I see it."

"I think a few months in New Zealand and I might be ready to come back here and have my own firm," Chris softly said as the driver pulled up to the apartment building.

Samuel frowned. "Really? You going to come home with me and we're going to explore what we have here and then you're going to just pack up and leave again? Almost everyone you care about lives there now."

They got out of the cab, and Samuel followed Chris back up to his apartment. "Yeah, but I don't. I figured I'd visit for a few months, come back here, then you could see me here and I'd see you and we'd switch off. That wasn't your plan too?"

Samuel tried hard to rein in his annoyance at Chris's flippant attitude toward their relationship. The challenges they had to face up to that point tested the strength of their young relationship, but adding a fucking long distance to it would most probably sink the ship completely.

"No, that wasn't exactly my plan." His good mood seemed to have been left at the memorial site, and for what the place represented, that was pretty screwed up.

Chris let them into his apartment without saying a word and walked over to the little boy sitting on the couch. As Samuel watched him, Chris typed something on his phone, the kid nodded, and a minute later he was closing the door behind himself and they were alone again.

"Then what did you expect? That I was going to move to another country? Completely ditch my life here?"

Samuel toned down his temper. "No, but I at least expected you to try. You know as well as I do that long-distance relationships in one country struggle to survive, not to mention those stretching over continents and oceans."

"What would make you happy here, then? Because three months is a pretty big fucking effort for me," Chris snapped.

Samuel glared at him. "No, it's temporary before you come running back to a place where you never belonged and probably never will. Where people treated you like shit, but maybe that's what you like. Relationships take work, and doing it over thousands of miles would waste my time as well as yours."

"What I'd like, asshole, is for you to get the hell out of my apartment. Now." Chris turned around and stormed into his bedroom, slamming the door behind him.

"Fine, Your Majesty number two! Don't ever fucking ask me to come back here. I'm done with this selfish, petty shit. You need to grow up and realize that life is not a perfect little fairy tale!" Samuel stormed into the room where Chris lay sulking on the bed, grabbed his duffle bag, and started shoving his belongings into it without folding them. The zipper almost didn't close, but with a final shove, he managed.

"That nickname doesn't even make sense," Chris snapped at him, sounding like a child.

"Figure it out. See ya!" Samuel turned around and left the room, pulling the door shut behind him with all the force he could manage. Satisfaction made him walk tall when he heard the doorframe crack. In the foyer he unzipped the front of his bag and threw the little box containing the present he had bought Chris in Bangkok on the table. The apartment door's weight made a large boom as he repeated his earlier action. The adrenaline rushing through his veins made it impossible to wait for the elevator, so he took the stairs to the ground floor.

When he flung the glass doors of the building open, a taxi pulled up and someone got out before Samuel got in. "JFK, please."

"Yes, sir," the cab driver answered him as they took off and moved into traffic.

Samuel's chest heaved with his upset, and he took control of it and forced himself to breathe deep and calm himself down. At this point he wondered if Chris was even worth his hurt, because up till now Chris had only cared about Chris, getting laid, his asshole of a father, Bran, and Misha. Samuel was not enough for the man to consider making some changes. Why he was surprised, he honestly didn't know. He had never told Chris about his last serious partner, Ian, who, after moving away, had thought it would be fine to just hook up on occasion. In no uncertain terms, Samuel had told him to go fly a kite. Now Chris almost required him to do the same things. Have a catch up every few months, fuck like bunnies to make up for lost time, and then live separate lives again for another few months. There was no way he would settle for a half relationship like that.

Thankfully the driver remained silent the whole way to the airport. At the international terminal, Samuel thanked the guy and handed him the payment before getting out. He made his way to the airline desk and spent the next few minutes shifting his flight forward, and despite the shitty night he'd had, he must have had some remaining luck stored up somewhere. The assistant informed him of a cancellation on a flight leaving in three hours, and he happily took the seat instead and went to check in.

With his car in storage at Auckland airport, he rang the parking company to inform them of his early return so they could collect him upon his arrival. With that sorted, he looked around at the shops and cafes. To keep his mind off the events of the night, and Chris for that matter, he bought himself the latest Stephen King novel and started reading it with a steaming cup of coffee as company.

As he had planned, the book hooked him by the end of chapter one, and when they called his flight, he frowned in annoyance at the interruption. This time his luck outdid itself when he sat toward the back of the plane with two empty seats beside him. A welcome bonus. In his present state of mind, he wasn't up to chatting with strangers.

He managed to finish his book by the time he landed in Auckland. Somewhere between Bangkok and home, he had lost his fight against sleep and managed to get some much needed rest. By the time he parked his car in front of the garage at home, his mood hadn't improved significantly, so he showered and got into bed. Tomorrow he would get back to work and let his friends know he was back. For now he wanted to be left alone, which was why he never switched his phone on after shutting it down at JFK.

The only reason he woke up at four in the morning was to empty his bladder, but he managed to get back to sleep after doing so. Unused to sleeping past sunup, he stirred as the weak morning rays filtered through small cracks in his curtains. He moaned and turned his back in that direction to snooze a bit more, but twenty minutes later his muscles complained from lying down too long.

A hot shower and his first cup of strong coffee helped shake off the fuzziness from the flights and the change from summer to winter and back again in such a short time. While waiting for his second cappuccino, he swallowed down some vitamin C to help his body cope with the stress of it all, because he couldn't afford to get sick and be off work even more.

His stomach revolted at the thought of food, so he guessed all the meals on the planes must've been enough to carry him through another few hours. When he sat down with his precious hot drink, he switched on his phone. A few seconds later, it sounded repeatedly as several texts and one missed call from Misha came through. Dialing voice mail, he sat back to listen to what Misha had to say and prepared to be pissed off all over again.

"Samuel, Misha here. I can't talk long, but got a text from a very upset Chris. What the hell happened, man? Don't let Chris push you around with his dramatics. I thought you knew how to handle him, because if you can't, then maybe you're not right for him after all. Never thought you'd give up so easily."

Without reservation Samuel dialed the number, which went straight to message. "Listen asshole, butt out of my business. Chris and his dramatics can go take a hike. We've tried to love, help, and support him, and the only thing we get in return is his selfishness. He's like a petulant child. I don't want to babysit anyone or handle anyone, as you call it. He needs to grow the fuck up. He's on the way to forty but acts fifteen. And I can't give up on anyone I've never had, mate." He disconnected the call and threw the phone on the coffee table. He picked up his cup and started sipping the hot liquid, once again trying to calm himself down before talking to Kaden, but by the time he finished the drink, he changed his mind about calling his friend. Nothing is quite as good as face to face.

When he came to a stop in front of Kaden's house, the door opened and both Kaden and Bran came out, their expressions worried, probably because he was back from Manhattan so early.

When he came to the top of the steps of the deck, Bran came forward and gave him a warm hug. "You look tired."

Kaden gave him a pat on the shoulder. "Come on in."

When they were all seated comfortably in the lounge, they sat across from him, waiting for him to talk.

"Have you heard from Chris?" he asked.

"Where is he?" Bran demanded instead.

"In Manhattan, where he obviously loves to be," Samuel spat, his temper already rising again. This shit was bad for his blood pressure.

Bran threw a pillow at him, surprising him.

"You weren't supposed to leave him there! He doesn't weigh that much. You could have dragged him. Seriously, what the hell, Samuel?"

The usual humor he felt at Bran's tactics had taken a hike today. "Listen, Bran. I'm in no mood for drama. I've had a truckload of that in the few hours I spent in New York. I'm not dragging anyone anywhere when it comes to being in relationship with me. They either come willingly or they can fucking stay where they are. Easy as that."

Bran glared at him, but it was Kaden who spoke up.

"Why don't you let Samuel tell you what happened?"

"It had better be good," Bran growled, crossing his arms over his chest.

Samuel glared at him. "Frankly, I don't give a shit whether you think it's good or not." He turned his attention to Kaden, completely ignoring Bran for his own sanity. "Maybe coming here wasn't such a good idea after all. I thought speaking to you in person might be better than a phone call or a text."

Kaden appeared sad. "If you texted me, I would've come to kick your ass. What's up, Sam?"

He took a deep breath. "Everything was fine the first night I got there. Misha and I paid Pavel a visit, and I put the fear of the Maori warriors into him, hopefully. Chris quit his job earlier that day, apparently. So Misha and I had a dual purpose for going there—to pick up Chris's personal belongings and to tell his father to leave him alone. Chris was cold towards me and obviously surprised to see me standing in his apartment, but once Misha said his good-byes and left for his next mission, we talked and smoothed things out a bit."

Kaden nodded. "That's when he called Bran for the first time since leaving here."

Bran nodded, for once not interrupting or demanding answers before someone could give them to him. He lacked any real form of patience.

"Yes. So we had a nice evening, talked some more, and he had a rough time throughout the night because of the emotional toll of what had gone down with his dad. He came to me, and we worked through it and he was better. I made us breakfast the next morning and decided to go do some sightseeing after. That's when he called Bran from the World Trade Center Memorial." Samuel rubbed a hand over his face, not believing this had all happened less than twenty-four hours ago.

"Sounds like a nice time, sort of," Bran quietly said.

It wasn't interrupting, not really. And his words didn't bother Samuel. He looked worried, and Samuel knew he had a right to be. Only Chris wasn't his problem anymore.

"He found it hard to be there, so we went back to the apartment. And that's when the whole thing came apart. From what I understand, Chris intended to come back to New Zealand for three months to recover before heading back there to start up a practice of his own. Oh, yes. He meant to pursue a relationship with me in that time and then continue as who knows what while he lives in New York and I here." Samuel started bouncing his knee as the indignant anger and hurt bloomed inside his chest.

"It is a sort of practical plan, though," Bran spoke up, earning himself a sharp look from them both. "What? It is. He's not a lawyer down here. The relationship would be shitty, but I mean… oh never mind." Bran wisely shut his mouth and went to cleaning his thumbnail.

Kaden shook his head slowly. "I'm sorry, mate. I know how you feel about such relationships after what Ian did to you, and I'm 100 percent on the same page as you. If Bran and I hadn't come to some sort of solution, we wouldn't be sitting here, because I wouldn't have settled for long distance either."

Samuel nodded his thanks for Kaden's support. "You know what makes me the maddest? That he decided all this before even talking to me. In his selfish world, the whole thing was planned out, as if he was the only one in the relationship and he had all the say. Who the hell does he think I am? On those terms, I'm literally looking forward to being his weekend lay once every three months. I thank God I didn't give in and have sex with him, because then this would have been so much worse."

He looked up to find Bran glaring at him again.

"First of all, I'm mad at you. Like completely mad at you. For Chris to offer that, it was a big deal to him. His longest relationship was six months. That's it. You think spending three months in a new country would be easy? Hell, I considered that kind of a plan too, but I had the sense to keep my mouth shut before saying anything to Kaden. Just because you've been with guys longer than him doesn't mean his way is wrong, and yeah, he should have said something more than that to you, but he works on negotiation. He says something, you say something, you two come to a compromise. That's how lawyers work. I'm calling this fight your fault."

Samuel felt his face heat up. Not good. "Kaden, keep your bitch on a leash, or I will leave here and you won't see me for a long time, if ever."

Bran looked like he wanted to say something, but Kaden clamped a hand over his mouth.

"Baby, it's okay. I know you're mad on behalf of Chris, but we weren't there. Let's take a breath. And Samuel didn't mean to be an ass to you right there. He's stressed. Aren't you, Samuel? Because you'd be mad if I called Chris a bitch. Wouldn't you?"

"I'm not stressed. I'm fucking pissed that every time Bran and Chris get confronted about their shit, they use their money, statuses, or emotional crap to excuse it. I mean, try going through what I went through and we'll talk again. They use their baggage to hurt people through their selfishness, and I won't smooth that over anymore. The bottom line is this. Chris may be a lawyer familiar with compromise. I'm not one. That's why a relationship consists of two people. In Chris's world there is only him and maybe you, Bran. And I won't play fucking second fiddle to anyone ever again. I want someone in my life who loves me and wants to be with me all the time. A person who can't wait to see me when we're apart and who couldn't imagine having a better time than spending it with me. And I know that is not a fairy tale, because it's possible and real. I've seen it in your parents' marriage. That's what I want, and if Chris can't give me a decent opportunity to try, then this is over before it's even begun. Listen, Kaden. I'm gonna go. I'm not fit for company right now." He rose from his seat, ready to leave.

"Is that what you think we do too?" Bran asked Kaden as soon as Samuel was done talking.

Kaden looked between them both. "Samuel, stay. You're fine. Bran, yes. I do. Sometimes you're exactly like Samuel just described. Chris has to own up to his own bullshit. Just like I make you do."

Bran got up and pulled out his phone. "Yep. Uh-huh."

"Babe…," Kaden called after him.

"I'm only going for a walk." Bran kissed him on his cheek and stood there looking at Samuel for a few seconds before coming over and hugging him. "Missed you. Glad you're home. Don't call me a bitch again unless you're playing."

Despite his annoyance, he managed a small smile for Bran. "I'm sorry."

"Don't be." Bran stepped back. "You've heard the kind of crap I've called Chris when I'm mad at him. Hell, I even smack him around a bit. You two have fun." He headed outside with his phone in his hand. Samuel figured he was probably going to try to call Chris.

"He'll be fine," Kaden assured him. "It takes time with them."

Samuel sighed and sat back down. "Time I don't have. Sorry, but you're much stronger than I am in that way."

"I'm really not stronger than you. Not at all. You think there aren't days when we don't talk to each other for hours?" Kaden laughed and shook his head. "Bran can get mad over nothing, like a wet towel on the floor, and I deal with it because I love him. We don't share our fights, but we have them. It's part of being in a relationship. And I believe that if you and Chris are supposed to work out, you will. Cooling down for a while will help, I think. And if you don't want to be with him after this, because I can tell you I wouldn't be okay with half the crap Chris does that I hear about, then that's on him. Not you. At least you tried."

"I know that, and I don't expect smooth sailing, but I'm not starting anything with Chris if he's already decided to put minimum effort into it. Then it's doomed to fail from the start. I'm not putting my heart at risk again without some promise of it paying off."

Kaden nodded. "And you shouldn't. Do you want a drink or anything? You don't have to stay if you don't want to. Just don't go home angry. I know you're tired, though."

"I've actually slept quite a lot, but it's the emotional ride that's getting to me. I'll have a glass of orange juice if you have any." Samuel could feel the strain of the last few weeks pulling him down.

Kaden got up. "Come through to the kitchen."

Once there Kaden poured them both a glass of orange juice, and they sat at the kitchen table to drink it.

"I know you. You're going to jump right back into work once you get home. Take a day or so and rest up. Do something senseless like watch movies or go for a hike to take your mind off things."

Samuel thought it not such a bad idea. "I may do that. I'll take my fishing rod and drive up to a nice spot and wet the line and see if I still have it."

Kaden grinned. "We must take out Trent's boat again soon. That way we can actually catch the big ones deeper in the bay."

"Sounds like heaven right now. I'm so over drama and conflict I could scream or pull all my hair out if I had any long enough." Samuel pulled his thoughts in line when he started wondering what Chris was doing. The sooner he forgot about the other man, the better off his heart would be, despite the hurt already caused.

Kaden pulled his phone out of his pocket. "I'll text Trent about it so he can work it into his schedule over the next week or so."

By the time Samuel finished his drink, Bran was still nowhere to be seen, and Kaden walked him out as he prepared to leave.

"Thanks, buddy. I'll see you whenever," he said as he opened his truck door and got in.

Kaden gave him a wave, his expression still worried.

He didn't know what the future had in store for him, but for now he had to get his head on straight. Chris might not need him, but his cows, the land, his friends, and family sure did, and it was time he started concentrating on that.

CHAPTER TWENTY-ONE

BY THE time Chris got up the nerve to drag his ass over to see all of them, a week had gone by. He wasn't particularly proud of that fact, but he'd barely been able to make himself get on a plane either, not when it seemed like everyone he cared about in the country wanted nothing to do with him. He'd promised Misha that he'd make a stop there, but he was being slow about it, and his brother wasn't happy about his delay tactics at all.

The motorcycle he'd rented rumbled under him as he drove slowly past Samuel's house. His truck wasn't in the driveway by the purple mailbox with the cow, so he kept going on down the road, figuring he would be at Kaden and Bran's house. As long as Trent was there too, Chris could handle seeing the rest of them. He didn't want any trouble, didn't feel up to arguing with them, and certainly didn't want to have a repeat of the last time he was in their house. He only wanted to get Misha's dog tag to Trent. His brother had already called him three times since he'd arrived in New Zealand a few days before, asking him when he planned to give Trent his present.

He'd been able to delay some, but Misha wasn't a patient man, and Chris generally tried not to be a coward. He turned the bike down a familiar driveway and stopped it, letting the bike's big engine rumble a little as he sat behind Bran's sporty white sedan. Samuel's truck was there too, along with a few cars and trucks he wasn't familiar with. He hoped one of those belonged to Trent and that he wouldn't have to get up the guts to come back out here again. One and done sounded like a much better plan to him.

Turning off the bike, he sat back and flexed his fingers a little. He'd kept his license up but hadn't been on a bike in over two years, and the constant vibration had gotten to him. It wasn't bad, though, and even though it was incredibly vain, he thought he looked fucking hot as hell in head-to-toe black motorcycle gear as he rode on the shiny black bike. He'd gotten more than a few appreciative looks while riding around Thames.

By the time he got off the bike, the front door had been opened and Kaden was standing there, watching him. Chris took off the helmet as he came up, revealing himself, and he saw Kaden's expression go from surprised to concerned.

"Is Trent here?" Chris asked him.

Kaden narrowed his gaze at him. "Working your way through my friends now?"

Chris snorted, then rolled his eyes. "Why, yes. That's exactly what I'm doing. I decided to break things off with Samuel, then make a move on the guy my brother is into. Be careful. Next up it'll be you." Joking with Kaden, even sarcastically, felt weird, and Chris quickly dropped the act. "It's a favor to Misha. I'll only be a few minutes. Then you won't ever have to see me again," he promised Kaden.

Shaking his head, Kaden let him in, and Chris stepped around him. "I can't believe you're willing to hurt Bran that much."

As much as Kaden thought he knew, there wasn't really anything to talk to him about where he and Bran were concerned. He headed into the living room, where he could hear people talking, and stopped short as everyone quickly cut off whatever they were going to say as soon as they spotted him.

Bran smiled at him, but Chris was paying far more attention to Samuel. Pulling his attention from Samuel's surprised expression nearly hurt. He wanted to be able to go up and kiss him, to slide into his lap and never leave. But that wasn't ever going to happen. So he turned his attention instead to Trent, who sat on the other side of Samuel.

Thankfully there was space on the other side of Trent, and Chris plopped himself down there on the comfortable leather couch.

"How long are you staying?" Bran asked him. "Want some lunch?"

Chris didn't think he could answer him, not really anyway, so he only shook his head and pulled his backpack off. "Trent, I have something for you, from Misha."

"Oh?"

Trent sounded wary, not that Chris could really blame him for feeling that way.

Chris nodded and brought out a small wooden box, barely bigger than the size of his palm and delicately carved with scenes of men fishing. "Here."

Trent took it from his hand and turned the box over in his fingers. "It's a lovely box."

"The present isn't the box. That's something I saw near my place in Thames and thought it looked nice. Open it up," Chris said. The others were all looking at him, the only exception being Trent, who had his focus solely trained on the small wooden box in his hands.

Chris looked only at him, trying to ignore everyone else, as Trent opened the box and the shiny silver dog tag fell out into his open palm. Chris heard his sharp intake of breath and hoped he liked Misha's gift.

"Tell him thanks for me?" Trent quietly asked him.

Chris nodded. "I'd like to say you can tell him yourself, but he doesn't really answer his texts or calls when he's doing missions. Try him anyway, though. His number never changes, and eventually you'll get through." He got up from the couch, glad to have been able to do this small thing for Misha and for Trent as he watched Trent slide the chain over his neck and pass the tag under his shirt. "If I talk to him before you do, I'll let him know you liked it."

He pulled one more thing out of his backpack, a small cloth bag he'd had tucked in the innermost pocket, and slowly started heading toward Samuel. He felt like prey, with his heart racing in his ears and his fingers shaking as he dangled the bag from them, but he wasn't some meek man. He was a rejected one, full of hurt, and by the time he dropped the bag into Samuel's lap as he sat there silently on the couch, Chris hoped that showed.

"Remember when I came to your house and I told you I didn't want you to pick me up? It was because I was getting this on my way. Keep it, toss it, at this point I don't care."

Walking away from Samuel as he fixed his backpack across his back, he tried not to think about Samuel, about how the necklace he'd just given him had the Maori word for love, *aroha*, engraved on it, or anything else as he headed toward the front door.

Of course it was Bran who stood in his way. Stubborn, beautiful Bran, who looked like he'd do anything to keep Chris from leaving. "Bye," Chris said, stepping around him. They'd talk later, when he didn't feel so vulnerable with Samuel so very close.

But Bran grabbed the front of his jacket, making him unable to move. Chris could have pushed him away, but he didn't want to do that to Bran.

"I challenge you to a game of truth or dare. Please."

Chris had no idea why Bran thought the game would be a good idea right then, or why he thought he had to add a "please" to it like he had to beg Chris for something so ridiculous.

"I don't drink anymore, so anything besides alcohol and I'm in." Bran's expression instantly lit up. "But! You have to get everyone else to play with us. If you can't, then I walk and I'll text you sometime."

Bran hesitated. "That's not exactly fair."

Chris couldn't help laughing at him. "And ganging up on me last time I was in your living room was? That's my deal."

He looked determined, though, even as he tried to touch Chris on his shoulder, and Chris moved out of his reach before Bran could put his hand down.

"I can't touch you either?" Bran began to snap at him.

"Not when the last time you did you took to smacking me. Look, Bran, we're friends. We're always going to be friends. Right now things just suck between us, and I can't do this with you all the time. Truth or dare is safe. I'll stay and play that, but if you can't get them involved, I'm going to go and I'll see you later. I'll be here for at least a month, so we do have time." Chris didn't want to hurt Bran, especially when his friend looked so concerned, but he wasn't up to just sitting around and making small talk either.

He felt broken open, and everything hurt, especially when he glanced back at Samuel and found the quiet man watching him. "What's your plan?" he asked Bran, though he was still staring at Samuel.

"Guys?" Bran raised his voice in order to call to them all. "Please?"

Chris turned away from Samuel to look back at Bran. "Don't beg. Not for this. It was a stupid idea anyway, thinking that they'd want to play our games." He started walking again and even lifted up his helmet to put it back on, but Bran grabbed him from behind, wrapping his arms around Chris's chest and stomach.

"Don't you dare walk out that door. Not again. Not like this," Bran quietly said. "I'm so fucking sick of you walking away from me lately."

The easy answer to that was that Bran needed to stop pissing him off. But that wasn't really fair. Sure, Bran had hurt him, and Chris had been so very angry with him, but having him close again made that seem like a stupid argument that he really should be letting go of. It wasn't going to be that simple, he knew that, but he and Bran had been friends for far too long for Chris to quit him so easily.

He took his free hand that wasn't holding his helmet and put it over Bran's on his stomach. "So you're letting me back into your country, then?" Chris quietly joked.

"Ha-ha."

Chris turned around in his arms and caught sight of everyone sitting at the dining room table as if they were waiting for them, before he hugged Bran tightly and buried his forehead against Bran's neck.

"I'm not giving you up as my friend, but this isn't going to be easy either. I'm mad at you."

"I'm mad at you too. I can't believe you were cutting again. I got so scared."

Chris nodded and pulled away. "I know. I'm not right now, though."

"For good?" Bran asked hopefully.

Chris wished he could give Bran the answer he so clearly wanted, but that would have been a lie, so he shook his head. "No. But I do plan to stop."

"That's better than nothing," Bran said optimistically.

Chris only shrugged. Better than nothing was too vague for him to really add any sort of comment. It could have meant he hadn't cut within the last five minutes, for crying out loud.

They headed over to the table, where Bran sat next to Kaden. Trent was on Bran's left, followed by Samuel, which left Chris sitting right between Samuel on his right and Kaden on his left. Bran could have been nice and sat between Kaden and Samuel, letting Chris sit next to Trent, but by the soft, nearly hesitant smile Bran gave him, Chris knew this latest bit of torture was intentional.

"Ready?" Bran asked them all, sounding anxious. Chris wished Kaden wasn't between them so he could have rubbed Bran's back or something to calm him down.

"Again, this was stupid. I'm going," Chris said, starting to get up.

Kaden put a hand on his thigh to stop him. "Chris, please stay. Let's play, okay?"

He looked to Samuel, but Samuel wasn't paying any attention to him that Chris could tell, so he took his seat again with a nod. "Normal rules apply. Take a drink each time you answer or do a dare, any question goes, can trade out one sexual dare for two smaller ones. Nothing is off limits." He didn't know what was in the pitcher Bran stood to bring out of the kitchen, but he really wished he was drinking again. He wouldn't have ridden the bike after, though, and there was nowhere nearby he would have wanted to relax for a while. "Kaden, you pour. Samuel, you ask the first question." He couldn't stay silent for long, not if he intended to play by Chris's rules.

"Trent, do you want Misha to come see you?"

Samuel started with a very innocent question, and Chris hoped this wasn't how the rest of the game was going to play off.

Trent predictably went beet red. "After the gift he just sent me, hell yes!" Trent downed his shot and smiled from ear to ear.

Chris smiled, glad he did. He took out his phone and sent a quick text to Misha saying, *He loved the gift. Visit him.*

Trent cleared his throat dramatically. "Damn, it's so hard to ask you all some questions, because it feels like a damn minefield." He appeared to think for a few seconds. "Okay, Bran. Seeing as Kaden likes sex in public places, where was the last more visible spot you two got nasty?"

Bran didn't even blush as he grinned over at Trent. "Dressing room at the mall. Kaden was trying on some boot-cut jeans, and I couldn't resist. His ass in those jeans was just wow." He took his shot.

"Chris. I missed you so damn much, wanted to say that first. Where are you staying?" Bran asked him.

"I rented a house in Thames. Right off the water," he replied easily before downing half the glass of water Bran had given him when he'd passed out the shot glasses for everyone else. "Samuel, gonna throw the necklace in the trash or keep it?"

"I'm not a child and I appreciate any gift I receive." Samuel didn't take the bait and calmly drank his shot. "Chris, how about the present I gave you?"

Chris had to stand up for that, which drew everyone's attention to him. He silently unzipped his jacket, hung it over the back of the chair, then dragged his thumb slowly up his stomach, lifting the thin shirt he wore to reveal his navel and the small silver ring in it.

"This present you mean?"

Intense satisfaction filled Chris when Samuel's eyes locked onto his stomach and filled with heat. When he dropped the fabric, Samuel's gaze shot up to his.

"Yes, that gift."

The big man looked away, and Chris sat back down with a smug smile.

"Bran, planning a wedding anytime soon, or did that invitation get lost in the mail when you kicked me out of your country?" Chris teased him, but it was Kaden who went red.

"Maybe.... We've talked about it." Bran took his shot. "Samuel, glad Chris is back or more wanting to strangle him?"

Samuel frowned at him. "Really? I'm glad he's back despite wanting to strangle him."

Chris laughed. That was exactly how he felt about Samuel in that moment. Samuel drank his alcohol and coughed a bit.

"Bran, do you regret moving to New Zealand?"

Chris knew what he was doing, and it didn't bother him at all. Instead it made him realize that Samuel might still want something, despite the tantrum Samuel had thrown back in Manhattan.

"It was hard at first. I mean, Chris wasn't here, and talking to him was different because of the time zones, and for a while there we were waking each other up in the middle of the night. And if I hadn't been here, he wouldn't have started cutting, but I got Kaden because I decided to make my life here, and I'm glad I did that. Chris—"

"I didn't start cutting again because you weren't there to take care of me," Chris interrupted him before he could ask his question.

Bran turned and glared at him from around Kaden's big body. "Sure seemed like it."

Chris rolled his eyes. "You aren't responsible for what I do. You can't take responsibility for the people I've screwed or the marriages I've ruined, so don't think it's your fault every single time I cut. Ask your damn question."

"I was going to ask you if you'd missed Samuel, but now I want to know if you've cut since the last time you were here," Bran grumbled.

For once Chris didn't feel bad for the answer he was about to give him. "No." He drank his water and got up to get some more. "Samuel, think my piercing looks sexy?" he goaded him.

Samuel didn't react much, which kind of pissed him off.

"Is that my question?"

"I did ask it," Chris retorted as he sat back down, trying not to give away his anger or his desire to have Samuel tell him how good the little ring looked on him.

"Yes, it does. I have good taste." Samuel grinned as he drank his next drink. "What did you tell Misha about me after I left? He sure left a lovely message on my phone."

Chris snorted. "I'm sure he did. Because he loves me and doesn't like people being mean to his little brother. Even if we don't share a mom. Thank God. I said you were a jerk, had a hissy fit because I wouldn't agree to move my life to New Zealand when we hadn't even really started a relationship, and that you got me a belly ring. Not sure which part of that bothered him most." He shrugged. Nothing in that was anything but the truth, though he was teasing Samuel a bit. It was simply too much fun not to as he watched that little tick start up in Samuel's jaw as he started getting annoyed at him.

He drank his water and decided to pick on someone else for a while. "Kaden. Hmm. What to ask you. Oh, I know. If Bran had said come move to Manhattan, when there was no real expectation of anything more than friends who made out sometimes between you, would you have?"

Kaden looked at Bran, who shrugged his shoulders in return. "Probably not, but it's not the sexual acts between us that would've done it for me either. It was about the depth of connection between us. On the other hand, our situation was different, because Bran's job was pretty mobile and mine wasn't."

They were pretty fucking adorable together, Chris decided, as he gave Bran a wink and got a grin in return. He took out his phone and texted Bran, *Romantic sap.*

Bran took out his phone as it beeped and texted him back. *If Samuel and you had started a relationship, would you be moving here?*

"Cheater, you can't ask a truth or dare question in text during a game," Chris said, calling him out on his tactics.

Kaden gave Bran a quick kiss before turning to Chris. "What would it take for you to come live in New Zealand?"

That answer was easy, but it freaked him out that he and Bran seemed to communicate telepathically now. It must have been a couples thing. "If Samuel and I were actually in a relationship and not friends with gray areas, then I would. That's not the case, though, and after his tantrum when I explained that, I don't think that's actually going to happen."

Samuel put his hand on the table and turned to Chris. "May I point out that every time we have an opportunity to work on those gray areas, you run away? Also, you were the one putting the brakes on having sex in Manhattan. So if it was up to me, we would have a proper sexual relationship if you stopped running."

"No, you may not," Chris snarked at him. "Also, not your turn. And I'm not running. I'm protecting you. Dumbass."

"I am big, fat, and ugly enough to protect myself, thank you. That position is filled," Samuel growled back.

Chris dipped his fingers in his water and flicked some drops at Samuel. "Say something mean about yourself ever again, and I'll bite you. Your boyfriend position is filled? By whom? Daniel?"

Samuel snorted. "All you do is deliver empty promises. I don't have a boyfriend. I fill the position of looking after me. And Daniel is as straight as a ruler."

Chris felt stupid for not understanding, but his opinion on the subject remained the same. "Until I know that you won't ever come home to a dead body instead of a boyfriend, even though I've never once been suicidal, I'm not dating you, which means I'm not moving down here permanently, and I'm not having sex with you because you don't fuck guys you aren't dating. Care about you too fucking much to hurt you like that. So fuck you."

"Well, there you go. We can't work on this relationship and gray areas, as you call them, or trust and emotional well-being, if you're sitting on the other side of the world. People have to actually spend time together to develop something deep like what Kaden and Bran have."

He might have been right, but then again he might have been completely nuts too. "You're so fucking stubborn. And we got off track. It was actually my turn to ask a question."

"You and Bran designed stubborn, so go look in the mirror at what it looks like. Ask your bloody question." Samuel shook his head as he spoke.

"I did look in a mirror before coming here, actually, and I looked damn sexy. Completely fuckable too, thank you very much," Chris snapped at him before turning to Bran and ignoring Samuel completely.

"Which one of them would you kill first in a zombie apocalypse, if they all turned at once?"

Bran laughed. "Probably you at this point, asshole."

"Bitch," Chris said, grinning back at him. This felt good, being able to play with his best friend again.

Bran's eyes got wide, and he leaned around Kaden on the table. "After we're done playing, I've got to tell you about when Samuel called me a bitch and actually meant it. If I had any chance in hell of causing him some real damage, I would have punched him."

The idea of Bran, who probably weighed a good seventy-five pounds of muscle less than Samuel, actually trying to hurt him had Chris snickering. "Ask your question."

Bran's expression went from playful to serious in a heartbeat. "Ever afraid Samuel would be abusive to you? Like Richard was to me?"

Chris instantly shook his head. "No way in hell. He wants to strangle me most days, I'm sure, but he'd never put his hands on me in anger." Taking a chance, he touched Samuel's knee with the tips of his fingers, though he didn't turn his attention from Bran. He thought of a question, though, and turned to look back at Samuel. "Was your hissy fit running back here really worth it? Right now we could be having hot chocolate on my couch watching bad movies if you hadn't overreacted like such a child."

"Listen, princess, I'm too old for this childish shit. You're out to bait me and still think it's a fucking joke playing with my heart. Fuck you too, asshole. Bran, Kaden, Trent. *Adios*. See ya later." He grabbed his wallet and keys on the foyer table and slammed out of the house, looking angrier than he had been in Manhattan. The doors in New Zealand must've been made of tougher stuff, because it only made a dull thud as it shut.

Chris slid back from the table and went to wrap his arms around Bran from behind. "See you soon. He's so pretty when he's angry."

"You did that on purpose?" Bran asked him, sounding shocked.

Laughing as he put his jacket back on and picked up the helmet, Chris gave him a nod. "Of course. I wanted to get him alone so we could talk. You and I should have lunch. We've still got loads of shit to work through. Text me."

As he turned away, Kaden stopped him. "Chris, I would recommend you give him time to cool off. He can be pretty dangerous if he's that mad. I've only seen it once or twice, and it's not pretty."

"If he's dangerous when I make him mad, then I don't want to be with him anyway, because there are going to be plenty of days where I piss him off. Thanks for the warning, though. If I call Bran up from whatever hospital you have around here, you'll know I made a mistake. Until then, I'm going to see him. Toodles, kids." He headed out and rode the bike the short distance down to Samuel's house.

The front door was slightly open, as if Samuel had been in too much of a hurry to close it. That suited Chris just fine, though, since it meant he didn't have to figure out a way to break into Samuel's house.

He turned off the bike and walked into the house as silently as he could possibly manage wearing full body armor and boots. He still made a ridiculous amount of noise, especially if he wanted to surprise Samuel with him being there, so he stripped off his jacket and left it and the helmet on the dining room table, then sat on the edge of the couch to take off his boots. He didn't like walking around in socks, so he pulled those off too and stuffed them in his boots.

Barefoot, he was much quieter and was even able to sneak into the large room at the back of the house, where he heard random thumping. Not being into sports in general, Chris wouldn't have been able to guess from the sounds that Samuel was beating the crap out of a giant punching bag. He had his back to Chris, which meant he could lean against the wall, stuff his hands in his pockets after making sure his phone was on silent, and watch Samuel all he wanted. All the sexy, bare-chested, already sweaty mess that he was. Chris licked his lips and had to adjust himself when Samuel brought up his knee to attack the bag some more. Poor bag, but damn, he was hot jumping around like that. Chris knew he had to make Samuel mad more often if this was the kind of performance he got afterward.

The jumping, spinning, punchy things Samuel did were beautiful, and Chris wished he knew what any of it was called. It would have been nice to have a conversation about something Samuel clearly practiced, if the controlled, graceful movements were anything to go by. Chris wasn't a complete klutz, but he knew he wouldn't look anything like Samuel did if he attempted to replicate any of what he was seeing. Sometimes

Samuel was so fast he didn't even understand what he was seeing to begin with.

Multitasking was something Chris did exceptionally well, and while he continued to stay focused on Samuel and what he was doing, Chris also let himself think about what a life here would mean. He'd looked into it, a little, and knew there would be tests to get licensed and he'd have to prove that his education and experience back home qualified him to be a lawyer in New Zealand. But what else would it mean? Getting to look at Samuel all the time? Maybe even living with him someday if they could stand each other that long?

He'd only ever lived with Bran, and that had been one crazy, messed up experience. He loved Bran, and he knew they would be friends again. That they could play together as they had back at the house proved that to Chris. But he didn't want to live with a roommate again. Maybe Bran was better now. Maybe he didn't throw a fit if a towel was left on the bathroom floor or if his toothbrush had been used by accident after a night of drinking anymore.

But living with someone meant giving up his privacy and his space. Sometimes maybe he didn't want to have someone else always on top of him. Maybe he wanted to watch his own movies and not share the remote. He didn't know what living with Samuel would be like, especially since they couldn't seem to go a day without arguing, but maybe if he lived close for a while, and Thames was only twenty minutes away so it qualified to him, then perhaps they could try things out for a while until they got sick of each other. Which always happened with the guys he was with. Six months was his limit, and maybe the only reason he'd been into Samuel for almost nine months now was because they hadn't been around each other that much. He didn't want to lose out on Samuel just because they got tired of each other.

He'd become a lawyer in New Zealand regardless, though, simply to see if he still knew what the hell he was talking about. He was qualified to practice in all but three states, because he liked proving how good he was and had wanted to make his dad proud. Maybe this time he could take the test to be proud of himself.

And New Zealand definitely had the lack of snow thing going for it. He'd looked up normal winter temps for the country, and after he'd figured out that he was looking at Celsius and not Fahrenheit, and therefore didn't have to panic, he realized they really weren't all that bad.

Samuel seemed to be slowing down, his harsh breaths rocking through him as he continued to beat at the heavy punching bag. Some people may have been afraid that the person they wanted could get angry enough to become this violent, this absolutely brutal. Chris was not one of those people, but he wasn't stupid either. Samuel had the potential to really hurt someone. And now he knew why Misha said he wouldn't want to face him in a match, because he was fucking dangerous.

But Chris's belief that Samuel would never hurt him intentionally was absolute, so he leaned back, enjoyed the show, and waited for Samuel to work out whatever it was that was bothering him this time. Chris had a pretty good suspicion that he was at the heart of Samuel's frustration at the moment, though, which he was okay with. He knew he was an asshole sometimes, and he'd intentionally pushed Samuel too far in order to get him alone. Wouldn't it just suck if his plan backfired on him now?

CHAPTER TWENTY-TWO

SAMUEL COULDN'T remember when last he had been this angry at a person and so sexually frustrated at the same time. The complete irony of the situation—he was sexually wired for a guy he wanted to throttle—should have been funny, but he couldn't find the energy to laugh at himself over his stupidity.

The best way to work it all off was over-the-top exercise to the point of pain. After leaving Kaden's house he came straight home to change into a pair of cutoff shorts and hit the workout room with a vengeance. Sweat soaked every piece of skin and ran down the side of his face. His heart pounded as adrenaline pumped into his bloodstream, his body in full combat mode. Pulling on his last reserves, he managed a few more roundhouse kicks to the rocking bag before grabbing it with both hands to stop its momentum.

Then he turned around and glared at Chris, where he stood by the door. "You don't want to be here right now."

Chris only smiled at him. "Actually, I think I do. I'm enjoying the view. Keep hitting the bag thing for a while. Your ass looks great when you do that." He pushed away from the wall and came toward Samuel, but instead of going to him, as Samuel had expected, Chris went over and poked at one of the larger punching bags. It swayed a little, and Chris nearly giggled. "It looks like fun." He looked back at Samuel. "I'm serious. Keep going. Mirrors everywhere here and I want to watch you. You're yummy to look at." He stripped off the thin shirt Samuel had wanted to peel off him back at the house and tossed it aside, giving Samuel a wink as he did.

All the workout he had done meant shit as he watched a cocky Chris walk through his exercise equipment—weights, treadmill, and a bench press, but when Chris bent over to lift up one of the smaller weights, Samuel lost the fight against his slipping control.

In two steps he rushed Chris from behind and full-body tackled him to the soft mats on the floor. Chris grunted an oomph as he hit the ground, but Samuel made sure to fall sideways to spare Chris his heavy weight. Before Chris could open his smart mouth, Samuel flipped him over and pinned his arms above his head. Only then did he look in his eyes.

"Should I be asking what you're doing?" Chris asked, making Samuel groan as he wiggled against him.

"I'm doing what I should've done a long time ago to shut you up," Samuel growled as he used one hand to hold Chris's arms and the other to loosen the button on his pants and started pushing them down over his hips.

Chris's smirk annoyed him, as did the kiss he blew him, as if he thought Samuel wouldn't follow through this time.

"If you wanted to give me a hand job, all you had to do was say so. You know I'm game for that. And if this is what I get every time I piss you off, I'll have to figure out more ways to annoy you. If I wash your reds with your whites and turn everything pink, would that do it for you?"

"Shut up! All you have to do to piss me off at the moment is open your mouth and speak."

Samuel slammed his mouth down on Chris's and roughly shoved his tongue inside to taste him. Chris took a second or two to respond, as if surprised to be kissed at all, and then all bets were off. Teeth clicked and tongues dueled, and at one stage Samuel tasted a bit of blood from a split lip, but tough shit. He'd waited a damn long time for this.

When he got Chris out of his pants, Samuel stood up and straddled Chris below him before pulling off his own shorts.

"Can I say something?" Chris bugged him.

"What?" he almost yelled as he lowered himself onto Chris's body, skin on skin.

Chris moaned a little at the contact and looked like he was enjoying himself. "The piercing is only from this morning. It looks healed, thanks to an awesome spray, but it's still raw, so try not to tear it out. Deal?"

Samuel pushed himself up and looked at the object of discussion. "Deal." Without further delay he moved back, stroking his palms down Chris's chest, abdomen, and over the amazing tattoo to his hips before taking his hard cock into a firm grip.

"Does begging count as talking?"

"I'll just ignore you," Samuel retorted. He wet his lips and took Chris into his mouth all the way to the base.

Chris laughed, but he wasn't laughing long as Samuel swallowed him. He didn't mind when Chris thrust as much as he could into his mouth, especially since he was only squeezing his shoulders with his hands, not pushing his head down.

"Fuck, you're good with your mouth. Whatever got into you, tell me so I can do it more."

Samuel held the root of Chris's dick and got to work on making him come. He applied all his knowledge and technique, which wasn't too much with his limited experience, but he did what he enjoyed done to him, and it worked, if Chris's exclamations and scratching nails were anything to go by. Samuel was sure he'd have long red scratches over his shoulders, but he didn't stop, even when Chris started to push him off.

"Stop," Chris gasped. "Not yet. Too soon."

He kept pushing, but Samuel refused to move as he worked his mouth over Chris's length, even as Chris whimpered and dug his nails sharply into Samuel's shoulders. He tasted Chris's precome and felt his cock harden more as his climax approached, and still he didn't pull off.

Chris must've realized there was no stopping, because he planted his hands on Samuel's head and came with a cry of surrender. His body bucked and shivered beneath Samuel, and Samuel swallowed some of the come before pulling off and jerking Chris to gather the rest on his hand.

While Chris lay there taking deep breaths, Samuel pushed his legs back slightly, giving Chris enough time to refuse if he wanted to, even as Chris smiled up at him and ran his hands down Samuel's sweat-drenched chest. Chris opened his legs farther, and Samuel took some of the release on two fingers and rubbed them around Chris's entrance.

Chris made a sound Samuel could only describe as a purr. For the first time he realized what a sexual creature the man before him was, and it made him regret holding out on Chris for so long. If they did end up together, Sam had his work cut out for him keeping this cat satisfied.

Using persistent pressure and gentle strokes, he loosened Chris's tight muscles enough to penetrate with first one then two digits.

Chris hissed and gave him a sexy smile. "I had forgotten how good that feels."

Samuel looked down at where he stretched Chris's ass and spread his fingers a little to prepare him some more. "I will feel much better."

With his left hand he added more come to the outside and worked it in, before adding a third finger.

"So damn good." Chris squirmed slightly, trying to push himself down on Samuel's hand, and he couldn't wait any longer. He leaned forward on one arm and lodged his cock at Chris's ready hole. "I'm clean. Got tested three months ago. You?"

Chris stroked his hands over Samuel's tattooed shoulders and upper arms, the appreciation of his body clear to see in his eyes. "I got tested before I came here. No one after my second visit to Montana. Nada."

Samuel kissed him as he pushed in slowly, lifting one of Chris's legs up to make it easier. Chris complied wonderfully by wrapping both long legs around his hips. By the third thrust, delicious tight heat enveloped his cock, and Samuel growled at the feeling of possessiveness that stole over him.

Chris surprised him by wrapping his arms around his shoulders, pulling him closer, showing he was just as desperate as Samuel was in that moment. He was as liquid metal under him, all hot and responsive, gasping with each slow movement as Samuel pushed into him.

Samuel sucked Chris's tongue into his mouth, their very breaths mingling in their closeness, and still neither broke it off. When breathing became too hard, he slid his lips down Chris's stubbly cheek and latched his teeth and lips onto the skin and tight tendon in his neck. He sucked the spot to make a mark and continued his journey down. He pumped his hips slowly, in no hurry to finish what they'd started and careful to avoid rubbing against Chris's belly piercing.

By far his most responsive lover, Samuel knew he wouldn't be able to give up this thing with Chris easily. Not when every ounce of pleasure was so easy to see in the tight lines of his face and his easy, breathless gasps. He seemed to hold nothing back, no part of himself, as he gave Samuel everything he had without a single word. Now he understood why Chris chose sex so long ago as an outlet, because it was one way he could let go of all his problems and give himself away fully.

Bowing his back Samuel licked and nibbled Chris's nipples, first one, then the other. Chris went wild beneath him, squirming and thrusting back up to deepen the penetration of his body. With every stroke Samuel took, Chris pushed up, and the desire Chris had for him made this so much better than any anonymous sex could ever be. Chris knew him some, they had kissed, cuddled and fought, but he wanted Samuel with a passion humbling to see.

"Look," Chris said in a breathless moan, and Samuel followed the direction of his gaze to see them gloriously naked and making love in the mirror beside them. Chris let go of him with one hand, and Samuel instantly missed the contact, but he watched as Chris pushed his hair back from his face, the soft curls growing tighter with his sweat as they clung to his skin.

"I want to—" Chris bit off before clamping his mouth shut again as if he was afraid to say what he wanted to. Instead he brought his hand back up to Samuel's shoulder and ran his fingertips down his arm.

"Tell me what you need."

Chris laughed breathlessly. "Need? What I need is you. What I was going to say was that we had so fucking much to talk about and I wanted to talk to you. That can wait until tomorrow, though. Right now I only want to enjoy you. Until you get pissed off at me again. Of course… if this is my reward for making you mad, I'll gladly do it every damn day."

Samuel smiled a bit. "Being mad at you doesn't change how much I want you, so if you piss me off I'll only fuck you again. So it's a good deal. We can talk tomorrow, because we're talking a different language right now." Samuel kissed him again, his lips red and swollen from their earlier aggressive kisses.

"Turn over. I want to ride you," Chris said, surprising him with his words and also the hard tap on his shoulder.

They'd have to separate for that, but Chris did look pretty insistent. Samuel carefully withdrew and rolled over Chris's leg onto his back, the mat cool against his sweaty skin.

As Chris balanced himself over Samuel, he couldn't deny how gorgeous and completely sure of himself Chris looked as he lowered himself back onto Samuel's shaft, hissing as he took him fully again. At first he didn't move at all, just knelt there on top of him, but when his slow movements came Samuel was nearly entranced as Chris gently moved his hips, the smallest motion rocking Samuel in him and making him gasp. Of course Chris looked smug, especially as he dragged his hand down his side, over his tattoo, taking Samuel's gaze with the movement.

"I knew you'd like this. Having me on top seems to be everyone's favorite. I don't mind. It's mine too."

Samuel growled in frustration. "No more talk of anyone else doing this to you. You're with me and only me. I don't want you doing this with another person, because as much as we fight, you know as well as I do, we can't deny this. What we have. The way we met, what are the chances?"

"I do so love that you consulted me on this decision," Chris said with a grin. He rolled his hips, increasing the movement, and laid his hands on Samuel's stomach. "The chances are slim. I'll give you that. And it's weird that really we've spent so little time together but I've been into you longer than anyone else in my life. Also, holding my wrists, I wouldn't have been able to go to even Bran for that. So you read into that all you want. But do it later. I don't want you distracted right now."

Samuel used his hands to touch Chris the way he wanted to when he first saw him without a shirt. Using a finger, he traced the lines of Chris's tattoo and a big circle around his navel, looking at Chris's face to see if it hurt him, but he only increased the pace. Samuel pulled his knees up and supported Chris's back, and it pushed him deeper into Chris's body.

Chris leaned over and sucked on his nipples, goose bumps rising all over his skin as his hips lifted involuntarily at the pleasure he got from it.

"You okay coming in me when you're ready?" Chris asked him huskily as he laid his forehead against Samuel's neck. "I think I'll cry if you say no."

"Why is it so important to you?" Samuel wondered.

Chris didn't lift his head. "Because no one ever has." He rocked himself over Samuel's hard length, no longer looking at him as he seemed only focused on giving Samuel pleasure, on making him come.

Samuel took his face between his palms, forcing Chris to look into his eyes. "It's a first for me too. I'm ready when you are."

"Don't get sappy on me now, old man," Chris teased him, even as he leaned down to kiss Samuel on his cheek.

He moved and caught Chris's kiss on his lips before sliding his tongue inside. He wanted to kiss this man as they both came. Nothing could be any more intimate than this. Chris lifted his stomach from

Samuel's without breaking their kiss, and Samuel began to feel the rough slide of Chris's knuckles against his belly as he stroked himself. Soon his soft moans turned into gasps and he began to tremble in Samuel's embrace.

"You better be close," Chris grunted against his lips before smashing his mouth back against Samuel's.

Samuel's whole body went hot and tight as his orgasm started to form. "With you," he managed to gasp against Chris's kiss.

With a strangled cry, Chris suddenly went still above him, and warmth splashed between them as he came. Samuel found his release only a second later, filling Chris and being with him in a way he'd never experienced with anyone else.

The moment was over far too soon, though, as Chris's phone began ringing and he started to pull away. "Leave it," Samuel said, trying to hold him.

"Nope."

But he was exhausted, and Chris was slippery with sweat, letting him escape as he got up and went over to his pants. Samuel felt an intense sense of pride as he saw a glistening line of come sliding down Chris's leg as he walked away.

He wasn't gone long, though, before he was back and lying on his side next to Samuel. "Hey," he said into his phone, which lay on the mat between them.

"What's wrong? You sound out of breath." Misha's concern was clear through the phone.

Chris gave Samuel a wink. "I'm fine. Just working out on the mats with Samuel. He's showing me some great moves."

"I don't need to know my little brother has a sex life, thank you very much," Misha groaned over the line.

Chris snorted and leaned forward to kiss Samuel. He pulled away before Samuel could get a hand on him, though. "Right. And here I was referring to some punchy kicky things. With big bags hanging from ceilings. But whatever, perv. Get my text? Trent wants you here." Chris pushed the phone a little toward Samuel as if he was saying that Samuel could talk to Misha too if he wanted to.

"Yeah. I got it. Thanks for giving him the tag. Only took you a fucking week."

As Samuel watched him, Chris turned bright red. "I was busy. Doing stuff."

"Sure. I'll see you later. Tell Trent I love him."

Chris rolled his eyes. "Tell him yourself. I'm not your fucking messenger."

Misha laughed, and Chris smiled down at the phone.

"Someday. But I'm going into a hot zone right now, and I want Trent to know that. In case."

"Nothing is going to happen to you. Don't think like that," Chris said with a dramatic sigh.

"See you. Don't piss Samuel off. I want you two to be friends, not you dead because you didn't know when to stop."

"Yep. Bye."

He hung up the phone, and Samuel was sure he'd get to hold him now that he was no longer talking to Misha, only that didn't happen then either as Chris stood back up and went to his pants, this time stepping into them.

"Where are you going?" Samuel demanded, shocked that Chris would leave him so soon. And part of him was terrified that Chris was running away again.

He had his pants zipped up before he answered him. "I have to go. See you."

Samuel grabbed his wrist before he could get too far, though. "Where are you running to now? And why?"

With a smile Chris softly kissed him. "I'm not running anywhere. I need to shower and change before I go to Renegade tonight. I promised Jeff I'd be there. You should bring the guys."

"Are you with him?" Samuel asked, instantly hating that he had to question that.

Chris's expression turned serious in an instant. "No. You're it for me. If we can figure out our shit before I go back to the States, that is. I figure a month should do it. Gotta go now, though. Thanks for this. You know I had fun." He quickly kissed Samuel, then bounced away before Samuel could grab him again.

CHAPTER TWENTY-THREE

RENEGADE WAS alive with hot bodies and thumping music when Chris walked in the door, waving to the bouncer on his way in. He'd been spending a few hours every night there since getting into New Zealand, and the guys at the door had started to recognize him. He wasn't there because he had started drinking again, or because he wanted to dance with the dozens of guys that hit on him every night, but because he genuinely liked Jeff and Aaron. And when Jeff had complained of not having enough help on his first night back for a quick drink of soda, Chris hadn't been able to resist helping him. He hadn't known them long, but they'd easily been brought into his small circle of friends. And being at the bar let him work off some of his energy. He'd been an anxious wreck while he'd been working up to seeing Samuel and Bran again.

He stripped off his jacket and shirt, pushing them under the bar as he came up beside Jeff as he busily mixed drinks. Aaron was only a few feet away, pouring a few beers from the taps.

"Already busy tonight," Chris said, smiling to some of the regulars he recognized. He didn't know their names, not yet at least, but he was good with faces.

Jeff gave him a nod before passing out the drinks to the guys at the bar. "Yeah. You look like you had fun. You're practically glowing."

Chris just shrugged at him. "Maybe I did." He liked the feeling of the bar, the music around him, and that he got to do something to help out a friend when the bar really started going. Aaron wasn't much of a help, though he did try.

And behind the bar, he felt like it was safe to dance and have fun while he poured drinks and flirted casually with the guys. "Aaron, come here," he called. Like a cute, eager puppy, Aaron was at his side in an instant.

"What's up?"

Chris grinned at him and pulled out a shaker. "I'm going to teach you a new drink. Pay attention. And remember, you gotta smile while making drinks." A whiskey sour was one of his favorite drinks, and he easily remembered the ingredients. Whiskey, lemon, sugar, and a lemon wedge for garnish after he'd shaken it all up and served it over ice. The man nearest to him hadn't ordered the drink, but he took it with a smile when Chris handed it to him. "Whiskey sour. Think you've got it?"

Aaron nodded, looking uncertain, but Chris had faith in him. He was a fast learner. Leaving him to it, Chris went to help Jeff.

"I'm amazed that he listens to you so well. I try to teach him the big industrial dishwasher in the back and he tunes straight out. You, he freaking idolizes."

Chris snorted and shook his head. "He wants me, even though he knows that is never going to happen. There's a big difference between attraction and idolization. But I'm happy to help out."

"Thanks. You're a great bartender. For a lawyer."

"Dated a guy. He was cute, horrible lover, but I picked up some skills. Also, spending a good part of my adult life drinking more alcohol than water probably helped." Chris went back to it, taking drink orders as they flew at him and mixing the drinks up when he had to, otherwise sending Aaron off to pour them if they were only beers.

When he got a few seconds, which wasn't often, he closed his eyes and danced, letting the music go through him and not really caring about anything else until either Jeff or Aaron tapped him on his shoulder, getting his attention again.

He could have been back with Samuel instead of here surrounded by random people, but if they were going to do this and actually try to have a relationship, Chris wanted them to have their own time to do their own things. That was important to him. It wouldn't always be just the two of them, or even the five of them. If this was going to work, then Chris would need his time. He was independent and stubborn, but it seemed like Samuel was too. So maybe they had a chance. He hoped they did. The sex had opened his eyes a bit, but if he was really being honest, he'd wanted to give some serious thought to being with Samuel since he'd gone in and asked Samuel to hold his wrists for him. Cutting was so much easier than that night had been, especially since he'd had to be so fucking vulnerable with someone he really did care about. That was nearly impossible for him.

He just needed to prove to himself that he could handle maybe just one week of being normal like everyone else and not wanting to cut. If he was okay with that then maybe he could make it to two, and then maybe he'd be okay at a month. It drove him nuts that he'd been fine, masking it all and dealing, for over a decade. But he hoped, and his ultimate plan, was to just stop it all. He wanted his crap gone and done with. When he had sex, hopefully with Samuel now that he knew just how good Samuel was, he wanted it to be because he was horny, because he wanted the other person... because, honestly, he was in love with Samuel and wanted to be with him. He didn't want his frustration, his pain, or the constant pressure on him to be why he found someone else and let them screw him. He only wanted Samuel, and he wanted to be good enough for him. No issues, no complications. Just him and just Samuel. He wanted to go on dates, to hold Samuel's hand as they went out to lunch, and not to feel like he had a volcano inside of him, just waiting to go off the minute he was pushed too hard.

He was still thinking about what he needed to do and how much he needed to work on himself an hour later when Samuel, Bran, Kaden, and Trent came through the double doors of the bar and headed straight toward him.

"Aaron, you're up," Chris said as he started on an order of three martinis. "Four guys that just walked in, get them whiskey sours. And if you hit on the guy with the tattoos I will claw your eyes out."

Aaron laughed. "I remember him. He the reason you're in such a good mood?"

Chris grinned but didn't answer him. "Get the drinks going."

"Don't even know why Jeff makes me listen to you," Aaron grumbled.

"He doesn't. You do that on your own. Soon as you stop thinking every guy here could be the right one for you and focus more on dating guys that don't just want quick hookups, he won't ask me to hang out and watch over you so much." It was just a guess, since Jeff was more than efficient when it came to running the bar from what Chris could tell, and they'd talked a little about the kind of mistakes Chris had made growing up. None of the worst of it but plenty of the small stuff.

He glanced over at Aaron, making sure he made the drinks well enough that his friends wouldn't get sick from them, then gave the martinis he'd made to Jeff to hand out. Aaron put the whiskey sours in front of them, and Chris took his spot. "Hey," he said, giving Bran a nod but Samuel a smile as he leaned over the bar to quickly kiss him. "Glad you came." He dragged the fingers of his right hand down the front of

Samuel's chest, loving that he'd worn one of those muscle shirts that showed off every bit of him again. He wouldn't be wearing it for long, though, if Chris could bring him home that night.

"Hey, nice tattoo, can I buy you a drink?"

Chris turned to face the unfamiliar man and gave him an easy, flirty smile. "Sure. I like vodka. Straight up. That good for you?"

The man gave him a smile, and Chris turned away from them all as he pulled down the most expensive bottle of vodka, grabbed a shot glass, and also a bottle of water he had hidden behind the pricey whiskey hardly anyone ordered. He poured himself a shot of water, hid the water bottle, and put the vodka away before turning around and making a big deal of shooting the water and having it burn like vodka. The guy laughed, his friends pulled him away, and Chris passed the money he paid over to Jeff, who gave him a nod of thanks.

He went back to Bran and Samuel, looking to Bran first. "How's noon tomorrow for you look? We need to talk."

Bran looked uncertain. "Why don't we talk now?"

They could, actually. There were plenty of dark places in the bar where they could go to talk, and it wasn't as if Jeff actually needed him there. He was pretty sure he was only there as eye candy and to help out sometimes, not that he minded. Or maybe it was that Jeff liked having someone around to talk to that wasn't a bull-headed twenty-two-year-old who seemed to know everything but absolutely none of it being important. "Sure." He turned his attention to Samuel. "I'd like you to come over tonight. If you can. I'll text you my address." He quickly did just that and got a little beep from Samuel's phone in return to let him know the message had been delivered.

Samuel nodded. "Okay, I'll be there."

Chris gave a little wave to Jeff to let him know he wouldn't be there for a few minutes, then lifted up the flap in the bar to get to Bran. They found a small, sort of quiet corner, and Chris crossed his arms over his chest as he tried to figure out where to start with Bran. "I want you to know I still love you, and I don't want to stop being friends. Ever. You're like a brother to me. I actually like you more than Misha 90 percent of the time, if not more."

Bran gave him a weak smile and laid his forearms over Chris's shoulders. Instead of pushing him away, Chris wrapped his hands loosely around Bran's back, resting them at base of his spine. "I can't fight with you anymore. I overreacted, I was stupid, and I'm sorry."

"I know you are," Chris said. Bran had apologized plenty enough already. "I'm mad at you because when you told me you screwed my brother, I forgave you. And when you didn't tell me that Richard had abused you, and then I got hurt by him, which could have been avoided had you actually told me the truth, I forgave you then too. But when I let you know that I was doing something that only ever hurt me, you threw me out of your life. That wasn't okay, Bran. I needed you, I've always needed you, and you pushed me away and treated me like I was nothing. Like you would rather that I screw strangers and hurt myself with other people and put myself in really dangerous situations, rather than just cut myself."

Chris waited for him to say something, to show that he understood why Chris had been so mad at him, and when Bran finally nodded and looked like he was about to cry, Chris was pretty sure he did get it this time. He pulled Bran tightly into his arms and closed his eyes as Bran held him just as close, digging his hands into Chris's back.

"I get that. And I'm sorry I did that to you, but I don't like you cutting. I wish I could stop you somehow," Bran quietly said, barely loud enough for Chris to hear him.

Chris nodded. "I don't like doing it either. I don't want to do any of it. When I told you, though, I only wanted you to listen, to try to understand, and it hurt that you couldn't do even that much for me after everything we've been through."

"I'm going to make this up to you," Bran promised him.

Chris didn't worry about that too much. Bran had been listening now, and by his tears, Chris knew he understood. "We're best friends. We're going to fight. I just wanted you to understand why I've been needing to punch you lately."

Bran laughed and pulled back. He wiped his cheeks, getting rid of his tears. "I don't blame you for that at all. What's your plan now?"

"I need to talk to Samuel for that." He took Bran's hand, and they headed back to the bar where Chris slipped behind it. Before he moved away, though, he leaned over and kissed Bran quickly on his cheek. "You're still a great friend. But you are stupid sometimes."

That made Bran laugh.

Chris served a few more drinks before Jeff came over to get his attention. "Thanks for the help, mate, but go so you can spend time with your friends. I'm sure you and your buddy over there will cause quite a stir on the dance floor by the looks of you together."

Chris saw him gesture at Bran and laughed out loud. "Oh, I'm sure we can. We used to dance like that all the time while in college. Just hope no one dares to touch us, or Kaden and Samuel may do some damage."

Jeff grinned at him. "If I hadn't worked my butt off to get this place, I would buy front row tickets. You guys are all smokin' hot. Go on. They're waiting for you." Jeff pushed him away with a hand on his shoulder.

He grabbed his shirt from where he stashed it under the bar and tucked it into his pants. When he reached his group of friends, Samuel's eyes latched onto his tattoo before moving lower to his navel.

"We gonna dance a bit?" he asked them all, but kept his eyes locked to Samuel's heated gray ones.

Bran was the one to answer his question. "Hell, yes. This music has me squirming on my seat to get moving."

Chris took Samuel's hand, pulling him onto the floor and immediately pressing himself against Samuel's chest, needing that contact. "So.... You okay with me being here? Random guys hitting on me while I walk around without a shirt on, or does this make your jealousy kick in?"

Samuel put his lips to Chris's ear, giving it a quick nip. "They can look all they like, but if they touch, all bets are off."

Laughing, Chris ran his hands down the front of Samuel's shirt, both loving and hating that he wore the skintight shirt again. It showed off everything, which was awesome, but then everyone else could see Samuel too, which made him want to yell at them all. "Good. Because I like it here. And we would have had another fight if you'd told me you forbade it or some shit like that. I don't really follow orders too well."

Samuel gave a deep laugh as he pulled Chris's hips closer and started moving with the beat. "I think I know that very well."

Chris looked to his left and quickly looked away again. "Don't look over there. I don't want you seeing my best friend practically screwing his boyfriend in public." He wanted to put a sheet over them and toss them in a bedroom somewhere, which was where they belonged, but

Bran and Kaden looked completely oblivious as Bran rubbed his ass against Kaden's crotch and Kaden kissed him from behind. It was hot, absolutely so, but Chris wanted to make sure Samuel didn't see them too. "Do you remember when Bran gave Kaden that lap dance back in Montana?"

"I was a bit drunk from the spiked vodka and orange juice you two made, but yes, I remember some of it." Samuel's hands went around his hips to grasp his ass and pull him into a pump-and-grind movement.

"Well...." Chris had no idea why he wanted to share an embarrassing fact with Samuel, but out it came anyway. "I was afraid you'd want him more than me after you saw him doing that. Clearly, I was wrong. But it was an insecure moment. We're both good-looking. I'm not blind or stupid about that. But Bran's got something all his own."

Samuel was doing a good job of getting him really horny.

"So do you. Why would I want Bran if I can have you? He belongs to Kaden and has since the very first day they met on Tobias's steps in Montana. I would never do that to my friend, and besides, Bran and I would've killed each other a long time ago. We are not a match. Believe me. What I want is right here in front of me."

Chris couldn't help blushing at Samuel's words. "Want to go to my place? It isn't far. Or did you bring the rest of them and now we need to wait for them before I can have you? There are bathrooms here, but I don't really see you being a bathroom screw kind of guy."

Samuel turned him around so Chris's back touched his front as they danced. His head fell back onto Samuel's shoulder, and he shivered when Samuel kissed his neck and jaw.

"Any bathroom but this one. I'll do you in Kaden's bathroom, Trent's—hell, even the one at our milking shed, but not here. Why, do you have a thing for bathrooms?"

"Hell no. Except that they're often the most convenient places to suck off random guys, but in general, they smell and are dirty. And let's not have sex in their bathrooms either. They probably have, and I'd rather not do that. I'm making that a rule. Unless we're absolutely desperate and can't wait to get back to your place or mine. But please can we get out of here? I can feel your cock through those jeans, and I really need you right now." Chris wasn't above begging if it meant getting Samuel naked in the bargain.

Samuel gave him a scorching openmouthed kiss with tongue, and Chris almost changed his mind about using the closest surface, but Samuel broke away far too soon.

"Okay, you go along, and I'll say good-bye to these guys and be there shortly."

"Great, bye!" Chris practically ran to his motorcycle, not bothering to say good-bye to any of them. If they cared, they'd understand with a quick explanation. He was pretty sure the only one who would have noticed him leaving, though, would have been Trent as he sat quietly at the bar, enjoying a drink and talking to Jeff.

CHRIS WAS on his second bowl of chocolate chip ice cream as he lay stretched out over the couch in front of some late night talk show when there was a knock on his front door. He sat up and peeked out the blinds, smiling when he recognized Samuel's truck.

Before Samuel had a chance to knock again, he'd tossed his bowl into the sink and stripped off the shorts he'd been wearing. There was an island across from the front door, and he leaned against it, propping himself up. "Come on in. Unless you're not alone."

Samuel opened the door, and Chris was glad to see the surprise so clearly displayed on his face. Chris smirked. "Mind closing the door? I think I have neighbors, though I have no idea who they are. And I'm not nearly as into public sex as Kaden and Bran seem to be."

Samuel quickly closed the door behind himself, and Chris wasted no time in going to his knees in front of him. He had Samuel's pants yanked down to his thighs before he remembered to kiss him first.

"Sorry, I'm eager," he explained as he stood back up and pressed his mouth roughly to Samuel's while also taking his dick in his hand and giving him a firm squeeze. "Any reason you don't want me to fuck you against this door tonight?" he asked Samuel as he pulled away and went right back down to his knees, where he began softly lapping at Samuel's sac while continuing to squeeze him.

"None at all. If you can reach, that is." Samuel hissed in pleasure at what Chris did with his mouth.

"Hmm. Good point. You are a good bit taller than the guys I usually screw." He quickly changed his tune when he saw Samuel's expression go dark. "Sorry. No talk of other guys when we're together."

"Damn straight."

That made Chris smile. "Then I'll just have you over the side of the couch. I do have one of those. Came with the house. I'm told it's comfortable, but really no one has been around to try it out." Done talking, he slid his mouth over Samuel's head, eagerly tasting him and working his tongue around Samuel's thick tip. When Samuel didn't do anything with his hands, Chris took him by his wrists and laid them over the back of his head, giving Samuel permission and a hint all at once. He liked to be controlled, to feel like someone he cared about, and especially someone he trusted, was taking possession of him. He didn't trust anyone like he trusted Samuel, so wanting to give him that power came naturally to Chris. He hadn't even considered any kind of an alternative.

Samuel was bigger than he was used to, but Chris went slowly, enjoying his time with him. They were past his six-month mark, with each day feeling like borrowed time and filled with uncertainty. He wouldn't focus on that now, though, not when he had Samuel exactly where he'd been wanting him for so long.

Samuel's fingers tightened around his head, and he carefully started moving in and out of Chris's willing mouth. Being on his knees in front of Samuel, being completely at his mercy and not caring one bit, that was bliss. And Chris absolutely loved it. He pulled back a little, releasing Samuel and smiling up at him as he slid his tongue up the underside of his shaft. "Don't come. Not yet. I have a lot more planned for tonight."

He slid his mouth back over Samuel's head, taking him as deeply as he could, and sighing the whole time. The hands on his head held him harder as Samuel slid his fingers into Chris's hair. Knowing the strength of the man made him weak and not scared—that Samuel held it so tightly reined in as not to hurt him, but Chris wanted him to lose his control a little bit. So he gave Samuel a bit of a bite, scraping his teeth along the underside of his shaft, right by the base. It wasn't enough to hurt him, not even a little, but if Samuel thought he didn't know how to bite, Chris hoped he remembered this moment.

Samuel moaned deeply, his thigh muscles bunching where he stood. "If you keep that up I am gonna come. Soon."

With a smug grin, Chris pulled back and got to his feet. "Thanks for the warning. Over the arm of the couch with you." He licked his lips, cleaning some of Samuel's precome off. This was fun, this getting to play with someone he cared about and trusting Samuel enough to know that if he did something Samuel didn't like he'd tell him right away. Chris didn't have to be careful with him when they were together. It was liberating to realize that.

Samuel shucked his shirt while toeing off his boots before pulling off his socks too. He walked toward the couch, and Chris watched his ass bunch and move, the muscles all tight and drool-worthy. He couldn't resist reaching out and giving Samuel a hard smack as he walked by. When Samuel looked back at him, Chris was quick to blow him a kiss.

"This is fun. You keep me around and we could do this a lot more. Even have naked weekends. Or more accurately, be naked all the time except when you have to work, other people are over, or in general someone could see you. New Zealand law seems to sort of frown on murder, which is what would happen."

Samuel grinned. "Naked all the time? Will take me some time to get used to that."

Chris shrugged and followed him over to the couch, where he ran his hands down Samuel's back as he got himself situated on the arm. It might not have been super comfortable for him, but it put him at the right height for Chris. And this was one thing he felt okay being selfish about. "Oh, you'll get used to it. I'll hide all your clothes, and then you won't have a choice if you want to come out of bed. And babe, I'm good, but I'm not breakfast in bed kind of good. I'm more the order food from down the street and put it on a plate and pretend I made it kind of guy."

He bent down and gave Samuel's right cheek a quick bite before he kissed down Samuel's spine to his entrance, where he began to gently swirl his tongue. Samuel jerked at the touch, and it made Chris wonder if anyone had ever done that to him. Since he couldn't talk about his previous guys when they were together, he wasn't going to ask Samuel that, but it did make him think. He rested his hands on Samuel's thighs, softly stroking him as he slid his tongue into him, getting him ready for what was to come next. He liked this part, though. Some guys skimped and rushed it, but he enjoyed taking care of the guys he was with and making them feel as good as they made him. Samuel had pretty much rocked his world that afternoon, so Chris wasn't going to give him any less than that tonight.

Samuel's glutes flexed, and Chris heard what sounded like nails scraping across the upholstery of the couch.

"That feels amazing. Wrong but wonderful," Samuel muttered breathlessly.

Frowning, Chris pulled back. "Wrong? You're going to have to explain that one to me." He went right back to licking Samuel's entrance. He may have thought it was wrong, but that didn't mean Chris wasn't going to continue on just like before.

"Just never thought it's somewhere someone would like to kiss and lick me, I guess." The back of Samuel's neck was flushed red, as if he was embarrassed.

Chris could kind of see that, in a way. But his position on how much he liked doing it still stood. "You've dated some whackos that needed to be taught some lessons, then. If you don't like it, I won't do it again. But I do kind of really like it so...." He shrugged and leaned back, knowing Samuel had enough lubricant from his saliva to make this easier for him. Chris could hardly hold still as he wanted to bounce around in anticipation.

Samuel sighed softly. "I said it felt amazing, so don't stop doing it again."

Laughing, Chris kissed him on the base of his spine. "Next time. Right now I need to be in you." He began stretching him as slowly as he could, even as his dick begged for attention and he kept bouncing up and down. "Been wanting you since the first day I saw you sitting there in the living room, looking like you wanted to kill me while I just wanted to kill Kaden for beating up Bran." Thinking back to that moment made him smile.

"Same here."

It appeared that Samuel wasn't much of a talker when he bottomed, because all Chris got out of him were a few broken sentences and lots of sounds. This time Samuel shivered and moaned as Chris prepared him.

"Oh? Did you want to kill Kaden too?" Chris joked with him as he withdrew his fingers and moved his hand to Samuel's hip. He was ready, though Chris would still hold himself back and go slowly. That afternoon on the mats was rough and wonderful, and he'd absolutely loved it, but they had time now, and Chris was determined to enjoy him during the hours they had until morning. He took his cock in his hand and swirled it around Samuel's hole, spreading the precome around to help smooth the way in. Every now and then he notched it in place and gave a little push but not enough to penetrate.

"How often have you done this?" Chris asked, even though he really didn't want to talk about Samuel's exes right then. They were history, old news, no longer existing on the same planet as Samuel as far as he was concerned. But the way Samuel tensed up each time Chris even got close to getting inside of him had him wondering. He smoothed his free hand down Samuel's spine, hoping to ease any worries or tension he might have.

"Only twice, and they weren't very memorable. I guess, like Misha, guys think I'm bigger and that I'm a top."

"Sucks for them. I'm loving this view." He leaned down and kissed Samuel between his shoulder blades. "You're beautiful. Just relax. I know what I'm doing. Oh, and one more thing, don't you dare touch yourself. I still want to swallow you after I come in you."

While he stayed bent over Samuel's back, keeping them together, he slowly eased himself inside. Samuel may have been trying to relax, but he really wasn't doing a very good job of it. Chris could work with that, though. He just had to slow down and be patient. For Samuel he was willing to do that.

"Good, you're doing fine," Chris said, showering light kisses over Samuel's back as he eased his way in a little more with small, slow thrusts. He was perfectly tight and deliciously warm against him, and Chris desperately wanted to go faster, but he kept reminding himself that he was trying not to be an ass. This was Samuel, and Chris wanted him to have a great time. He desperately needed to be memorable to Samuel more than he needed to come.

Finally he felt Samuel begin to relax, and the viselike grip on his cock eased away. He was still unbelievably tight, but he wasn't crushing Chris nearly to the point of pain either. He stayed over him for a few more minutes, gently easing into him with short thrusts that left him gasping as he felt Samuel tremble beneath his hand. When he was mostly in and Samuel hadn't tried to kick him off, Chris figured it was safe to lean back, put a hand on either side of Samuel's tight hips, and stroke into him with some actual speed.

He grunted softly as he watched Samuel's skin flush with pleasure, though he wished he could see Samuel's face. That would be for next time. After so many months of denying himself any pleasure that wasn't from his hand, this felt freaking amazing. And Chris dreaded how quickly he would end up coming. It seemed like when he was with Samuel, he always came embarrassingly fast.

And that night was sadly no different as he dug his hands into Samuel's hips, only afterward realizing that he might have actually hurt him, and emptied himself into Samuel's body as he panted out a cry. He wanted to drift lazily off, to relax for a few minutes and just bask in the feeling of how good it had felt to take Samuel and how often he wanted to do that from now on. But right then he wasn't going to be an ungrateful dick, and a horrible lover at that, while he left Samuel hanging, waiting for his own orgasm. He brought Samuel over to the couch, onto his side, then further to his back, so that he could kneel between Samuel's open thighs.

He looked needy, which made Chris smile as he took him back into his mouth, bobbing his lips over Samuel's swollen cock as he balanced himself with one hand and stroked him from the base up with the other. He was quickly rewarded with Samuel's loud groan and a mouthful of warm come, which he happily swallowed.

"I had fun. And if you had fun too then we're doing that a lot more often," Chris said as he sat up next to Samuel and struggled to catch his own breath. He took Samuel's hand in his and leaned his head back on the couch as he waited for his heart to stop racing, all the while smiling.

Chapter Twenty-Four

THE NEXT morning Samuel sat by a table at their favorite coffee shop and bakery in town with Trent and Kaden opposite him. Farming was the topic of conversation until the waiter served their large strong coffees in cups as big as soup bowls.

"What's up?" Kaden was the first to ask.

Trent looked around, taking in their surroundings, appearing completely disconnected from their talk, but Samuel always thought it was a trick. No one was more aware than Trent.

"Well, we haven't exactly had much time alone since getting back from the States, and a hell of a lot has happened since. Thought it would be good to catch up." Samuel saw Trent reach up, take Misha's dog tag between his fingers, and stroke it with his thumb. No one had heard from Misha since he had started his latest mission. No one even knew where he was in the world. Samuel respected Trent for his quiet strength, because he sure as hell wouldn't have been so calm about it.

Kaden watched Trent too, a small frown of worry creasing his forehead. "Fair enough. These American boys sure took our lives on a tailspin. How's things with you?"

Trent snickered, not even looking their way. "He's getting laid, so he'll be sweet as."

Kaden chuckled. "Besides that?"

Samuel sipped his coffee before clearing his throat. "I've fallen for him. Big time."

Trent's grass-green gaze swung to him instantly. "No shit!"

Samuel ignored him. "The problem is he hasn't spoken of his future plans after his month or so here is up. If he's going back or staying here. Back in the States, he said he meant to go back and possibly start up his own practice, but he's never mentioned it since. I'm in the dark here."

Kaden also drank from his cup, licking the foam off his top lip. "Didn't you make it clear to Chris that you're not willing to pursue something serious with him unless he gives it a chance by being closer to you?"

"Pretty much."

"Well, you've made your point. Leave it, then, and trust he'll do the right thing. He knows where you stand, but don't push. You know he's as skittish as a horse around a snake when you force him into anything," Trent added wisely, his cup already half-empty.

Samuel's frustration rose. "I hope Misha gives you hell."

Trent's white smile flashed as he turned to look at the passing pedestrians, his attention caught by a young boy with a small dog on a leash. The pug stopped by Trent's legs, and he reached down to give it a pat. When the boy walked off, Trent spoke. "Oh, I'm completely convinced he will do exactly that. He's not a cuddly soft teddy bear. That much I know. More like an exotic wild cat wrapped in thorns and thistles."

Samuel actually felt sorry for the man. "Better you than me."

"That's what I say about what you two have" came the witty reply.

"Samuel," Kaden sighed, "I know both Bran and Chris have these hard as brick exteriors, but inside, all they want is to be loved and accepted. Give Chris time. By what he's told us, he hasn't ever been loved just for who he is."

Samuel thought about it and agreed with Kaden. "Okay, there's nothing I can do but give him what he needs, then. Oh, yes. Trent, we'd all like to go out on the boat whenever it suits you. Let us know and we'll help with fuel and bring some eats, and we can spend the day on the water and maybe catch a few big ones for the pan."

Trent smiled brightly. "That's a good idea. I haven't taken her out for a while, so it will be a nice change. Maybe this weekend?"

"Sweet, I'll tell Bran." Kaden pushed his empty cup away.

Samuel did the same. "And I'll tell Chris."

Trent snickered. "Awww, how domesticated you two sound."

"Shut up," they both growled at him before getting up.

After saying good-bye to them, Samuel got in his truck and had an idea on his way home. First, though, he had to know Chris's plans before making such a serious decision. Hopefully he'd know sooner than later whether Chris would be making his home in New Zealand with Samuel or going back to Manhattan.

His phone started ringing, and he answered it with a touch on the display in his truck. "This is Samuel."

"Hey."

Samuel smiled instantly at the sound of Chris's voice.

"I did something bad. You're not going to like it. Not one bit."

His good mood vanished in a single rapid heartbeat.

"What did you do?" Samuel asked, fearing the worst—that Chris had started cutting himself again and had done so terribly, and now he was in trouble.

"Can I come over?"

Even though Chris couldn't see him, Samuel nodded. "You don't have to ask if you can. Do you want me to pick you up?"

"That's not necessary. I'm on my way to you right now. See you soon."

Before Samuel could say anything else, Chris had already ended the call. Samuel was quick to dial Kaden.

"This is Kaden," he said, answering Samuel's call on the first ring.

"Chris did something to himself. I think having Bran over at the house might help."

Thankfully Kaden didn't need to be told anything more than that. "We'll be right over. I'll call Trent too. It won't be like last time. We'll all handle it much better this time around. I promise we will be able to help him."

Samuel needed to hear that from him. He had to have that reassurance from one of his two best friends. "I'll see you there. Thanks."

"Of course."

Hanging up on Kaden, he raced his truck home. He hoped to find Chris there waiting for him, but everyone else was instead. He got out of his truck and headed up to let them all in. Bran paced. Kaden tried to silently comfort him. Trent sat down on the couch and simply looked worried. Samuel stood right inside the front door, waiting for Chris to come in.

A few minutes later he heard a motorcycle pull up, and he expected Chris to knock. Instead he opened the door and instantly started stripping off his helmet and jacket and kicking off his boots, as if he couldn't get naked fast enough.

"Hey. Didn't know you were having a party," Chris said as he got his socks off by balancing with his shoulder on the wall.

Samuel looked him over, expecting something to be wrong, but Chris looked fine. Happy even. Especially when he came over and gave Samuel a kiss on his cheek. And he was wearing a button-down shirt, along with a tie, over the tight black motorcycle pants that perfectly showed off his ass.

"Are you okay?" Samuel asked. Bran had stopped pacing, and Samuel could see him staring at Chris too.

Chris frowned at him, then began undoing his tie, and once it was off, he started removing his shirt. "Of course I am. What did you think? Oh...."

Samuel watched him shift his attention over to Bran, before coming back to himself.

"You thought I was cutting again. Didn't you?"

Samuel gave him a slow nod. "Yes. From your call I assumed you'd slipped and made that mistake."

"And then this would be an intervention. Again. Right.... Can we go upstairs?" Chris asked him, looking again to Bran, then to the others.

Bran stepped up. "No. We're here to help you. Let us."

Chris snorted, sounding a little like he was laughing at Bran, finished unbuttoning his shirt, and tossed it with the rest of his discarded clothes over the back of one of Samuel's dining room chairs. And that's when Samuel noticed the shiny new ring in each of his pierced nipples. He couldn't help staring, instantly wanting to touch Chris, to bring him upstairs, where Chris had asked him to go with him.

"Since everyone is already here and apparently going to know anyway," Chris said, raising his voice along with his sarcasm, "I was in Thames this morning and got carried away with the piercings. I didn't think to ask about giving you head with my tongue pierced until after she'd put the stud into my mouth. The bad thing I did was getting pierced, and now I can't suck you off for two weeks while this thing heals." He rolled his eyes and stuck his tongue out at Samuel, showing off a shiny metal ball in the center of his slightly swollen tongue.

Bran walked up and gave him a hug, which Chris returned, but Samuel could see him flinch before he pushed Bran away.

"Nipples are sensitive right now."

Bran's face lit up. "Can I touch?"

"No!" Kaden snapped at him from the living room where he and Trent sat on one of Samuel's big couches.

Bran laughed. "Can I see your tongue, then?"

Chris stuck it out for him too, and Samuel came up to get a closer look as well.

"Slut," Bran teased.

Chris closed his mouth and smiled at Bran. For Samuel, he grinned wickedly. "Saw you boys having coffee. Looked yummy. I was meeting someone in town anyway, in case you thought I was stalking you. Not that I wouldn't if I was curious enough."

"You should have come over to join us," Samuel said.

Chris shrugged. "Didn't want to interrupt. It's important that couples get their own time apart."

Bran laid his head on Chris's shoulder, obviously looking for attention, but Chris's gaze didn't stray from Samuel's. "You came in wearing a shirt and tie," Bran said, wrapping his arms around Chris from the side.

Smirking, Chris nodded. "I did. Amateur stripping competition. I won a hundred bucks."

By the wink Chris gave him, Samuel knew he was joking.

"Actually, I had a meeting with someone. Not anything I can really disclose to you, not details anyway, but it was business related."

"Lawyer related?" Bran pressed.

Chris stepped out of his arms and went to Samuel instead. "Something like that. A guy… a custody thing… someone paid way too much to be as incompetent as he was…." He ran his hands down Samuel's chest, to the front of his pants, and continued to drag his fingers along Samuel's waist as he slowly circled him. "Were you worried?"

"Of course I was," Samuel easily admitted.

Chris moved behind his back and wrapped his arms around Samuel from behind. It was good to be held and better to feel Chris lay his head against his back after Samuel felt him kiss his spine.

"Sorry. I'll remember to give you some kind of hint when I want to surprise you about something. Are they sexy, though? I tried to make sure they matched the belly button ring you got me, since I know how much you like that one. You'll have to be gentle with me, though, for the next two weeks. You're supposed to be nice to me and get me ice cream and brownies whenever I ask for them, while the new holes in my body heal. It says so on the aftercare instruction sheet I got."

Samuel grinned at Chris's pouting face. "I think I can manage to be gentle with lots of ice cream and chocolate brownies for two weeks. After that, though, no promises."

With a loud laugh Chris pulled his stuff into his arms and started heading upstairs. "I'm putting all this in your bedroom. No reason to have my boots and things in the dining room when I'm just going to be naked up here later."

"Are you putting on a shirt?" Samuel asked him as he watched Chris go up the stairs.

"Too rough on the nipples. You're just going to have to suffer for a while until I'm healed up," Chris called back down with a laugh.

"We should play a game!" Bran declared as soon as Chris came back down the stairs. "I propose Never Have I Ever, with screwdrivers."

"We haven't played that game in forever. Make the screwdrivers weak. Very, very weak. I mean it, Bran," Chris said as he joined them all in the living room.

Samuel made room for him on the couch beside him, and Chris instantly joined him, pressing up against his side as if he couldn't stop touching him, which was perfectly fine with Samuel since he had to have his hands on Chris as well. "Are you drinking again, then?"

Chris turned to look up at him, appearing uncertain. "Am I okay to be here? Even if I piss you off or I want to kill Bran? I won't ride if I've had any. That thing's a beast to control even in the best conditions."

Samuel wrapped an arm tightly around him. "You'll always be welcome here."

"Then I'll drink. A little," Chris said with a soft smile.

"How is this likely ridiculous game played?" Trent asked Chris as Bran went to go mix the drinks.

Chris leaned his head back against Samuel's shoulder, and Samuel wished he had Chris sitting in his lap instead, the way Bran instantly did with Kaden as soon as he came back into the room with a pitcher and a handful of glasses.

Chris answered him as Bran started handing out glasses and pouring drinks. He didn't get off Kaden's lap, so there was a lot of passing the glasses down between them until they each had one. "Someone says 'Never have I ever…' fill in the blank. For instance, I'd say 'Never have I ever fallen off a horse.' Then if you have, you take a drink. Try to make them more interesting than that, though. I don't want to be bored."

Bran laughed. "No, we can't bore you. And if no one has done the thing you say, then you take the drink. Simple enough, though not nearly as direct as truth or dare, but you can get a lot of secrets fast if you ask the right questions. Like I would say 'Never have I ever had sex in a zoo.' Then we could see how many of you are perverts."

"Aside from you?" Chris asked him with a snort, and Samuel smiled over at him, getting a wide grin and a kiss on his chin in return. "Samuel, you start. Then we'll go around in a circle. What is something that you've never done?"

Chris moved onto his back, stretching his legs out over the side of the couch and laying his head on Samuel's thigh. It was comfortable, and even though they hadn't done this, having Chris lying over him felt familiar. He rested his hand on Chris's chest, right between his shiny silver-pierced nipples, and felt Chris's heartbeat thump against his palm.

Samuel had to think a bit before he could start. "Never have I ever kissed a girl."

"Clarification, are we talking kissing like you would a guy, or just a kiss on the lips or cheek?" Bran asked.

"Well, I've kissed Martha, Kaden's mom, on her cheek, and also Kylie, but no romantic girl kissing."

Bran nodded, and the only person that took a sip of their drink was Chris. When Samuel looked at him, he shrugged.

"I was drunk. She stuck her tongue in my mouth. I count that."

Samuel shivered. "Okay, if you say so. Doesn't sound like you had fun, though."

"I've very rarely had actual, honest fun when I've been flat out drunk. Trent, your turn," Chris said, shifting attention away from himself even as Samuel continued to watch him.

Trent sat forward, also taking his time. Then his face lit up. "Never have I ever taken a leak against a post and zapped my willy against the electric fence."

Both Kaden and Samuel took their cups and drank from them.

Bran looked shocked, while Chris just laughed. "And I thought we were stupid," he said to Bran.

"Apparently not as much as these two," Bran said, shaking his head. "Thank God there wasn't any lasting damage. I'd be heartbroken. Kaden, your turn. It'll give me time to think of one of the few things I haven't done yet."

Kaden glared at Trent. "Never have I ever passed out hugging a fencepost for most of the night in the middle of winter."

Trent had a drink and cleared his throat after. "Hey, if your bed is empty at home, a fencepost is a great substitute."

Bran shook his head. "You're all crazy. Fine, I've got something. Never have I ever kissed my best friend. Booyah."

Chris took a drink, drawing Samuel's attention. "Huh?"

Shrugging, Chris smiled up at him. "I have, hence the drink."

"Who else are you best friends with?" Bran demanded.

Chris rolled his eyes. "You, moron. We've kissed, though I'm not surprised you forgot, since you were drunk off your ass stupid that night."

Bran looked like he didn't believe him. "Prove it."

"Right. God, you're stubborn. Fine. You were seventeen, first party we'd ever been to, right after winter break, you lost your virginity, I got my first kiss. Do you remember the guy in the Santa hat? The one you gave that sloppy wet kiss to?" Chris asked him. Bran only stared at him. "It wasn't worth mentioning, still isn't."

"I was your first kiss?" Bran sounded shocked.

But Chris only shrugged. "Yeah. And I spent half an hour getting the taste of whatever the fuck you were drinking out of my mouth after you went upstairs with whoever that was. Believe me, you weren't a great kisser back then. At least not when you were drunk off your ass. I hope for Kaden's sake you've improved a bit. No one likes being kissed by a slobbering idiot." He batted away the pillow Bran threw at him. "My turn now. Never have I ever said 'I love you' to someone romantically. Drink up, boys."

Everyone except Chris took a drink.

Samuel sat forward. "Never have I ever rimmed someone."

"Now we're getting somewhere," Chris said, taking a drink, along with Bran and Kaden.

"Never have I ever…," Trent almost singsonged out, "been handcuffed while having sex."

Chris and Bran both burst out laughing as they took their drinks, sharing some secret memory that only they knew and Samuel wasn't sure he wanted in on.

Kaden shook his head at Bran. "Do I even want to know about it? No, never mind."

Bran snorted and put his glass aside. "Good choice. You really don't want those details."

Kaden continued with his turn. "Never have I ever been given head while driving."

Surprisingly, no one else drank. When Samuel looked down at Chris, he merely smiled up at him. "I've given the head. I haven't gotten it while driving. Of course, that might have something to do with preferring to be driven places except when I'm on the bike. Kaden, you drink. No one else has either. Sad day for all of us poor, pathetic saps."

Kaden looked proud to have asked the question no one seemed to have done and drank some.

"I'll be fixing that soon," Bran said with a smirk. "Never have I ever considered having kids. Fuck no. Can you imagine me as a dad? Just… no. That kid would be so screwed up. Plus I'm selfish and lazy."

The first one to drink was Trent, his cheeks all pink as he did so. Chris came next, earning a stare from Bran and a smile from Samuel as he also drank from his glass. "Before you get to thinking I want a whole football team or something, it was only briefly, and only because the neighbor kid you met is pretty much the ideal child. He needs work on cleaning up after himself, but he can make his own food and doesn't order porn when I give him control over the remote," Chris clarified for him.

They all laughed at how Chris described the perfect child. One of their phones started ringing, something poppy coming out, and Samuel was about to make fun of whoever it was for having that tune when Chris shifted his weight and pulled his phone out of his pocket.

"Hey, missed you."

The call was too quiet for Samuel to hear who was on the other end of the call, and he wondered who Chris could be that happy to talk to as Chris smiled and closed his eyes.

"Yeah, just hanging out with the guys. It's pretty nice. Haven't killed him yet. But he is on my shit list."

Ah, probably Misha, then, Samuel realized.

Suddenly Chris sat up, his smile gone instantly. "What's wrong with you? And what the fuck was that? It sounded like a gunshot, and don't you dare fucking lie to me. I went to the range enough times with you to know what that sound is."

Chris looked up at Samuel, looking worried, before he got up and took the phone over to Trent. "I'm putting you on speaker. No, you don't get to argue. Not while you won't tell me anything." He handed the phone to Trent. "My brother, the asshole, wants to talk to you." Leaving his phone with Trent, he went to sit back down next to Samuel, leaning into his side.

"Trent? Did my idiot brother actually listen to me for once?" Misha asked.

Trent got up and started pacing up and down. "Hey. Sorry, but no. You're on speaker."

"Fuck it. I don't have time to play games. Chris, you're a child. Trent…. So much to say. I've been thinking a lot about it lately, actually."

There were gunshots behind Misha, completely clear and enough to make Chris shake beside Samuel.

Trent's eyes were wide, and his usual blushed complexion had gone pale. "What can I do for you? Are you in trouble? Are you okay?"

"What? The guns?" Misha laughed. "That's the guys practicing on some targets. Don't worry. I'd like to see you when I'm done here. This is going to be my last mission. I'm retiring. But I want to see you. Can I?"

Something in Misha's voice didn't sit well with Samuel. He sounded desperate, like Chris had the first time he'd called after eight months of silence. Samuel imagined him to be rattled, and maybe there were even tears in his voice, but he didn't know Misha well enough to be sure. But looking at Trent, he knew his friend could tell something was wrong as well.

"Sure, of course you can. Where are you? When did you want to come see me?"

"Can't tell you that, and I'll be there as soon as I'm done here. It'll be good not to have the two morons around all the time. Or your friends either, for that matter. I've been wanting you alone for months now. I can say that I'll be flying out from Sydney, though. You'd better be ready," Misha replied.

Instantly Trent went bright red at the suggestions in Misha's words. "I hope I'll be ready. If you're in Sydney, it's only three hours flight this way. Will you let me know when and where to come pick you up?"

Samuel heard the smile in Misha's voice and saw it reflecting on Trent's lips.

"Sure. I will text you. Sorry I haven't been responding. I didn't really know what to say. We'll talk much more when I'm done here. I'll be around so much you'll get tired of me."

Trent's whole face practically glowed. "I doubt that."

"He's such a jackass," Chris muttered.

"I heard that. Stop worrying, Chris. I'm fine. Routine stuff here."

Chris shook his head. "You say that every goddamn time. How many new bullet holes do you have in you now?" He took Samuel's hand, nearly crushing his bones with the force of his squeeze.

They all heard Misha's loud sigh.

"I promise I'm done after this. And Trent, I know you'll think I'm crazy, and maybe I am, but I've seen so much, and I want you to know…. Shit! Chris! Why do you have to be so selfish? Can a man not have some privacy?" Misha's voice took on an urgent tone, and Trent sat down on the edge of the chair, his eyes wide. "Trent?"

"I'm here."

"I've seen too much to let this opportunity pass me by. I love you. I think I fell for you the first time I saw you blush in Montana. And I know it's quick and I don't expect it back, but I wanted you to know. Anyway, see you soon, Trent. Little brother, try not to make Samuel kill you."

He hung up before any of them could say anything else, and Chris got up to take the phone from Trent, who sat there staring blankly at nothing.

"Bran, are you still getting waxes?" Chris asked him.

Bran nodded. "Yeah. Need a distraction? I'll get us in tonight."

Chris sat down heavily beside Samuel, who put his arm around him. "Yes, please. Book me for the manwhore ultimate, just like back in Manhattan. Anyone else want to come? My treat." He began to shake, and Samuel held him tighter. "Fucking Misha. I'd punch him if I thought my hand wouldn't break on his chest."

"Have you ever considered talking without cursing?" Samuel asked him softly.

Chris shot him a glare. "You don't mind my mouth so much when I'm sucking you off." He frowned and shook his head. "Never mind. Sorry. Like I've said, I get bitchy when I'm upset. Does the cussing bother you?"

It did, a little, but he didn't want to ask Chris to change that about himself. "I'd prefer not to hear 'fuck' from you unless we're in bed together."

Chris gave him a slight nod. "Sure. I'll try. No promises, but I can try."

Samuel smiled. "That's all I can ask for."

Trent started carrying the dishes out to the kitchen, where he rinsed them and loaded them in the dishwasher. When he came back out he was as restless as Samuel had ever seen him.

"I guess I have to go and get ready for Misha's arrival. Do some cleaning and stuff."

"He'll be at least a few days, by my guess. Come out with us tonight. Get something waxed. There's something absolutely perfect about getting your balls waxed," Chris tried.

Trent looked horrified. "What? No! Sheez, you two will drive any man insane."

Bran winked at him. "Kaden's certifiable. And Chris gets even more waxed than me, so it won't take long for Samuel to be just as crazy. He's got some kind of phobia against having hair or something."

"It's true. Come out with us," Chris said with a smile.

Samuel could tell he was trying hard and hoped Trent went along with them.

"No, definitely not. I'm going home, where things are normal."

Samuel chuckled as a beet-red Trent headed for the front door.

Chris got up, and though Samuel couldn't hear what he said to Trent, he did see them hug and Trent smile, though only a little, before he left and Chris came back to them all.

"Bran, you get us in?"

Bran nodded and got up as well. "Yeah. You ready? I'll drive."

Chris looked over at Samuel. "Am I coming back here tonight?"

"I would like you to." Samuel pulled him close for a hug and a kiss.

Chris grabbed a handful of his ass before stepping back out of his arms. "Bran, we need to stop by my place on the way back from the salon. I need clothes and things."

"You can borrow some of mine," Bran offered, putting an arm around his shoulders as they headed toward the front door.

Chris shuddered. "Hell, no. You'll just give me back those neon T-shirts I punished you with in Montana. No thanks."

Samuel watched them join hands, and he could hear Bran laughing the whole way out to his car.

CHAPTER TWENTY-FIVE

THE NEXT morning, over a group breakfast at Bran and Kaden's, Bran said, "We should go out on Trent's boat for the afternoon. The guys can fish, and we can work on our tans."

Chris smiled, and just like that they were lying out on the bow of a boat two hours later, the salty breeze wafting through his hair as he rested with his eyes closed and his hands behind his head. Samuel, Kaden, and Trent stood nearby, fishing poles in their hands as they quietly talked together. It was a perfect sunny morning, the kind Chris knew he'd get a lot more of if he and Samuel worked out.

Bran knocked his hip against Chris's leg as he got up. "I'm getting a drink. You want anything?"

"Naw. I'm good." He was practically blissful.

The boat bumped along as the sun warmed his skin.

"What the fuck is this?" Bran yelled, and Chris opened his eyes to see what had pissed his friend off.

His eyes went wide as he saw his kit in Bran's hand and his friend staring angrily at him, along with everyone else. "Bran…." He slowly sat up. He flicked his gaze to the case, then back to Bran, and finally over to Samuel, who looked just as shocked. "It's not what you think. I—"

He didn't get to finish what he was going to say, as Bran pulled his arm back and launched his kit as far away from them as possible, deep into the shining blue waters.

In an instant Chris was sprinting down the bow of the boat, then diving into the water. The icy splash practically hurt his overheated skin as his heart raced. The water was dark, and he only had a vague idea of where Bran had thrown his kit, but he was desperate to get it back. He searched for it as long as he could, then came back up for air, where he could hear them yelling at him. He ignored them, though, diving back under the water and going even deeper than the time before. His lungs hurt, and he gasped, nearly choking himself, as he got lucky and finally managed to close his fingers around the box.

Chris held it tightly as he surfaced and swam the few yards back to the boat. Bran tried to grab it out of his hands, but Chris pushed him away before he could manage to take it away from him again.

"I can't believe it. You're an addict. When the hell did that happen?" Bran seethed as he fell heavily on the deck.

Chris still hadn't fully caught his breath when he put the kit on the deck and opened it up for them all to see. "The case is waterproof, my brother is getting shot at, and this phone is my only way to talk to him," he snapped at Bran, and the rest of them too since they were all staring at him. There was no knife in there; he'd left that back at the house. Only his phone, which he quickly locked back into the case as soon as he knew it hadn't been damaged. Then he got up on shaky legs.

"Turn the boat around and take me back," he demanded before settling his gaze on Bran. "And you, stay the fuck away from me. You want to know what it's like to be thrown away by your best friend? Like you did to me? Well, here you go. Enjoy it, asshole."

He walked as far as he could away from them and pulled his knees to his chest as he looked out over the water. It didn't take long for his hands to start shaking, though, and soon the tremors worked their way up his arms until he was tightly clutching his knees to keep from scratching at himself, but that only let him dig his short nails into his skin as he ground his teeth together. He needed to get away from them, and he needed to ease his problem. But he couldn't do any of that while he was stuck on a fucking boat in the middle of some ocean or whatever it was they were in.

"Samuel?" he called, hoping he'd answer him and not be pissed off at him like the rest of them were. He needed help, and he hated that he was breaking apart in front of them all. He closed his eyes tightly and shook, even as Samuel moved his big body behind his and slowly covered Chris's hands with his own. He knew it was Samuel without having to look at him. No one else was that comforting, that warm, or that absolutely perfect when he needed them most.

"You should talk to Bran," Samuel said, coming forward to rest his chin on Chris's shoulder.

He really did not have any intention of talking about or to Bran anytime soon, if ever again. "Or you could just hold me and pretend that he isn't on this boat and that we aren't trapped here. Maybe we're in bed instead. Maybe you've just gotten done fucking me and now we're all sweaty and you're holding me."

"Or...."

Chris opened his eyes to see Bran sitting across from him, his feet nearly touching his own. He was blushing deeply and looking rightfully ashamed of himself. "What part of stay away from me didn't get through to you?" Chris nearly yelled at him. But Samuel tightened his arms around him, holding him close, silencing some of his rage. "Why isn't the boat moving?" Chris asked, turning his head to the side to see Samuel.

"We don't want you to run. Not again," Samuel said.

Chris wanted to struggle, to get away from him, but Samuel was too strong, and fighting him was quickly proving to be useless until finally he stopped trying and let his chin fall to his chest in defeat. "Fine. Let's get this shit over with, then." He lifted his head to look at Bran. "You're up. Talk. Only way I'm getting off this boat, apparently."

"I don't even know where to start. It's like everything I thought I knew about you is wrong." Bran tried to touch him, to cup his cheek, but since Chris couldn't smack his hand away, he bit instead, landing a hard nip on Bran's thumb that had him yelping and pulling back.

"Why can't you just trust me?" Chris demanded. He was so tired of fighting with him all the time, with him harping on this one thing that Chris did that had absolutely nothing to do with him, like he had any kind of say in what Chris did to himself.

"Because I don't want to bury you," Bran hissed at him, holding his thumb.

Chris was happy to see a few drops of blood coming from Bran's thumb where he'd bitten him.

Chris rolled his eyes. He wasn't going to repeat that he wasn't suicidal to them all. Not again. He'd said it enough already.

Bran reached toward him again, this time going for his ankle where Chris couldn't bite him or even kick him because of how Samuel was holding him. "Just get rid of your kit. We're all here for you. You don't need it. When you need some help now, you've got us."

"Except when you get mad at me and kick me out of your life. Or when Samuel gets tired of me."

"Chris, you need to know that isn't ever going to happen," Samuel softly whispered in his ear before landing a soft kiss on his neck.

He would have loved to believe that. He wanted that with his whole heart. "My longest relationship was six months. We've been friends for longer than that now. And every single day I expect you to tell me it'll be the last. I can't lose you. You're the best, the absolute best, Samuel. And I need you in my life."

He felt Samuel kiss the back of his neck, and Chris started to relax against him for a little while.

"I'm not going anywhere. I promise you that. I love you."

No one had ever said that to him before, outside of his family and Bran, and he closed his eyes and softly smiled at the sound of those words coming from Samuel. "I love you too."

"So now you can get rid of your knife. And everything can be better," Bran said excitedly.

Chris rolled his eyes, but he didn't stop smiling as he looked over at Bran. "I will. I was already planning to. But in my time. Not when you say so."

Bran held up his pinky, and Chris laughed at the absurdity of a pinky promise right then. But Samuel let his right wrist go, and he tightened his finger over Bran's.

"I'm sorry," Bran said.

Chris was so tired of hearing him say that. "No more of that." He turned to look back at Samuel. "I'm okay now, if you want to let me go."

While Samuel did release his wrist, he didn't go anywhere, and Chris leaned his head back against him. "Just fucking ask me if you want to know something. Any of you. I'll tell you the truth. But I'm done trying to defend myself against you all. It's exhausting."

"Deal."

Bran smiled at him, and Chris gave him a small smile in return.

"I really am—"

"I swear to God, Bran, you say you're sorry one more time and I will throw you off this fucking boat," Chris warned him.

Bran shut up instantly, but he did smile.

"Also, going into private, personal property for the sake of snooping without a warrant or probable cause, or the owner of the property's permission, is still against the law here too. I've never had to defend you for a criminal offense, so don't make me start now."

Kaden frowned at him, taking a seat next to and slightly behind Bran. Trent joined them in sitting as well. "How do you know that?"

"I was on a plane, sitting in an airport, or in the back of a taxi for over thirty hours earlier this week. I read up on New Zealand law. What else was I supposed to do?" He'd been bored out of his mind and anxious to see Samuel and Bran again. The reading had distracted him a little, enough to let him sit still for hours at a time, at least.

Bran looked insanely happy about that. "Are you taking the test? Getting licensed here?"

"I was thinking about it," Chris hedged, not sure why Bran suddenly grabbed him in a tight hug.

"So you are moving here!" he nearly shouted in Chris's ear.

He was quick to push Bran off him, though. "I never said that. I'm a lawyer in most of the States, figured I could be one here too. Doesn't mean I'm not going back the second Samuel says he's done with me."

"I just said—"

Chris cut him off. "You can't know what the future holds. I could piss you off tomorrow."

But Samuel just laughed. "You can't know that either, and you piss me off every day. And yet I'm still here."

Well, there was that. Chris grinned and reached back to put his hand on Samuel's hip. "So am I. Despite how ridiculously stubborn you are. You're lucky you're so good-looking."

"Ha-ha." Samuel gave his hair a light tug. "You're lucky I love you so much."

That was true too. "Yeah, I guess I am," Chris softly replied. "Samuel, if we're really going to do this, you need to know that I like having my space sometimes. If I'm out and not answering your calls, I want you to try Bran before assuming I'm dead. And I want a key so that I can surprise you in the middle of the night. And I'm not moving in for at least a few months. But I will move in with you."

"I understand about needing space and about the other thing—I'm hoping that how you feel about me is enough for you to want to stay alive."

Samuel winked as he spoke to soften his words, Chris guessed.

"But ultimately, I would love to have you around all the time, but once you feel ready."

Chris froze. "So…. All the time meaning…." He swallowed thickly. "Marriage? Is that what you ultimately want from me?"

"I won't ever ask for anything you're not comfortable giving, so let's just leave talk about marriage if it scares you so much right now."

"It scares the crap out of me." He glared at Bran, who was smiling at him like an idiot. "Go away. Right now. I want Samuel time. Not Samuel, Bran, Kaden time."

Bran gave him a pout, but they did leave.

"Just so you know I'm serious here, I have one more present for you. It's in the bottom right drawer of your bathroom vanity. Bright red ribbon. You can't miss it."

His words genuinely seemed to surprise Samuel. "I look forward to opening it. Thank you."

Chris nodded, though he doubted Samuel would like it all that much. He didn't need it anymore, though, and had left it there for Samuel to find eventually. It was the drawer with all the random junk in it, so he figured it might have taken Samuel a while to find his knife wrapped up with a bright red ribbon.

"Woohoo! I got a big one!"

Trent's voice rang out from the stern of the boat where he stood alone fishing. The end of his fishing rod bowed almost right down, and it shocked the hell out of Chris the strength such a simple tool could have. Kaden hurried over to Trent, grabbing a landing net on his way.

Samuel craned his neck to see better, and Chris took pity on him. "Go on. I can see you want to."

Samuel chuckled and gave him a quick kiss as he also went over to where Trent wrestled with something strong at the end of his line.

"I can't see the appeal," Bran said with his upper lip almost pulled up. "The smell alone makes me want to spew."

Chris laughed. "Me neither, but hey, I haven't actually tried fishing, so who knows? I'll give it a try once and see."

They sat back down on the roof of the cabin and watched the action unfold from a distance. At one stage Trent handed the rod over to Samuel so he could take his shirt off and wipe the sweat out of his eyes before taking control of the fishing rod again.

"Hmmmm." Chris watched Bran turn his head almost sideways as he looked at the men going crazy about a fish.

"What?" Chris followed his gaze, trying to figure out what his friend was on about.

"Look at him without his shirt on, leaning back and fighting whatever is on there. I would've never thought he was that buff. Misha is a lucky man."

Chris focused on Trent, as he was the man in question. He wasn't particularly impressed, but then again it was hard for any man to catch his attention next to Samuel. "You've seen him shirtless before in Montana."

"Maybe, but I didn't notice then. I'm noticing now. Not in the wrong way, though. It's just a surprise. That's all."

Chris nodded. "Trent's height detracts from his build. He's very buff and, from what Samuel has said, freakishly strong, but he's such a softy. I hope he's strong enough to handle my brother. Otherwise he'll be run over, flattened like a pancake."

Bran grimaced as if he agreed. "Only time will tell. I hope it works for them and, I guess, for all of our sakes, because if it didn't, things can be pretty awkward at family gatherings."

Just then Kaden stretched over the side of the boat and Samuel grabbed him by the waist of his pants to keep him from going over too far as he reached out to net the catch. When they placed the massive pinky-red fish down on the deck where it flopped around, all three men whooped and high-fived like little boys.

"Bloody hell, Trent. He's huge!" Kaden said in obvious awe.

"Let's weigh it." Kaden bustled around, and they watched the men weigh the fish, measure it, and take some photos from different angles.

"Let's put him back where he belongs, hey?" Trent looked like he was tempted to kiss the ugly beast in his hands.

"After all that, you're gonna let it go?" Chris called out.

Kaden, Trent, and Samuel looked their way, but it was Trent who spoke.

"This is a breeding male snapper, and we always put the biggest ones back so they can continue to breed. We've got a few smaller ones from earlier on ice that we can make for a late lunch."

"Aaah, okay. Makes sense," Bran mumbled.

Neither Chris nor Bran, it seemed, were all that interested in fishing. Chris liked fish well enough, but he liked them deep fried with french fries and some malt vinegar, not dangling from a hook at the end of a pole and line.

With the excitement over, Trent fired up the small tabletop BBQ grill and pan fried the fresh catch for them. Kaden and Samuel made a couple of salads, and they all enjoyed the lovely meal with a glass of wine or beer as the warm day started turning cooler with approaching nightfall.

"Wow, Trent. That was amazing," Chris thanked him when he swallowed the last bite. "At least I know my brother will be well fed. Come on Bran, let's clean up, seeing as these guys made the food."

It didn't take long for them to wash the few dishes and secure them in the small wooden cupboards in the cabin. When they were done, Kaden and Trent seemed deep in conversation on one bench, and Bran walked over to join them.

Samuel had gone up onto the deck, and Chris made his way up there too. He went around and lowered himself between Samuel's legs, his back resting against his man's chest. Samuel's tattooed arms came around him to hold him closer as they stared out over the glass-like water. The sun had lowered on the horizon, and beautiful hues colored the sky.

Chris sighed. "It's so beautiful here."

Samuel's chest rumbled behind him as he chuckled in agreement. "It is, and I remind myself often to be grateful for it."

Chris leaned his head back to see Samuel's face, using one arm to pull him down for a kiss. As always, it didn't take much for the heat to spike between them. Samuel fondled him through his shorts, and Chris gasped as his neck was nipped and licked at the same time, making him nearly animalistic as he rubbed himself against Samuel, desperate for contact.

"You make me want to strip down and have sex right here."

Samuel groaned deeply. "Maybe another time, without an audience."

On cue they heard snickers. "Get a room!" Bran yelled at them.

"As if you can talk!" Chris retorted. They withdrew and turned back around to appreciate the view. "We gonna be okay?" He was frightened and uncertain, needing Samuel's reassurance, even if all Samuel could give him were his words and the promises in them.

Samuel kissed his ear. "We're gonna be fine."

CHAPTER TWENTY-SIX

AFTER THEY docked the boat back at the marina later that evening, well after the sun had set, Samuel wanted Chris to come back home with him. But Chris went to his bike instead, pulling on his helmet as he walked away from the rest of them. Samuel went to him anyway, hoping to convince him to come over. "You can load the bike into the back of my truck and I'll take you back to my place," Samuel offered.

Chris flipped up the visor on his helmet so they could talk. "Look at my present first. And I didn't mention how much I like seeing the necklace I got you around your neck. It's hot." He reached up and touched the small jade pendant, and Samuel took his hand before Chris could pull away.

"I'd rather have you come back with me."

Laughing, Chris shook his head. "Present first. Come over tomorrow morning if you want to."

Of course Samuel would want to. He wanted Chris to come over now, though. It wasn't just that he wanted to have sex with him, it was that he wanted Chris close by. He wasn't ready to say good night to him just then. "If you insist on not seeing each other until tomorrow, I'll respect that."

Chris took off the helmet and gave Samuel a soft, lingering kiss. "Don't sound so sad. I need to do a few things, and I want to think a little too."

Samuel frowned at him, and Chris smiled as he put the helmet back on.

"See you tomorrow."

Samuel stepped back, giving Chris some room. "I'll be there in the morning."

Chris gave him a nod and took off down the road, the bike kicking up dirt and loose gravel in its wake. Samuel shook his head and turned to see Bran watching him as Kaden and Trent loaded up Trent's truck.

"He does care about you, despite whatever it is you're thinking," Bran said.

Samuel didn't doubt that at all. "I know. It was good to hear him say he loves me. It would be nice, though, to be let into his life, to feel like I have some place in it."

"You do. May not seem like it, but you are in his life in a big way." He took out his phone and started typing. "I really shouldn't do this, and Chris would probably kill me if he found out, but here, he sent me this text while you were all cooking dinner. He didn't want us to be overheard."

Samuel walked over to him and looked at the text Bran had pulled up on his phone. *If Samuel asked me, I'd say yes. Help me plan it? Not sure what passes for a wedding here, and I don't want a cow as a best man. Freaking out but surprisingly not feeling crazy. Glad he can't tell. Also, and don't you dare mention this, but I start therapy again on Monday. Don't make it a big deal.*

Samuel grinned and wanted to go find Chris that minute, to take him in his arms and hold him close. He knew Chris wasn't ready for marriage, but it was enough to know that he was thinking about it, that he'd thoroughly considered it, and that Chris wanted to say yes to him. He was also going to therapy. It was going to be hard for him not to ask Chris about how it was going.

"Told you so," Bran said, smiling at him. "Fucking divorce lawyer probably getting married before me. He always was the romantic one between us, though, despite his aversion to a piece of paper and a ceremony. The party part was never an issue. Talk to you later." Bran went over to Kaden since Trent's truck was loaded up, and took his man's hand.

AT HOME, Samuel went straight to his bathroom and pulled open the drawer Chris had told him to look in, and for a while there he could only stare at the small knife, still tucked away neatly in its sheath, with a bright red ribbon wrapped around it. The knife was a present, clearly, but it was so much more than that. Samuel took it as a promise that Chris wasn't going to be cutting anymore, and that he knew he had family there in New Zealand to help him when things did get to be too much for him.

Samuel understood the overwhelming need to release the tension inside of himself, and he took care of that need with martial arts. It was healthy and constructive and something he hoped to introduce Chris to someday, because he knew Chris would still need some way of helping himself if life got to be too much for him. His hands shook as he pulled the knife from the drawer and considered what to do with it. He didn't want it anywhere near him or anywhere Chris could find it again either. Picking a place where it couldn't be used ever again, he took it downstairs and tossed it in the trash bin outside of his house. Chris had better ways of coping now, and he had all of them to lean on when he needed some support. They were his family, and someday soon Samuel intended to be his husband.

I got your present. Thank you, Samuel texted him.

The reply was nearly instant, but it wasn't anything like what Samuel had been expecting to receive from Chris.

Which of these paint chips do you like most?

Along with the text was a picture of six pieces of colored paper, all taped up against a cream-colored wall Samuel didn't recognize. Most of Chris's walls were light blue, and he was renting the house anyway, so he didn't understand what Chris was doing with paint chips to begin with.

What are you painting? Samuel texted back.

Doing this myself would require getting dirty. I don't do that unless it's sex. Pick a color.

Samuel wanted to know what was going on first. *Tell me what you're doing. Then I can help.*

His phone lit up, and he answered it, glad Chris had called him. Maybe he could get some answers while Chris was on the phone.

"Come over," Chris said before Samuel could speak. "I want to see you. It'll be fun. Stuff to talk about. Might even let you play with my piercings if you're good."

Samuel's body reacted instantly to the thought of Chris's new piercings, but he sounded distracted, despite the softly teasing note in his voice.

"So... you coming over? I don't really have clothes on to get to you."

"Well, if you put it that way, don't go to any trouble. I'll be right over." Samuel chuckled at the image of Chris strutting around naked in his house.

Chris groaned, sounding like he was stretching. "Great. Door's unlocked. You can help me eat this ice cream."

"Leaving now. See you soon." Samuel grabbed his keys off the foyer table and locked the door. The drive to Chris's place didn't take long, and he pulled in behind the motorbike where it stood in front of Chris's garage door.

The lights were on, all of them, which Samuel thought was strange as he turned off the engine in his truck and headed up to the front door, which had been painted a pretty dark blue since the last time Samuel had seen it. The door was unlocked, just as Chris had said, and he came inside to find Chris sitting at the island, wearing only a pair of black boxers. He had a carton of ice cream beside him and a pile of papers in front of him. In his right hand he twirled a pen between his fingers.

"Hey," Chris said, looking up at him.

Samuel put his wallet, keys, and phone down before walking up to him to give him a kiss, tasting the sweet coldness on his lips. "Hey. I missed you."

"Missed you too. Even though it's only been a few hours. I figured we'd talk tomorrow… but I was up, you were up, and paperwork is always less boring with a sexy distraction. Start distracting me. I still have six pages left to do." Chris gave him a light shove away, smirking at him.

"Six pages of paperwork is a lot. What are you doing?" Samuel was curious.

Chris bit his lip as he turned the papers toward Samuel without saying a word, and Samuel started reading for himself. They were immigration papers, filled out nearly completely. The only things Chris had left to fill out were the references. The rest of it, Samuel saw, were the laws he'd have to abide by. He stared at the forms in astonishment before looking up at Chris.

"Wow, that's a big step for you."

Chris shrugged, looking like it wasn't as big of a deal as it was. Only Samuel saw the worry in Chris's eyes.

"You okay with this? I'm not just doing this to be near Bran. You're going to have to put up with me being around a lot more than only at holidays. The guy I'm renting this place from, he said I could make my law practice from here if we ever do move in together. Which would be into your house, in case you were wondering. I'm not giving up living there. Not a chance in hell."

"I'm glad you like my house, then, and this is perfect for a law office. What were you planning to set up here?"

Chris slid off the barstool and, seemingly nervous, took Samuel's hand. "C'mon, I'll show you what I've been doing since I got off Trent's boat a few hours ago."

He pulled Samuel into a small room that Samuel hadn't even noticed before since the door had always been closed, but now that Chris had let him in he saw a shiny brand new desk, a bookshelf half-full of law books, and Chris's degrees and awards hanging on the walls.

"Welcome to my office. I was hoping you could help me pick a wall color. I hate white walls. So boring." Chris let go of his hand and stepped back, still looking worried.

"You have been busy. It looks really nice and professional, but the walls look a bit dull, I agree with you. Where are the color charts you texted me earlier?"

Chris smiled at him, obviously relieved. "In the bedroom. I figured that if I was going to go through the trouble of getting one room painted, the others should be done as well. I'm glad you're okay with this. With me starting over here. Misha made me realize, when he told Trent he loved him, that all of my family is here now. And there's nothing left for me in Manhattan. My neighbor will visit, but my dad isn't speaking to me, and my mom hangs up on me. If Misha really is ready to stop, I don't want to be away from him. Bran and I aren't perfect, but we've been texting all night. And then there's you...."

Samuel could see the concern all over Chris's face, and he wanted it gone, so he teased him a bit. "Oh? What about me?"

"Kaden was right. It is a long way for a quick screw. Guess if I want you all the time, I better be here," Chris said, his scared smile giving way to a grin. "I want to see you more than once a month. More than once a week, even."

"You mean you just want me for my body?" Samuel mock frowned.

Chris snorted. "Maybe not just your body. Kind of want your heart too, seeing as how you've had mine for the last eight months. And I've put holes in myself for you. Four of them. That should count for something."

Samuel pulled him closer until their hips met. "You had my heart a long time ago, so it's yours. And I can't wait to start exploring your holes."

Chris laughed loudly. "Ha. Then you really had better follow me into the bedroom. Oh, and no telling Bran that I'm staying just yet. We're getting coffee at that place you guys went to in Thames. That's tomorrow morning. I'll tell him then." Chris pulled out of his arms and started heading down the hallway with Samuel close behind him.

"I won't see him before tomorrow anyway," he told Chris as he followed him into the bedroom.

Chris rolled his eyes and closed the bedroom door behind them both. "I was more worried about you texting him. I figured you wouldn't be seeing him after midnight unless you were all at a club. Colors are on the wall there. I have it narrowed down to six. I guess. I've never had to choose paint before so, really, they could all be wrong."

Samuel wasn't looking at the paint, though, not when Chris was pushing the boxers down his hips, appearing completely at ease with the idea of being naked with him around.

"Like any of them?" Chris asked as he started lotioning up his arms now that he was naked.

Staring at the colors, Samuel shook his head. "Do you honestly expect me to concentrate on paint if you're naked next to me?"

"You said no more nudist beaches. I have to get my naked fix somehow. What? Is this *hard* for you?" Chris asked him with a snicker.

"You have no freakin' idea how hard it is." Like steel, in his pants.

"Maybe you need to be closer to the paints, then," Chris teased him, pulling a random color off the wall and bringing it up to Samuel's face. "How's this? Still hard?"

It could have been an accident, but Samuel figured he'd spent enough time around Chris to know that his hand brushing against the front of Samuel's pants was completely intentional.

Chris giggled when Samuel turned around with a growl and half picked him up as he stepped over to the bed, where he dropped Chris on the duvet before climbing on top of him.

"Very hard for me, so very good for you."

"I'd like to think you get something out of it as well," Chris said with a laugh. Samuel shut him up with a kiss, then quickly made coherent speech impossible for the next few hours.

SAMUEL LEFT a groggy Chris early the next morning to head back to the farm for the morning milking. For the last few days he'd had this idea but hadn't wanted to follow through until he knew for certain whether Chris had made up his mind about some things, such as their relationship and possibly making a home in New Zealand.

His phone beeped a few hours later, and he looked down at it, surprised to see a text from Chris this early.

Doesn't anyone in this country sleep in? You weren't here, and Bran woke me up with a text telling me it was going to rain so I should bring a jacket. I'm not five. I blame the cows. You all and the cows.

Samuel smiled at the whiny tone he could practically hear Chris using through the phone.

He rushed through a hot shower and chomped down a large bowl of cereal before heading out. For this mission he drove to Hamilton, because the city would have many more options for what he was looking for. His first stop was a pet shop and after that three more with no success. The two animal shelters also couldn't help him, and though he was relieved most of the cages were empty, it made him worry his trip had been a waste of time.

As a last resort he used his phone to find all the farm veterinary clinics in the city and drove to them one by one. Almost four hours later he walked into a small clinic on the outskirts of town, and by the size alone he doubted he would have any luck.

The young girl behind the counter perked up when she saw him, her eyes taking on a calculating gleam. "Hi there. How's your day been?"

Samuel sighed. "Hey. It's been a long day so far, so I'm hoping you can help me."

She turned her head slightly sideways and played with a curly strand of hair hanging by her ear. "Well, I can do my best. What were you after?"

Samuel looked around the small shop attached to the veterinary clinic, not seeing any pets on display. "I am on the lookout for a gift for someone—a puppy to be exact. Do you have any for sale here?"

She shook her head slowly, and Samuel felt like walking out of the store without another word.

"Not here, no. But someone came in here yesterday and left this here for us to advertise. I haven't put it up on the notice board yet, but you can look at it."

She held out a sheet of paper, and Samuel stepped closer to take it.

The moment he laid eyes on the puppy in the middle of the three on the photo, he knew his search was over. "Where do I find these?"

She smiled and gave him another once-over. "It's a local farmer who owns them. Their farm is about twelve kilometers from here."

Doing his best to keep his distance, Samuel got the directions and a phone number from her and drove over there straightaway. By the cows in the paddocks next to the farm's driveway, he knew it to be a dairy farm. He came to a stop behind another parked vehicle and got out.

He got another text from Chris. *Bran's happy. Be prepared for a party or something. Bring me some energy when you come back. Only fair since you took it all away last night.*

Before he could knock on the massive wooden door, it swung open to reveal who Samuel assumed was the owner. The graying man wore shorts and a singlet with wooly gumboot-style socks on his feet.

"Hello. What can I do for you?"

As Samuel watched, a beautiful larger version of the puppy on the advertisement came to sit down by his master's feet.

"Hello. My name is Samuel. The lady at your vet clinic gave me this"—Samuel showed the pamphlet to the man—"and I was hoping you would have some puppies left?"

The man smiled. "I sure do. In fact, they're all still available, because I left those in the shop only yesterday. Let me grab my boots and we can go around to the back deck. The mum is lying there in the sun with her babies."

Samuel's excitement was almost uncontrollable as he followed the man to where they were going. They rounded the house to display a large timber deck, climbed up the few steps, and there was a huge soft dog bed with the blue heeler female and her pups.

"Hey, Sheeba, we may have found a home for one of your kiddos." The man spoke to her affectionately. He turned to Samuel. "Have a look at them. She won't mind as long as I'm around."

Samuel went down on his knees a few steps away from where the puppies played with each other. They noticed him almost immediately, but two continued wrestling and growling as they bit each other's ears. The last one, however, came running to him, and it surprised him that it was the puppy he had singled out on the photo. Well, it seemed it had chosen Samuel too.

He sat still as the little dog climbed all over his arms and tried to lick his face. He started scratching the tiny ears, and it lay down and rolled over. It was a girl, and he thought she was perfect for Chris.

The man chuckled above him. "She has been the shyest of the lot, but she isn't shy with you at all."

Samuel scooped the little ball of mischief up in his arms as he got up. "Because she knows I want her." He smiled at her persistence to try to reach his face.

"Well, she's eight weeks old, so all yours if you want her."

Samuel gave the little puppy over to the man to hold while he pulled out his wallet and paid for her.

Twenty minutes later he left the vet store with Blue, as he called her for the moment, in one arm and a bag with all the necessary goodies for a new puppy, from a food and water bowl to a bed and blanket, plus toys, in the other.

In the truck he placed the blanket on the passenger seat and placed Blue there, where she sniffed a bit and lay down. He pulled out his phone.

Where are you now? Samuel texted him.

Chris's reply was nearly instant. *Watching some singing show on the couch. This kid is Maori too. Decent voice, not a clue what he's singing about.*

I'm heading over.

Good.

It took him nearly an hour to get back to Chris's little white house with the blue trim, while the puppy lay on the seat next to him the whole time. Chris's door was unlocked again, and it was something Samuel wanted to talk to him about. But not when he had a squirming puppy in his arms.

He didn't see Chris at first, but the TV was on, so he let the puppy go play so he could look for him. He didn't get far before he heard sharp puppy yips and the sound of Chris laughing.

"Hey, cutie. How'd you get in?"

Samuel came around the side of the couch where he'd been lying so that Chris could see him.

"Hey. When did you get a puppy?"

Samuel smiled at him and joined him on the couch. "I didn't. She's a present for you, now that you're staying here for good."

Chris looked shocked for about two seconds before he sat up with the puppy held tightly in his arms and gave Samuel a soft kiss. "Thank you. She's perfect. A fluffy little cloud. That's what I'll call her. My little Cloud."

Samuel smiled as he watched Chris love on the speckled blue ball of fluff.

"I've never had my own pet before."

"I know. I wanted you to start here."

Chris shifted around on the couch so that he was sitting beside Samuel with the puppy bouncing around on the couch too. "She's adorable. Seriously, thank you. I love you."

Samuel wrapped his arm tightly around Chris's side, holding him as close as he possibly could. "You're welcome. I love you too." Chris laid his head on Samuel's shoulder, and Samuel smiled, knowing everything would be all right now.

EPILOGUE

IT WAS a perfect New Zealand day as Chris stepped into Samuel's arms and said his vows as he promised to love him forever. There was rain expected later, but the breeze was warm and it carried Samuel's rich scent all around him.

And there, all around them, were their friends. They'd chosen to go without best men, simply having everyone they knew and loved standing with them as they stood on the beach with the water quickly coming in around them.

Samuel's kiss was warm and gentle, exactly what Chris had needed on a day that could have been stressful, but had ended up being anything but. Bran had handled it all beautifully, with Kaden's help to keep him in check when he'd started talking about something ridiculous. At one point there had been mention of a new car or a parade or something. Chris really hadn't been sure actually.

Misha was the first to come up and give him a hug as soon as he'd stepped out of Samuel's arms.

"I'm so proud of you. For everything," he whispered.

Chris gave him a watery smile. "Thank you. I'm glad you decided to completely retire, and for good this time. Trent seems really happy."

Misha chuckled. "He makes me happy too."

"Stop hogging him!" Bran called out, and Misha gave way to Bran, who hugged him with such intensity that he was sure his bones would be bruised later. "Love you," Bran said.

Chris hugged him back just as tightly. "I love you too. Thank you for settling here and bringing us all together."

Bran said nothing and Chris held him for a long time. They'd been reckless and foolish before coming to Montana and now, with their friends all around them, Chris knew that they were right where they should be. It had taken them moving across the fucking planet, as Bran liked to say, but they'd found their way home.

KARA NASH makes her home amongst the stunning islands in the South Pacific. Writing is a passion, but so is reading, a good cup of steaming coffee, and the love and company of friends and family. While life carries on around her in a bustle, her mind is filled with the voices and antics of the characters in her next creation. Kara is an absolute romantic at heart and happy endings are precious, which is why she chooses to tell stories of couples fortunate to find and hold on to love. And cats! Kara adores these furry creatures and the sense behind "too many" escapes her when it comes to them.

CAITLIN RICCI was fortunate growing up to be surrounded by family and teachers who encouraged her love of reading. She has always been a voracious reader and that love of the written word easily morphed into a passion for writing. If she isn't writing, she can usually be found studying as she works toward her counseling degree. She comes from a military family, and the men and women of the armed forces are close to her heart. She also enjoys gardening, hiking, and horseback riding in the Colorado Rockies she calls home with her wonderful fiancé and their two dogs. Her belief that there is no one true path to happily ever after runs deeply through all of her stories.

Website: www.CaitlinRicci.com

KARA NASH & CAITLIN RICCI

DARE TO RISK

DARE: BOOK ONE

Dare: Book One

For successful businessman Bran Wilson, selling the large Montana dairy farm that has been in his family for generations is an easy decision. He hates the farm, the land, even the cows, and wants nothing to do with any of it. But there's a glitch in his plan: a stubborn cowboy from New Zealand who is as sexy as he is aggravating.

Kaden Barker loves the Wilson farm, and respected Bran's grandfather up until the day he died. With his two best friends, he's taken over working the farm and caring for the cows, and he'd happily spend the rest of his days doing it.

When Bran charges into his life, telling him he's selling the farm and there's nothing Kaden, or his friends, can do about it, the animosity between them is instant. But so is the attraction, and only one extreme can win out.

www.dreamspinnerpress.com

reckless

caitlin ricci

When his best friend, Lee, offered him his sub as part of a bet, Colton Prier never expected more than a clean condo from the boy. But Tate Nicholson is well-trained, eager , and he likes rope play as much as Colton enjoys tying him up. It should have ended after one night, but they begin meeting in secret, and Colton can't stop thinking about Tate. It's a betrayal of his friendship with Lee to fall in love with Tate, but Colton can't help wanting the sub for himself.

He's not alone in his feelings, either. Tate thought he was happy with Lee. Not completely fulfilled, but happy enough. But as he spends more time with Colton, he realizes Lee isn't capable of giving him what he wants anyway. Lee demands his full submission, but Tate doesn't want to be a lifestyle sub. Colton expects his obedience at times but gives him his freedom more often than not, which is more in line with what Tate wants.

When Tate really needs his Dom and Lee isn't around to help him, he reaches the tipping point and needs to choose who he wants to give his submission to, and to accept the consequences of his choice when he does.

www.dreamspinnerpress.com

FOR
MORE
OF THE
BEST
GAY
ROMANCE

DREAMSPINNER
PRESS
dreamspinnerpress.com

www.ingramcontent.com/pod-product-compliance
Lightning Source LLC
Chambersburg PA
CBHW051637260626
47170CB00004B/1221